ROD

CW00402508

The Year 1071
~Resistance and Revenge~

The Harrying of the North Series
Book Two

Hindrelag Books

THE YEAR 1071
~RESISTANCE AND REVENGE~

For Serena and Leyla
– two very special granddaughters-

Contents

Author's Note

My motivation for writing the tale of Hravn and Ealdgith, and their experience of the Harrying of the North, was a desire to leave something for my family's future generations that brings to life an early and easily forgotten period in our past. My parents' families, the Flints, Martins, Wilsons, Mattinsons, Pattinsons, Curwens et al can trace their lineage through 1000 years of life in Cumbria and the Borders, as far back as the nobility of the pre-Norman north, and through Gospatrick to Earl Uhtred of Northumberland and King Ethelred 2nd of England.

Modern Western societies are increasingly equal and diverse in their social attitudes. The Anglo-Saxon and Norse societies of pre-Norman England had evolved from pre-Roman Germanic cultures and followed an Orthodox English Christianity. They were more equal in their attitude to women, and their legal status, than the strongly Catholic, constraining and more misogynistic society that developed under the Normans. I wanted my two heroes to reflect all that is good about today's society whilst remaining true to their own time.

Whilst writing, I have tried to use words that are authentic and made a deliberate effort to avoid those that have a French or post-invasion origin. That is why 'stake-wall' is used instead of the French word: palisade.

I live in Richmondshire and chose to use the traumatic time of the Harrying of the North as a vehicle for the tale. The geography speaks for itself; these are the places I have known and loved all my life.

I have based the second story in the series amidst the rolling hills northwest of Richmond. I have assumed that these remote hills and valleys were still largely wild woodland and upland pasture in the early 1070s. They could have been home to refugees from the harrying.

Today, this is high desolate moorland that has been much damaged by centuries of intensive lead mining. Lead mining destroyed woodland, clearing it for production of pit-props and use as fuel for smelting. Topsoil was stripped away to access the veins of lead and the ground was poisoned by lead waste, smoke and toxic rain. The ground is now impoverished, though a few strips of woodland cling on in narrow valleys and on a few hill tops.

I would like to thank all those who have supported and encouraged me, not least in the laborious task of proof reading and for helping ensure that the story is understandable to all. In particular, my wife Judith for her support and encouragement; my mother Clarissa, herself a true Cumbrian and incredible font of family history; my daughter Lara, always full of enthusiasm for the tale and in some little way a role-model for Ealdgith; my brother Paul and his meticulous attention to detail; and my good friend Rachel Howe, for her advice as one who is of an age with Ealdgith.

My thanks are also due to Andy Thursfield for his graphic design and art work, and to Kathleen Herbert whose book, 'Spellcraft – Old English Heroic Legends,' recounts the tale of Hildegyd and Waldere, that I drew upon in Book 1.

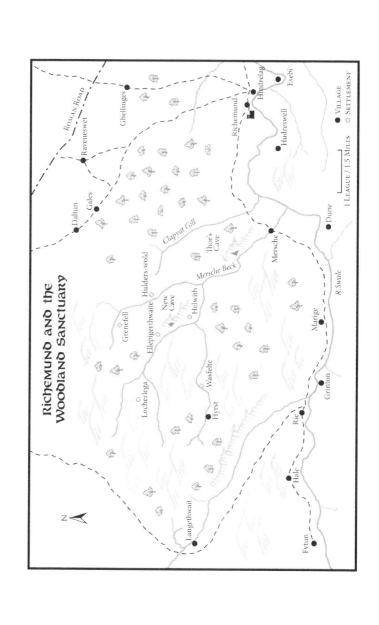

Richemund and the Woodland Sanctuary

N

ROMAN ROAD

Ghellinges

Raveneswet

Dattun

Gales

Hudders-wold

Clapyat Gill

Thor's Cave

Hindrelag

Esebi

Richemund

Hudreswell

Dune

Mersche

Mersche Beck

Grenetell

New Cave

Ellepigerthwaite

Helwith

Marige

Locherlega

Wasfelte

R. Swale

Hyrst

Grinton

Rie

Hale

Langethwait

Fytun

1 LEAGUE / 1.5 MILES

● VILLAGE
○ SETTLEMENT

Place Names

Place names are those shown in the Oxford Dictionary of English Place-Names. I have used the name for the date nearest to 1071. Where a similar name has several spellings, I have chosen a common one in order to avoid confusion. Places that existed in 1071 but aren't listed retain their present name.

Alnewich. Alnwick. Dwelling on the River Aln.
Aluretune. Northallerton. Farmstead of a man called Aelfhere.
Aplebi. Appleby in Westmoreland. Village where apple trees grow.
Ascric. Askrigg. Ash-tree ridge.
Bebbanburge. Bamburgh. Stronghold of a Queen called Bebbe.
Bogas. Bowes. The river bends.
Carleol. Carlisle. Celtic; fortified town at a place belonging to Luguvalos.
Corbricg. Corbridge. Bridge near Corchester.
Corburne. Colburn. Cool stream.
Crosebi Raveneswart. Crosby Ravensworth. Manor with a cross owned by a man called Rafnsvatr.
Cumbraland. Cumberland. Region of the Cumbrian Britons.
Curnow. Cornwall.
Daltun. Dalton. Village in a valley.
Dune. Downholme. Place in the hills.
Dyflin. Dublin. Norse, derived from Gaelic 'Dubh Linn', meaning 'black pool'.
Ellintone. Ellington. Farmstead at a place where eels are caught.
Elreton. Ellerton. Farmstead by the alders.
Esebi. Easby. Village of a man named Esi.
Euruic. York. From Celtic; probably meaning yew tree estate.

Federbi. Fearby. Farmstead at a place frequented by flocks of birds.

Fytun. Feetham. Place at the riverside meadows.

Gales. Gayles. Place at the ravines.

Ghellinges. Gilling West. Capital of the Wapentake of Ghelliges-scir.

Ghellinges-scir. Approximates to Richmondshire. North Yorkshire local government district embracing Swaledale, Arkengarthdale and Wensleydale.

Grinton. Grinton. Green farmstead.

Gunnar's Saetr. Gunnerside. Summer pasture belonging to a man called Gunnar.

Hale. Healaugh. High clearing or wood.

Hagustaldes-ham. Hexham. The warrior's homestead.

Haugr-Gils. Howgills. Hills and narrow valleys.

Hep. Shap. Heap of stones.

Hindrelag. Richmond. English name before 1070. Origin not known.

Hotun Rodebi. Hutton Rudby. Farmstead of a man called Ruthi.

Hudreswelle. Hudswell. Place at a spring of a man named Hud.

Hurdewurda. Hurworth. Enclosure made with hurdles.

Hyrst. Hurst. Place at the wooded hill.

Jor. River Ure. Origin not known.

Kelda. Keld. The spring by the apple tree.

Kircabi Lauenesdale. Kirkby Lonsdale. Village with a church in the valley of the Lune.

Kircabi Stephan. Kirkby Stephen. Village with the church of St. Stephen.

Kircabi Thore. Kirkby Thore. Village with a church in the manor of Thore.

Langethwait. Langthwaite. Long clearing.

Loncastre. Lancaster. Fort on the River Lune.

Lundenburh. London. Celtic; place belonging to Londinos.

Lune. The River Lune derives its name from the Old English word Lon which has its origins in an Irish Celtic word meaning health giving.

Marige. Marrick. Boundary ridge.

Massan. Masham. Homestead or village of a man called Maessa.

Mersche. Marske. Place at the marsh.

Meuhaker. Muker. Narrow cultivated spot.

Middeltun. Middleton-Tyas. Farmstead in the middle.

Morlund. Morland. Grove in the moor.

Mortun. Moreton on Swale. Farmstead on marshy ground.

Penrith. Penrith. Chief ford.

Ravenstandale. Ravenstonedale. Valley of the raven stone.

Raveneswet. Ravensworth. Ford of a man called Hrafn.

Richemund. Richmond. Norman name after 1070; meaning strong hill.

Rie. Reeth. Place at the stream.

Ripum. Ripon. Territory belonging to the tribe called Hrype.

Romundrebi. Romanby. Village of a man called Rothmundr.

Routhebiria. Rothbury. Stronhold of a man called Hrotha.

Smidetune. Great Smeaton. Farmstead of the smiths.

Snotingeham. Nottingham.

Stanmoir. Stainmore. Rocky or stony moor.

Sedberge. Sedburgh. Flat topped hill.

Schirebi. Skeeby. Village of a man called Skithi.

Swale. River Swale. Old English 'Sualuae', meaning rapid and liable to deluge.

Thorntune. Thornton Steward. Thorntree enclosure. 'Steward' was appended later.

Tirnetofte. Thrintoft. Thyrnir's homestead.

Tresch. Thirsk. A marsh.

Twisla. Haltwhistle. Junction of two streams. The old French, 'Haut', was added latter.
Ulueswater. Ullswater. Lake of a man called Ulfr.
Westmoringaland. Westmorland. District of the people living west of the moors (Pennines).

Woodland Settlements. All are north west from Richmond.

Ellepigerthwaite. West House. A clearing in a glade of alder trees. Old Danish: home of the alder tree girls, where they dance and lure young men to their death.
Grenefell. Long Green. The top of the hill is bare, grass covered.
Helwith. Helwith. Hel's wood. Where the dead souls go.
Hulders-wold. High Wallgate. In Norse mythology, the hulders were seductive forest creatures, kind to charcoal burners, watching their fires while they rested.
Locherlega. Lockley Wood. Woodland clearing of a wood keeper.
Wasfelte. Washfold. The place where sheep were washed.

Principle Characters

*Historical character

Ealdgith's Family

Thor. Father. Thegn of fourteen manors including the manor of Hindrelag. Killed in the Harrying.
Earl Uhtred*. Earl Uhtred The Bold of Northumbria. Great grandfather. Killed in 1016. Ealdgith's grandmother, Ecgthryth, was his first wife.
Earl Gospatrick*. Earl of Northumbria 1067-69 and 1070-72. Grandson of Earl Uhtred and his third wife, Aelfgifu. Aelfgifu was the daughter of King Ethelred 2nd of England. He is Ealdgith's second cousin.
Lord Gospatrick*. Ealdgith's uncle. Brother of Thor. Thegn of nine manors.
Aethelreda*. Earl Gospatricks wife. From Wessex.

Hravn's Family

Ask. Also known as The Bear. Norse heritage. Held the manor of Raveneswet for Thorfinnr*. Now leads those taking refuge in the wild woodland.
Freya. Ask's Norse mistress and, after the Harrying, his wife. Hravn's mother.
Bron. Ask's mother, Hravn's grandmother. Herbalist and healer. Cumbrian.

The Resistance

Ulf. Former housecarl to Thor.
Orme. Former stable hand for Thor.
Frida. Agnaar's daughter
Ole. Agnaar's son.
Cyneburg. From Grinton

The Settlement Leaders

Leofric. At Helwith
Agnaar. At Hulders-wold.
Aelf. Woodcutter at Locherlega.

Normans and Bretons

Count Alan*. Count Alan 'Rufus'. Relative of William the Conqueror, and commander of Breton forces at the Battle of Hastings. First Lord of Richmond.
Lord Enisant*. Count Alan's Constable.
Riocus. Reeve.

The Others

Father Oda. Priest at Esebi. Earl Gospatrick's agent.
Father Ealdnoth. Priest at Hindrelag.
Alfhildr. Birthing woman at Hyrst
Ealhstan. From Grinton. Cynburg's father.
Elfreda. Cyneburg's mother.
Esma. Aelf's wife
Ada. Twelve year old girl.
Edric. The Bear's assistant. Recruited to the resistance.

The Harrying of the North

The Year 1071 – Resistance and Revenge

Aere Yule 1070

Chapter 1

Ealdgith cursed the cold as she lay prone under the edge of a dense holly bush. She longed to wiggle her fingers to stimulate some warmth, but she was also willing a squirrel to come closer and so she stayed perfectly still. The squirrel's red tail glowed in the dawn sunlight as it dug into the earth and stuffed nuts from a winter stash into its cheek pouches. Despite the protection of her padded leather jerkin and leather helmet Ealdgith was chilled to her bones from lying still for so long. Only the warmth of the two wolfhounds, snuggled either side of her, stopped Ealdgith from shivering. The wolfhounds were as still as Ealdgith, their gaze fixed, not on the squirrel but on a young roe deer that scratched the frosty grass on the other side of the track. Trained to hunt, they couldn't understand why their mistress ignored the deer.

Both hounds twitched suddenly as the deer and the squirrel looked up, then bolted.

Ealdgith flicked her eyes back to the track. "Damn!" She swore under her breath.

A Norman soldier, helmeted and armoured in chain mail, rode towards her down the track from the direction of Richemund. He was already well clear of the bend, that was a half furlong away, and three others followed. Ealdgith cursed the squirrel for distracting her and wondered to herself why Norman soldiers always patrolled in fours? Hravn would know.

Ealdgith placed a restraining hand on each of the hounds' shoulders and lay still, watching. The wolfhounds tensed, their hackles rose. The last time they had encountered Norman soldiers was in a mortal fight. The wolfhounds were called Sköll and Hati, named after two characters from the tales of Hravn's Norse heritage. Sköll and Hati were evil wargs that chased the sun and the moon. Cunning and strong they succeeded in their quest; just as the two wolfhounds had fought alongside Ealdgith and Hravn and saved their lives three times in the past year.

The soldiers were a danger, but they didn't pose an immediate threat unless they turned off the Richemund to Daltun track and followed the small rough path that led into the wild wood. Ealdgith was confident that her woollen cloak would camouflage her on the woodland floor; its green, russet and purple pattern blended well with the red-berried holly bush. Nevertheless, she moved her hand gently down her left side to loosen the thong that held her long seax in its scabbard.

Ealdgith was skilled in the use of the seax and the bow, having been trained to fight by Oswin, a warrior turned hermit-monk, who lived in a cave in the wild Mallerstang forest. He had given Hravn and her sanctuary when they had fled the valley of the Swale a year ago and, in the three months that they had stayed with him, she had learned to fight and survive the brutality of a man's world. Oswin was a Dane who had served the old king, Cnut, and then fought for the Byzantine Emperor, before turning his back upon violence to become a soldier of Christ. But, he was a soldier at heart and had made sure that Hravn and Ealdgith had mastered the skills of armed and unarmed combat before they embarked upon a journey that had seen them return finally to the hills of Ghellinges-scir barely a month ago.

Now, having turned fifteen last summer, Ealdgith was betrothed sworn to Hravn, her cousin by marriage and her life-long friend. Although not formally married they considered themselves to be so and were accepted as such by all who knew them. Hravn was himself only sixteen, but they had both grown from childhood to adulthood in their year-long flight and, despite her youth, Ealdgith was already known as 'My Lady' by those of her father's people who had survived the slaughter.

The day before, some of these people had stolen three sheep from the village of Daltun. They now lived in the wild woods that covered the hills above Richemund, having been forced from their village of Daltun just after last year's Yule-tide feast, when the Normans had harried the North of England in brutal revenge for an uprising against King William. The harrying had been a vicious slaughter in which thousands, maybe tens of thousands, had died and many more had later succumbed to starvation after the devastating destruction of their homes, livestock and granaries.

In the ensuing mayhem, the Anglo-Scandinavian population of Ghellinges-scir had little option other than to submit to their new Norman overlords. Many of the surviving English gentry had lost their lands and been forced into servitude. A few had thrown in their lot with the Normans, paid a high price to retain their estates, and worked their people hard to raise the taxes their Breton-Norman overlord, Count Alan, demanded.

Those who had refused to submit had fled to the woods that cloaked the hills between the valleys of the Swale and the Tees, banding together in new communities. Their leader was Ealdgith's future father-in-law, Ask. He had held the manor of Ravenswet until his own lord, Thorfinnr, had sided with the Normans. His people were now close to starving.

The track that Ealdgith was watching led from the new Norman castle and military camp at Richemund, through Ravenswet and on to Daltun and the other small villages that still scraped a tenuous existence on the northern slopes of the valley south of the River Tees. Richemund was a new settlement, built on the site of Ealdgith's family home, the hall for the manor of Hindrelag. Her father, Thor, had perished there, along with all her family. His hall had been burned, and his people forced into servitude. Richemund was now the centre for Count Alan's military domination of the North.

Ask, known as The Bear by his people, was concerned that the rustled sheep could trigger a reaction from the Norman garrison. The sheep had been led along the track, and then up a small path into the woods. Although the rustlers had taken care to cover their tracks, using brushwood to clear away any marks that risked leaving a sign for a search party, The Bear could not risk Norman interest in his people's woodland haven.

The soldier slowed, his eyes taken by something on the ground. He reined the horse to a halt and dismounted slowly, taking care not to disturb the track. Then, kicking the ground with his boot, he bent down and flicked the remains of a semi-frozen sheep's dropping with his gloved fingers. He straightened and looked along the track, checking the undergrowth on either side, and then glanced towards his colleagues who were watching quizzically from a distance. He shook his head and shrugged before he remounted and waved the party of soldiers forward. Ealdgith held her breath as she watched them trot towards Daltun. She smiled grimly as the low Aere-Yule dawn sun cast a blood-red light onto their polished conical helmets.

*****

"Go Sköll, find Hravn!" Ealdgith sensed the wolfhound's eagerness to rejoin his master. She had walked most of the two leagues back to Hulders-wold, the small charcoal burners' settlement on a high wooded spur, where Hravn and The Bear were discussing the night's rustling with Agnaar, a miller and refugee from Daltun. It was Agnaar who had planned the rustling and, in so-doing, earned The Bear's ire for risking the safety of the people, within the six settlements, for which he was responsible.

As Ealdgith walked into the woodland clearing her eye was caught by the two charcoal burners' huts and the recent collection of small shelters that had been thrown together by the dozen or so refugees that had fled there last winter. She could see how roughly made the shelters had been, and could tell how desperately uncomfortable the families must have been in the two months of snow that had followed. The shelters had been reinforced during the summer, and walls of interlaced branches, with mud and moss filling the cracks, would at least keep out the wind and rain; if not the cold. But what really drew her attention was the fire above which a cooking pot was suspended. She could smell the sweet aroma of a broth over the sharp tang of the wood smoke, and was suddenly hungry.

"Hey, Edie!" Hravn called to her from the group of shelters. A tall, broad, black-haired and black-eyed youth waved at her to join them. He was flanked by The Bear. Although Hravn had grown quickly during the last year he was still dwarfed by his father who, despite the generous salting of white in his dark hair and beard, was still very deserving of his nickname. Ealdgith didn't recognise the third man, who was squat and bald, but assumed that he was Agnaar. As Hravn walked over to Ealdgith, Agnaar shrugged his shoulders resignedly, nodded to The Bear and turned back towards his shelter.

The Bear smiled at his daughter-in-law as he watched her pull off the tan-coloured leather helmet and shake her long fair hair free. Her green eyes caught the low sun, enhancing her beauty, and he realised why his people were already referring to her as 'the wildcat' behind her back. He was reassured. There was a deep respect in the name, respect for a young woman who they recognised as a warrior as well as the lady who should, by rights, have inherited much of the land south of the Ghellinges-scir hills. He knew many of his people were unsure why she wore breaches and boots in the fashion of men, but he wasn't concerned; why would she wear a dress and wimple? Ever since she could ride a fell pony Ealdgith had worn boys' clothes when hunting and exploring the fells with Hravn. What did it matter, now that all their lives were in turmoil?

Ealdgith studied Hravn as he walked towards her. He looked every bit the young warrior that he was proving to be. His woollen cloak, of a similar pattern to Ealdgith's, draped from his right shoulder, partly covering the chain mail shirt that their Norse friend, Gunnar, had given him whilst they stayed in Morlund. Another symbol of the depth of that friendship was the long sword that hung from his left hip. The sword was

6

called 'Nadr,' and Hravn had already proven that he could wield it with the lightening lethality of its venomous namesake. Ealdgith was pleased that Hravn wore the mail shirt. She knew that he didn't do it for vanity, rather, he needed to build up his strength to get used to its weight. She was also very aware that he was now at constant physical risk and would doubtless have to defend himself many times in the future.

Hravn took Ealdgith's helmet, stooped to give her a kiss and passed her a wooden bowl. "Come, have what's left of the broth. You'll need it. You must have been frozen out there."

Ealdgith sat down on a tree stump by the fire whilst Hravn ladled broth into the bowl. The broth smelt better than it tasted. At least it was hot and wet and warmed her from the inside. It was the day before yuletide and she remembered last year's feast in her uncle's hall. That would never happen again. She feared that they would never have that sort of food again either. The thin broth of mixed leaves, grain and just a little meat, that she thought was hare, was a poor substitute. But it was all that they had in their woodland refuge and she feared that it would not last the winter. She wondered just how the five score or more people that depended upon the wooded hills would survive? She and Hravn had already lost weight since their return three weeks ago. She could feel it herself, and see it on Hravn. "Come on Edie, have some bread." Hravn passed her a small flat-loaf, and she wondered if he had saved his share for her.

She knelt closer to the fire as she chewed the rough bread. The warmth from the burning pine logs soaked into her and her mind wandered as she stared into the glow of the embers. She recalled their meeting with Earl Gospatrick on the week after their return.

7

Ealdgith had always thought of Earl Gospatrick as one of her uncles, although Hravn, who knew her family history better than she did, said that he was really her first cousin once removed. The relationship sounded complicated, but at least it stopped confusion with Lord Gospatrick, her father's brother, who now sided with the Normans and still held his lands along the River Swale and south into the Vale of Euruic.

Hravn's understanding of her family history intrigued Ealdgith and she had spent much of her last year trying to piece it together. The more she understood, the more she realised just how much their lives were now being governed by it. Her great grandfather was Earl Uhtred the Bold. He had been known as The Lord of the North and was from an ancient Anglo-Saxon family that ruled from the centuries old Northumbrian fortress of Bebbanburge, far to the north of the River Tyne. When the Danish King Cnut had taken the English throne after the death of the late King Ethered's son, Edmund Ironside, he had schemed that Earl Uhtred should be killed in a blood feud and replaced by a Danish Jarl.

Earl Uhtred had married three times. Her dead father, Lord Gospatrick and The Bear's first wife, Hild, were all grandchildren from Uhtred's first marriage. Uhtred's third wife, Aelgifu, had been King Ethelred's daughter, and their daughter, also named Ealdgith, had married the Cumbric Prince Maldred. Ealdgith's son was Earl Gospatrick. Earl Gospatrick had a claim upon the northern English lands of Yorkshire, Durham and Northumberland as well as Cumbraland, Westmoringaland and Scots lands in Strathclyde.

Ealdgith mused that Wyrd, the web of fate woven by the three Norns, had really entangled her in its mesh. Earl Gospatrick had finally regained his northern earldom a few years ago, purchasing it for a high fee from a revenue-hungry King William. But he wasn't the King's man and he quickly sided with the Atheling, Prince Edgar, who was the great grandson of King Ethelred and the strongest claimant to the English throne. The young Atheling was only in his teens and had needed strong guidance. With Earl Gospatrick's support, and the aid of King Malcolm of the Scots, he had risen against King William three years earlier in 1068. The rebellion failed and Gospatrick had lost his earldom and fled to Scotland. Months later, the North again rose against Norman rule and, with the support of King Swein of Denmark, the Atheling and Gospatrick took Durham and York. King William's retribution had been swift and brutal, and the harrying in the Aefter-yule of 1070 had destroyed support for the uprising. The Atheling had fled back to Scotland and Earl Gospatrick had been lucky to escape and retain his Northumbrian lands around Bebbanburge.

Following their winter with Oswin in the Mallerstang Forest, Hravn and Ealdgith had fled to Westmoringaland to try and find Hravn's Cumbric family or join Earl Gospatrick if he was there. They had instead been taken hostage by Uther Pendragon, a brutal Cumbric warlord. Ealdgith had protected herself from harassment by pretending to be a boy and they had been obliged to work for the Pendragon clan by scouting and planning raids on wealthy manors in the Norman-held lands south of Westmoringaland. They were successful and, in so doing, earned the hatred of Uther's bullying grandson, Owain. When Owain discovered that Ealdgith was a girl he attempted to rape her and, in the ensuing fight, Hravn, Ealdgith and the hounds had killed Owain, his father, and several others. They had fled into the Eden Valley and taken sanctuary in the church at Morlund. It transpired that the parish priest was Earl Gospatrick's agent. He had reported that

Hravn and Ealdgith were intending to return to Ghellinges-scir to join a resistance against the Norman oppression or, if that was not possible, seek to serve Earl Gospatrick in Bebbanburge.

Earl Gospatrick was playing a dangerous political game, befriending Count Alan on the one hand and encouraging resistance on the other; and had arranged a meeting with Hravn, Ealdgith and The Bear within days of their return to Ghellinges-scir. The Earl had been surprisingly open with his cousin and her family, and had explained that he wanted to generate unrest to pin the Normans' attention to their lands in Yorkshire and Durham and deter unwanted interest in Northumberland. He intended to keep his lands free, as a possible base from which he could mount a further rebellion with Scots or Danish support, and he had wanted Hravn and Ealdgith to be his 'eyes and ears' in the vital Richemund stronghold. He had even gone so far as to write them a signed and sealed letter of introduction to Count Alan.

The letter, written in Latin and English, described Hravn as a freeman of Ravenstandale and Ealdgith as his wife. Hravn couldn't read or write, other than to make his own mark, but Ealdgith was literate in English. She thanked God that her mother had insisted she learn, saying 'a wife who can read and write is invaluable to a husband who can do neither'. Ealdgith had smiled when she read that she was Hravn's wife. They weren't married, but were sworn to each other and, although they shared the same bed, they had never made love as married couples do for fear of bringing a child into their turbulent world. That would have to wait.

"Edie! Are you nodding off there?" Hravn's sharp nudge jerked Ealdgith back to reality. "N...No. I was just thinking about our meeting with Earl Gospatrick and what we must do next."

"Me too." Hravn shuffled closer to her, his mail shirt rustled metallically. "The Bear and I were talking things over when you were on watch. Agnaar's foolishness has rather brought matters to a head, but it's also made me realise what we must do."

"Go on." Ealdgith half turned and smiled as she raised a quizzical eyebrow. Hravn knew that she had probably guessed his plan.

"Well, Gospatrick said that he wants to create many small points of resistance across the North. 'Cells', he called them, and he wants them to be independent of each other so that if one cell is taken then they won't be able to inform on the others, even if tortured."

"Yes..." Ealdgith was hesitant. She was confident in her ability to fight, but torture terrified her. She had resolved never to be captured, but she wasn't sure what she would do if she was. It was a thought she kept pushing to the back of her mind.

"He wanted us to form a cell here. He said that Brother Patrick's reports about our time with the Pendragons had convinced him that we could do just the sort of tasks that he needs. Remember how impressed he was with the way you shot the two soldiers when I was knocked unconscious. He knows that we can do it. I, we, just need to be confident in ourselves; though I'm not sure if I'm ready to use my Cumbric to ingratiate myself as a translator for the Breton knights that are based here. The languages are similar, but not the same, and I don't want to be face to face with these...bastards... every day. I know that I would certainly be his 'eyes and ears', but-"

Ealdgith interrupted, "So, you're thinking that Agnaar's rustling was an act of defiance, or resistance, that we didn't control and therefore placed us at risk?"

"Exactly. If we are to form a resistance cell, then we need to be very sure that we are in control. That's what The Bear was saying just now. I know he's keen to support a resistance, but he doesn't want to put his people at risk. It's hard enough for them just to survive. What The Bear wants, and I agree with him, is for us to form a cell, but place ourselves away from his settlements. We must choose a small team of volunteers, create a secure camp of our own, and then control all acts of defiance. The Bear says that he will make sure that his people provide us with the food and support we need. He trusts us and doesn't want to know what we are doing. If he is taken and questioned he can't be forced to tell what he doesn't know."

"Yes, and..." Ealdgith was seized with enthusiasm. "...we can raid for food, just as Agnaar did, give it to our people so that they see that we aren't a drain on what little that they have, and gain their support. We can also ambush and rob, just as Pendragon trained us to do, and pass the money back to The Bear."

Hravn nodded. "You've got it Edie. I knew you would. We will choose when and where to raid, we'll be responsible for the risks we take, and we can make sure that we don't mess on our own doorstep. We should target those of our own who have sided with the Normans. Your uncle for one!"

"I know," was all that Ealdgith could reply. She couldn't understand how her uncle could have sided with those who had killed her family; his family. He had always been a strong supporter of the rebellion. Why was he now such a traitor?

Hravn's confidence grew as he enthused about the plan. "The people are close to starving so we need to start now if we are going to stop them doing any more foolish raids. We need a group of at least four, maybe a couple more. Orme is with us, I know. The Bear suggests that we tour the settlements and find at least one more to join us, we can build the team up from there as we go."

"What about a camp?"

"Aha! I'm ahead of you there Edie. I know just the place. Thor's Cave, in the cliffs above Mersche, is just outside the boundary that The Bear has placed on his people's movement. Look, I'll show you."

Hravn levelled a large patch of cold ash and, taking a stick, started to sketch the outline of the Ghellinges-scir hills.

"This, Edie, is the line of the River Swale. Here is Arkengarthdale, then Langethwait, Hyrst, Daltun, Raveneswet, Ghellinges, Richemund, Hudreswelle."

Hravn placed larger stones to represent the villages and then small ones for the settlements that The Bear's people had created. He then scored deep lines in the ash to show the steep valleys that cut through the wooded Ghellinges-scir hills.
Finally, he named the little settlements.

"In the north, we've got Grenefell, it's that bald headed hill that overlooks the Tees, the settlement is in the woods on the north slopes. Grouped in the middle from left to right there's the woodcutter's clearing at Locherlaga; Ellepigerthwaite, you know – the glade in the alder wood where the elven girls entice hapless young men, or so it's said; then there's Hulders-wold, where we are now. To the south there is The Bear's settlement by the sheep wash at Wasfelte and finally there's Helwith on the edge of the steep valley. If you follow the river down from Helwith, you come to Mersche, just north of the Swale."

Ealdgith nodded, adsorbing the details of the sketch in the ash and trying to relate it to hills and woods she had known all her life. She knew that Hravn had a real knack for creating a bird's eye view of the surrounding land in his mind, but it was a skill she was still trying to master.

"Right, do you see how all our settlements are in the western woods? The Bear has said that his people can't live or hunt to the east of Throstle Gill, or the Mersche Beck, for fear of coming across a Norman work party or, far worse, a hunting party. It's a risk he won't take. He's also very aware that smoke from cooking fires can be seen from a long way off and wants all of us to be very careful where and how we make them."

Hravn paused, "Well, Thor's Cave is on the eastern slopes of the Mersche Beck, high up in the limestone cliffs at the top of the wood line. It has a good view of the valley below and from the high ground above we can see over some of the wooded hills towards Richemund and Hindrelag. There's a deep dry cave and we can build a shelter on the front to help camouflage it."

"That sounds good, although I hope you are game for carrying water up from the beck all the time." He laughed, "There's a spring just fifty feet away, that'll be why it was once lived in."

Ealdgith was intrigued, "Why is it called Thor's Cave?"

14

"Ah! I wondered if you would ask that?" Hravn gave Ealdgith a cheeky grin. It was a grin that usually won her over. "It's The Bear's name for it really. When he was a lad he found three skulls there. Human skulls. He said they must have been a sacrifice to the old gods, Thor maybe."

Ealdgith pulled a face. Hravn laughed.

"They're still there, or they were a couple of years ago, resting on a ledge. It would be unfeeling to move them after all this time, don't you think?" He ducked quickly, just missing the flick that Ealdgith aimed at his ear.

Aefter Yule 1071

Chapter 2

Yuletide passed unremarked, save for the slaughter of the three sheep. Their carcasses were scraped clean of anything that could be eaten or used, and the bones boiled for stock. Hravn and Ealdgith rode back to The Bear's settlement at Wasfelte to plan the start of the resistance and the formation of their cell. They rode the same fell ponies upon which they had fled a year ago. The ponies were more sure-footed and nimble than a horse, particularly on rough moorland and in denser woods, where their riders could duck under low hanging branches.

As they trotted towards the settlement the hounds ran ahead, alerting a stocky, blond, youth who was in his late teens. He turned and waved across the clearing, "Hey, Hravn. Good hunting?" Pausing, he added with a cheeky grin, "...and My Lady?" Ealdgith gave him a stern look, then poked her tongue at him. "Orme, if I didn't know you better, and didn't owe you a debt of gratitude, I'd say you were chancing your arm. Come over to our hut, we've an idea to put to you."

Ealdgith's jocular relationship with Orme was based on strong mutual respect. He had worked for her father and assumed that she had been killed in the harrowing. When Hravn was knocked unconscious in the climatic fight that had almost prevented their return, Orme had come to her rescue, disposed of the Normans' bodies, recovered their weapons, armour and horses, and then proclaimed her martial ability in front of The Bear's people by presenting her with the arrow heads with which she had killed two soldiers with clean shots though their eyes. Very loyal to her family, and instinctively cocky, he held Ealdgith in awe as heiress to her father's estates and as a proven warrior, but he couldn't resist teasing her.

The two men ducked under the entrance of the A-framed shelter and squatted on the earth floor. Ealdgith sat on the low wood-framed bed whilst the hounds stretched across the entrance, placing their heads onto their paws with a long yawn.

Hravn glanced at the door to check that they weren't overheard. "Orme, we've decided what we are going to do. There's no shame if you want to back out, but, we would very much like you to join us in forming a special group to resist Norman rule."

Orme nodded, looked them each in the eye, then beamed, "Hravn, why ask? I'd follow you anywhere, and Edie, My Lady, I swore to you on the day you returned that I would serve you like I served your father. We've a lot to revenge, as well as resist."

Hravn clasped Orme's shoulder, "Well said, I knew you would, but we couldn't assume. Don't underestimate the risk, particularly if caught. I want you to help us choose a fourth member. Now let us tell you what we have in mind."

*****

"Damn! Ugh!" Hravn pushed himself up onto an elbow as he lay on the crude mattress of dry ferns covered with an old sheep skin. He shook his head to clear away the fuzziness of sleep and realised that water was slowly dripping through the sloping wattle, moss and fern wall above his head. He rolled over and gently shook

Ealdgith's shoulder. "Wake up Edie. My waterproofing skills aren't what they should be, and we need to move if we're to stay dry."

Ealdgith roused, squinted at Hravn, looked up as another drip glistened in the half-light and nodded in sleepy agreement.

Hravn was up and peering through the gap in the A-frame. "It's time we got going anyway, we need to rouse Orme and start our circuit of the settlements. The mist's down, it's as thick as a Herdwick's fleece, but at least the rain has stopped."

"You go and give Orme a shake. I'll blow on the ashes, get the fire going and warm some broth for us all." Ealdgith splashed some cold water from a bucket onto her face, pulled on her wool-lined leather jerkin, wrapped her cloak around her shoulders and took the last of their bread out of the covered pot in which she kept it, making a mental note to ask Hravn's mother, Freya, for some more. Ealdgith was now so used to living in the wild that she had almost forgotten the comforts of her former life as a wealthy thegn's daughter. Sköll stretched, yawned with a deep sigh, and ambled out to look for Hravn. Hati continued to lie by the bed, watching his mistress through large doleful eyes, willing her to throw him a tit-bit.

The broth was simmering when Orme ducked under the A-frame. "Morning Edie, that smells good," he said more out of politeness, than enthusiasm for their daily staple meal. "Hravn will be here in a moment, he's telling The Bear about our route. We'll head north to Locherlaga and Grenefell and come around in a circle to finish at Helwith. I think we'll have to stay over at Hulders-wold, he doesn't reckon we'll do it in one go in these short days."

"Here we are Edie." Hravn squeezed his way into the shelter. "Moder was baking whilst the rest of us slept. She's given us fresh loaves to take with us."

Ealdgith looked up, smiled and passed Hravn a bowl of broth in exchange for the loaves. "Let's eat up and get going."

*****

The mist hung low over the Ghellinges-scir hills. Only the valley bottoms were clear, but so little daylight penetrated, even they were in a permanent gloom.

Orme led the way as they rode towards Locherlaga. The mist dulled all noise, even the strike of the ponies' hooves on the earth sounded oddly muffled. Small droplets formed on the outside of their cloaks, and they shook themselves frequently before the water started to soak in. Ealdgith quipped that they were just like the hounds, who constantly shook off the cold damp drops glistening on their coats.

Hravn was impressed at the manner in which Orme followed a route hugging the edges of the broad wooded spurs that dropped into the valley bottom.

"You must know this area well? I'm amazed at how you navigate without any land marks."

Orme grinned and flicked a drop off the end of his nose. "Ah! There are, but I'm glad you can't see them." Hravn gave him a quizzical look.

"It's The Bear's idea. We've marked two ways that link all the settlements together in a circuit. An outer route follows the higher ground and this one runs through the valleys. There are two more ways that cut cross-wise, linking the settlements at the opposite corners. We've marked the routes with flashes cut into the trees; horizontal ones for this, vertical ones for the outer circuit and diagonals for the cross routes."

Hravn studied the ground ahead, his eyes drawn down in the manner of a tracker. "Where?"

Orme laughed again. "That's the beauty of it. We've cut them higher up, above the eye line. We stood on each other's shoulders to do them. It took us half the summer to do it. See!" He pointed to an oak tree that was just looming out of the mist.

"I've got it!' Hravn laughed. "Just below the fork in the trunk, a single broad slash. I'm impressed. Once you know where to look its easy, and quick to follow too."

Hravn's expression suddenly changed. He frowned, momentarily lost in thought. "But, we won't mark any routes to Thor's Cave. No one must be able to find us there. We'll havc to make sure we don't wear a track into the ground and make sure we always take different routes in and out."

Ealdgith had remained silent until now. "You're right, we can't risk the Normans, or anyone working with them, getting an inkling of where we are based. It's where we are most vulnerable. We can't even risk our own people knowing."

"You're right Edie." Hravn changed the subject. "Orme, do you think any of the lads that have been working with you will want to join us?"

Orme thought for a moment, then shook his head. "No, they haven't the confidence. Edie will tell you how

20

nervous they were when we came to find you. I think they saw too much violence last winter. We all did. They're happy with the challenge and excitement they get from working for The Bear, and he's going to need them to take his messages around the settlements and keep watch from the tops on clear days.'

"Mmm, that's rather what I thought. We need those who want revenge and will take risks."

"Yes...but revenge tempered with common-sense and the desire to survive," Ealdgith interrupted, adding, "and to support the Earl in his plans for a further rebellion. We need to choose carefully, and they will need to believe in us as much as we will have to trust in them."

The three fell silent, lost in their thoughts of what their plans really meant for their own futures.

*****

Hravn reined his pony to a halt and held up his hand to stop the others, before pointing to the hounds. Both had frozen and, their hackles raised, were staring fixedly towards a clearing to their left, in the direction from which the mist slowly drifted towards them. He turned, mouthed "deer" and slipped silently off his pony. Ealdgith did likewise, removed the bow that was slung over her shoulder and gestured to Orme to stay mounted, but still. "Watch," she mouthed silently.

The deer, a solitary roe buck, was nibbling the shoots off a sapling and was blissfully unaware of the down-wind threat.

Hravn drew Ealdgith towards him. She nodded as he whispered in her ear. They separated, each with their respective hound. Hravn unslung his bow. Ealdgith stooped down and moved a stone's throw further on, along the edge of the clearing, just in sight within the confines of the mist. She raised a thumb to Hravn and then bent down to Hati. Hravn did likewise with Sköll.

Both hounds moved, cautiously, silently, heads down as they looped around the opposite sides of the clearing towards the upwind corners. The buck continued to nibble.

Ealdgith knelt to the side of a gorse bush, rubbed her fingers tips together in her warm breath, then slowly eased an arrow from the quiver behind her right shoulder. She fitted the arrow to the bow then pulled, bracing herself and aiming at a point midway between her and the deer. When the deer bolted, she could quickly adjust to the left or right and ensure that the arrow hit the deer at the optimum range for her bow. She glanced sideways and saw that Hravn was similarly in position near to where the ponies stood, silent.

The deer's death was quick. It suddenly looked up, ears erect, sniffed the air and bolted straight towards Ealdgith. She tracked it momentarily, there was no need to aim off because it was moving straight towards her. Her arrow hit the deer cleanly between its eyes, piercing its brain. As the deer stumbled Hravn's arrow ripped into the side of its neck. The deer crashed through the saplings that it had so recently stripped of their buds and rolled onto its back, legs thrashing.

Sköll and Hati tore through the undergrowth, trailing briers from their coats. "Off boys! Off!" Hravn's urgent command saved Hati from a violent blow from a flailing hoof. Hravn grinned up at Orme, amused by his stunned expression. "Come on. We need to make sure it is dead."

Hravn took his spear from the holster on the side of his pony and ran forward. He waited until the deer's death throws had stopped and then prodded its neck to test for a reaction. It was dead. Ealdgith ran from the ponies with two lengths of rope. "Here, Orme, help lash the hooves together."

Hravn looked across at the others, "By rights, we should cut its throat and gut it now. But, it's so cold and there are no stomach wounds, so we might as well sling it over Orme's pony and slaughter it as soon as we get to Locherlaga. It can't be far now, can it, Orme?"

Orme shrugged, "To the woodcutter's place? Twenty minutes, or so." He was bemused as to why he'd been chosen to share his pony with the carcass. Perhaps it was an honour?

*****

"Yo! Aelf!" Orme's call shattered the stillness. A thick-set man, with nut brown weather-beaten skin and the last vestiges of blond hair on his balding head, ran towards them from a robust log cabin that stood in the middle of a clearing surrounded by oaks. A few pigs snuffled in the dirt beneath them.

Aelf slowed, wiped his hands on his breeches and then looked in puzzlement from Orme to Hravn, Ealdgith and the hounds. His eyes rested on the deer slumped over the back of Orme's pony.

Orme was enjoying his momentary fame. "Aelf, let me introduce Hravn and Lady Ealdgith. Hravn is The Bear's son. Lady Ealdgith has the rights to her father's lands along the Swale, but as we know..." He tailed off as Hravn interrupted.

"Aelf, you must remember us, we hunted these woods when we were children. We fled last year and have returned to hunt a different prey, though we would like you to take a share of our fresh venison. Is your good wife here to give us a hand to butcher it?"

Aelf stepped forward, an expression of recognition spread slowly across his face. "Hravn! Welcome. Come. You've changed so, both of you. Esma will want to see you, 'Little Edie'."

Orme looked stunned. He turned to Hravn, saw the broad smile on his friend's face, and laughed.

Ealdgith dismounted from her pony with a light spring. Pulling her helmet off she ran into the cabin to surprise Esma.

Later, the deer having been disembowelled, its blood drained to make black pudding, and its skin carefully removed, they stood talking to Aelf and Esma whilst Hravn tied two thirds of the meat into a tight bundle. They still had two more settlements to visit before nightfall, and would take some venison as a gift for each.

"I understand what you are planning to do, Hravn and, in my youth, I would have done the same." Aelf held Hravn's hand and looked him in the eye, speaking slowly, thoughtfully. "But the Normans have imposed the King's will in a way that no southern king ever has before. I can't see how we can ever break the hold that they now have, but if you can make life unpleasant for them, and help sustain those who have taken refuge, then you have my support."

Hravn nodded. He held Aelf's eyes, "I appreciate that."

"I fear that you won't find many willing to join you. So many starved, or were forced into servitude after the winter, that few are now likely to risk what little security they have left to them. I've heard that some who would fight have already gone into the hills south of the Jor or to the Mallerstang forest, where they are far away from the soldiers who are here, and where they can prey on Norman and Northerner alike. Those places have become wild and wicked lands, a home to reavers, and I would stay clear of them."

Hravn frowned grimly as the meaning of Aelf's counsel sank in. "Thank you Aelf," he said sombrely. Then added, his eyes alive, "But, we have work to do hereabouts." He clasped Aelf firmly on the shoulder before turning and, placing his foot in the stirrup, mounted nimbly onto his pony. "Grenefell awaits us."

*****

Grenefell was a disappointment. The refugees there had listened to Hravn, but he had failed to inspire them. He fell into a mood of gloomy introspection as they headed towards their last call of the day.

The mist was yellowing and the trees were little more than shadowy skeletons as they finally approached Hulders-wold. Ealdgith guided her pony with her knees, her hands tucked into her cloak to try and keep her fingers warm. Hravn blew on his, steamy warm breath mingling immediately with the mist that swirled around him. "You're doing well Orme. You know these woods better than I ever did. I couldn't say where we are within half a league yet you've brought us straight here. Tree-marks, or no marks, I'm impressed."

25

Orme grinned, then chuckled. "There's a reason, and you'll guess, but for the life of me, don't say anything to Agnaar."

Hravn threw him a sideways look; puzzled.

"Frida, perhaps?" Ealdgith asked, in a teasing tone. "Jet-black hair and innocent eyes? It was her father that was behind the rustling, wasn't it? I couldn't help but notice how your eyes followed her when we were last here." Despite the gloom, she could see Orme blush.

"Take care," Hravn teased. "I hear he's very protective."

As if on cue the trees parted and they entered the small clearing. A man was hunched over an open hearth trying to rekindle flames in the still damp air. He turned, startled.

"Hey, Agnaar. A boiling pot is just what we need for this meat we've brought you." Hravn's call was as much a reassurance as it was a greeting. He sensed that Agnaar would still feel sore from the tongue-lashing The Bear had given him and he wanted to gain his support for his plans.

Agnaar stood, stretching stiffly. "The damp is getting into my bones."

"This venison should help with that," quipped Hravn. "We need to pay for our keep tonight." Agnaar nodded his assent, smiled to the three-some and called to his daughter. "Frida, come and take this to your moder. We'll eat well tonight, and let the others know." Frida ran forward, glanced shyly at Orme and said quietly, "Thank you My Lady," as she took the hide-wrapped bundle of meat from Hravn. Ealdgith swung herself swiftly off her pony "Edie, please. Just call me Edie. Wait Frida, I'll come with you."

The light faded rapidly. Agnaar called to a young lad hovering to the side of them, "Ole, build the fire up and bring some stools. I can see Hravn has something on his mind."

"Yes, fader."

"Your son?" Asked Hravn.

"Yes, I forget whether he's twelve or thirteen. He's growing that quickly." Hravn could sense the pride in Agnaar's voice.

Ole returned with dry wood. It caught quickly and created a warm circle of muted light. Frida and Ealdgith came forward carrying a large pot on a pole that they slung across the side of the fire. Hravn saw more faces gathering around the edge of the circle and sensed that their interest was perhaps more to do with the pot, than his conversation with Agnaar. He gestured to Orme to join him and smiled to himself as Orme chose to settle himself as close as possible to where Frida was tending the pot; Orme's attention to Frida, and Frida's attention to the pot, was one of almost domestic bliss.

As Hravn explained his plan he glanced surreptitiously at the faces around him. From the solemn nod and shake of heads he could tell that there was support for the idea of his raiding for food for the benefit of all, but little enthusiasm to take part. The only exception was Ole, whose wide blue eyes reflected the firelight as he leant forward, buying into every word of Hravn's plan. He was his sister's double.

Hravn finished talking. Agnaar straightened up on his stool, glanced around at the men of his settlement, and gripped Hravn firmly on the forearm. "Hravn, I speak for all here when I say that we can't let these Norman bastards grind us into servitude. We support you and will do all we can to help you, just as you will be helping us all by bringing meat and grain. But, and I am ashamed to say this, none of us can risk what little future our families have by fighting alongside you."

Hravn nodded. "I thought as much. It is what Aelf said."

"Fader? Can I?" Ole asked earnestly. His voice was boyish and not yet broken, his tone pleading, but determined. Ealdgith glanced across to Frida. The blue of her eyes was innocent, gentle, almost seductive, whereas her brother's had the penetrating intensity of hard determination. She knew instinctively that Ole would be an asset.

Agnaar looked at his son with pride, and sadness, in his eyes. "We lost your two brothers last year. We can't lose you too."

"But, Fader..." Hravn interrupted Ole's plea. "I agree with your fader, Ole, all of us are at great risk. I am sure he will need you here, now that your brothers have been slain. It's not a boy's game."

Ealdgith stood up from where she was kneeling by the fire. "No, it isn't a child's game. But, we were barely out of childhood ourselves a year ago. I respect Ole's desire to resist and revenge his brothers." She looked around. "It's what we all want, if we are honest with ourselves."

Then she turned to Hravn with a very determined expression and said pointedly, "If we are to succeed, we will need all the support we can get. We have weapons to keep clean and sharp, mail to scour, ponies and horses to look after, and we will have a camp to keep. Remember Bran? He was the Pendragons' stable and errand boy. They couldn't do without him, though they never thanked him."

Hravn nodded reflectively. "Edie, well said, you're right." He turned to Agnaar. The question was in his eyes, unspoken.

Agnaar studied his son. He could see the boy's pent-up desire to revenge his brothers' deaths. He knew that it was an honest request. He knew also that it would be a small step towards restoring his family's honour.

"Very well, but you are not to raid outside the woods, and must come to see your moder every few days. She will find it very hard, I'm sure."

Hravn stood up, shaking Ole's hand in his. "Thank you Ole. I'll call for you when we are ready. It won't be long."

*****

Cold swirling mist continued to lock the woodland sanctuary in upon itself. Looking back, the three-some saw no sign of the broad high hill that sheltered the little settlement of Ellepigerthwaite. Ealdgith joked, as their ponies' hooves skittered on the steep gravel slope leading them away from the settlement, that the dour look on the settlers' faces must have scared away the elvish maidens who were rumoured to haunt the clearing in the alder-wood. "More like it's the weather that has soured their humour." Hravn's mood was little better than the settlers'.

"Cheer up. We've still to visit Helwith. Let's push the pace and get there quickly." Orme shouted with forced enthusiasm as he urged his pony forward through the sparse trees above the bank of the beck.

The stiffening breeze blowing up the narrow valley lifted their spirits and the mist.

"There! See it?" Orme pointed. "The clearing on the little plateau, halfway up the slope."

"Yes. There's rising smoke mixing into the cloud above." Hravn's gloom had gone.

"Halt! Who goes there?" The sudden challenge froze them.

"Sköll, Hati! Hold!" Hravn's counter-caution stopped the hounds from lunging at the tall well-built man that stepped from a tree to their front. He held a spear levelled towards them.

"Rest casy, Ulf. Put that spear away before you hurt yourself. I've someone for you to meet." Orme's unafraid good humour relaxed Hravn as he eased his half-drawn sword back into its scabbard.

"Ulf. Meet Hravn and Lady Ealdgith. We ... rather, they, have something to put to you."

Ealdgith pulled her helmet off, jumped from her pony and held out her hand. "Ulf! It's been a long time. I never thought to see you again."

Ulf's mouth gaped, then smiled. A broad grin creased his ruddy face. "Lady Ealdgith!" He took her hand and then pulled her to him in an embrace, "And not a ghost, for sure!"

"Hravn! You too?" Ulf glanced across to Hravn who was unbuckling his helm. "This day is certainly brightening up. Come, I'll walk you up to meet Leofric and his people."

As they walked Ulf turned to Ealdgith. "My Lady, before you ask, you have to know that my greatest sorrow is that I didn't die alongside your father."

Ealdgith slowed and glanced at Hravn. He walked further on, nudging Orme to follow. She stopped and took Ulf's hands in hers. "You're here now. Surely that is what matters? But tell me what happened."

"My Lady, on the day of the harrying I was on my way to Ghellinges on your father's business. When I saw the smoke from Hindrelag and the other manors I realised that our lands were being attacked and took to the woods. It was nightfall before I could get around the Norman patrols and return. I was too late. The hall was burning, as were all our houses."

Ulf saw tears on Ealdgith's cheeks and stopped.

"We too saw the hall burning. Hravn and I were hunting on the high moor south of the river. That is why we fled, to Westmoringaland and back. We only returned this month past."

Ulf nodded, sharing Ealdgith's grief.

"I found your father's body and those of his other huscarls. Normans too. Our men's lives had not been taken cheaply. I found my Adelind and our son by the remains of our house. There was nothing left and no one alive. I retreated to the woods. Others did too. After the killing stopped it was obvious that the Normans wanted to impose their own order on the land. Many returned to work in bondage, but some of us preferred to scrape a living in the wild. I found Leofric's settlement, and stayed."

Ealdgith continued to hold Ulf's hands in hers. She had known the blond, ruddy-faced, man for most of his adult life. His courage and loyalty were beyond question. Five years ago, in his late teens, he had fought for her father as a fyrd-man at the battle of Fulford, helping to save his life when the Danes broke the Northumbrian shield-wall. Having proven his worth as a soldier, her father had selected him personally to train as a huscarl and join his household bodyguard. Ealdgith knew that the shame Ulf felt at not dying alongside her father hurt him as much as the death of his own wife.

"But what of you and Hravn, My Lady?" Ulf glanced down at Ealdgith's leather helmet and smiled shyly. "You were always a headstrong girl, but never one to carry a seax and wear armour. Hravn too. He is every bit the warrior, by the look and sound of him. What happened in Westmoringaland?"

Ealdgith looked up at Ulf. Her face was serious, but her eyes smiled. "A lot happened, Ulf. Enough for half a lifetime. I'll just say that we've returned to take our revenge. Let Hravn tell you what we have in mind and then let me know if you will serve us as you once served my father. Come. Just call me Edie." She released his hands with a tender squeeze of her fingers and picked up her helmet. Hati whined and nuzzled Ulf's hand.

*****

"Well, that's our plan." Hravn raised his palms and looked around the group that had gathered by Leofric's hearth. "Leofric, I shan't ask if any of your people want to join us. I think that they have a duty to care for their own families, but, I will ask you, Ulf." He stood up and grasped Ulf's shoulder. "Edie and I have learnt a lot, and fought and taken lives, this past year, but we don't have your skill and experience...or maturity." He added, with a wry grin. "Will you join us?"

Ulf took Hravn's offered hand. The big man barely contained his emotion as he glanced across to Ealdgith. "I will serve you as I served my Lord Thor. Thank you. You've given me my life back and a purpose that I thought was lost."

He turned to Leofric. "I think you know why I can't stay. I'm a warrior at heart, but I'll never forget your kindness in giving me shelter. I'll gather my belongings and take my leave."

Hravn waved an acknowledgement to Leofric, then turned to Orme. "Here, take my pony and go and fetch Ole. We'll walk back to Wasfelte with Ulf. Mind you don't dally with Frida, we've a lot to do before we move to the cave."

Chapter 3

"Right! We'll leave at first light. Orme, can you make sure young Ole's settled in your shelter." He gestured to where Ole was slumped in sleep against a tree stump by the fire. Ealdgith and Hravn excused themselves from the small group that huddled around the dying embers of the communal fire. The hounds stretched and rose to follow as they walked back to their shelter. The Bear and Freya watched them go, a shared look of pride and concern on their faces.

Hravn turned to Ealdgith as they lay snuggled under a sheepskin, with the hounds lying close to their sides. "Edie? Are you happy with the idea of living with four men in a cave?" She giggled. "I dare say it wouldn't be quite the same as you living with four women in a cave, would it?"

Eadgith paused, then added, "Of course I'm happy. I spent most of last year living amongst men whilst I pretended to be a boy – now, that was difficult! Anyway, the others can live in the cave and we can live in the shelter outside the entrance. That way I won't attract attention when I need to go outside and the hounds will be more alert to unusual noises." She poked Hravn in his ribs, "Just make sure that the new roof doesn't leak like this one!"

"Do you think Ulf and Orme will get on?" Ealdgith asked with sudden concern. "They were both sworn to my father. Do you think that's the only reason they are joining us?"

She sensed Hravn shaking his head, "Don't worry. They are each cast from the same mould, of course they'll get on together. Although Orme's eight years younger, he'll want to learn from Ulf. You watch. He'll take his lead from Ulf just as he would from an elder brother. Anyway, you've forgotten that they are both sworn to you now. They're driven by the same resentment of the Normans as we are, and want to do something about it. You do realise that they would both die for you, don't you?"

Ealdgith took a deep breath. "Yes, I do. It's something I want to avoid. The responsibility is hard to think about. It's not like you and me; theirs is a commitment made out of duty."

"No," countered Hravn, "it's a commitment of strong affection and belief in you and what you represent. It's not duty. You have to understand that."

"I, I do." Ealdgith was still awed at the thought and struggled to understand the influence she held.

"We must keep the vow we made to Oswin. It might be hard for Ulf to understand." Ealdgith referred back to their promise to only use their martial skills, that Oswin had taught them, in the justified defence of those at risk of harm.

Hravn was grave. "He will. He's a huscarl. We must ensure that Orme follows his lead in that. I'm sure he will. I value Ulf. He is a leader of men, but he also wants to be directed."

"I know." Ealdgith interrupted. "That's your strength. You have the mind for planning and quick thinking. It's a great strength and you have a strong personality. I am sure Ulf will respect it and follow your lead. He

35

understands the leadership you provide. I can see it when you talk. Orme too."

Hravn smiled at her. "Thank you. Believe me, I have no hesitation in taking Norman lives. Not gratuitously, but for a purpose. They have taken everything from our people. We will still fulfil our vow to Brother Oswin if we are forced to kill to take food to feed the starving. If we burn a Norman granary, or the hall of an English lord that has sold-out to the Normans, then so be it. Oswin was a soldier. He would expect it."

He paused for a moment, thinking. "I won't take from our people, only from those who have sold-out. We should concentrate on raids and ambushes for robbery. Call it 'hit-and-run'. We mustn't let revenge cloud our judgement, though I will take revenge for my sisters and I am sure Ulf will be avenged for Adelind and his son. Come, let's sleep. There's a lot to do in the morning"

*****

The dawn was grey, but at least the mist had lifted. Low clouds drifted above the woods, clipping the tops of the high hills at Greenefell and Ellepigerthwaite.

When Hravn looked out from the shelter he could see shadowy figures by the light of the communal hearth. Last night's fire had already been brought back to life. The Bear was talking to Ulf, and Hravn thought that he could see his mother just beyond. Since their return, he had wondered why his mother had seemed unnaturally distant from him. He realised suddenly that she had withdrawn into herself only after he had explained their intention to contine resisting the Normans. He knew the pain of losing him again was hard for her to bare. Casting a backward glance to where Ealdgith was

36

rolling up the sheepskins, he ducked under the low entrance and strode across to Freya. As she turned he pulled her towards him in a deep hug, "Moder, this isn't farewell. It's just something I have to do. We will always be close by. Please, do not fret."

Freya held his eyes with hers. She nodded, not trusting herself to speak.

Hravn turned to The Bear. "Fader, come, please give us a hand to load the ponies. We've the mail coats and weapons from the dead Normans to move, as well as the sack of arrow heads we brought back from Morlund. Your help would make all the difference."

The Bear clasped his son's shoulder, pleased that the sombre mood had been broken and grateful to help.

Hravn was surprised at how quickly they were able to move to Thor's Cave; with four horses and six ponies to carry the loads, they were lifting the saddles off the animals by midday. "You were right to insist Ole joined us." He caught Ealdgith's eye and nodded towards where the lad was lugging the sack of arrow heads into the cave. "He hasn't stopped laughing and talking all morning. If he's always this enthusiastic he'll save us a lot of work."

Ulf reined his horse to a halt and swung down. He, too, was in high spirits. "Well, Hravn, I never thought I'd wear a mail coat again. That dead Norman was just the right size." He rolled his shoulders, relishing the feel of the metal rings as they slipped around the padded waistcoat that had also been taken from the dead soldier. "I still can't believe that you killed them both with a shot through the eye, Edie. Just make sure I never get on the wrong end of one of your arrows," he teased.

Hravn looked around, then raised his voice slightly. "Right! We've still got half the day. Ulf, can you stack everything in the cave, whilst Orme and Ole start to make a wattle and moss shelter outside. It needs to be big enough for Edie and me, and the hounds of course. We can't have your snores keeping us awake, can we! It must blend with the trees along the base of the crags. See if you can transplant some ivy to grow into it."

He turned to Ealdgith. "We'll find a spot to make an enclosure. I think we'll use the narrow flat ground at the base of the cliff. We'll fence off the steep side, where the trees drop into the valley, and we'll have a gate at either end. For a start, we just need a stack of straight branches and I'll link them together."

As the light began to fade cold air filled the valley and Ealdgith scavenged for dead wood. She was about to make a fire outside the cave when Hravn called across to her. "Edie, the best place is inside the cave, towards the back. There is a crack that leads up to the top of the crags. It's a natural chimney and an escape route if we need it. I forgot to show you all." He paused to see if everyone was within ear shot. "Hey, Ole! Leave the shelter, you can finish it tomorrow. Take one of the torches that The Bear gave us, set a spark to it. Go and find the chimney, then help Edie set the fire."

Ulf looked up and nodded approval to Hravn. "Good idea. The warmth will help keep the cave dry and will be better for storing the weapons, armour and the saddles. It'll also make sure that light doesn't show and the smoke will be filtered by the trees above."

Hravn grinned back, pleased to have the huscarl's praise. "That's what I thought. Once Ole's made a decent shelter we can have a small hearth outside to keep warm by, but not for cooking. I want everything to be invisible from twenty paces. When we finish, even the enclosure will have to blend into the woods and the crag, it's going to..."

Hravn was cut short by a boyish scream from within the cave. It was choked off almost immediately as Ealdgith shouted, "Hravn! Just what are you doing about these skulls?"

Hravn gave Ulf a sheepish grin and raised his eyes, saying, "Come, meet our ancestors."

He nipped into the cave. Twenty paces inside, Ole stood holding the torch. Its light reflected off three skulls that were perched on a ledge by the side of the chimney. The three heads, with yellow teeth, stretched parchment skin and clumps of brittle hair, stared down from their eyeless sockets. Although he had seen them before, Hravn's heart still missed a beat.

Ole turned towards Hravn. Ealdgith simply glowered. "I'm sorry Hravn, they just took me unawares." Ole was worried that Hravn would be cross at his sudden loss of nerve.

Hravn stepped forward, gave Ole a reassuring squeeze on his shoulder as he took the torch from him and then, with an apologetic, boyish, grin at Ealdgith, held the torch aloft so that Ulf and Orme could also see the skulls. "Meet Thor's men. Mayhap they were our ancestors and served the old gods. They've guarded this passage for many a year and they will guard us whilst we are here too. They're an ugly bunch but if ever we have to flee this way let's hope they scare the Normans as much as they did you, Ole." He paused to smile at Ole, "Why not show them who's the boss and give one a rub on the pate whenever you go up the chimney?"

Hravn was as pleased to see Ole's sheepish grin as he was to see the look on the others' faces. Ulf gave a wink and a chuckle and Orme's bemusement turned to a quick smile, whereas Ealdgith pulled a face of wry disgust. They all sent him the same message: they trusted him as their leader. "Let's leave them in peace and get the fire going."

As they turned to go Ealdgith muttered to Hravn, "At least they might do more for us than our current god. The women in Hyrst are saying that the bishops now want the priests to set their wives aside. Where is God's love in that?"

*****

It was completely dark by the time Ealdgith and Ole had prepared their meal of thin soup. Ealdgith had found old hearth stones at the base of the cleft in the cave wall and it proved to be the ideal place for the fire; a slight draught from the cave entrance carried the smoke straight up the natural chimney. Flames from a blazing log cast long ghoulish shadows around the cave walls.

Hravn perched on a low ledge and cleared his throat to attract attention. "Now that we are here we need to agree how we are going to work. There is a lot to do before we are ready to raid, but it's vital that we have an early success and can show our people that we can help provide for them."

Ulf nodded. "We need to train. My weapon handling skills are rusty and I doubt Orme's had any real teaching. Edie and you have the best recent experience."

"I agree." Ealdgith interrupted, with an apologetic glance at Hravn. "I can teach each of you the unarmed skills of the Byzantines. Brother Oswin was a master of them. Ole is still too slight to really wield a seax, so it is best he learns to fight as I do. But, sorry Hravn, let's hear your plan."

"Thanks Edie. I want us to have a routine. We'll rise and eat at first light. Then we'll start our tasks or training for the day. At last light, we'll get together to confirm exactly what we've done, set tasks for the next day and plan for the days ahead. Ulf's right about training. That has to be our priority once the shelter and enclosure are finished. Ulf, you're the huscarl. What do you advise?" Hravn was keen to show Ulf that he valued him."

The big man paused, thinking, before he spoke. "Well...I think we have an interesting challenge. You and Edie have a different experience of fighting to me, and the Normans do not fight as we English fight. I fought in the shield-wall or as part of a tight group around Edie's father. You fight as individuals or a pair. You've learnt also how to reave. That's a very different skill. The Normans fight on horses; we just rode them to battle and fought on foot. I think we have to work out what works best for us, develop the skills we need and decide how we can gain best advantage over the Normans."

Hravn chuckled. "Ulf, well said. You've hit the nail right on the head. Edie was right too. She needs to teach Ole to use the small seax and unarmed self-defence. She can teach both of you too." He glanced across to Orme. "There are some moves a large man can use to good effect."

"Right, this is what we'll do." Hravn lent forward and drew their attention.

"Ulf, you can teach Orme and me how to lock shields. We have three Norman shields that we must learn to use. We must practice as a threesome, with Edie and the hounds guarding our backs. Ole can practice standing alongside Edie."

"Ulf and Orme must train as a pair. Edie and I will always fight and work as a pair. You will form the second pair."

"You are right about the Normans fighting on horseback, Ulf. We saw them do that with brutal effect at Hudreswell. Brother Oswin learned that skill fighting in Byzantium. He taught us to fight with the javelin, riding the ponies and guiding them with our knees. We must all learn how to do that on horseback. Edie and I will show you how to hold and thrust the javelin, but we all need to improve our horsemanship. We should plan to ride the ponies in the woods, where they are nimbler around the trees, but we must go on horseback outside the woods, where speed will count more. I don't intend that we will fight on horseback, but we must be prepared to do so."

He turned to Ole, who was watching, awe-struck. "Ole, I want you to make us four man-size targets please. Long stakes bound with a thick thatch of ferns should do. I noticed some pollarded willows by the river bank, use the new growth for rods and weave some baskets to make the torsos. We'll set these up at intervals and then ride at them. Once we are happy with the javelin we will practice with the sword."

Ulf interrupted. "I'll make wooden swords to practice with, the same length as ours. I'll make wood seaxes too, of varying lengths."

"Thanks, that's a good point. Steel would be too sharp." Hravn smiled as he saw his unintended joke register with the others.

"Ulf, can you show Orme and Ole how to look after the armour, weapons and horses' tack? It will be Ole's task in the main, but Orme can you lend a hand when he is pushed, please."

The three nodded their agreement.

Ealdgith looked across to Hravn. "I think Ole needs his own pony if he is to run errands through the woods and stay in touch with his parents." Hravn nodded as Ealdgith continued, "Ole, choose one you like, but I suggest that the mare with the while fetlocks has the best nature. They can all be a bit stubborn at times, mind."

Ole beamed. It was as if he had received the best of Yule-tide and name-day presents all at once. He felt that he really was a member of their select team.

Hravn continued, "Before we start training, Orme can you take Ulf and Ole on a quick tour of the settlements? They need to know how the trail markers work and how to get around the woods quickly." He knew that the chance to visit Hulders-wold and see Frida would raise a smile from Orme. He wasn't disappointed.

Ealdgith added, "We also need lanolin if we are to care properly for the tack and keep the mail oiled...and tallow for candles too'

Ulf laughed, interrupting, "...and for that we need a sheep, or rather, we need its fleece to boil and its fat to render."

Hravn chuckled at Ulf's joke. "Well, that's our first mission and initial plan. Tomorrow, we'll finish setting up here. On the day after, you can do a very quick circuit of the settlements and Edie and I will hunt, as we need meat. I'll then give us ten days to practice horsemanship and swordsmanship. It's not long, so we will have to work hard. Then, we'll do a circuit of Mersche, Grinton and Marige to scavenge. We need a selection of pots, a large one for boiling a fleece, smaller seax and…a sheep or two. It will give us a chance to see which, if any, of those vills are still lived in."

"Good plan Hravn. I like how you think," Ulf paused, "your brains and my brawn go well together."

Ealdgith nodded agreement, pleased to see Ulf's reaction. She caught sight of Ole's concerned expression, "Yes, you can come too. It's called scavenging, not raiding. Just don't mention it to your fader."

Chapter 4

"Yo! Fader! Come and give us a hand with this buck." As they rode into the clearing at Wasfelte, Hravn called across to The Bear, who was sitting on a tree stump repairing a leather harness.

The Bear laid his work aside and stood up, stretching stiffly, and shivered from the effect of sitting still for too long in the cold and damp. "I was just fettling a harness so that the ponies can plough." He laughed at Hravn's bemused expression. "It's how we Norse ploughed before the English persuaded us that the ox was a better beast. I've acquired a plough. Now I need to adjust a harness so that one of my ponies can pull it."

Hravn laughed. "Well, I have a different beast that needs your attention. If you can help butcher this buck, I'll swap half for some of Moder's oat cakes." The Bear grinned at his son. "It's a fair swap, worth more oat cakes than we have, I'm sure, and a fine beast too. Where-"

Hravn interrupted. "You might not want to know. I sent Orme to show the others the track markers, so Edie and I took a careful ride into the woods towards Hindrelag, almost as far as the long west-fields." He knew that this was well beyond the limit that The Bear allowed his people to hunt or forage for fear that the Normans might discover them.

"We stopped on the high hill that overlooks the vale of the Jor, towards the moors and Euruic. Great tracts of the woodland there have been felled all around, save for a clump of old oaks on top of the hill. We didn't see anyone, but work parties have been there in the last few days."

The Bear nodded slowly, grim faced. "I'm glad you took a look. I'm not surprised. The lads keeping watch from the hill above Ellepigerthwaite said that the skyline there seemed to have changed and I've heard that they've built a large timber frame around this Richemund castle they're building. It's to help them haul blocks of stone into place on the walls. There's also a high stake-wall around the whole of the plateau that Ealdgith's hall was on. They'll need a mass of timber, and more yet, I'm sure. They'll be quarrying too, somewhere."

"I agree, but there's worse. We saw no wildlife at all, not even a hare or a bird. I know the woods have been disturbed, but it looks as if they have been hunted out."

The Bear was silent for a moment, as he let the meaning of this news sink in. "Where was the buck from?"

"The hounds caught him almost by chance, at the foot of the crags in Clapyat Gill. They had him at bay and Edie took him with a clean head shot."

"Good...good," he said absentmindedly. "You do realise that this means they could start hunting closer to us now. I must warn my people. We all need to take even greater care not to be discovered."

*****

Dusk was falling as Hravn and Ealdgith made their way slowly along the slope north of the cave. They moved quietly, keen to avoid attracting attention, wanting to check just how concealed their hideout was. They saw the enclosure first. It was well hidden, but the movement of the animals gave it away.

"I can't see any sign of the cave. Ole's done well", Hravn whispered.

"Make sure you tell him in front of everyone. You need to build his confidence. I can smell wood smoke though," Ealdgith whispered back.

There was no sign of light until they slipped behind the wattle and moss screen and into the cave.

"Ah, Hravn! Let me tell you what we heard." Ulf turned to greet them as Ole pushed past to have a look at the sack that Ealdgith carried. She lifted the oatcakes in the air, "Later, and don't try using your sister's charming eyes on me. Get the broth going first. We have some venison to add to it."

"Another head-shot, Edie, I bet." Orme shouted his praise from the hearth where he was getting the fire going.

As Ealdgith went to give Orme a hand, Ulf took Hravn to one side. "I spoke to Agnaar whilst Orme was busy making eyes at Frida. He was the miller at Daltun."

"I know. He still has contacts there. The Bear had to rein him in over some rustling."

"Be that as it may, he's got a good feel for what's going on. He said that when the Normans came it was as if Thorfinnr had an agreement with them. Most of his better manors suffered little harrying. The mill and granary at Daltun were untouched and it was Thorfinner, not the Normans, that threw Agnaar off his land. He gave the mill to Osberht, who he says is lazy and as sly as a weasel."

Hravn smiled, knowingly. "It was Osberht's sheep he rustled."

"Well," Ulf continued, "There's more than sheep to take from Osberht. Agnaar says that the Normans take all his wheat. They won't touch oats or barley by all accounts. Those stay in the granary for Thorfinnr's use. For some strange reason the Normans will only eat bread made from wheat. They think bread made from anything else is not worthy of their status...arrogant bastards!" Ulf spat.

"Go on." Hravn sensed where Ulf was leading.

"The granary floor is unsound. Agnaar intended to fix it. He didn't and Osberht is too lazy. He probably doesn't even know it's rotten. The granary is raised on limestone blocks to keep it dry and the rats out, but the floor at the back is rotting. Agnaar says that we could easily break a way in and clear sacks of grain from the back of the granary, through a hole in the floor. If we make sure we don't touch the sacks at the front nobody will know, not until Lencten anyway, when the stock runs low."

Hravn doubled up, laughing. "Ulf, you're a genius. It's simplicity itself. Mind, we need to plan our routes in and out carefully, but it is just the quick hit success that we need. If we can get a couple of sacks of oats to each of our settlements we will have proven our worth in their eyes. We'll talk this through after our meal, but I think we need to adjust our plans a wee bit, don't you?"

Their meal over, they stretched out on the cave's dry earth floor, soaking up the warmth that the fire threw out.

"Ulf's right." Ealdgith said, when she had heard his suggestion. 'There's more to this than you might think. We can afford to slip training and scavenging round Grinton for a few days if we can get sacks of grain to the settlements, where they're desperate for it. But if Agnaar is right about the Normans and wheat, then that is how we can hurt them. Their granaries will be half empty now and there's half a year to go until the next harvest, when they can re-stock. If we can find them, we can burn them. They won't lower themselves to eat oats so they will have the choice of starving or-"

"Carting grain in from elsewhere." Hravn interrupted, then caught sight of Ealdgith's raised eyebrow.

"Sorry Edie, but you're brilliant. I taught you well when we were raiding for the Pendragons. Ouch!" He winced as the toe of Ealdgith's boot caught his ankle bone.

Ulf picked up the conversation, with a cheeky grin across the fire towards Ealdgith. "Lady Edie. I now know why the people call you Wildcat. Hravn's right, that is brilliant. If they have to bring grain in by the cartload, they will need a lot of them. More than they can guard properly, I'm sure. That will give us the opportunity to hit them again." He paused, then lowered the tone of his voice as he looked them each in the eye to emphasise his point, "but our training and planning have to be faultless. If we make a mistake we won't live to make another."

They all nodded, sobered. Orme cleared his throat. "Edie, I think we all know which granaries to raid..."

"Yes, I know, Orme, my uncle's. We just need to find out which hold his wheat. I don't want to deprive his people of their barley and oats, but if he is holding stocks for the Normans then he can pay the price of replenishing that stock when we burn it." There was a hard edge to her voice. "Are we agreed?"

Hravn spoke for them all. "Aye, Edie. Of course, we are. We'll see Agnaar tomorrow and do the Daltun raid quickly. Afterwards, we'll scavenge around Grinton because we are going to need sheep to render down to tallow for torches when we burn the granaries. After that we need to train hard, like we planned, and then work on seriously reaving your uncle."

He glanced over to Ulf. "Ulf, you and I will plan the Daltun raid and Edie and Orme can plan the scavenging. I want you both to understand how Edie and I think. We can then get into the detail of the raids on Edie's uncle whilst we are training. It's two weeks into Aefter-Yule now and nigh on the full moon. I want us to be ready for the next full moon, we just need to pray that there is no snow."

*****

"There, that's the granary. See how it faces east to catch the warmth of the early sun and is built close into that crag behind to shelter it from the north winds?" Hravn and Ulf nodded as Agnaar pointed from the cover of the scrub line on the edge of Daltun.

"It couldn't be better sited, that crag screens it from the rest of the vill." Ulf was enthusiastic.

"Aye, and we can get the ponies as far forward as here and hold them behind the scrub whilst we break through the granary floor. Where is the rotten patch,

Agnaar?" Hravn quickly visualised the scheme of the raid. It was almost too easy.

"On the far-left side. It'll be the damp at the base of the crag that's caused it. We'll have room to work mind you." Hravn had agreed that Agnaar would come with them on the raid. His knowledge and strength would be very useful.

"Ulf, you stay here. Agnaar, we'll go forward and have a look at just where we are going to break in. We need to make sure we've got the right tools tonight. Come on."

*****

The fading glow from the dusk sun caught the top of the crag, hiding the granary in a blue shadow as Hravn, Agnaar and Ulf doubled forward from the scrub, leaving Ealdgith, Orme and Ole to look after the six fell ponies.

They rolled onto their backs on the turf between the granary and the crag and shuffled under the building. Hravn placed a rush-candle at the base of a staddle stone and, taking some tinder, sheltered it with his hands whilst Ulf struck a spark from flint and steel. The tinder caught and Hravn lit the candle. It would give them just enough light to work by, but would be well screened.

"Here, give me elbow-room to cut the rot out with this." Ulf shuffled under the rotten planks and began to stab rotten wood with his short seax.

"I'll take the end of the next plank. If we can cut a hole big enough to drop one of the sacks, we'll be able to slowly clear a way in. Thank the gods that I never got around to fixing this in the past."

"Aye, so are we, Agnaar, so are we." Hravn added under his breath.

The rotten planks fell apart with surprising ease and Ulf suddenly rolled to one side. "Thor's bollocks!" He cursed as a sack of grain fell through the gap, almost pinning his head to the ground. Hravn and Agnaar massaged the sack out of the hole and rolled it under the base of the granary and onto the turf at the bottom of the crag.

"Here's another coming." Ulf warned as a second sack slipped through the hole.

Within minutes they had six sacks lined up at the back of the granary. Hravn gave a low owl hoot.

"That's the signal, Orme. Take the first pony down. I'll send Ole with the next when Hravn hoots again." Ealdgith spoke quieter than needed, but she knew how sound could carry on a cold, still night.

Hravn and Agnaar had already tied two sacks together with stout hemp rope and strained as they lifted them, to hang them either side of the pony's saddle. "I reckon he can take another two. With six ponies, we should clear twenty-four sacks." Hravn hooted again and, as Orme led the pony back up the hill, Ole led the next one down.

Hravn rolled back under the granary. "We'd best check inside. I'm probably the slimmest." He passed Ulf another rush-light. "Here, light this and pass it up to me once I'm in."

Hravn choked back a cough as he pulled himself up into the dusty air. The sweet smell of grain mingled with the sharp odour of rotten wood. As he reached down for the candle he realised that he would have to be very careful that the dry dust didn't catch alight. This was one granary that they couldn't risk burning down.

"Phew!" He flinched as he straightened up and raised the candle, almost catching the bottom of a bulging sack with the flame.

"Ulf, tell Ole that we need Edie and him to manage the ponies, and to send Orme back down here. There's a mass of sacks above me and they'll collapse if we are not very careful. I need you in here with me, to prise them down, and then Agnaar and Orme can roll them out from underneath."

"Got it. Don't move 'til I join you." Hravn could hear Ulf shuffle backwards and whisper to the others.

"Ye gods! I see what you mean. It's like a small cave." Ulf was impressed. "I saw a stone mason build an arch once. As long as we can keep the pressure from the sides working on the central sacks we should be alright."

Hravn and Ulf choked and sweated as they gradually eased sacks down from above.

"I reckon that's got to be the last one." Hravn half spluttered on the dust as they lowered a sack down to Agnaar. "If we take anymore the whole lot will cave in on us."

Agnaar peered up and sucked his teeth. "You're right. We're lucky to get this many. We've a score I reckon." He laughed. "Osberht will never know he's been robbed. When they get this far the whole lot will collapse through the floor and he'll take the blame for not fixing the rot. That's sweet justice, for sure."

Agnaar helped Orme and Ealdgith to load the remaining sacks onto a pony whilst Hravn and Ulf cleared all signs of rotting wood. Ulf chuckled. "Osberht's day of reckoning may come sooner that Agnaar thinks. The rats will get stuck into this and bring the whole lot down before you know it."

The waxing moon rose just as they led the ponies away from the scrub and back to Hulders-wolde.

Hravn clasped Agnaar on the shoulder. "You're a good man Agnaar. I hope we've helped you even the score a wee bit. I shan't tell The Bear you helped us, but you deserve the lion's share of the spoils. We'll take a sack. Keep four yourself and I'll give the rest to The Bear to share around the other five settlements. Young Ole's a great lad too. He's a credit to you."

Agnaar turned to Hravn with a grim smile. "I admire you Hravn and what you're doing. I wish I could do more. It's a fine balance between keeping ourselves alive and making the bastards pay. In truth, I can see no happy end, but I'll be damned before I give in."

Chapter 5

It was a cold, clear morning. The grass on their side of Mersche Beck was in the shadow of the crags and still thick with frost. Orme blew on his fingers and cursed the cold as he helped Ole saddle the horses, Ole's pony and two pack ponies.

They made their way cautiously down into the valley bottom. Ulf and Hravn paused waiting for Orme to catch up. Ulf grinned across to Hravn and then called back to Orme, who was still struggling to come to terms with riding whilst wearing a mail shirt and steel helmet. "We'll make a warrior of you yet Orme. Two weeks from now, you'll feel a different man."

Hravn and Ealdgith laughed and joked together. "If the pain of Brother Oswin's training is anything to go by, he certainly will."

Orme scowled, then, seeing the truth in the jest, grinned at Ulf. "Just wait huscarl. I bet you're rustier than you think. I'll put a coin or two on Edie against you."

It was barely a league down to the vill of Mersche. Hravn led as they rode cautiously down to cross the track that linked the small vills north of the river. He paused, and pointed down to the ground, as they crossed the track. "Look at those weeds. They tell a tale."

"Aye," Ulf nodded, "It's usually too busy for weeds to grow in the ruts. A cart hasn't passed by here for a year since."

They slowed as they approached the cluster of thatched cottages. The silence was telling. No dogs barked. The only movement was a couple of cats that slunk away around the corner of a building.

Ealdgith rode close to Hravn. Memories of the destruction of Hudreswell and the brutal slaughter of the people of Dune, who had been burned alive in a barn, crowded her mind. "Let's not stop. It's deserted. We can always come back if we don't find what we need elsewhere."

"Hravn! Look there!" Ulf called across in a low voice, pointing with his spear to a pile of rotting rags at the edge of a barn. Bones poked through the rags. "I heard that most of the people here were forced to go to Richemund, but there's at least one who didn't."

Hravn was sobered by the gravity of the moment. "Edie's right. Let's head on to Grinton. This place is on our doorstep. We now know its deserted and can come back at will, if we need to. Take the lead, Edie. Ulf and I will bring up the rear."

Ealdgith tweaked her reins and led off at a trot.

Riding through the open fields and deserted pastures was unnerving after being cooped up in the woods. Orme peered all around, "I feel as if we are being watched, but by whom?" He called back to Hravn, "Do you think it is safe? Won't we stand out?"

Ulf chuckled and shouted forward from where he and Hravn were riding at the rear of the group. "All I can see is a party of men-at-arms escorting a lad on a pony. I think anyone hereabouts is more likely to be scared of us.'

"Look yonder!" Ealdgith, as sharp-eyed as ever, pointed to a distant group of figures by the river bank, just to their side of Grinton.

"It looks like three men and two ponies are ploughing, or trying to plough." Hravn shielded his brow with his hand, as he tried to make out what they were doing.'

"We'll soon tell by their reaction if they think we are Normans." Orme was rather more confident after Ulf's reassurance.

"Lead on, Edie." Hravn called forward to her. "We'll go and put their minds, and ours, at rest."

The men froze as they saw the party riding towards them. Two walked slowly forward, shielding the third who was holding the ponies behind him, protectively. Theirs mouths dropped open as Ealdgith reined her horse to a halt and pulled her helmet off, shaking her long hair free. Orme smiled inwardly at their reaction. Was it because Ealdgith was a woman, or because she wore armour and a weapon, or was it just the beauty of her golden hair burnished by the low sunlight?

"Relax. We're not Norman, though I am reassured by your actions that you thought we were." Orme hung back slightly, letting Ealdgith speak, sensing that she would gain their confidence better than he could. He turned and motioned Hravn and the others to join him.

"I'm Ealdgith. You would maybe once have known me as Lady Ealdgith, before my father was slain and our lands taken." She turned, waiving behind her. "These are my friends. We've just returned and taken sanctuary in the high woodland. I want to know who our neighbours are?" She looked at them questioningly and glanced across towards the vill behind them, as if inviting an answer.

The men stared at her, grim faced, but resolute in their ragged clothes. Two were well into middle age, the one guarding the ponies was older, stooped and white haired.

One spoke, at last. "I'm Ealhstan. I speak for those of us who are left. I do not recall you, lady, but if your father was Thor then I knew of him. He was a good man, unlike his brother, Gospatrick, and Thorfinnr, our own lord." He spat at the mention of their names. "I mean you no offence, lady, but they are cruel and beyond cursing. They've taken most of those of us who survived last winter and forced them to work on their other lands down the river. We few, the old and sick, are all that are left. At least they have left us alone since. We scrape at the soil as best we can."

Ealdgith nodded. The plight of these people sickened her. She felt only cold hatred towards the Normans, and contempt for what her uncle was doing. "What you say only confirms what I have heard about my uncle and other of our, so-called, lords. We too, are scraping by, but we will do what we can to help you. Tell me, where are your livestock?" She peered around.

Ealhstan cleared his throat. "First, lady, tell me how it is that you, a woman, are here, armed and armoured, to all intents one of a Norman party?"

Ealdgith smiled and waved Hravn forward. He bade the hounds to stay with Ole and urged his horse forward, removing his helmet.

58

"Ealhstan, this is my husband, Hravn, son of The Bear, once of Raveneswet. The Bear and his people also took sanctuary in the woods. They sustain us whilst we seek to take what we can back from the Normans and give it to our people. As I said, I am reassured that you thought us Norman men-at-arms, for that is our guise."

Hravn had already hung his helmet from his saddle pommel. He sprang down and offered his hand.

Ealhstan continued to look from Ealdgith to Hravn, scrutinising the group. Ealdgith was unsure, but then Ealhstan's frown slowly relaxed into a broadening smile. He shook Hravn's hand. "Welcome My Lady, and you my lord. Maybe, at last, we have something to smile about."

"I hope so," Hravn said, "But what of your livestock? The fields hereabouts are empty."

The old man with the ponies spat. "Norman bastards. Slaughtered the lot. Even the oxen."

Hravn nodded. "That explains ploughing with ponies. My father is doing the same."

"My uncle's not quite right," Ealhstan contradicted the old man, "They slaughtered what they saw, but weren't here long and weren't thorough. They killed those that we needed to work with: oxen, dogs, my bull and many of the cattle. The sheep and pigs scattered. One barn was fired too, but we saved the grain in the other, so we did have some seed corn to sow. The ponies were on the fell. We've got the pigs back and penned, and some cattle, but without the dogs we haven't been able to round up many sheep."

"But they graze yonder." Ealdgith pointed to the fellside beyond the vill.

"Yes, My Lady, they are hefted to the fell, but we're too few, or slow, to herd them and they scatter."

Hravn pursed his lips, thinking. "Ealhstan, we are after sheep to render down and their fleeces to boil for lanolin...oh, and their meat!" He added, chuckling. "Our hounds are bred for hunting rather than herding, but I'm sure we could manage to bring most of that flock off the fell for you. We also need domestic items. If we bring the sheep in, would you be happy for us to scavenge the empty houses for what we need?"

"By all means try, My Lord." Ealhstan was sceptical. "Take what you need."

"Thanks. We will talk more when you have a pen full of sheep. I also want to know about you neighbours up the valley."

Hravn remounted, tipped a casual salute towards Ealhstan as a gesture of thanks and, waiving to the others to follow, led off at a trot to the wooden bridge that crossed the river to Grinton.

*****

"God! That was a struggle! I'd forgotten that sheep could be so bloody minded," muttered Hravn as he rode at the end of the extended line that shepherded three score sheep down the fellside, towards the cluster of thatched timber houses that formed the vill of Grinton.

"We've the hounds to thank. There's no way we could do it. I can see why the old man sounded unsure." Orme shouted across from where he rode ten paces to Hravn's left.

Both glanced to their right as they heard Ealdgith's shrill command to Hati, urging him to encourage a recalcitrant young ram to stay with the flock.

Hravn laughed, "It's a daft tup that argues with a wolfhound…see!" As Hati lowered his head and glared forward, the ram turned suddenly and fled back to the flock. The ewes followed, bleating, as it ran ahead leading them to the pen that Ealhstan and his uncle held open.

As they swung the gate closed Hravn turned to Ealhstan. "Can your men give Orme and Ole a hand to slaughter the three sheep we need, whilst we talk with Edie and Ulf?" Ealhstan nodded, deferring to Hravn's authority. "Come inside. My wife and daughter will be there."

Hravn nodded to Ulf to join them.

As he followed Ealhstan he thought to himself just how much the past year had changed him, giving him the confidence to lead and direct men with considerably more maturity and experience than he had. He knew that he had an instinctive self-confidence and ability to think and plan clearly. Maybe that was it. He knew that he thrived on the challenge of leading others, but it was a responsibility that daunted and tired him too.

"This is my wife, Elfreda." Ealhstan gestured, too dismissively for Ealdgith's liking, towards a grey haired and rather gaunt lady by the hearth. "Our Cyneburg is hereabouts too."

Ulf spoke first. "Before we ask about what is happening at Rie and Marige, I think we can help you with the question of dogs." Ulf smiled at Hravn's surprised look.

"Do you know Leofric of Helwith?" The stocky huscarl dominated the room as he spoke. "No, but I know of Helwith. It is some years since I was there, mind."

Ulf laughed, "I doubt it's changed. Leofric has half a dozen working dogs and a bitch that has just pupped. His problem is that he has no sheep. I think you might be able to help each other there. Tell him Ulf sent you."

Hravn glanced at Ulf then turned to Ealhstan, "Tell him also, that The Bear knows. He insists that his people don't go outside the woodland without his say-so. It's for the safety of all, though Leofric will need to come here to swap sheep for dogs."

"Aye, my lord, 'tis not a problem. Thank you."

"Good. Now that's settled, what can you tell us of Rie and Marige?" Are the vills inhabited and, if so, by whom and how do they cope?"

Ealhstan shrugged and pursed his lips before speaking. Hravn noticed the glazed, watery look in Ealhstan's eyes as he spoke. He could tell that the memory hurt. "Same as here. Grain burnt, livestock slaughtered, men taken later. Bastards at Rie raped more than here though, and much of the vill was burnt. At Marige they killed instead. Quite a few, especially the sick and the children, starved in the winter. Some fled up the valley to Westmoringaland. There's nowt but a few families left at each. They survive, as we do."

Hravn paused, narrowing his eyes as he thought. "Mmm. If you see anyone from there you can mention us, but warn them to hold their tongues. We'll visit soon enough, we haven't the time just-" He broke off and turned as the cottage door opened.

A mousy-haired, bare-footed, girl hesitated in the opening. Hravn was struck first by her unusual prettiness. Her high cheekbones, wide-spaced blue-grey eyes and snub nose gave her an exotic, almost sultry appeal. Her heavy state of pregnancy was the next thing to impress him.

Ealdgith happened to be watching Ulf and saw how he tensed and his eyes widened when he saw the girl in the doorway.

"My daughter, Cyneburg." Ealhstan announced gruffly. "Come in girl and go through to the back." His voice was hard, cold, without affection.

Ealdgith held her hand out to her, "Was your husband taken by Thorfinner too?"

The girl paused and glanced at her parents. Her mother spoke. "No, she has no husband. Men-at-arms came after our men were taken. They wanted men for work at Richemund. When they found that there were none, they took Cyneburg for their sport instead. Three of them."

Cyneburg dropped her head, stifled a sob and rushed to the door at the back of the cottage. Ealdgith glanced at the frozen faces around the room and dashed after her. She caught Cyneburg's elbow with her hand and pulled her to one side just outside the door.

Cyneburg stopped and stared at Ealdgith, looking her up and down. "Who, in Freya's name, are you? I thought the men were Norman, at first, but you?

63

Dressed like that?" Her tone was almost aggressive, but Ealdgith sensed that the girl was more scared and self-conscious.

"Just call me Edie. Hravn's my husband. Ulf was my father's huscarl, 'til the Normans slew my family."

"Huh! Aye. They slew all our families too, but that doesn't explain-"

"Our armour, my clothes?" Ealdgith interrupted. "No, it doesn't. We're here to fight for those who can't fight. To take what we can and give it to those who need it...you." She let the thought sink in.

Cyneburg nodded, a slight smile twitched her lips. "It's a bit late for me. Those bastards took what they wanted and left me with this." Her hand rubbed the front of her extended tummy. You haven't asked, but Eostre, I think, I must be due about then...I...I..." Cyneburg stammered, then paused.

A tear trickled slowly down the side of Cyneburg's nose. Ealdgith took the hand that lay on Cyneburg's tummy and held it in hers. "The child? What of its future?" She asked gently.

"Fader will not talk of it. I know Moder will take it to lay on the fellside. Both say that we haven't the food for another mouth; and why should we feed a Norman bastard?" Cyneburg was sobbing now. Months of pent-up grief and worry welded up within her, triggered by the first act of simple kindness since the trauma of her rape. Ealdgith pulled Cynbeburg to her and held her. Moments turned into minutes; at last she pulled slowly away and, taking Cyneburg's hand in hers, led her back into the cottage.

"Thank you Ealhstan. I'll speak to The Bear about Leofric. We'll check the outlying cottages and then be on our way." Hravn turned as the back door scraped open, "Edie? We are just...what is it?"

Ealdgith stood, still holding the girl's hand and stared forcibly from the father to the mother. "There's been too much death in this valley already. If you are going to survive you will need a new generation. Sort out dogs and sheep and you'll have sufficient food for a little mouth. There is a birthing woman in Hyrst. I will make sure that she sees Cyneburg in time." She turned to Cyneburg, "and I will come and see you again too."

Hravn and Ulf were somewhat taken aback at Ealdgith's abrupt tone. She left them in no doubt as to her frame of mind when she said, "Right Hravn! We still have work to do. Thank you Ealhstan and mind you care for your daughter." No one doubted that, as the one-time heir to much of the land in the valley, she was not to be gainsaid in the matter of Cyneburg's unborn child.

Ulf hung back as they left the cottage. The big man grasped Ealhstan's shoulders. "Make no mistake. My Lady means what she says. Send word through Leofric if you need help...I will be back too." He looked directly at Cyneburg as he spoke.

Hravn rode alongside Ealdgith as they rode away from Grinton. Ulf and Orme led the pack ponies that laboured under the weight of the slaughtered sheep, a couple of very large cauldrons and several wooden buckets.

The day had clouded over, bringing warmer air that now turned to ground-mist. They quickened their pace instinctively as the light faded quickly.

"You were a bit terse back there. What got into you?"

Ealdgith turned square-on to Hravn and gave him a forceful stare. "Think! For one who is normally so thoughtful, Hravn, I'm surprised you didn't see Cyneburg's anguish. Men can be very hurtful and selfish towards women. It wasn't Cyneburg's fault that she was raped and I doubt Elfreda would expose the child on the fellside unless Ealhstan directed it. That's what got me. If Cyneburg wants to keep the child, then it's right that she does."

She paused, then added, almost thinking aloud, "I'm going to see Bron and have her teach me what she can about healing and birthing. Hers is a skill we need. It's best I learn it, else it will die with her."

Hravn smiled and Ealdgith relaxed as she looked into the warmth of his raven-black eyes. "That's good, Edie. You learn quickly and you have a natural way with people." He paused, adding, "But make sure my grandmother teaches others too. We need you with us, you can't be tied to the settlements."

"I know. I will."

Chapter 6

"Edie?" Ealdgith detected a plaintiff tone as Hravn hugged her from behind. "Would you be happy smoking the mutton whilst the rest of us get the training ground ready? I want Ole to finish making the thatched targets as soon as he can."

Ealdgith turned and poked her tongue at him, "Mmm...I wonder? The boys aren't all off to play, are they?"

"No...you'll be in the thick of it tomorrow. I promise." Hravn squeezed her, teasingly. "I rather think that Ulf isn't persuaded about the benefit of fighting on horseback. We will need to give him a little demonstration, you'll be good at that." She poked him in the ribs and raised a questioning eye-brow, "Sounds interesting. Tell me more later. I'll just need Ole to shift the carcasses and then he's yours."

Ole listened carefully whilst Hravn described how he wanted the targets making and then ran off to gather a mass of dead bracken and long grass from the river bank. He was keen to please Hravn. In his mind's eye, he saw himself as a warrior's swain, looking after his master's weapons and supporting him in battle. He wanted to serve Hravn and Ulf like that. Ole worked quickly and before the sun reached its zenith he called proudly to Hravn that he had five targets for him to inspect.

The targets were identical, each the size of a man's torso. A hollow lattice framework of young, green, willow rods stuffed with dry ferns and bound by tough river grass. Four were mounted on stout stakes. The fifth was attached to a long rope so that it could be hung from an over-head bough and swung.

Hravn lifted each in turn and turned to Ole with a wide smile and nod of approval. "Well done, Ole. Just what I need. You'll get a chance to test one yourself in a day or two. Now go and give Edie a hand smoking the mutton. I fear she'll be half-kippered herself by now."

As Ole ran off, Hravn turned and began to pace out the size of the water meadow that lay between the river and the wooded slope up to the cave. He placed two targets fifty paces apart and two closely staggered, left and right of a central line, with just ten paces between. The fifth target he hung from a broad oak that overshadowed the meadow. A sudden anguished cry drew his attention to the far end of the meadow where Ulf and Orme had started sword training.

Orme lay flat on his back. He rubbed his arm and laughed as Ulf bent forward and offered him a hand. They had spent the morning carving wooden swords that matched the size of the ones with which they they were armed. Hravn had insisted that they used wooden weapons in all their training, as they couldn't risk cuts and minor stab wounds. He had also insisted that Orme was not to wear his mail shirt until he had fully mastered use of the sword; not that he was unfamiliar with the weapon, but he had never been trained formally and had several bad habits to overcome.

Hravn had discussed a training plan with Ulf and agreed that Orme would have priority. He wanted the young man to be confident with a sword within a week. In the second week, he would progress to fighting whilst wearing mail and on horseback. If time permitted he would then work with Edie learning self-defence and archery. In the meantime, Edie would teach those same skills to Ole.

"Hey! Edie!" Hravn waved to Ealdgith as she staggered down the bank through the trees. "I hate to say it, my love, but you are going to curse me as much as you cursed Oswin when he trained us last year. Now just be gentle with that log." He stepped back quickly as Ealdgith slipped the log from her shoulders towards his feet.

"Mmm! You'll be cursing yourself too before the week's out. I dare say that humping our individual pet logs up and down this fellside all the time is going build up our strength, but just make sure yours is a damn sight bigger than mine. Remember that you've grown this past year, I haven't."

Hravn held out his arms to hug her. "By God! You smell smoky! How's the mutton coming on?"

"You really know how to inspire a girl, don't you?" She teased him as she pulled back from their embrace. "Now, tell me how we are going to impress Ulf with the merits of mounted fighting. It's three months since we last trained at Morlund, and that was when we only had the ponies. It'll be very different on horseback and I want to practice."

*****

Ulf grimaced as he washed a piece of gristly smoked mutton down with a mouthful of spring water, and then shook his head. "The fyrd always fought on foot. Our strength was the shield-wall and feet planted firmly on the ground."

"And that's the problem." Hravn jerked the edge of his hand to emphasise his meaning and his frustration. "The fyrd lost at Hastings, and we've never won a fixed battle with the Normans since. Man, on man, yes, I grant you, no-one could better us, whether we be English or Dane. But, a man against a mounted knight? No. You didn't see how they were when the vills were destroyed. We did. Knights just rode people down. Height, speed, the weight of the horse and armour. It's a brave, strong, man that will stand against the shock of that." He paused, not wanting to fall out with his friend, but convinced that the huscarl had to embrace change. "We'll say no more, not yet. Wait until Edie and I show you."

"Alright, what do you have in mind?" Ulf hesitated. "I am open to change, but I do need to be convinced."

"Go down to the meadow and stand five paces behind the first target, facing along the length of the meadow. Wear mail and your helm, and for Thor's-sake, keep your arms well tucked in. Just don't move. I think you will see what I mean by 'shock-action'." Hravn stood up and nodded to Ealdgith. "Come on Edie, we need to saddle the horses. Oh! Orme. Take Ole and go with Ulf, but stand well to the side of the meadow."

Ealdgith paused as she saddled her horse. "Are you sure about this? If one of us makes a mistake Ulf could be injured."

"No, he won't, nor will we make an error. Even if one of us misses the target with our lance he is still five paces off. Anyway, I've bound the lance heads with a piece of fleece so there's no risk of a glancing cut."

Ealdgith nodded, controlling her nerves. She knew she could do it. It was just that moments such as this always reminded her why they were training. She wondered how she would feel riding against a Norman man-at-arms and forced herself to focus on today instead, on attacking the wicker target. She had to forget that her friend stood just beyond it.

Hravn led the horses slowly down through the wood and chose a sheltered spot to the side of the meadow. "Edie, I want us to gain as much surprise as we can. Ulf has to see that a foot soldier really is out-classed when faced by cavalry. Once he understands that he will doubtless become a force to be feared."

The oaks that bordered the meadow were wide-spaced and their branches were high enough for them to ride under without risk. "Look, Edie, we'll gallop under cover of the trees and veer through that gap, straight towards the target. Keep your lance low, clear of the branches, and then brace into position as soon as you are free of the trees. Focus on the target, not Ulf. Keep on my left and keep the target on your right. You'll find it easy to veer off and miss Ulf. I'll pass the target on my left, stab down and then veer. That's where the challenge is." He reached across and held her forearm. "You'll be fine. Now, helmets on...ready? Let's go!"

Ulf stood five paces behind the target. He felt very exposed and glanced across to Orme, who gave him a thumbs-up and nod of encouragement. The thrum of pounding hooves echoed across the valley. The mist-shrouded ridge-tops seemed to loom over him. Where was the sound coming from? A flock of jackdaws burst from the tree tops and tore towards him as if it was a whirl of wild black smoke. He flinched as the high pitched metallic 'kaaaar' sound of their call reverberated around his head and he cursed Hravn for his raven-eyed looks. Could he really summon the black birds to do his bidding? The thought was dismissed for the foolishness that it was, but Ulf felt suddenly disorientated, alone, almost scared.

Light glinted off Hravn's helmet as they broke clear of the trees and Ulf grimaced as the two riders lowered their lances and hunched forward over their saddles. The horses were closing on him so quickly that he found it hard to focus properly. He moved his arms in front of his body and hunched his shoulders inwards, minimising his size as he flicked his eyes to the wicker target.

Ulf braced himself as Ealdgith appeared to hurl herself towards him. A white-tipped lance with a cat-like mask behind. He feared that the tip of her lance would rip through the target and continue to run straight through him. He suddenly panicked. How would he cope if the threat was real? Surely a drawn sword would deter the rider...surely it would? The thatch and wicker exploded from the top of the target as the horse disappeared in a swerve to his right, outside his sword arc.

Ulf suddenly flinched and fell to his right. He had been so intent on Ealdgith's direct charge that he had failed to focus on Hravn. The target disintegrated in a mass of flailing thatch as the bulk of Hravn's horse flashed past Ulf's left side in a warm, brown, blur. Hravn wheeled tightly and cantered back. Ealdgith followed.

"You alright, Ulf? Persuaded yet?"

Ulf pulled himself upright, his hands on his hips, and breathed deeply as he looked from one to the other. "I'm persuaded. How did you do that?"

Hravn pulled his helmet off, chuckling. "Edie held her lance under arm, driving it straight through the target. I held mine over arm. As I passed I stood in the stirrups, turned, learnt to my left and stabbed down into the target. The rest is history. I guess a man-at-arms would be too."

Ealdgith turned in her saddle and bowed towards the ripple of applause from Orme and Ole. She grinned widely, elated and relieved, her self-confidence flooding back. The flash of her green eyes behind the tan coloured face guards of her helmet prompted Orme to shout, "well done, Wildcat." Ole just stared, open mouthed.

Ulf was shaking his head in disbelief as he held his hand out to Hravn. "I can see that I've a lot to practice. Knight against knight would be interesting," he mused.

*****

Ole stared at Ealdgith, wide-eyed and slack-jawed, as she edged slowly around the square of clear turf, facing Ulf's intimidating bulk. He held his breath, captivated, frozen. How could Ealdgith hope to beat Ulf? How could Ulf fail to hurt her? His weight alone would pin her to the ground, let alone a blow from his wooden sword. Ole felt a surge of nausea, how could he face Ulf? He was no taller, or stronger, than Ealdgith.

Ealdgith's words of advice echoed in his ears: 'watch his eyes, read his thoughts, keep his hands, his feet, in the periphery of your vision, but his eyes will tell you what he will do next'. It had all sounded so simple when Ealdgith had sat him down and talked him through the basic moves. 'Come on, I'll show you,' she had said. 'I'll topple Ulf, believe me. Soon you will too'.

As she edged slowly around Ulf, swaying gently from left to right, her hands spaced apart and a short wooden seax grasped in her right, Ealdgith felt rather less confident. It was three months since she had beaten her Norse friend, Gunnar, and six since she had killed Pendragon's henchmen. Ulf was intimidating; the tallest opponent she had ever faced.

For all his strength, bulk and experience as a huscarl, Ulf was far from happy. He knew he could beat Ealdgith, but not without hurting her. That was something he could never do. She was his friend, his Lady. Hers was the life he had sworn to protect.

Ealdgith sensed his hesitation. Perversely, it gave her confidence. In past fights her opponents had always goaded her, either for real or in jest. Ulf wasn't goading her now. She knew that for their training to be successful, to have meaning, they must fight, regardless of the risk to themselves. If they were sensible, careful, and followed the rules that they had set themselves then any injuries would be minor, or so she hoped. Ealdgith had to lure Ulf into attacking her.

"Come on, big man. How can a huscarl fail to take a girl?" Ealdgith slowly reversed the grip on her short wooden seax. She would make her move soon and she couldn't risk falling on its sharp point when she broke inside Ulf's sword circle. She edged forward, slowly, testing Ulf. He stood his ground as the gap between them closed.

Ealdgith held Ulf's eyes. "Come on, Ulf, I'll topple you yet. But you have to move first, else it'll be a long day." She twitched the fingers of her left hand, beckoning him. Ulf sensed that Ealdgith was poised to move, but how? His own move was swift. Ealdgith almost missed it, distracted by her own goading. Ulf thrust his sword directly towards her seax, attempting to knock it from her hand.

His sword swept through empty air. Ealdgith had disappeared. He lurched forward, his momentum carrying him when he felt his legs swept from under and he fell flat on his face, winded. As he gasped and rolled onto his back a weight hit him, winding him again. Green eyes laughed down at his stunned expression, the tip of Ealdgith's wooden blade pressed hard against his cheek as she straddled his chest with her knee in his stomach.

Ulf lay back and laughed loudly, relieved that he hadn't hurt Ealdgith and highly amused at how she had caught him out. He accepted her hand and stood up, bracing his shoulders. "I think I need you as my body guard, Edie. How, in Thor's name, did you do it?"

She turned to the open-mouthed young lad beside her. "Tell him, Ole."

Ole grinned. "The mighty fall the hardest. Edie used your weight and momentum against you. She read your eyes, anticipated your move against her and dived through your legs as you lunged forward. The rest, as they say, is history." Ole ducked to miss Ulf's good natured cuff towards his ears.

Ealdgith giggled. "Good anticipation, Ole. That's you beaten, again, Ulf." She paused and nodded towards the patch of trampled grass, "Come on Ole. I'll go through some throws with you, then we can spar."

*****

Several days later they lay in front of the hearth in the cave. Orme and Ole nursed several bruises and Ealdgith raised an eyebrow when she saw a yellow weal on Orme's upper arm. "My fault," he laughed, "I was too

75

slow and Ulf taught me a sound lesson. It's not as sore as it looks."

Ealdgith nudged Hravn's ankle with her toe. "I think it is holmganga time, don't you?"

"Yes, Edie, I think it is," he replied with a wry grin towards their three friends. Their blank stares confirmed that, as Angles, they hadn't a clue as to what they were talking about.

"They'll enjoy it, won't they?" Ealdgith's reply was more a tease, than a question.

Orme looked at Ealdgith. The reflected fire light made her eyes twinkle with a look of devilment. "Ah! Edie! Why is it I feel like a baby lamb being led to slaughter?"

She paused, enjoying the moment. "It's a Norse competition. Single combat in a marked space, often to the death. But, this time, maybe not. Just the three of you. Ole and I will judge. It'll be a good way to finish off our sword-work, before we start on horseback." Hravn was nodding, smiling, watching the others. "Oh...and by the way, Hravn always wins," she added with a giggle.

Ulf sighed, shaking his head in mock despair. "You win Edie, but I wouldn't wager any silver if I were you."

Ulf's words of caution were prophetic. The competition started early the next morning. Each had to face the other two. The rules were simple. The loser would be the one who stepped outside the marked boundary of ten paces by ten, fell to the ground or sustained more than two, clear, sword blows. Orme drew successive short straws and faced Ulf, followed by Hravn. Both applauded his valiant efforts, but it was clear that although he was now a capable swordsman, he would need much more practice to face a competent man-at-arms. Orme accepted defeat with good nature and settled himself on a tree stump to watch the climax. He knew it would be close-fought.

Both men wore leather jerkins and steel helms, but were unencumbered by mail. Hravn knew he faced a challenge. Ulf was a good head taller and his bulk and strength would mean that any sword blow would have real force behind it. Hravn remembered his last fight and how the repeated blows from the Norman soldier had quickly tired his wrists, but he couldn't recall how the Norman had landed the blow that concussed him. He reasoned that he would have the edge in speed and agility. He would have to keep moving, force Ulf to waste energy in making hard blows against empty air, and use his sword to deflect rather than block. Would he be able to tire Ulf before his own constant movement tired him? Thank Thor that the swords were wooden.

Hravn's tactics seemed to be working. He moved constantly, changing his lead foot, twisting and spinning as he deflected Ulf's blows with either the seax in his left hand or the sword in his right. Their force was brutal. He knew he would really feel it if one landed on him. Ulf's foot skidded on the dry earth as he turned to follow Hravn's twisting body. Hravn saw his opening and he got in the first telling blow, suddenly crouching and swiping at Ulf's left leg with a sword cut that could have hamstrung him if the blade was steel.

Ulf's response was immediate and overwhelming; his sword crashed down onto Hravn's helmet as he stepped backwards in acknowledgement of the strike on his leg. Hravn staggered and rolled, raising himself on one knee with his sword covering his head; he blinked, trying to clear his head.

"Hold!" Ealdgith jumped up. "It's a draw! Hravn you were concussed just two months ago. Another blow like that could be fatal."

Hravn nodded, slowly, still blinking. Ulf turned to Ealdgith. "You're right, Edie. We've nothing to prove to each other. I'd trust my huscarl's back to Hravn any day." He bent forward and grasped Hravn's shoulders in his hands, raising him slowly. "Come, my friend, sit on that stump young Orme is hogging and clear your head. I'll save my blows for a Norman bastard."

Ealdgith turned to Ole, "Ole, run down to the wet-land by the meadow and cut some mint. Mint tea will help with his headache."

They called a halt to the day's training and, as Hravn rested, Ulf took Orme and headed to see Leofric to tell him to take his working dogs and seek out Ealhstan at Grinton.

Hravn was sitting outside the shelter enjoying the peace of the post-dusk evening, waiting for Ulf's return, when he heard the sound of hooves in the valley below. Light from the half-moon broke through the broken clouds and reflected from the river. Although he couldn't see the ponies, Hravn noticed that the moonlight was reflecting off his friends' faces and bare hands. It was an effect that he had never noticed and he realised that it was something he had always taken for granted. It now worried him. He watched his friends make their way slowly up the fellside, leading their ponies to the enclosure.

"Edie, Ole, come here a minute. Ole, bring some cold charcoal from the hearth too." Hravn called quietly, back into the cave, where they were preparing a meal.

"See how the low moonlight reflects off their faces?" They nodded. "It's got me thinking. When we raid your uncle's barns, Edie, it will be a full moon and our faces will really stand out. It's a risk we can't take. Now, Ole, come here and give me the charcoal. Stand still whilst I improve your handsome features even more."

Ole stepped forward hesitantly, a bemused expression on his face. Hravn took the charcoal, scratched the surface to check that it was loose and carefully blackened the lines of Ole's nose, chin and cheek bones.

"Why not just blacken his face?" Ealdgith was intrigued.

"I wondered about that, Edie, but I thought a solid black shape would stand out more. Just look around. Everything is made of irregular shapes and lines with shadows and shades of light and dark. I think it's better just to break up the outline of a face."

He paused, "There, Ole, that should do. Run down to meet them and walk back with them. I want to see how your face contrasts."

Ole laughed and ran off, enjoying the intrigue. Ealdgith giggled when she heard Ulf's sudden exclamation from the edge of the wood. "What the! Ole! You daft bugger! What's with your face?"

"Well done, Ole!" Hravn shouted, partly to praise the lad and partly to reassure Ulf. "Now, look this way." Hravn stared. He could see Ulf's face clearly, and Orme's just behind him. He wasn't sure about Ole's. "Hold your hands out Ole. That's it. I can see you now. Come on back."

"What's up, Hravn?" Ulf looked at him quizzically. Hravn leaned back, grinning up at his friend. "I could see your faces beyond the river and coming up through the wood. The moonlight was shining off them. We can't risk that on a raid, so I broke up the outline of Ole's with some charcoal. It's quite an improvement, don't you think?"

Ulf looked from Hravn to Ole, pursed his lips and nodded. "Mmm, you should get a blow on the head more often. It obviously helps you think. You're right." He chuckled as he slapped Hravn on the shoulder. "And I'm meant to be the soldier here!"

*****

The mist had returned by the following morning. It clung to the fell tops in a wafer-thin layer that drifted into the valley bottom. Early morning sun penetrated through to give the meadow an ethereal feel and a sense of unreality as they began to practice fighting on horseback.

Hravn was impressed at how quickly Ulf and Orme progressed. Both had ridden when they served Ealdgith's father and they teased and goaded each other as they practiced controlling their mounts with their knees. Hravn showed them how to ride with a long spear, or lance, held vertically, then lowering it as they progressed to a charge at the wicker target. He and Ealdgith showed them the techniques that Oswin had taught them, which he had learned whilst serving with the Varangian Guard in Byzantium.

The easiest skill to master was riding with the lance held, couched, under the right arm. They then progressed to holding the lance couched, but laid across the front of the saddle, with the butt braced against the cantel at the back of the saddle. This gave the lance power and support when it hit its target and would, when they learned to ride with a shield, help protect them when riding against a mounted enemy. Finally, they mastered riding with the lance held overarm, as Hravn had done in his demonstration with Ealdgith.

"I think you've finally got it, Ulf.' Hravn shouted across the meadow as the huscarl reined his black stallion to a halt.

"A day and a morning is quicker than I thought." Ulf stretched his back and rolled his shoulders to ease the muscles. "But I need a lot more practice yet; it's got to become instinctive. I know I'm not there yet."

"You're good though, you've a natural poise," Hravn continued to encourage his friend. "Now, on the next run take out the first target however you want, then discard your lance and go straight for the staggered pair of targets with your sword. See if you can take them left and right of you with alternate swings. The one on your left will be the challenge."

Ulf shook his head in mock despair, then sat back in his saddle and looked intently at the line of targets. He trotted slowly back to the start line, flexed his fingers within his gloves and carefully eased the sword that hung in the scabbard suspended off his left hip. He checked the line to follow. The first target was on his right and the second on his left. Although fifty paces further on, it would be only a few strides for his stallion. He decided he would take the first target with his lance couched under-arm and let go just as the tip touched. His right hand would then be in the best position to flash across his pelvis, draw his sword and immediately switch it to his left hand for an upward thrust as he passed the second target. The momentum of his arm would then enable him to switch hands again and cut down and backwards as he passed the third target. Timing and momentum would be the key.

"For Adelind!" Ulf's battle cry echoed across the valley as the black stallion reared and surged forward at a gallop. His lance already lowered, Ulf hunched forward in the saddle urging the stallion straight down the line. He tensed, holding his breath, and as the lance sliced through the first target his years of training as a huscarl kicked in. His body moved instinctively and he thought and acted as the soldier he was. Ulf found that he was focusing on the targets and the line ahead whilst his thighs directed the charging stallion and his sword moved around him in a single, controlled, purposeful movement. As the third target disappeared in a blur of shattered wicker and grass he wheeled hard to his left and cantered back, his sword held above his head.

Hravn glanced at the three open-mouthed faces behind him and gave a loud whoop of praise. "I couldn't beat that, Ulf! Never!"

*****

The last day of their training was dedicated to archery. Hravn and Ulf watched as Ealdgith patiently taught Orme and Ole the use of the hunting bow.

"Edie has a rare skill. I saw earlier how she can ride and shoot successive arrows into the target within the blink of an eye." Ulf commented to Hravn as he applauded Ole's first strike upon the centre of the woven-grass target. "But the hunting bow lacks the power to drive an arrow into a man-at-arms wearing mail."

"I know," Hravn agreed soberly. "Good as we are with the sword, close battle is too risky, unless we're forced into it. Surprise and a hail of arrows from behind cover is what we need to think about. We need war bows, and someone to make them. We have the arrow heads that I brought from Morlund, but we need a skilled bow maker and wood, hemp, glue...I just don't know."

Ulf gave Hravn a serious look. "To be fair, I think you and Orme probably lack the strength for a real war bow. You would struggle to use it properly without intensive training, and we lack the time for that. Anyway, they would be too cumbersome to run with through the woods."

Hravn laughed, taking the criticism in good heart. "You could well be right, Ulf." He paused, "How about this? Aelf at Locherlaga, he's a wood cutter, has lived his life hunting in the woodland, and he makes hunting bows. Why don't we see just how large he can make them? A large one will have more power than those Edie and I use. A heavier arrow, at shorter range, might then be all we need to punch a hole in a mail coat. Why don't we ask him?"

Ulf nodded. "We've nought to lose. Anything that punches a hole in a mail coat will do for me."

"And talking of mail, when the lads have finished their lesson with Edie let's get them preparing those fleeces. They need boiling to make lanolin, and sheep fat needs rendering for tallow. Ole has mail to oil and torches to make, before we raid Edie's uncle's granaries."

Chapter 7

Hravn perched on a ledge by the side of the hearth and looked down at the faces of the others as they lay enjoying the heat from the dying embers whilst waiting to hear his plan for the raid on the granaries. Hati dozed with his head in Ealdgith's lap, Sköll yawned and watched Hravn.

"I've checked with The Bear. As far as he knows all Edie's uncle's manors above Richemund have been destroyed and those downstream are only producing wheat. I think we can assume that the granaries will be part full, though I doubt any were anywhere near to being full after last year's haerfest. There wasn't much seed corn left after the harrying."

"Nor many men left to work the land." Ulf added, sourly.

"Aye, that's why he's taken men from the vills by here. Anyway, Ulf, tell me if I'm right. He has granaries on his manors at Corburne, Elreton, Mortun, Thorntune, Ellintone and Federbi?"

"Correct. I know where they all are, I used to escort the reeve to stock-taking. They all stand just outside the vills, on the edge of the fields and away from the hazard of house fires. That will work in our favour. We're less likely to attract attention from dogs and can be away quickly before alarm is raised."

"Good, but Mortun, Thorntune, Ellintone and Federbi arc well to the south. Mortun is east of the Swale, Thorntune is on the east bank of the Jor and the last two are next to each other on the west bank of the Jor."

Orme gave a low whistle. "That's a long way. At night, too. Are we going to lay up and do it in two stages?"

Hravn shook his head, he had a confident smile. "What do you think, Edie?"

Ealdgith pursed her lips, looking at Hravn. "I think we have to do it in one go. Once the alarm is raised the hounds of Hel will be unleashed." She grinned at Hravn, "But that's why we will do it over the full moon. We have to pray for a clear sky." Ealdgith raised her eyes, thinking. "What route would you suggest? I think Corburne is too close to here though, we should avoid it."

Hravn spoke. "I agree. Ulf?" The huscarl nodded.

Hravn continued. "Well, if we lay up near Elreton, start at dusk and hit each one in turn until we finish at Federbi, we'll give the impression that we were reavers that came from the south and are returning to the woods beyond Ripum. That should send the 'hounds of Hel' running in the wrong direction."

Ealdgith continued her line of thought. "I reckon it will be just over thirty leagues. It's a lot to ask, but we could ride that and be back to Grinton by dawn. But, you've already worked that out, haven't you?" She cocked a raised eyebrow at Hravn.

"Ulf did, to give him his due," said Hravn. "We planned it between us. If we keep the horses at a steady trot between vills, approach cautiously and allow half an hour for each granary, all we'll need to do is to light a couple of torches and fire the thatch. We shouldn't have too much problem."

Ulf interrupted. "The problem will be crossing the two rivers. I know several fords over the Jor, but if we get heavy rain in the days before we will be forced to use the bridge at Massan. It's several leagues further south and a bigger vill to get around. The bridge at Mortun should be alright, if we get clear of the vill quickly. I can't see anyone being about at that time."

"Thanks, Ulf. Now, that brings me to our tasks. Ulf, I want you to lead throughout. You know that land better than any of us and we can't afford a mistake in finding the granaries or the fords."

Ulf smiled. "Revenge is sweet," he murmured, half to himself.

"Edie, you and I will ride twenty paces behind Ulf. Far enough back to keep in the shadows if there is a problem, but close enough to keep Ulf within bow-shot. If we are stopped by mounted men we'll shoot their horses and cover Ulf's withdrawal. If needs be we can set Hati and Sköll against horses, that should cause them to throw their riders."

"The wildcat and the blackbird together," she joked, grinning at Hravn.

"Or Valkyrie at my back," he teased, using his pet name for her.

"Orme, I want you to cover our backs and give warning of any movement behind us. I also want you to be responsible for the torches. Make sure you have plenty of tinder, flint and steel. Work with Ole and make a score of torches. I'm planning on just two for each granary, but we will need spares and we might need light to cross the fords. I hope not, but we must plan for it. When we get to each granary, go forward to Ulf and we will cover you both. Ulf will direct you where to set fire to each of the roofs."

Orme gave a serious smile. This was resistance and he craved its challenge.

"Ole, last but by no means least. I have to honour my pledge to your father, but you aren't forgotten. I want you to keep the camp secure and have a pot of stew or broth boiling at first light. We will be in need of a good meal and a sleep when we get back, and the horses will need tending. It's not quite as glorious, but it's every bit as essential. We can only fight if we have a good man to rely on to keep us in the field. Can you do that?"

Ole nodded, grinning.

"Now, our dress for the raid." Hravn continued. "We won't wear mail, but we'll wear steel helms. We need to keep our weight down so as not to tire the horses and, if we are pursued, we should be that bit faster. In the half-light, or dark, we have to look like a Norman patrol. We will carry the shields that Orm gathered after the fight at Langethwait.

Ulf gave a grunt. "Those kite-shaped Norman shields will be bugger all use if we fight on foot and they will get in the way in the dark. They're good if fighting mounted, I grant you."

Hravn nodded, Ulf was right. "We need to carry them so that we look the part at a distance. You're right. Leave them hanging from the pommel when you dismount."

"So, how soon do we go?" Ealdgith was enthusiastic.

Hravn glanced at Ulf, prompting him to speak. "I've been watching the moon. I say that we get ready tomorrow, rest the morning after and then leave as the light starts to fail. It's a few leagues to Elreton and we ought to take a longer route. We should swing around and approach from the south east, just to confuse anyone who might see us."

"My thoughts exactly." Hravn was keen to fully involve his deputy. The more that he could delegate to the huscarl, the more he could concentrate on planning their next raid.

*****

Ealdgith rode alongside Hravn as they skirted a wood just to the east of Elreton. She could smell an early frost in the air. The cold gave an added clarity to the bright moonlight bathing the broad valley and she wondered at the beauty of the halo surrounding the full moon with a blue-white glow. "So far, so good," she whispered to Hravn. "The weather has held and we will be able to ride more quickly without fear of a horse twisting an ankle."

"I know," he responded. "It's almost too clear. If anyone is about when we get to a vill, there is a good chance that they will see something. Keep an eye on Ulf, we must be almost there."

Ulf stopped, his silhouette blending with the shadows of the trees. They reined to a halt and Ealdgith called the hounds quietly to heel as Hravn turned and waved Orme forward. As he joined them, Hravn signalled for him to ride forward to Ulf. He could already see that the huscarl had slipped from his horse and, leaving it tethered, he had moved forward, crouching down.

Orme crouched alongside Ulf, keeping low by a gap in a wicker fence. He could see the dark outline of the granary's long sloping roof half a furlong away. Smoke from the vill of Elreton curled quickly upwards another furlong beyond the granary. Distant domestic sounds carried on the still air. There was no sign of life nearby.

Ulf placed his hand on Orme's shoulder, partly to reassure him and partly to hold him close so that he could keep his voice as low as possible. "Go straight forward, and mind that there is a small ditch half way across the field to the granary. It's shallow, but you might get your feet wet. Get right under the lee of the roof and light just one torch. The air is so dry that the thatch should take quickly. Start at the far end, then light the side all the way along, back to this end. I'll wait here. Remember the ditch on the way back. Now, go!"

Orme ran forward. He kept the shadowy bulk of the granary between him and the smoke from the vill. He saw the ditch, half thought about jumping it, then decided that the risk of a slip was too great. He winced as the freezing water in the bottom soaked through the leather of his boots. "Damn!" He cursed to himself. Wet boots were the last thing he needed on a freezing night.

The granary was built around two great wooden A-frames, one at either end. The steeply pitched thatched roof overhung the low side walls to within three feet of the ground. Orme snuggled his back against the end door, quickly dried his boots on his cloak as best he could and took out the leather pouch that held the dry tinder, flint and steel. He scraped a patch of dry earth by the shelter of the door, struck a spark into the tinder and as soon as it caught dipped the wick from the torch into it.

The tallow spluttered alight and the flame lengthened as the fat melted and flared. Orme didn't hesitate. He stuffed the flint and steel back into his pouch and, sheltering the torch flame with his hand, ran to the far end of the overhanging roof and touched the flame to the thatch. The dry reeds and turf caught alight instantly. He gasped. The roof was burning more quickly than he had expected. He ran back along the line of the roof, lighting the thatch in a crazy fiery line as he went, then flung the torch onto the top of the building. The flames at the far end were already higher than a man.

He sprinted back towards Ulf, cleared the ditch in a long leap and barely paused as he headed back to the horses. Ulf was close behind. He could hear the huscarl chuckling as he ran.

The vill's dogs were already barking when the two men reached Hravn and Ealdgith. "Lead on Ulf, we've only moments before the first men get to the granary. That went up much quicker than I expected."

Ulf grinned, the charcoal lines on his face giving him an eerie, Hel-like, expression. He led off at a brisk, steady, trot.

"Well done Orme, that was perfect." Ealdgith gave him the sort of smile that she knew would inspire him. Hravn simply gave him a nod and a thumbs-up, motioning for him to follow on as before.

The pair galloped to catch up with Ulf. They had gone barely fifty paces when they heard a loud crack followed by a blast of warm air. A brief crazy light lit up the trees around them and threw dark shadows into the woods. "Don't look back!" Hravn shouted at Ealdgith, urgently, as she started to turn in her saddle. "You'll lose your night-sight. Just calm Hati...and your horse." He gripped the reins, eased his mount back to a slow trot and rubbed its neck reassuringly.

"What was that?" Ealdgith turned to Hravn with wide, concerned, eyes.

He grinned. "The roof beam broke and collapsed into the grain below. My guess is that the force threw the grain into the air and it exploded as it caught alight. I hope no-one was too close."

The bright light faded as quickly as it came and he turned at the sound of distant shouting and cries for water buckets. As he did so, he saw Orme's silhouette ten paces behind. His friend was rubbing his eyes. "Hravn. Edie. I can't see a damn thing...just bright lights. I saw the roof explode and then that was it."
Hravn laughed and rode back to take Orme's reins in his hand. "You've lost your night sight, that's all. It'll take a while to come back. Keep your eyes open and focus on me. I'll lead you 'til you can see better. Now come. We can't tarry."

Ulf realised that there was a problem and waited for them to catch up. "It's best the pair of us ride ahead," said Hravn. "If we meet anyone, speak in Cumbric and claim to be a Breton. Edie can lead Orme, but he should be fine before too long."

Hravn agreed and bade Sköll to stay with him. They led off on the track to Mortun

The raid on Mortun was far less dramatic. The granary was on the far side of the vill and Ulf led them around in a cautious loop, keeping far enough away from the cluster of thatched wooden houses to ensure that the dogs weren't disturbed. Orme struggled, however, to set light to the thatch. Unlike the granary at Elreton, which must have been thatched only a couple of years ago, the one at Mortun was in desperate need of rethatching. The roof was damp and moss covered, and the thatch refused to catch alight. In the end, he used his sword to prise a gap in the bolted double doors and was able to push a lit torch inside. The dry, dusty, hemp sacks soon caught, although he waited until he was sure that the flames had set light to the underside of the thatch roof before he ran back to Ulf.

Ulf laughed to himself and nodded his appreciation to Orme when he saw thick smoke starting to billow through the roof. He was impressed by Orme's diligence and determination to complete the task. "Three to go, you're doing a grand job, let's get going again."

He paused as he rode back past Hravn, "We'll try the bridge, rather than fording the river. It's that cold we need to keep our boots dry as long as possible."

Hravn left Ealdgith to hold his horse's reins as he walked carefully out along the bridge. It seemed sturdy enough but he wanted to be certain that there were no gaps between the four great oak trunks that formed the trackway. Reassured, they led the horses across. The bridge lacked side rails and they followed the centre line with caution, keen to ensure that the horses weren't spooked by the black waters of the Swale swirling beneath them.

Ulf led them quickly towards a low ridge dominating the horizon in front. The earth was now frost-hard under the horses' hooves and Ealdgith sensed the still air resonating with the hoof-beats of their passage. She turned and gasped, as they reached the crest of the ridge. "Look back!" She called ahead to Hravn and Ulf. The moon-lit land of eastern Ghellinges-scir lay behind them. Two bright beacons stood out on the blue-grey landscape. "Even Elreton is still burning."

"Which means," Hravn added soberly, "that if the Normans have any sentries out on high ground, they can see what we can see."

Hravn and Ulf kept their route along the low ridge, heading west to avoid several vills that lay on low ground to either side. Ulf raised his hand as he reined to a slow walk. "Thorntune isn't far off. Look, there is the line of the Jor, winding around the foot of the hill."

Ealdgith and Orme closed in, their horses steaming from exertion in the frosty air. "I can see the vill, there, that shadowy line just beyond the trees."

"Yes." Ulf confirmed, "and there's your uncle's manor, half a league off to the right." He answered her question before she asked it, "The granary is at the other end of the vill. You can see it, at this end of the long field, in the gap between those two strips of wood."

"Where do we cross the river, Ulf?" Hravn asked, thinking ahead to their escape route.

"You can't quite see it from here. It's around yon bend in the river." Ulf pointed off to their left. "The ford is about three leagues down from here."

Hravn nodded, "Lead on, Ulf. The moon's still high. We're making good time, but the ford might slow us up."

Thorntune's granary was similar to Mortun's, roofed with an aged mossy thatch that Orme struggled to light. He again resorted to prising the doors apart and pushing a blazing torch inside. He leapt in fright as three black rats ran squealing between his legs, then laughed at himself. He wasn't the only living thing raiding a granary that night. Ulf chuckled as Orme ran back to him. He signalled for Orme to pause and wait until they were sure that the inside of the granary was well alight.

"The fire will suck air in through the hole those rats got in by. They did you a favour. See the sparks falling out from under the floor." Then, tapping Orme on the shoulder, he dashed back to their horses and started to lead the way down river to the ford.

"I'm glad you know the route, Ulf. This ford's a God-send. Still, are you sure it's safe to ride across?"

Ulf grinned, the charcoal on his face was now streaked with sweat. "Oh Aye, it's safe enough." He turned to face the three of them. "Just make sure you keep heading toward the right hand of those two willows. That's the centre line. There's not much of a current, either. The hounds should manage alright." The sound of a distant crack and sudden lightening of the sky beyond the low hill behind them prompted them to start to cross.

"There goes another one, you're getting good at this, Orme." Ealdgith joked.

Hravn rode up to Ulf at the top of the river bank. "We've had a good run tonight, but I think we need to change the plan. Ellintone's just the other side of these woods, isn't it?" Ulf nodded. "and Fedebi is another two leagues down river? I think that with the way these granaries are lighting up the sky we need to cut and run once we've torched Ellintone."

Ulf could see Ealdgith nodding agreement. "I agree," he said. "Our route back is within a league of Ellintone. We don't know what force the Normans have down here. We can't risk a patrol on our escape route. There's bound to be some sort of reaction once they realise that Thorntune and Ellintone have both been fired."

Ulf led the way on foot, snaking through the open woodland until they came to the edge of a long field. "The granary is just on the left edge of the field. You can see the roof-line, there."

Hravn and Orme nodded. "That column of smoke, at the far end of the field; is that the vill?"

"Yes, it's about two furlongs away." Ulf paused. "We'll have to go close to it, or through it, to reach the ridge beyond. We need to follow the ridge to get back into the vale of the Jor."

Hravn gave a low whistle. "It would be quickest, no doubt, to gallop through the vill. Ulf, is there a track?"

Ulf nodded. "There was. I assume there still is."

"Orme," Hravn spoke in a low voice. "Make your way around to the granary and check on the condition of the thatch, as quick as you can." He turned to the other two. "I think we should escape through the vill. If we try and cut around it, we might get slowed up and enmeshed in the alarm. If we go straight through it, we will probably trigger the alarm and should be clear on the other side before there is a reaction."

Ulf looked at the distance to cover. Hravn could see that Ealdgith was thinking. When she bit her lip, it was always a giveaway sign. "What is it, Edie?"

"I agree, but we should start from the other side of the granary. We'll stay mounted, fifty paces beyond. Orme can run to us once he's done his work. I'll hold his horse. Then you and Ulf lead the way through."

"Aye, you're right, My Lady." Ulf spoke with sudden respect. "We should have swords drawn ready, too. You take the right side, Hravn, I'll take the left. Edie, you follow with Orme right behind. Have the hounds run either side of you."

Hravn glanced from one to the other. "It's a plan."

As he spoke, Orme ran, crouching, back across the field. "Its new thatch. If it's like Elreton, it'll go very quickly."

"All the more need for speed, then." Hravn turned to Orme and explained the plan to him.

Orme was right. The thatch burned very quickly. He hid behind the covered side of the granary, lit two torches and then flung them onto either side of the steep roof, before sprinting to where Ealdgith held his horse. The four turned and galloped towards the vill. There was no need to look back at the granary. Crazy wild shadows danced all around them. The granary was ablaze. The vill awoke in a cacophony of barking dogs.

Ulf led their mad charge towards the vill's central track. They were halfway through the small cluster of thatched houses before the first door crashed open. Ealdgith caught site of a man's naked torso as he stumbled out clutching his breeks. Hati snapped at him and he staggered back; then she was past, their horses' hooves thrashing the dry earth as they tore up the hill and into the wood.

Ulf didn't ease up on their pace. He led the way along the woodland tracks until he reached a cross-track at the foot of a ridge of hills and paused for the others to catch up. He leant across to Hravn, "We should follow the edge of the hills and will need to cross the Covre beck at Covreham, there's a small mill there and a bridge."

Hravn looked concerned. "Is there not a quiet ford somewhere? We don't want to be noticed, and for an association made to our route north."

Ulf shook his head, "Sorry, it's the first crossing above the Jor. The Covre flows through a steep gorge and is fast flowing. Once across we'll head directly to the foot of Penhill. It dominates the valley."

Their track split and Ulf chose the left fork that took them higher up onto the edge of the hills. As they climbed they could see three beacons of light. The fourth granary was now just a dull red glow, far off to their north. Ulf halted, the ground dropped away quickly in front of them.

"That must be Penhill?" Hravn pointed to the silhouette of a table-top shaped hill that dominated the southern entry to the vale of the Jor.

Ulf nodded. "And here is the vill of Middelham. You can just see the dark line of the Covre gorge this side of it."

"Ulf! What's that?" Ealdgith's low, urgent voice gripped their attention. "On the hill to the left of the vill."

Ulf gasped. "The bastards be damned!"

"It's like the one they built at Sedberge. An earth motte with a wooden castle on top and a stake-wall around it. God only knows how hard they drove the people to build it." Hravn clenched his teeth as he spoke, muttering his words.

"This was Gillepatric's manor. I expect he was dispossessed and his people forced into servitude as villeins, rather than slain. That's how they have the manpower to build something like that and grow the food to keep a garrison." There was a bitter sadness to Ulf's voice.

"Edie, how many knights were there at Sebderge?" Hravn asked.

Eadgith replied, "I think Elfreda said twenty, or so, with over a dozen horses. Remember, there were others based in the outlying farms, as we found out."

"Listen!" Orme held up his hand. The clear call of a horn carried on the still night air. The sharp blast of an alarm call was followed by sound of commotion: shouted orders, running feet, horses.

"Keep close to the edge of the wood, we don't want to be seen up here." Hravn walked his horse backwards into the cover of the trees. The others did likewise.

The rasp of heavy bolts being drawn was followed by sudden light from the front of the castle. Horses galloped from the castle gate down towards the bridge over the Covre. Ulf breathed a deep sigh. "Thank the gods you spotted the castle Edie. If not, we would have been down there now. How many do you think there are?"

Ealdgith had the sharpest eyes. Using her hands, she shielded them from the moon and star lit sky. "Ten, no, a dozen."

"That's the same as at Sedberge. It probably means that there are at least a half dozen men-at-arms left guarding the castle. Where are they headed, Ulf?"

"They're following the track at the bottom of the hills, to Ellintone."

"So, those are your hounds from Hel, Edie." Hravn quipped. "Thank Thor we didn't meet them down there." He nodded towards the plank bridge by the mill.

They sat quietly, watching the castle and the bridge for a few moments longer. Hravn realised that they were waiting for his lead.

"They'll be a while yet. The castle looks quiet, although there'll a guard or two watching, I'm sure. If you say that we have to cross the bridge, Ulf, then so be it. We should follow along the edge of this this wood until it drops into the valley. With luck the trees by the beck will screen us from the castle. We need to ride across as quickly and purposefully as we can. The miller will expect the patrol to come back, so we won't surprise him. Then we'll follow the far bank upstream for a while and keep well clear of yon cursed hill." He said, with a lot more confidence than he felt. "Ulf and I'll lead, then Edie with the hounds, and Orme close on her tail. Let's go."

There was no sign of life at the crossing, other than the frantic barking of a dog in the barn by the mill. "They'll be keeping their heads well down," Ulf muttered as they rode across the plank bridge and turned sharply to keep in the shadow of the trees lining the river-bank. They headed away from the mill towards the wood at the foot of the next hill.

The full moon dropped below the horizon and the night was suddenly darker, with just the cold starlight left to guide their way. It cast an icy blue reflection off the thick hoarfrost that now coated the grass and copses. Ealdgith shivered, blew on her fingers, tucked her free hand under her armpit and pulled her cloak tighter; her mood dropped along with the temperature. She closed up on Hravn and Ulf as they took a wide looping route towards the slopes of Penhill. "You know what this means, don't you?" She said to them as she rode between them. Both gave her a questioning look.

"They're building a castle in stone at Richemund, from where they can command the valleys and the routes to the north, west and south. They are building smaller, wooden, castles in the valley mouths, just like that one behind us. We know that many who escaped the harrying and servitude are living as reavers in the upper valleys, hills and higher woods, just as we are."

"I know, Edie." Hravn continued her line of thought. "You're right. They are controlling the fertile valleys, where they can grow their precious wheat, and separating the people there from those who they don't control."

"Which means," Ulf interrupted, "you're the brains here, so tell me if I'm wrong, but I reckon that if the Normans' control the manors, hold the people in bondage and keep them away from those who could pose a resistance, then there can be no resistance. Without food and the freedom to move and talk, then those who do resist will be isolated and starved out."

"Or live as reavers and outlaws." Ealdgith added.

Hravn sounded dejected. "I agree, you're both right. We need to speak to the Earl. He needs to know about this rash of castles across the land."

Ealdgith looked at them both. "Don't sound too defeatist. This doesn't change what we must do. We are my uncle's eyes and ears and we must provide for our people. Any wider resistance may struggle, but that doesn't stop us. We just have to be very careful not to bring the hounds of Hel down on us. We saw how quickly they reacted just now. We just have to out-think them and keep all our actions well away from our home ground."

Ulf rode close to Ealdgith, reached out and squeezed her forearm tenderly. "Well said My Lady. I know you were not close to your father, but you are Thor's daughter sure enough, and true to your family's honour and the honour of your people.

Hravn just smiled, content in the warmth of the bond that held this new family together.

*****

The hazy light of the false dawn rose above the eastern horizon behind them, as they crested the ridge south of Grinton. Hravn reined to a halt and turned to face the yellow-blue light that backlit the distant moors. "Just look at that! This may be a sad land, in mourning for all that is lost, but it is still beautiful."

Pausing for a moment, whilst past memories pulled at his heart, he turned again and spurred his horse forward. "Come on, we'll be back at the cave by the time true dawn breaks. Let's see if we can catch young Ole abed!"

Chapter 8

"I'm sorry, Ole. I owe you an apology." Hravn rubbed the young lad's shoulder as he pushed open the fern and wicker door at the cave's entrance. "I told the others that we would catch you asleep, but you've done us proud. I can smell that broth from here." Hravn had caught sight of Ole's worried face as he walked back from the enclosure. He guessed that the lad hadn't slept and had probably had the broth simmering for an hour or more, waiting for their return.

Ole grinned, feeling suddenly heavy eyed; relieved and tired after a long wakeful night. "You know me, Hravn. Up with the lark! Here, I've broth and bread. Grab a seat and I'll pass it across."

Hravn waited for the others to come in, then said. "Let's get Ole's broth, but before we get some sleep I want to go over my plans for what we must do next."

They listened, nodding, as they ate. The hounds gnawed a couple of raw marrow bones left over from when the sheep had been rendered.

"Edie's uncle has a problem now, and a famine on his hands. He will have to buy grain in from wherever he can find it, or bring it from his other manors. He might work his people hard, but he can't afford them to starve. He will also have to bring in seed corn for them to sow."

Ealdgith nodded, swallowing a broth-soaked crust. "Most of his lands are well to the south of where we have just been, or to the south of the moors. But he did have at least one manor to the east of here, near Hotun Rodebi."

Ulf caught Hravn's eye. "If you are right, and we've led him to think that the raids came from somewhere in the vale of the Nidd, then he's not going to risk carting grain from his lands in the south. He might cart it around the edge of the moors, but that is a long trip. I think he's more likely to bring it from Hotun Rodebi."

"I agree." Hravn nodded his thanks. "In which case that is the road we need to watch. It's going to take him a couple of days to make plans and sort out a new granary, though I'm sure there will be empty barns that can be used." He paused.

"Tomorrow, Ulf, you and me, we'll ride out, dressed as Normans, and look for a site for an ambush between Aluretune and Mortun. They will have to pass that way. The four of us will return the next day and hide and wait. Ole, when we leave can you go and stay with your fader and warn him that we might arrive with a cart of grain within a few days. It's not a certainty, but if the gods stay with us, we will."

Hravn caught sight of Ealdgith stifling a yawn with the back of her hand. "Come on, let's get some shut eye. Ole, shake us at midday. We need to sort ourselves out for the morrow."

As he turned to go he noticed Ole kneeling by the pot at the hearth, grass was poking through the thin soles of his leather boots; he must have lined them with grass to cover the holes in their soles. Hravn knew it was another problem he had to address. They all needed better footwear.

Hravn cursed and grunted breathlessly as he placed the back of his shoulders against the old cart and pushed it onto the narrow track that lead from Aluretune to Mortun. Ealdgith assisted, standing between the ends of the shafts and heaving sideways to slew the cart across the track. Hravn stopped, stepped back, satisfied that the cart blocked the way to other wheeled traffic. The trees either side of the track prevented anyone from driving a cart around the blockage.

"That'll do, Edie. We'd best get in place before Ulf and Orme return. At least they'll give us a few moments warning of the grain carts' arrival." Ealdgith nodded her agreement, still breathless from the exertion of pushing the empty cart down the track from the abandoned farmstead where they had found it.

The foursome had ridden out two mornings before and patrolled the track to the west of Aluretune. Some of the land was still farmed and they kept well clear of the little settlement at Romundrebi, but Tirnetofte was different. They could tell from the overgrown fields and charred remains of a barn that the vill had borne the brunt of the harrying, although, as at Grinton, a couple of haggard stooped men were digging in a field by the one cottage that appeared unscathed. The land was waste, certainly not being farmed and all but deserted. Hravn knew it was suitable for an ambush. Yesterday two carts, laden with sacks of grain and escorted by two Norman men-at-arms, had passed by the vill, making their way slowly towards Mortun. They had returned, empty, just before dusk.

Hravn was hopeful that the delivery would be repeated, estimating that it should be about midday before the carts would have ground their way slowly across the dozen leagues from Edie's uncle's manor at Hotun Rodebi. He planned a simple ambush in a wood beyond the vill, where the track wound around the foot of a low hill, and had chosen a spot carefully where the carts would be confronted suddenly by a blocked track, unable to turn around and screened from view.

Ealdgith called the hounds to heel and crouched down behind the old cart. Hravn, wearing Orme's old cloak over his mail shirt, looked every bit like a villain, down on his luck, his horse having bolted.

The dry earth track was rock-hard after days of constant frost. Ealdgith rubbed her chapped fingers, their tips tingled painfully as the blood returned and she glanced at the clouds looming from the northwest. "Have you noticed the weather, Hravn? Those massive yellow clouds remind me of when we were caught in the blizzard on the tops above Mallerstang, last Lencten. You know what happened then!"

Hravn turned and looked back over the top of the cart. "Hel's teeth! Edie, you're right. I give it an hour or two before snow comes in." The sound of galloping hoofs reclaimed his attention. "Here we go, my Valkyrie. Keep down and keep the boys calm until I give the word."

Ulf and Orme galloped around the corner. Orme took up a position to the side of the track, screened by the bulk of a fallen oak. Ulf paused by Hravn, "two carts, two guards, two minutes," he shouted. Hravn cocked a raised thumb and Ulf turned, spurring his mount up the short slope. He remained mounted, hidden by a thick holly bush on the opposite side of the track to Orme.

Hravn crouched by the cartwheel, his back to the approaching carts and their Norman escorts. He busied himself, pretending to examine a damaged axle hub.

Adrenalin surged through his body and he controlled his breath, calming himself and slowing his heartbeat as he listened. The rumble of approaching carts and the beat of hoofs striking the hard earth, echoed in the little valley.

"Cur! Move this. Now!" The voice was harsh, used to being obeyed. Hravn stood, slowly, and turned to face the two horsemen. He wondered how the Normans could ever communicate with the English, other than by brute force, but he understood the soldier. He had spoken in Breton, as had the soldiers that he had fought, and Ealdgith had killed, in their last battle three months earlier.

Hravn held his ground, erect, and looked from one to the other. Both wore mail and held lances that pointed at him.

He raised his hands and smiled, answering in Cumbric. "I would move this, with pleasure, but I can't. The wheel has jammed and my horse has bolted. Care to help?"

One of the soldiers spat. "Care to help! You're an insolent sod! I want to see you push it, now!" His spear jerked to emphasise the point. The other held up his hand to stop his partner. "You speak Breton, but with a heavy accent. How so?"

"I am English, and we English are not the ignorant dogs that you seem to think we are. We are many races, Saxon, Angle, Dane, Norse, Cumbric. We've learned to live together, at last, and some of us speak the many tongues of our forefathers. I am part Cumbric, a race from whence you Bretons once came, or so I have been told."

The first soldier spoke again. "That maybe so, but we sit here with spears at your throat. So, cur, move the cart."

Hravn shrugged and dropped his hands to his sides, ready to draw the sword hidden under his cloak. "Edie!"

Ealdgith had been listening to the gist of the conversation, straining to understand the language that she was still trying to master. She gauged that the moment was close and, as Hravn shouted her name, released her grip on the hounds' collars. "Go!"

Sköll and Hati tore around opposite ends of the cart and lunged directly at the lower legs of the two men. Their horses reared, panicked, throwing the soldiers from their saddles. One seemed to hang, momentarily, in the air then tumbled landing on the back of his head with a loud, hollow, thud. He lay still, blood trickling from his ears. The other, the first to have spoken, twisted and slid slowly down, his right foot caught in his stirrup.

"Off boys, Off!" Hravn threw himself at the hounds, hauling them off and away from the flailing hoofs of the horses. He was worried, too, that the more they fought men the more likely they would be to acquire a taste for human blood. So far, Ealdgith and he had always succeeded in controlling the hounds, but it was a constant worry.

Hravn threw off Orme's old cloak, drew Nadr and held it at the soldier's throat. The man stared back, a mix of shock and contempt in his eyes. "Edie! Control the boys and release his foot, please." Ealdgith had anticipated his curt command and was already pulling the entangled foot from the stirrup. She let the leg drop, stepped back and pulled the hounds after her. The man winced as his twisted leg hit the ground.

"Whoa, steady there, steady." Hravn glanced up, surprised by the calm reassurance of Orme's voice. He had forgotten that Orme had once worked in his lord's stables; his natural affinity for horses was a God-send. Orme controlled his own mount, urged it next to the panicked horses and gently reassured them. He led them slowly down the track, towards the two stationary carts.

The rasp of hooves on the hard earth bank behind him reassured Hravn that Ulf had joined him. "Here!" He called over his shoulder. "Guard him whilst I take stock of things."

Ulf remained mounted and lowered the tip of his spear to the Norman's throat. The man lay still, very aware that Ulf could have him trampled to death, or slit his throat, should he make the slightest move.

Hravn looked back down the track to two carts that had stopped fifty paces away. He could see that Orme had already tethered the soldiers' horses to a tree and was calling on the two drivers to dismount and control their own horses. "Hold them there, Orme," he shouted. "Reassure them that they are safe so long as they cooperate. I'll speak to them in a minute." He kicked the prone body of the soldier that had fallen on his head, confirming that he was dead, and turned to the man that Ulf guarded.

A wave of nausea gripped his stomach. Hravn feared suddenly that he would lose his confidence. He had never killed with cold deliberation before. Taking a deep breath, he stared into the man's eyes, determined not to betray his emotions; and spoke at last, with an authority that surprised him. "You will die, soon, you can be sure of that. How you die, depends upon you." Hravn paused, he could see the meaning of his words

108

register as the soldier's eyes twitched wide, before nodding his head. He could feel Ulf's eyes upon him too. He knew that the big man couldn't understand the conversation, but he was reading their body language.

"Who is your lord?" Hravn demanded. The man breathed deeply. Hravn could see that the soldier still held him in contempt, but was now very aware that if he answered the questions put to him that he would die quickly and painlessly. A slashed throat was infinitely preferably to a gashed stomach.

"Your lord?" Hravn prompted.

"Enisant, Count Alan's constable." The soldier's words were forced and, to Hravn, his accent sounded coarse, but at least they understood each other.

"For whom do you move the grain then?"

This time the soldier replied without hesitation. "Gospatrick. He's one of your Saxon lords. Count Alan is his over-lord now."

Hravn scoffed, "Angle, not Saxon. But, no matter." He nodded slowly, thinking. "Why do you, who serves Enisant, work for another lord?"

The soldier smirked. "Why do you think? Some Saxon lords may still hold their lands, but why would my lord trust them with their own men-at-arms? I serve Enisant and Gospatick pays him for my services. Silvatici raided his manors several days back, burning his granaries and now he needs to bring in fresh grain from his other manors – but you must know that."

Hravn continued to nod slowly, a slight smile on his lips. "Silvatici? Who are they?"

"It's a Norman word, or maybe Latin. Not Breton anyway. It describes the likes of you, 'men of the woods'."

Hravn laughed. "Really? You think so? Where did these silvatici come from then?"

"Ripum and the vale of the Nidd, or so my lord believes." The soldier paused. "We did not expect you here."

Hravn's expression hardened. "Thank you. I believe you." He flicked his eyes towards Ulf. The huscarl had watched him throughout and knew what was expected of him.

"For Adelind," he muttered softly, almost to himself, as he flicked his wrist and the razor-edge of his spear head slit the soldier's throat. Hravn turned his head away as the soldier jerked sharply upwards, then collapsed back, blood spurting from the gash with a gurgle. Ulf didn't hesitate. He stabbed the spear through the man's mail shirt and into his heart.

"Thank you, Ulf." Hravn turned back to his friend, sensing that the grim act had forged a new bond between them. "Can you strip them of their mail and weapons whilst I speak to the carters? We'll need to hide the bodies and scrape earth over the blood. The longer we can conceal what's happened here the better it will be for us. At least they seem to think we came from the south. Get their crossbows too," he added as an afterthought. "None of us has used one, but I'm sure we can work out how to."

"Will do," Ulf called back with a cold professionalism as he started to strip mail from the soldier he had just killed. "I've heard that crossbow quarrels are very good for punching through mail at close range. Just my sort of weapon."

As Hravn strode towards the carts Ealdgith ran after him, the hounds following. She had remained behind to see what happened and to hold the hounds in reserve in case something went wrong. She was surprised at how detached from the violence she felt. "You did right, Hravn. I understood most of what was said. He had to die. You didn't break your vow to Oswin. His end was swift and painless. I doubt he would have treated us the same," she added.

Hravn stopped and turned to Ealdgith. "You're right, Edie. I nearly lost my nerve, but it had to be done. I have no regret. None. In fact, I've crossed a line I had to cross. If we are to survive, it's the only way. Ulf knows that too."

Ealdgith took his hand and squeezed it. "I know."

*****

The carters proved to be very cooperative. Both were Danes from Aluretune. They had been freemen until their livestock was slaughtered in the harrying. After which, starvation and the need to provide for their families, had forced them into servitude. Both had chosen to move to Hotun Rodebi and serve an English, rather than a Norman, master. Ealdgith said nothing about her uncle.

Hravn paid them both in silver, bidding them to say that a dozen wild men from the woods above the Nidd had killed the escort and driven off the carts. He also told them to take the dead soldiers' boots, as he was sure they needed them.

Ulf was less convinced about their loyalty and made a point of reassuring them that he would find their families if he heard it said that the raiders had come from anywhere other than the lands to the south and west. Hravn sensed that both Ulf and Orme would have preferred to keep the dead men's boots, but Hravn argued that it would help ensure the carters' silence if there was a risk that were seen to have benefited from the death of the soldiers. Wearing Norman boots would be a luxury that they would have to keep quiet about. "Anyway, I have a plan to solve that little problem," he had added with a wink.

Ulf and Orme hitched their own horses, along with those of the dead soldiers, to the back of the two carts and followed Hravn and Ealdgith in a long route north, past the derelict manors of Smidetune and Hurdewurda, before turning west through the empty land around Middeltun. Hravn was developing a feel for the manors that were empty, or farmed only by a handful of half-starved families, and those that seem to be over-stocked with labour, under the tight grip of a Norman overlord. He cursed the poverty that stalked much of their land, but was thankful that the neglected manors created corridors through which they could move with some security and secrecy.

"By Hodr! It's cold!" Hravn cursed the Norse god of winter, shouting across to Ealdgith who was hunched up with her cloak clasped tight around her throat to keep the wind out and trap her body warmth within. She glanced back to the cart behind, where she could see Orme rubbing his hands together, relying on the horse between the shafts to follow the horses in front without his control. She marvelled at his confidence.

Ealdgith turned her attention back to the route ahead. "Snow's coming. Look, you can see it falling ahead. It'll be here before we get back to the woods."

"Don't worry." Hravn grinned as he shouted back, his voice whipped away by the strengthening wind. "We might leave some tracks, but they will be buried quickly. Hodr has a sack-full of it to dump on us by all accounts."

Hravn reined to a halt and waited for the carts to catch up, gesturing to Ulf and Orme to close up on him, and then dismounted. "We'll be hit by the storm any minute now. Ulf, I want you to lead. Edie and I will bring up the rear in case we have any problems with a cart. Take the route through Ghellinges. We saw the other day that the vill is all but destroyed and there's a bridge over the beck there, and then follow the track to Gales. From there it is straight into the woods and over the top to Hulders-wold. The track through the woods should be wide enough, just. At least the trees will stop the snow drifting and it won't lie as thick, not for a while yet. Orme, it's your job to persuade Frida to get a pot boiling." He added with a wink. "Let's go!"

The snow caught them just as they passed through Ghellinges. The white flakes clung to the stark black ribs of the burnt buildings and the sudden biting cold added to the sense of melancholy that overshadowed the manor that had once been the bustling capital of Ghellinges-scir. Hravn thought he saw smoke coming from the roof of a small cottage at the edge of the vill and wondered at the tenacity of the family clinging to life in the dead place.

Heavy wet flakes soon covered the ground, blanketing the track. Hravn and Ealdgith urged their mounts forward past the carts. "Just trust in me, and follow,"

Hravn shouted to Ulf. "I'm hefted to this place. Even if we lose the track, I can still read the route.

The huscarl was sitting, hunched, a frozen ice-warrior, caked in white snow.

Ealdgith was surprised at the confidence in Hravn's voice as she was beginning to doubt her ability to see the way ahead. As they rode Hravn kept calling out the next point to ride towards. "Edie, make for that loan oak - keep to the right of the craggy mound - stay left, it's marshy in that hollow." She wondered if he was just reassuring himself, then cursed her doubts; they were a betrayal of Hravn. "There Edie, see the wood's edge? We follow it for half a furlong then we'll find the track to Hulders-wold. See! There it is." She sensed the relief in Hravn's voice, but it was nothing compared to the flood of relief that surged through her.

Hravn left Ealdgith to lead the way and dropped back to check the carts. Ulf and Orme looked identical, their hunched bodies encased in white shrouds, with faces blue rather than white. "I'll go ahead and get Agnaar and Frida warming a pot. He'll feed you all the meat he has when he sees the grain we've brought in. Well done!"

As Hravn cantered along the narrow track he felt as if he was rushing into a darkening tunnel. The trees crowded in from the sides. Their branches inter-twined above, holding the snow off the track to form a white canopy that robbed the last of the day's light.

His horse skittered to a halt as he burst into the clearing at Hulders-wold. He was pleased to see Agnaar sitting on a stump by a fire at the entrance to his hut. Ole and Frida squatted beside him, just sheltered from the falling snow. It was heavy and wet, already three-fingers width deep in the middle of the clearing. Hravn's heart leapt, with surprise and relief, as a tall bearded man stepped out of inner gloom of the hut.

"Fader!" He called, "What a surprise. You've saved me a trip to fetch you. We have two carts of grain for you." He led his horse across to the hut and gave The Bear a warm embrace before turning to Agnaar. "Ulf and Orme are frozen driving the carts, and Edie and I are little better. Please can you ask Ole and Frida to get a pot going?"

Agnaar grinned, clasping Hravn warmly on his shoulder. He had anticipated the request. "Frida, my girl, that broth should be ready now. Go and prepare a meal for your sweetheart."

Hravn gasped, then laughed. "You old fox, Agnaar. How long have you known?"

Agnaar shrugged. "He's a good lad and Frida's of an age. I didn't need to be told. Even a father has eyes and was young once."

"Ole, get the torches your fader prepared and we'll go and meet them." The Bear spoke with a natural authority. "Hravn, we've made a shelter for the grain too, on yon side of the clearing. It'll save the grain from too much damage in the snow." Hravn glanced across to see a long, turf-covered, A-frame shelter. He was impressed. His father's preparations had been thorough and he gave a secret prayer of thanks that he had been able to seize enough grain to fill the new granary.

Lencten

Chapter 9

Ealdgith woke early. The four tallow lights that Ole had made in the natural pits in the limestone of the cave wall were kept burning constantly and they threw a faint flickering glow that reflected off the walls. It was enough for her to find her clothes at the foot of the bed that she and Hravn had moved back into the cave from the shelter outside the entrance. It was now simply too cold out there. She pulled on her cloak, wrapped a wolf skin around it then, tucking her breeches into her boots, she quietly moved the wicker screen and stepped outside. Hati followed, nuzzling her hand.

The cold dry air hit her, catching in her throat, before the beauty of the scene took her breath away. In the three days since their return the snow had frozen into a hard, white crust that glistened, reflecting the starlight. As the sun's first light caught the higher tops of the fells across the Swale it cast a pink light that contrasted beautifully with the stark black and white etching of trees and rocks in the valley below.

Scraping hard snow from one of the tree stumps that they used as a seat by the outside hearth, Ealdgith sat and thought. She felt ill at ease, but couldn't think why.

The weeks of Aefter Yule had passed in a blur of activity, but the snow had forced them to stop and this gave her time to think. She reflected on how her life had changed once again. For most of the last year it had been just her and Hravn. They had shared their every thought and moment, with little need to worry about anyone, or anything, else.

But, now? She lived amongst four men. She shared their banter, their jokes and, at times, their bawdy humour. Ealdgith knew she had a rare and privileged place in their lives. She was one of them. They didn't see her as a woman to do their chores. She was their Lady. She was as much their leader as Hravn. She led them and they did the chores for her, without bidding. She smiled as she thought of Ole as a man, but he was, or soon would be. But she was more than just a leader of a group of men, she was a woman too. This was something she had to resolve by herself. Hravn's attention was, rightly, no longer just on her but on their safety, resistance, a future for them all. What was her future? Her role?

As the sun's light moved slowly down the far fellside Ealdgith let her mind wander. She could sense the dawn illuminating the shadows in her emotions and she began to realise what she wanted, what she needed. She needed Hravn, she needed her love for him to be fulfilled. But it was more than just that. Ealdgith remembered Cyneburg, and her promise. She sat up with a jerk.

That was it! She must see Bron. She had told Hravn that she would learn the arts of the herbalist from her, and she must. First, she would learn how to prevent conception; she had overheard women talk of rue and wild carrot but didn't know how they could be used. Her need for Hravn had to be fulfilled. Then, she would learn the art of healing and the herbs to use. Finally, she would learn what she could of childbirth, even if it was only enough to advise women in need and enable her to understand and help the birthing women.

Hati's ears pricked up and Ealdgith turned as Hravn pushed the wicker door open. Ealdgith didn't rise, she waited for him to come and stand behind her, wrap his arms around her and gently kiss her head. She took his hands in hers and drew them to cover her breasts in a soft caress. As Ealdgith lay backwards against him, relishing the warmth and their private moment, she knew her decision was right.

"I'll ride and see Bron after we've eaten. It's best I go alone, there are things I must ask her." Ealdgith turned and smiled up at Hravn. Her eyes told him that which she didn't speak.

"Come," he said, taking her hand in his.

*****

Hravn watched Ealdgith's pony as it surefootedly trotted through the snow across the valley then he turned back to the threesome. "Right, Ulf, unlock the mysteries of the crossbow for us, if you can." It was a tease and a challenge.

Ulf perched on a tree stump and held the crossbow across his lap, his brow furrowed in concentration as he examined it carefully, turning it over and moving the trigger mechanism gently. "Go on, Ulf. Show us what it can do." Ole lent so close that his head almost got in Ulf's way.

He flinched when Ulf tweaked his ear. "Patience young Ole! It's easy to injure ourselves with one of these if we don't handle it correctly, and I've still to work out just how to use this tickler safely. Just sit back and watch." He pointed to the trigger mechanism as he spoke.

Ulf glanced up and smiled when he saw the intensity with which Hravn and Orme were also watching him. "I've handled one of these only once before, but never had the chance to use it," he admitted. "The Normans used them at Hastings. They can be lethal at close range. Good for hunting too," he added. "Some have a simple pin as a trigger but this one is quite impressive, look." He held the crossbow up and pointed to a small barrel shaped piece of bone that rotated in the centre of the stock.

"That is the nut and it's controlled by the tickler. It's the key to how the crossbow works. See how there is a notch cut into it at the top, with a groove through the centre of the notch?" They nodded. "There's another notch on the bottom that the tickler butts against. Watch."

Ulf stood up, placed the toe of his boot into the metal stirrup that projected from the end of the stock and pulled back on the bow string. "The bow has short prods so it is more of an effort to draw it back. Clip the string into the notch in the nut and make sure that the end of the tickler is wedged against the bottom notch. There, see?" He held the crossbow up and turned it so that they could see the string was held in place. "This long handle underneath the stock is the tickler. When it's squeezed up against the stock it disengages from the nut, the nut spins around and the bowstring is released. Stand back and watch."

Ulf placed the end of the stock against his shoulder and, supporting the front of the stock with his left hand, used his right hand to squeeze the trigger. The bow string snapped forward with a loud crack that made the three watchers jump. He lowered the crossbow, beaming. "Well, now I know how it works. Ole, fetch the target we used for archery practice and go and place it in front of the broad oak. I rather think that the bolt from this will need more than the target to stop it."

Whilst Orme helped Ole position the thick wicker and thatch target, Hravn passed Ulf one of the crossbow bolts that they had taken from the dead Norman soldiers. He weighed it in his hand, "Its heavier than you would think." He spoke to himself as much as to Hravn. "See how the dense shaft leads neatly into the metal head. There are no barbs, unlike an arrow, because it needs to slide smoothly along the groove in the stock."

"And just two fletches, on either side," added Hravn, "I'm sure we could get some made and fitted with the bodkin arrow heads I brought back from Morland. They'll be easier to make than an arrow-"

"And even more lethal against mail," Ulf interrupted with a smile.

Ulf glanced across to the target. "Stand well to the side lads. Let's see what this little beauty will do." He hefted the bow string back and secured it with the nut, laid the bolt carefully into the groove so that the cup in the end of the bolt rested against the nut, then raised the stock with his left hand, balancing it at the centre of gravity. He took aim by looking along the length of the bolt. Controlling his breathing, he squeezed the trigger gently with his right hand, taking care not to disturb his point of aim. The prods snapped forward, the only sounds were the twang of the bowstring and the simultaneous sharp thwack of the bolt smashing through the target and into the bark of the oak tree.

Ulf nodded slowly, still looking at the target. "Mmm, I like it. Save for the effort of drawing the bowstring, it's much easier to use than a bow. Even Ole could manage it."

Ole glanced sideways at Ulf. "How could I draw it?" He asked nervously.

Ulf laughed. "Easy. I'll show you. Here, take the bow. Lie down and put your feet on the prods, either side of the stock. Now, push forward with your legs whilst you lie back pulling the string towards your chest. Use your body's weight."

As Ole drew the bow string back Ulf lent forward and slipped the trigger into place. "See, that's it. Not too difficult even for a weak stripling like you." He teased Ole and rubbed his head fondly. Ole grinned. His mind raced as he worked out that even if he wasn't strong enough to hold the crossbow in the aim he could probably shoot it sitting down whilst balancing his elbows on his knees, or resting the weapon on a tree stump. He was determined to succeed.

They spent the rest of the day taking turns to shoot the crossbow. Hravn insisted that after each turn they dug out the head of the bolt from the bark of the oak tree. Their stock of bolts was limited to a couple of score and they couldn't risk damaging many until they had arranged for Aelf to make some more. The gnarled bark of the oak tree was soon criss-crossed with deep scars from where the bolt had embedded itself.

*****

The pony trotted briskly along the track. Ealdgith was relieved that the snow was sufficiently deep and crisp to give its hooves sound purchase, with little risk of slipping. She made good time and the little vill of Hyrst had not long awoken when she trotted across the small fields that surrounded it. Hyrst was tucked into a fold in the hills and had been untouched by the harrying. Ealdgith was unsure how long it would remain unknown to the Normans, but thankful that it was. It was now home to The Bear's mother. Too frail and aged to live in the woodland, Bron had been taken in by the villagers who venerated her skills as a herbalist.

Bron was Cumbric by birth. As a young woman, she had escaped the clutches of the renegade Cumbric warlord, Uther Pendragon, when he had seized her family's lands at Ravenstandale and sold her family into Viking slavery. Uther had taken her younger sister, Rhiannon, as his wife's servant. Ealdgith and Hravn had discovered her last year when they had been held hostage by the Pendragon clan. The two elderly sisters were almost identical: small with long thick wavy greying-brown hair, pinned into a bun, dark brown eyes and an inner resilience that belied their frail stature and aging years. Ealdgith loved them both.

Ealdgith dismounted and led her pony along the track between the thatch and turf roofed cottages that formed the small vill. She saw Bron from a distance, working at a long trestle table sheltered under the protruding eves of a small cottage. Ealdgith marvelled at the old lady's fortitude, but as she got closer she appreciated that Bron was making the best of the light in order to sort many dried herbs and seeds into little pockets stitched on a long length of fabric.

Bron turned at the sound of hooves and raised a hand in greeting. She wasn't surprised to see her new granddaughter, she knew that she would visit. "Come inside, there's a fire in the hearth and pottage to warm through." They embraced warmly, then Ealdgith hobbled her pony and ushered Hati through the door and into the dimly lit cottage.

It was their first real opportunity to talk since Ealdgith's return from Westmoringaland, though The Bear had already told his mother what he knew of their adventures in the last year. As Ealdgith spoke about Rhiannon and her years in captive servitude, Bron's eyes glistened with tears for the long-lost sister that she still loved. When Ealdgith paused, wondering if she should go on, the old lady sat up suddenly. "Come my dear, let us eat. I know we are too old to ever meet again, but to know that Rhiannon is alive, safe and knows that she still has a family who think of her, is a gift I never thought to receive. Thank you, and thank Hravn from me too."

As they ate the pottage Ealdgith asked about Bron's skills as a herbalist and wise woman, and enquired whether she might be able to acquire even the basic knowledge necessary. Bron smiled knowingly, placed her bowl to one side and took Ealdgith's hands in hers. I've known you since you were a babe, Edie, and you were the brightest child, though don't tell Hravn. You've an enquiring mind and compassion for others that is rare to see, so I've long expected you to ask. Beware though, an intelligent woman with knowledge that men don't share is not always thought of fondly.

Ealdgith laughed. "Most men don't like warrior women either, though they might think twice before saying so to my face. I intend to help those who I can, men and women, especially women."

Bron squeezed her hands and stood up. "Good, come outside. I have something for you." Ealdgith followed, wondering just how Bron had anticipated her request. Did she really have Cumbric second sight, as some rumoured?

Bron showed her the fabric roll on the trestle table. It was a square of bleached linen, four hand-spans across, that had been folded into thirds. Two of the thirds had been stitched together to give a series of narrow pockets. The remaining third made a flap that secured the pockets, and the whole could be rolled up and secured with two ribbons. Each of the pockets contained individual herbs, seeds, leaves or powder. Ealdgith's eyes widened. It was a work of art, and very obviously old. Muted stains coloured the different pockets where, for many years, the contents within had left their individual marks. Upon each pocket, there was a small embroidered image of the content and other little symbols that puzzled Ealdgith. She recognized some: garlic, balsam, mint, valerian, but there were many that she did not know. The roll was backed with a fine calf leather, burnished by time and many hands.

"Edie, this is now yours." Bron folded the flap and rolled the fabric into a scroll. "It has been in my family for many years. It is all I have from my life in Westmoringland. My skill was my mother's, and hers before her. I was buying medicinal herbs at the Kircabi Stephan market when the Pendragons struck and took my family. I had no daughter to pass the knowledge onto, until now. Maybe it is Wyrd's way."

Ealdgith stared momentarily in consternation and, bending forward, embraced Bron tightly and lightly kissed her cheek. "It's a privilege and a treasure, and so unexpected. Thank you, Ealdmoder."

Bron was a good teacher, calm and methodical. She led Ealdgith meticulously along the row of little pockets and explained how the little symbols showed the purpose of each. Ealdgith marvelled at the simplicity of the system. After Bron had explained the first ten she made Ealdgith repeat the explanations until she was confident that they could progress further. Ealdgith learned quickly. Much of her knowledge was lodged already at the back of her mind from watching the women of her childhood.

"You are doing well, Edie. Once you can show me that you are familiar with them all, I will show you how to use them. Some can be used for both good and bad, and so you must know just how much to administer, and when, where and how."

"Such as foxglove?" Ealdgith asked. "It controls the heart, but can bring delirium and death, can it not, and may be confused with comfrey?" Bron looked up and smiled, recognising her instinctive ability.

Ealdgith stayed with the old lady until the light began to fail. She knew that she would have to leave soon if she was to navigate safely along the track back to the cave. At least the snow would reflect the moonlight. "I'll return in the morn, Ealdmoder. Hravn and I have agreed that I will learn all that you can teach me." She paused, then added, "There is a girl in Grinton who is with child. She was raped and I fear her mother will not help her. Can you teach me the ways of the birthing bed?"

Bron hesitated, placed her hand on Ealdgith's wrist, then said, "I will, but you will need our Alfhildr for that. She is our birthing woman now, and very good. I will take you to her tomorrow...and, yes, I'll talk to you about rue and wild carrot too."

*****

A thick mist had descended upon the snow-clad woods and great balls of wet snow fell from the branches as the thaw set in. Hravn rode with Ealdgith as far as Wasfelte, then he lent across to kiss her briefly before she continued the next league to Bron's cottage in Hyrst. She had already spent four days with the old lady, enjoying the challenge of learning as well as getting closer to Hravn's ealdmoder.

Hravn had sent Ulf and the others to see Aelf at Locherlaga with a request to make arrow and bolt shafts and fit them to Hravn's sackful of arrow heads. In the meantime, he wanted to speak to his father. His half-sisters' fate had begun to play on his mind, the urge for revenge growing and gnawing at him from within.

The Bear was just about to ride over to Helwith. "Come Hravn, ride with me. I was on my way to speak to Leofric about his new flock of sheep." Hravn sidled his fell pony alongside as they rode across the clearing.

Pigs rooted up the earth in an enclosure, clearing the undergrowth. Hravn wondered if The Bear's people would stay there long enough to fell the trees on the cleared ground and plant crops. He rather doubted it. A group of women squatted by a bread oven to one side of the cluster of huts. Two were bareheaded and wore breaches and a tunic instead of the conventional cloak and under gown. The Bear glanced at Hravn and laughed at his expression. "Your Edie has a lot to answer for. More than a few of the women have taken her lead and wear men's clothing. It is certainly far more practical for this way of life."

"I can't blame them," Hravn replied smiling. "What's good for Edie is good for everyone, but do their men accept it?"

The Bear pursed his lips in a mock frown. "Many see the sense, though there are more than a few who resent their women's freedom. It's one matter in which I'm not going to get involved."

The ponies ambled slowly down the track, finding their own way. Both men found it easier to talk without the need to concentrate on the route, but able to look ahead and avoid seeing the sadness and distress in each other's eyes. Hravn's question about his sisters' fate had stopped The Bear in his tracks, after which he rode on slowly.

"Six younger women were held to one side, then forced onto a cart and driven off. We were kept back at sword point. Alfr tried to reach Asta and was slain on the spot. I could do nothing. The shame nearly broke me."

Hravn placed his hand on The Bear's wrist, causing him to look at his son. He spoke gently. "There's no shame, Fader; only the guilt of the brutal bastards that took them. Did you-"

"Yes," The Bear interrupted. "We found them two days later, in the woods. All but Cori. They had all been abused brutally, before being slain." Hravn stared into the distance, his mind numbed. "What of Cori?" He asked, hesitantly. Cori was the youngest of his three half-sisters and only a year older. She was also the prettiest.

The Bear took a deep breath. Hravn sensed that he was steadying his voice. "I don't know. There was no sign. I fear she was taken to become a whore. Death would have been better for her, though I doubt she can still be alive." He added, almost under his breath.

Hravn reined his pony to a halt and grasped his father's wrist with an urgency that jerked The Bear out of his introspection. "Fader. Did you see who was in charge? Was there a knight, or just men-at-arms?"

The Bear stared at Hravn, his eyes looking through him as he forced himself to recall the horror a year ago. "A knight? Yes!" He spat, hatred in his voice, in the phlegm that hit the dirt track. "An arrogant red-headed bastard with a scar across his cheek. His shield was red, marked with the head of a black boar with yellow eyes. He rode after the cart when it went."

Hravn shook his father's arm and stared into his eyes, pulling his mind back to the present. "If he serves Count Alan we'll find him, Ulf and me. My sisters will be revenged."

Chapter 10

"Hravn! There's a rider coming, quickly." Ole almost fell through the wicker screen into the cave. His breath came in laboured gasps. It was obvious that he had clambered halfway up the hill to warn Hravn. "There's one, I think, but he has yet to cross the ford."

Ealdgith pulled Ole to one side and sat him on a rocky ledge as Hravn and the others slipped quickly past the screen and out into the dusk, securing it immediately to minimise the risk of stray light revealing the cave's location. Ulf raised his hand, ensuring silence. He pointed to the wood below the enclosure and mouthed to Hravn, "One man, on foot. His mount is tethered at the foot of the cliff." A feint whinny confirmed his statement.

Hravn gestured to Orme to remain by the cave and led Ulf to the trees at the edge of the enclosure. The man was making no attempt to disguise his arrival as he laboured up the unfamiliar slope in the gathering dark. Hravn grinned and whispered to Ulf, "He's not a threat, whoever he is. But I want to know how he knows we are here."

Ulf nodded agreement. "Aye, we can't risk being compromised."

They waited until the man was almost past them before stepping out behind him. He turned, and gasped as Hravn's sword point touched his breast. "H..Hravn, I'm Edric."

"I know you. You were at Ellepigerthwaite," Ulf almost growled.

Edric nodded. He was stocky with red hair and a dense beard that hid half his face. His grey eyes sort Hravn's with an urgency that was unsettling. "The Bear sent me, and told me where to find you. You must come, now. Our lord is with your fader."

Hravn was taken aback. "Lord? Gospatrick?"

Edric nodded. "Yes. He has men-at-arms and pack horses too. He must speak with you now. That is why The Bear told me how to find you."

Hravn glanced at Ulf, who raised an eyebrow quizzically and shrugged. "We'd best make haste and take Edie too. He is her uncle after all," he said.

Hravn laughed, the tension broken. "Welcome Edric, you did well to find us. Come, quench your thirst whilst I get the others." He shouted. "Orme, fetch Edie and Ole, and get five ponies saddled. We need to get moving."

Despite the urgency with which they had been summoned they rode cautiously along the woodland tracks, taking care to avoid a stumble in the dark. Hravn thanked the gods for a starlit night as Ealdgith rode up alongside him. "My uncle must surely have business with Count Alan. I can't see him risking a visit to us without a reason to explain his presence so far south."

Hravn nodded agreement. "I'm sure you're right. I'm glad we have news for him. We can show that we haven't been idle and prove that his faith in us is justified."

Ealdgith smiled back, "Of course it is. You'll see."

As they rounded the bend in the track that led to the clearing at Wasfelte, Hravn could see that the fire in the hearth was larger than usual. The flames lit the silhouettes of a sizable group of men seated around it, and reflected off the flanks of several pack ponies tethered just beyond.

Hravn reined quickly to a halt as a shadowy figure, armed with a stave, stepped in front. "Hold there Edric. Hravn, Lady Edie, I'm sorry but The Bear directed that all are to be stopped until the Earl is warned that there are visitors. He has a guard on all the tracks."

Hravn watched as a second figure ran from the shadows, crossing the clearing towards the fire. He turned to Ulf, "I'm impressed. Fader's beginning to think more like us." A sharp whistle caught their attention and the guard stepped back, allowing them forward.

Earl Gospatrick stood up as Hravn and Ealdgith stepped forward together. Taking a pace towards them, he drew Ealdgith to him in a warm embrace and then placed both hands on Hravn's shoulders in a gesture of warmth and affection that surprised him. "Hravn, it is good to see you recovered and fit. I'm pleased to say that you have a reputation that precedes you."

Somewhat taken aback, Hravn was thanking Gospatrick when Ealdgith interrupted. "Uncle, does this mean that you have heard from Count Alan?"

Gospatrick laughed with a deep chortle. "Indeed, it does my dear Edie. Indeed, it does. Come sit here. There is much I have to tell you both." He settled back onto the length of a fallen oak trunk upon which he had been sitting.

Ealdgith looked again at her uncle. Tall and well-built with the deeply tanned face of one who spent most of his time outside, he was balding and just entering middle age. A neatly trimmed brown beard framed his jaw, complemented the rounded shape of his face. It was, however, his warm, dark brown eyes that always drew her attention. She felt that they always saw deep within her. It was if they inspired her love and trust whilst searching out her inner thoughts. The flames reflected off the coat of mail that he wore. He was a soldier and a leader of men. Ealdgith knew that his calm presence in the beleaguered wood inspired them all.

Gospatrick held his hands out towards the flames to warm them, then turned to the young couple who had settled on the grass beside him. Ulf, Orme and Ole joined The Bear, standing a respectful distance to one side. He smiled at them both, then grinned at Ealdgith. "You were always very smart Edie. I've spent the day with the Count, though that wasn't my main reason for coming here. I could not risk a visit without seeing him and it is of course good to see the ground from the enemy's position – even if he does count me as a friend," he added, with a laugh.

"He told me that there have been raids on my cousin's lands, granaries burnt and grain stolen. Even two of his constable's men-at-arms are missing presumed murdered. I of course shared his concern and asked for my sympathy to be passed to my cousin." Gospatrick continued, with a glint of mischief in his eye. "I was beginning to suspect that he might be talking about your efforts, Hravn. So, you can understand my relief when he explained that it was the work of the silvatici in the untamed woodlands between the Wharfe and the Nidd."

Eadgith giggled and glanced at Hravn. "Oh uncle, I do so love it when a plan comes together. Or rather, when Hravn's plan comes together."

"Thanks Edie," Hravn responded. "Although, to be fair My Lord, it was as much to Edie's credit as mine."

Gospatrick laughed again. "I care not whose plan it was, but it does prove to me that you are mastering the principles of war: surprise, deception, sound planning. You're both justifying my faith in you." He glanced across to where Ulf was standing beside The Bear. "And I can see that the morale of your team is strong too. Well done." He paused, catching their attention, his eyes glinting in the firelight. "I want you to build upon the Count's misunderstanding. Direct your attention south of here. Raid, kill his men, keep his eyes looking south. I want a free hand in the north. I'm asking a lot, I know, for you must kill all whom you engage with. You cannot risk them surviving, for they will talk and identify you. Concentrate on the area around Massan, Ripum and Tresch. I don't have any cells there and so you can focus his attention without fear of reprisal against others who resist."

Hravn's stomach tensed. A sudden coldness in Gospatrick's eyes forewarned of unwelcome news. "One thing you both need to know is that the King has revived Cnut's law of murdrum, but this time for the hidden killing of any Frenchman, be they Norman or Breton. If any bodies are found, and seen to be French, the lord of that manor must find the murderer within five days. If he fails to find the murderer, forty-six marks of silver must be paid to the King, or those under the lord's control must pay." He held their eyes. "This means that any bodies must be stripped and hidden. Without a body, no-one can claim murder. The King has also ordered that no one shall be executed for crimes they have committed; but if they are guilty of a crime, they will be blinded and castrated. The consequence could be worse than death. It is a risk you need to understand, and so do those whom you lead."

They nodded soberly as the full implication of the Earl's orders sank in. Hravn spoke first. "You said that the Count spoke of the silvatici. One of the men we killed spoke of them too. Who are they?"

Gospatrick chuckled, "Ah, it's what the Normans call the resistance: the 'men of the woods', and that brings me to another reason for my visit."

They could see a mixture of mischief and intensity of purpose in Gospatrick's expression, he continued. "The Count might call you, us, the silvatici. I call you the 'green men'. It's a term that is catching on elsewhere. I saw, when we last met, that you both wear cloaks that blend with the undergrowth. Those that live and fight in woodlands must be dressed to survive, and to survive you must be able to hide. Come." He stood and gestured for them to follow him towards the pack ponies.

"Weapons can be taken from those whom you kill, but clothes are a different matter, especially those that help conceal you." Gospatrick unbuckled the lid of a pannier on the side of a packhorse and, pulling out a roll of clothing, he tossed it to Hravn. "Here, open it and tell me what you think." He signalled to one of his men to hold a torch closer.

Hravn caught the cloth, shook the roll open and held up a woollen cloak, woven with a random weave of green and brown, waterproofed with lanolin. He gave a low whistle of surprise whilst Ealdgith's face broke into a broad smile. Gospatrick held up his hand. "There's more. Catch, Edie," he grinned as she caught the small roll of light material. Ealdgith flicked it open, revealing a leaf-green light-linen hood. "Have a look at the bottom, Edie, there are draw strings to secure it over a helm, if you need to, and to mask your face."

The quality of the cloak and the hood amazed Hravn. Only a man with considerable wealth could have had them made in such numbers. The cloak was perfect for their needs: warm, waterproof and camouflaged. The hood was light enough to cover a head without constraining hearing or being unbearably hot when active. He wondered if he could push his luck and ask the Earl to bring bodkin-tipped arrows and crossbow bolts when he next came.

Ealdgith laughed. "Green men, Uncle? We'll become the stuff of nightmares, Norman nightmares." Gospatrick hugged her shoulder. "I hope so Edie." He turned to Hravn. "I have sets of these for all my cells between the Tees and the Aire. How many do you think you will need?"

Hravn pursed his lips in thought. "A dozen, if you have enough? I want to expand the group. I'm sure our success will inspire more to join us, as will your visit. I know the people welcome it." He paused and grinned cheekily as he glanced across the Ulf and Ole, "I could do with different sizes."

Gospatrick nodded. "Have your men choose their own, and take a baker's dozen. I have enough."

A sudden concern nagged at Hravn's confidence. "My Lord, how do I get a message to you if I need to? As we get more engaged with the Normans there is every chance we will discover information that will help your cause, our cause."

Gospatrick, suddenly serious, drew Hravn to one side. "You are right. I should have told you before now, but I need to be very careful before I can disclose the links in the network. You do understand the risk of such knowledge, don't you?" He looked earnestly into Hravn's eyes.

"Yes, Lord. Is there not also a risk if I don't know?"

The Earl chuckled, "Of course. If you need me seek out Father Oda at Esebi. He, like Father Patrick, does not favour the increased influence of the Pope in Rome that the church is being forced to accept. He will do all he can to return the North to the way it was. He has his own way of getting a message to me within a matter of days."

Gospatrick turned back towards The Bear and placed his hands on the couple's shoulders. "Come, we have a lot more to talk about. Tell me how you fired my cousin's granaries."

*****

Ealdgith was lost in thought as she sat on the tree stump by the cave entrance. Her uncle's visit had reminded her where her duty lay, but she was determined to also do what she could for the women of her community, particularly Cyneburg whose time must be almost due. She jerked with a start as an arm suddenly wrapped around her, holding her tight. Her panic passed as quickly as it had come as she settled her back against Hravn. She smiled as his left arm also encircled her, his hand presenting a posy of fresh primroses. "Lencten's here Edie. Just think how far

136

we've come since last Lencten and our time with Oswin."

The spring sun warmed their faces as they enjoyed the quiet moment; the recent cold and snow seemed an age ago. "Hravn, I must go and see Cyneburg. I promised to help her and her time must soon be due." Ealdgith half turned to look up at Hravn.

"I know, you must. Go this morning and take Ulf; I rather sense that he too wants to see her again."

Ealdgith couldn't help noticing the look of surprise and the sudden secret smile when she asked Ulf to accompany her. "Of course, My Lady," he said with sudden formality in an attempt to hide the blush that swept his cheeks. He laughed, though, when Ealdgith poked him in the ribs and stuck her tongue out, teasing. "Don't be shy Ulf, we can all read the signs."

They led their horses down through the wood, mounted, and cantered along the flat ground towards Mersche. They slowed as they came to the deserted vill. Ulf glanced around the buildings and along the cross-track before walking his horse slowly forward. "There's a sadness here that I can never get used to," he said, almost to himself. Then, turning to Ealdgith, his mood brightened. "I'll be open with you Edie. There is something about Cyneburg that draws me to her. I can't say what. Her face is strangely beautiful and I feel her eyes look deep into me. I felt it as soon as I saw her. It's an attraction I can't explain. Maybe we sense we each have a pain that we need to share. I don't know..." Then added quickly, "she's not a bit like Adelind."

Ealdgith smiled back, but her voice was serious when she spoke. "She's very fragile, you do understand? The child was forced upon her and I fear her parents will insist she kills it. They'll have no love for a Norman bastard."

Ulf nodded, soberly. "I know, Edie, but hers is a tragedy we must all share. She invites tenderness, from me at any rate." Ealdgith nodded, understanding. They rode in silence, Ulf thinking about Cyneburg; Ealdgith about the plight of women in general.

As they rode into the small vill of Grinton they could see Ealhstan in the distance, training a sheep dog. "At least he's taken your advice and seen Leofric, and we can talk to Cyneburg without him." Ulf sensed the relief in Ealdgith's voice.

Tethering their horses at the edge of the homestead, they dismounted and were about to walk across the ragged line of flags covering the muddy ground to the door when Cyneburg came around the corner of the building. One hand carried a pail of water, the other clutched the bottom of her very extended stomach.

"Come, let me!" Ulf immediately, and instinctively, leapt forward, took the pail from her and placed his free hand around her waist to help support and guide her gently towards the door. He stepped in the mud whilst she followed the paving. Ealdgith opened the door and stepped back. Cyneburg looked surprised, before quickly recovering to smile thankfully at Ealdgith then, quizzically, at Ulf.

Ealdgith spoke quickly. "Cyneburg, I'm sorry, I promised to come back before your time, but you're further on than I thought. You do remember Ulf, don't you?" She added, realising that the sudden intrusion of a man into her time of late pregnancy might unsettle Cyneburg.

Cyneburg breathed out deeply as she lowered herself onto a stool, and glanced quickly at Ulf, with a smile of tenderness and gratitude. "Yes, I do, thank you. You're very gentle."

Ealdgith smiled as Ulf blushed, then quickly moved the subject on. "When do you think that you are due?"

Cyneburg shrugged. "I've never been with child before. Moder thinks maybe two weeks. She could be right, for I have contractions but have had no pain, yet."

Ulf surprised both women by speaking. He glanced at Cyneburg. "I think she is right. I remember how my Adelind was with my boy. I lost them both in the slaughter."

Ealdgith giggled to break the sudden tension. "Ulf, I never knew that you were a birthing woman as well as a huscarl."

As Ulf's mouth dropped open, Cyneburg came to his defence, and leaning forward placed her hand on his. She said quietly, "Ulf, thank you. I barely know you, but you are surely the gentlest, most understanding, man I have known, and one of the strongest."

Ealdgith watched as Cyneburg held Ulf's eyes with hers. "Ulf spoke first. "I will speak to your father before I leave. When you feel the pains of birth coming he must send immediate word to me, through The Bear. Edie and I will come."

"As will Alfhildr, the birthing woman from Hyrst." Ealdgith added, feeling suddenly almost superfluous in the matter of Cyneburg's birth.

Still holding Cyneburg's hands Ulf said to Ealdgith, "Edie, spend time with Cyneburg and talk about those things that I do not know about, whilst I search out Ealhstan and make sure he knows what he must do." He turned back to Cyneburg. "And your moder, where will I find her?" He released her hands with a gentle squeeze as the girl said, "She was in the byre. You'll find her there."

*****

Ealdgith and Ulf were lost in their own thoughts as they rode over the bridge at Grinton and turned towards Mersche. "It's a beautiful time, isn't it Ulf? The days are lengthening and sumor could almost be upon us. Look how the leaf buds are bursting with new life?"

"Hah! Just like Cyneburg," he quipped, in reply, then blushed, embarrassed.

Ealdgith's next comment sent a sudden shiver down his spine. "This dale is so peaceful, it's like our own private place."

Ulf reined to a sudden halt. "No, Edie. The dale may be beautiful, but it can be a dangerous place. Let's leave it and ride back over the hill above Marige. I could do with having a look at Fremington and what the dale looks like from higher up."

Although Ulf appreciated the dale's beauty he saw it as a trap. A soldier's sixth sense warned him away from it. Ealdgith didn't demur as he turned his horse northwards, towards Fremington and the hill above Marige. She understood the folly of her comment. "I'm sorry Ulf, that was foolish. I can never forget how the Reeve's men caught us at Langethwait, nor those who raped Cyneburg. All will have ridden this way."

The horses found it hard going as they zig-zagged slowly up the steep fellside above the almost deserted vill of Fremington. Ulf and Ealdgith helped them as best they could, leaning forward in their saddles and guiding them across the more even patches of turf.

"Hati! What?" Ealdgith turned in her saddle and froze. Hati had spun around and was stood erect, still, hackles raised, growling deeply. His nose and eyes pointed towards the woods below them, where the fellside dropped steeply into the dale below, where Ealdgith had expected them to go on their journey home.

Ulf reacted first. His eyes caught sight of a bird diving swiftly. "Edie down! It's a hawking party. Get your horse to yon crags." He nodded towards a small outcrop thirty paces below them, "And get it to lie down." He leapt from the saddle and ran, leading his horse to the crags that were no more than a man's height in size. "If we're low and still, we'll blend with the ground," he panted, as he urged his mount down, reassuring it as he forced it to lie prone.

Ealdgith could feel her heart racing. She could almost hear her blood pumping as she strove to control her breathing and listen. Her eyes were sharper than her ears. "Look, Ulf, to the right of the gap in the trees." They watched as a solitary rider in a scarlet cloak made his way noisily along the edge of the wood.

Ulf nodded, his face a stern mask. Ealdgith could see the loathing in his eyes. "It's a knight's squire. He's putting pigeons to flight, those hawking will be in the dale below." He paused. "They'll have followed the route we always take from Mersche to Grinton." His next words were spoken softly, but coldly; his meaning was not lost on Ealdgith. "This is what The Bear has

141

long feared, that hunters find our settlements by accident."

They watched in silence as the loan rider picked his way along the line of trees below them, disappearing slowly down into the dale. "Come, Edie, we'll cut across the spur, then hug the edge of the woodland and get back to warn Hravn. He bent down instinctively and took Hati's large head in his equally large hands, gently ruffling the dog's ears, "Well done Hati, lad. You saved your mistress again."

Later, as they sat in the cave by the hearth's glowing embers, Ealdgith spoke for them all. "We can't let this stop us, but we have to be more careful when we are outside the woods. I was too confident today, it was Ulf's sixth sense that saved us."

"You're right Edie," Hravn agreed, "but we can't rely on a sixth sense. We need to use the ground more sensibly, just as you did, Ulf, taking cover in the shadow of the crags. We need to observe open ground before we cross it, move quickly when we do, and stay under cover or in shadow where we can. The shortest route certainly isn't the quickest or safest."

Ulf nodded, "Aye, you have it Hravn. But my worry is what will The Bear do when the settlements are found? They will be, sooner or later."

"I know, Ulf, but that's for my fader to decide. I'll talk to him. He has to know about what has happened. My thoughts are that the people may have to move to a vill further up the dale. From what Frode told us when we were at Kelda last Haerfest, the vills above Rie survived. Maybe they could go there and even start to rebuild Rie."

"But would the people accept them?" Ealdgith interrupted. "Remember how poor they were in Kelda. They hosted us, but only for a few days. Even if our people were to take everything they have, it might not be enough to sustain everyone."

Orme had remained silent until now, his eyes flicking from one to the other as they spoke. "You're right Edie, some will succumb, but the strong will survive. Maybe that is all we can expect. Hravn's right, let The Bear decide. I know it has been on his mind ever since we came to the woodland." Ealdgith glanced at him, surprised at his fatalism and his maturity.

Hravn stood up quickly with sudden resolve. He had to break the mood of despondency. "There are yet more pressing things to deal with. Look at young Ole's boots. I've never seen so much grass growing from someone's feet. I'm going to Richemund in the morn, and Edie and Orme are coming too. We're going to find a cobbler and order boots for us all. Edie, can you bring the letter of authority that your uncle gave me? I might just need it."

He turned to Ulf and raised his hand gently to stay the huscarl's look of surprise. "Ulf, I fear you might attract too much attention there. Orme can keep our backs for us. Can you show Ole how to clean up all the armour and weapons we took off the dead Normans, and then match them up with a cloak and hood? If we can recruit some more 'green men' I want them to each to have a full set of clothing and arms. Let's see what we have that will fit Ole, too."

Chapter 11

Ealdgith shivered. It was early, with a spring-time nip in the air. She slipped from her pony, cursing the dress that had ridden up over her thighs whilst she rode, feeling distinctly self-conscious. Hravn smiled, teasing her with his eyes, but careful not to say anything that would goad her temper. He knew that she disliked wearing a dress, even if it was the very flattering green one that Rhiannon made for her last sumor. Orme kept a very straight face, thinking that, if only Ealdgith realised how pretty she looked, she might feel a lot more confident.

Hravn squeezed Ealdgith's hand, glanced back towards Orme, raising his eyes in mock despair, then said calmly, "Edie, remember, wrap your cloak around you, keep your shawl over your head and lower your eyes. God forbid that anyone recognises you. I have Earl Gospatrick's letter of introduction and will speak in Cumbric and bluff my way as a Breton if we are challenged." He turned his head to Orme again, "Orme, keep a few paces behind and guard our backs. You're my man and I'll speak for all of us. Let's see what this new vill of Richemund is all about."

Having tethered their ponies in the copse on top of the hill dominating the adjacent vills of Hindrelag and Richemund, they walked down to the track that ran through the long west-field. The still-rising sun threw long shadows across the terraces and the lines of stooped, hard-worked, peasants. Hravn glanced sideways at Ealdgith. He could see anger in her eyes. "Look! That stake-wall around my family's manor is more foreboding than we thought, the whole plateau is enclosed by it. There's no sign of our house now. They're so brutal..." She bit her lip, then continued. "See the stonework where they're building above the cliff? It's already above head height." Hravn winced as she swore unexpectedly. "God's teeth! That castle will be a hellish oppressive place."

Hravn nodded, then paused for Orme to catch up. "Aye, you're right, Edie. I can see why your uncle is keeping a close eye on the Count and what he is doing." He pointed. "See? This side of the stake-wall. They've cleared the little wood where we used to play, and knocked down the barn. That line of thatched roofs must be the new vill of Richemund."

"Hindrelag is still there, it's not been burnt." Orme chipped in. "The church of Our Lady, with its little wooden tower, and the jumble of houses going down to the river. They've not changed. There're people down there too."

"And in Richemund. It looks like a small market, I think," Ealdgith added hesitantly.

Hravn glanced across the fields to where a line of men in tattered clothes had stopped hoeing the ground and were stood watching. "Come on, we're attracting attention. Let's walked briskly, it's only half a league."

As they got closer they could see the familiar outline of what was once Ealdgith's manor. The west-field track met the gallows-field and east-field tracks just above the hotchpotch of houses, huts and pigsties that was Hindrelag. The collection of turfed roofs and mossy wooden walls was dominated by the little church tower and just beyond, to the right, they could see the reflection of the fish pond that had once helped sustain

145

her father's table. The plateau above the cliffs at the bend of the broad river, from which her father's hall had once looked down upon the vill, was now enclosed by a high wooden stake-wall with a large gate on the northern edge. The freshly cut timber of the new buildings of Richemund stood out starkly in a straight row, running westward from the gate.

The track was rutted and muddy, scourged by heavy cart wheels. "No wonder it's in such a state, think of all the trees that have been hauled down here to build that enclosure, the castle and the vill. That's why the wood back there is so damaged." Hravn grumbled loudly with ill-concealed anger. As they reached the line of new buildings forming the growing vill of Richemund the track improved where cart-loads of river cobbles had been trodden into it. A noticeable smell of sewage hung in the air.

Ealdgith faltered, taking Hravn's arm, as a group of children ran by barefoot in the mud. "It's not just us, or those children, that need a cobbler. Look at yon women by the stall." She gestured with her head to three women, one barefoot and two with thick wads of grass above bark soles tied to their feet, forming rudimentary clogs.

"Aye, and their clothes are threadbare too," Hravn said quietly.

"They're no better off than our people in the woodland," Ealdgith whispered back. "And, if you look carefully, there is precious little produce on the stalls, and what they have they are bartering, not selling."

Ealdgith stopped. "That man, beyond the women, the one bent double under a stack of firewood on his shoulders. He was the reeve for Hindrelag, I'm sure of it."

Hravn gripped her hand. "They're no better than slaves now, that's why we have to resist."

They turned as Orme tapped Hravn on the shoulder. "Look, at yon end of the vill. There's smoke from a forge and it looks like the sign for a cobbler next to it."

"Well spotted, Orme, it could be that the craftsmen are closest to the gate into the enclosure." Hravn gave him a quick grin.

Ealdgith turned to them both with sudden resolve. "Let's go. Walk as if you own the place. If we act cowed well be treated as such. Come on Hravn, be my Cumbric lord in a foreign land."

Orme was right. As they strode along the broad track, the central row of rickety market stalls between the ramshackle huts gave way to a sound surface of recently laid cobbles. A double row of well-built houses lined either side. They were framed in stout oak with sound wattle and daub cladding. The people had changed too. Their clothes were finer, clean and well presented. Ealdgith felt less conspicuous and Hravn could tell by the voices that English had given way to Breton and a strange, lilting, tongue that he guessed was Norman. The hounds trotting obediently behind drew occasional glances, the threesome were ignored.

The enclosure was closer too, only a furlong or so beyond the forge. The high gates were fixed open and a constant flow of people, men and women, moved in and out under the watchful scrutiny of four men-at-arms standing guard. A clatter of hooves caused the threesome to pause, each feeling a momentary panic, as a troop of four horsemen galloped out, their chain mail glistening in the weak sunlight. The horsemen didn't pause, wheeled to the right, took the track towards the east-field. In doing so, they brushed against a labourer who fell back to save himself from the flailing hooves. "Bastards!" Hravn cursed, before remembering where he was.

As they passed the acrid smoke of the forge, they paused in front of a crudely painted image of two leather boots that hung above a trestle displaying rows of footwear. The door was half open and a strong smell of newly cut leather wafted from within. Ealdgith looked at the two men beside her. "Well?"

Hravn pursed his lips, thinking. "They must be made for the garrison, and those who work for them. I can tell by the voices that there are more Bretons and Normans, than English, at this end of the vill." He glanced around, checking that they weren't attracting attention. "Right. Let's go in."

They blinked as they stepped in, the lack of light momentarily blinding them. A bell fixed to the back of the door tinkled loudly. "Bouônjour à matîn, beinv'nu," a voice called from an inner room, in what Hravn took to be Norman. "Sorry, I speak Breton, not Norman." He called back in Cumbric, with a confidence that he didn't feel. They took a quick glance at their surroundings. The room was small, lit by a smoking oil lamp hanging from a rafter and by a low fire in the central hearth. Some light permeated through two small vellum-covered windows. Freshly tanned hides hung from the rafters, partitioning a second room from where they heard low voices and the sound of leather being scraped. A long trestle table displayed rows of boots of a uniform pattern in various sizes. More ornate shoes, some for women, were laid out on a smaller table.

The hides were pushed to one side as a man, swarthy and wearing a heavy apron, stepped through, then paused, obviously surprised to see a well-dressed woman, two men with swords at their waists and two wolfhounds. Ealdgith placed her hands on their collars to calm them.

Hravn stepped forward, his hand extended in greeting. "I work for Count Alan," he bluffed, speaking Cumbric, hoping that the Norman cobbler would speak Breton.

He did. "I understand you, but you are not Breton? What is your business here? I only serve the garrison."

Ealdgith's eyes flicked from one to the other as she tried to understand the gist of the conversation. Hravn drew her in. "My wife, and man-servant..." He paused, gathering his thoughts, as he strove to make their presence seem perfectly normal. He drew the scrolled letter of authority from inside his cloak. "I too, am from the garrison. I am Cumbric and serve the Count by translating the English tongue for him and my lord Enisant, his constable." He learnt forward, conspiratorially, and lowered his voice. "I move within the English and report what they say. You understand?" He raised a questioning eye brow. "This is my authority." Hravn unscrolled the letter and, without letting go of it, showed it to the cobbler.

Ealdgith could tell from the movement of the cobbler's eyes that he couldn't read. She hoped that Earl Gospatrick's large red seal would suffice to impress. It did.

The cobbler stared at the seal, raised his eyes back to Hravn and nodded. "Very well. How can I serve you?"

149

Hravn laughed, breaking the tension. "It is simple. You're a cobbler and I need boots, for my wife and all my staff. May we?" he gestured to the trestle tables and, without waiting for a reply, hefted a stout pair of boots in his left hand, before bending down to try them on. The cobbler didn't demur, giving Ealdgith and Orme the confidence to follow suit.

Ealdgith had measured Ulf and Ole's feet against the palm of her hand and had a fair idea of what would fit. She chose accordingly then, on a whim, said quietly to Hravn, with a cheeky smile. "Frida and Cyneburg too?" Hravn raised his eyes, then nodded, cursing inwardly that he had no idea how big his father's feet were.

Visibly pleased with the size of his sale, the cobbler relaxed and happily answered Hravn's questions about where he could find a tailor and saddle maker. He even provided a stout leather sack to carry the shoes in when Hravn unquestioningly paid the asking price in silver coin.

Taking the opportunity of the cobbler's good nature Hravn casually asked about life in the vill and how business was going. He talked as if he already knew the answers to his relaxed, open, questions and gathered quickly that the new castle had two baileys: an inner one for the garrison, with wooden fortified buildings lived in whilst the stone castle was being built, and an outer one where stonemasons and craftsmen from Normandy and the south of England were housed. Some even had their families with them. Others, a few only, had taken local women as their wives. The household was run by Count Alan's steward, a man called Scolland. The talk of women led the cobbler to mention that an English widow, 'Ola the Ox' they called her, now kept a brothel in a house by the fishpond. Girls that were found in the outlying villages were taken there and kept for the men of the garrison. Hravn wondered about Cori.

Hravn's next question, about the cobbler's business, killed the conversation. The cobbler answered casually, grinning. "Business? Good. Now that the count has engaged another thirty mercenaries to destroy those silvatici in the south, it is going to get even better."

Hravn looked up sharply and forced a smile to hide his shock. "It certainly will! Now, thank you for your time. We must depart, though I will doubtless return."

Ealdgith was thankful to leave the cobblers shop. She felt very vulnerable so close to the burgeoning garrison, with its castle and foreign tradesmen. It was as if she had stepped into a strange country on the land where her family once lived. Orme, too, felt threatened by the babble of foreign voices. They followed Hravn out of the doorway, bumping into him as he paused mid stride. Hravn was staring across the cobbled street to where a Norman knight berated the firewood-carrying former reeve that Ealdgith had pointed out earlier.

"Come Hravn. Let's move on, quickly." Orme urged Hravn on as Ealdgith stepped beyond them and walked briskly back towards the cluster of market stalls.

Hravn gathered his senses and caught them quickly. "Stop Edie, one minute. Orme, take a look at that bastard back there and remember his face. That's the one that sacked Raveneswet and raped my sisters. Fader described the same man: red hair, tall, blue eyes, scar across his cheek, wears the boar crest on his tunic and has a red shield marked with a yellow-eyed black boar. It's him alright. Arrogant murdering rapist bastard! Remember him Orme. One day you, Ulf and I will kill him." He paused. "You're right Edie, it's time to go!"

*****

"Well, we did it! We entered the wolves' lair and survived," Orme said cheerfully as he swung himself onto his pony's saddle.

Hravn and Ealdgith grinned back, their spirits and self-confidence boosted by the flow of adrenalin and sure knowledge that they had overcome another challenge. But doubts still nagged. "Aye, you're right Orme, we've proved ourselves again. Though don't forget what the cobbler told us. Gospatrick wants us to raid into the south, and that's to be another wolves' lair by all account."

Ealdgith heard the note of caution in Hravn's voice. She nodded, adding, "Yes, and we've seen how our people have been dragged into servitude. That will happen to us all if we don't resist."

Hravn turned to Ealdgith. "We need to talk this though with Ulf, Edie. Raiding into the south is a challenge and a risk."

She nodded, thoughtfully. "Mmm...the bigger challenge will be avenging your sisters."

Hravn spurred his pony forward. "Let's go! I want to see Ole's face when he puts his boots on."

Ole's expression surpassed Hravn's expectations. When Ealdgith handed the boots to him he stared, whooped, then embraced her in a tight hug. "Thanks, Edie." Then, remembering that Hravn had bought them, he punched

Hravn playfully in the chest, "And you too, Hravn. Thank you."

Ulf was equally pleased. Ealdgith grinned as he eased his feet into them, rubbed his hands gently over the soft leather, then stretched his legs out, waggling his feet, "By Thor! That feels so...oo good!" This reaction was nothing compared to when Hravn gave him the boots for Cyneburg. Ealdgith was sure she saw a wetness in his eyes as he accepted them gently, saying, "I'll keep them until after she gives birth. Thank you, Edie."

*****

Ealdgith was felt unusually elated after their early morning trip to Richemund. The sun was only just past its zenith and, with a cloudless sky, the day was the warmest of the year, so far. She turned cautiously to Hravn and raised herself to whisper in his ear, "Come, let them get used to their boots, there is something down by the falls that I want you to see." She took his hand firmly in hers and led him across the sward and down into the trees below the enclosure. Hravn followed, intrigued.

Ulf caught their disappearance out of the corner of his eye and smiled secretly. He turned to the others. "Right, lads, to work. Ole, it's a while since you saw your moder. Gallop over there now and show her your boots." Ole turned, grinned and, without further bidding, ran down to fetch his pony.

"Now, Orme, let's get these weapons, mail and cloaks sorted once and for all. Fetch the dry sand whilst I get the lanolin and a handful of fleece. Hravn and Edie have things to do. We'll get it done before they get back."

Ealdgith, still wearing her green dress, led Hravn down to the meadow and along the river bank to a series of low waterfalls over each of which the water tumbled in a glistening curtain. A large ash hung over the broad pool and grassy bank, and a swathe of delicate primroses clinging to the bank were reflected in shimmering yellow streaks across the pool.

She ran ahead and, as she did so, Hravn could see the green of Ealdgith's dress catching and mingling with the yellow and blue reflections. He paused, struck by the sudden beauty of the scene and was about to call to Ealdgith when he saw her slowly slip her dress from her shoulders. As this dropped below her waist she eased off her under shift, let her clothes fall to the ground, and turned towards Hravn. She opened her arms in a welcoming embrace. "My love, it's time," she said gently. "Bron has told me what to do and I am ready. Take me, I've held you back for so long – I know we can wait no longer."

Without a word, Hravn stepped forward and pulled Ealdgith to him. Her lips sort his as one hand gently stroked the back of her neck whilst the other caressed the small of her back then, dropped, to stroke her buttocks, pressing them towards him. She moaned softly then pulled back, grasping at Hravn's clothes, pulling their fastenings, urging him out of them.

Naked, they stood, hugged together, until Hravn slowly lifted Ealdgith and gently lowered her onto the cloak he had spread over the grass and flowers. "Edie, you truly are the most beautiful woman and this the most beautiful place. Let us make a beautiful memory together, to share for all our lives." Ealdgith rolled on top of him, silencing him with her tip of her tongue.

Sköll and Hati kept a respectful distance, lay down and snoozed.

Chapter 12

Ole galloped along the woodland tracks, enjoying the thrill of speed and marvelling at the green of the young leaves bursting forth all around him. He knew the route but still kept glancing up to check that he could see the way marks blazoned on the upper tree trunks.

He was barely half a league south of Hulders-wold when a scream shattered the peace of the woodland idyll. His pony slid to a halt as he strove to steady his breath and listen. The scream had come from his right, off to the east. He was sure of it. Yes! Through the raucous call of disturbed crows, he could hear distant galloping. One, no, several horses were on the track that cut around the top of Clapyat Gill then south to Hindrelag. They were heading away from him.

Sudden panic seized him. His family! The horses were galloping away from Hulders-wold. Ole urged his pony into a frenzied gallop. He knew before ever he reached the tiny settlement that something was wrong. He smelt the smoke before he saw it, rising lazily through the trees in a gentle blue haze that belied the violence that had caused it.

He saw the people next, his father's people, standing in a cluster in the little clearing. Several women wept, clinging to each other. Ole jumped from his pony and ran into the crowd, pushing his way through, fearful of what he would find; inwardly knowing it was too late.

Agnaar lay on his back; a seax in the hand of one of his outstretched arms. A bloody tumble of guts oozed from the gash in his stomach; sightless eyes stared at the sky. Ole's moder lay across her husband's feet, her half-severed head hung grotesquely.

Ole collapsed, retching. He stumbled forward, desperate to reach his parents, but fell, unconscious, alongside his mother.

*****

Orme read the look in Ealdgith's eyes as the couple walked hand in hand from the enclosure back to the cave. He knew. As he gave Hravn a big boyish grin, his expression turned to one of surprise. "Hravn! Look! Is that Edric galloping this way?"

Hravn knew instinctively that something was wrong. Ealdgith ran to change out of her dress, her inner-peace shattered, whilst Ulf and Orme followed Hravn in a slithering descent through the wood to the ford.

Edric's pony splashed through the river and then skidded to a halt on the loose clay bank. He took a moment to gather his breath, then looked them all in the eye. "It's bad news. A hunting party rode into Hulders-wold earlier. It was pure chance by all accounts. Agnaar put himself between them and his people, but they saw Frida and pulled her out. She was the only girl there and it was obvious what they wanted. Agnaar threw himself at them, wounded one, but was then slain where he stood; his wife too. The others were spared. They torched the huts and left, taking Frida. Ole arrived just after. He's badly shocked and was taken to Wasfelte. The Bear's ordered everyone to move back from Hulders-wold and to join him. He also said that he recognised the description of one of the knights in the party. You'd know who he meant."

"*Skíta*!" Orme punched the tree next to him then crouched down, his head cradled in his arms. Ealdgith crouched next to him, her arm around his shoulder.

Hravn stared at Edric momentarily, before reacting with authority and urgency. He knew what must be done, but how to do it? "Ulf, get the ponies and lead them down." He bent down to Orme and placed his hand on his shoulder and, as Orme looked up, said, "We are going to get her back, tonight." Then, glancing at Ealdgith, "I need to think this through Edie, but we can guess where Frida will have been taken. We have to speak to The Bear first and see Ole. I must speak to those who were there." Ealdgith nodded, enraged, supportive, but daunted. She had never seen such cold resolve in Hravn's eyes.

"Stay close to Orme," he said. "I need to get a clear plan in my head before we speak to The Bear. We will need to be back here, armed and away by dusk."

Ulf slithered back down the slope, panting, leading a string of ponies. They mounted and galloped after Edric.

Dismounting in the clearing at Wasfelte, Ealdgith ran straight to The Bear. "Ole?" He pointed to his hut before striding to meet Hravn. Ole was sitting on the ground by The Bear's hearth, Freya's arm around him. Seeing Ealdgith he ran to her and flung his arms around her, sobbing. She held him as a mother would, gently rubbing his head whilst his tears flowed. "Hravn will get Frida back," was all she could say to him. The death of his parents was too much for her to talk about.

Hravn was quite blunt when he spoke to his father. As far as he was concerned their options were limited and he didn't have time to debate them. "Fader, this is a disaster on three counts: Frida has been taken to be a whore, Agnaar is dead and the security of the settlements is compromised. We can do something about Frida now, Agnaar and his wife must be buried, and we have to think seriously about the future of the settlements." The Bear nodded, surprised at his son's cool forthrightness.

"I will rescue Frida tonight. I'm sure I know where she is and how to get her away. The settlements are another matter. Edie's already had a brush with hunters and we now know what they will do when they find a settlement. Sumor's coming and they will hunt further west now that they've destroyed the game in the woods above Hindrelag. I suggest that you will have to think about moving away, possibly to the vills above Rie, but that's your call. I have to stay here to carry on the Earl's work."

The Bear looked at his son, stern faced, then clasped him on the shoulder. "I agree, it's been on my mind since we spoke about the state of the woods. How you rescue Frida is your business, but if you fail there could be sudden consequences for us all. Once I know all is well I will send Edric to look at the vills in the upper dale. As you say, you must do as the Earl bids and lure the Normans eyes away from us."

Hravn smiled grimly. "Thanks, Fader." As he turned he noticed Ealdgith standing with Ole. Ole spoke first. He was still ashen faced, but Hravn sensed that he looked older. "Hravn, I will come with you tonight."

"No, I would-"

Ole persisted and interrupted. "I am no longer bound by my word to my fader to stay in the woodland. Frida is all the family I have left. The Normans have killed them all and I will either save Frida, or die for her. It is that simple." Hravn bit his tongue, then stepped forward to embrace him. The Bear nodded his approval. Ole had come of age.

As Hravn released Ole, The Bear pulled him to one side. "How do you know where Frida will be?"

Hravn was stern faced. "We were in Richemund this morning and heard of a brothel where girls from the vills are taken. Ulf knows of the woman that keeps it." He looked his father in the eye, "I will see if Cori has been there."

Ealdgith walked beside Hravn as they returned to the ponies. "I am coming too, Hravn. The girls you find will be scared of armed men in the night. They will be scarred, too, by what has been done to them. You will need a woman with you." Hravn put his arm around Ealdgith's shoulder and hugged her to him as they walked. "You're the 'Wildcat' and my Valkyrie, why wouldn't you be there?"

*****

Dusk fell as they rode quickly through the woods, for the second time that day taking the route to the copse above the west-field and Richemund. Hravn and Ulf had agreed to leave their chainmail behind so that they could move quickly and quietly through Hindrelag's back lanes and ginnels. Each wore a steel helm and carried a sword and a seax. Ealdgith wore her padded jerkin and leather helm. Orme and Ole each managed a grin, pleased to see the Wildcat again; her green eyes glinting behind the tan eye and cheek guards.

Hravn had called a quick meeting on returning to the cave to prepare, telling them, "I want to get to the copse before last light, it will save a lot of thrashing around in the woods. We've a half-moon and broken cloud, so visibility won't be good, but it will help us with getting into Hindrelag."

"When do you want to enter the house?" Ulf had asked. "I want to get a good look at it first."

Hravn had acknowledged his concern. "Agreed. I think we need to go in three hours before first light. We need to leave Hindrelag and get back to the copse in the dark, then move through the wood at first light." He had then added, as a thought struck him, "Orme, bring two spare ponies. One for Frida and another in case we find anyone else. Bring spare cloaks too."

Hravn had explained the plan. "Once it's dark we'll follow the high ground above the west-field then take the gallows-field track down to Hindrelag. It'll be quiet by then and I can't see anyone being afoot, other than around the brothel. What do you think?" He had asked Ulf, who had simply nodded in reply, confident in Hravn's planning. Hravn had continued, "We'll lie up in the churchyard whilst Ulf has a look at the house. Ulf, my initial thoughts are that you and Orme should go in through the door to the cess pit, its sure to be unlocked, then I'll go to the front door with Sköll. Edie, follow with Ole once I'm in. Both of you, find the girls and tell them they are free to leave. Orme, find Frida. Ulf and I will deal with Ora and any men that are there. Hopefully they will have left by then. I'm sure the hounds will quieten any that are there."

Hravn's last words had not surprised them, and no one had disagreed. "Any Normans there will be killed. If they live they'll retaliate. I doubt we'll find any locals."

Ole rode next to Orme, their shared grief drew them closer. The sense of purpose, and the urgency with which Hravn drove them, calmed them as each focused on the task ahead.

Hravn moved into the copse, dismounted quickly and then tethered his pony under the trees. The others joined him, thankful that the frantic dash through the wood was over. The last of the day's light faded quickly, leaving just an intermittent low glow from a half-moon through broken clouds. Ulf flashed a grin at Hravn, his teeth reflecting the moonlight. "It's a perfect night for a raid. Just enough light, plenty of shadow and a stiff breeze to mask our noise." They left the copse to follow the ridge that dropped slowly down to the east-field, north of Hindrelag.

Ealdgith felt unusually vulnerable in the open, at night. Smoky black shadows and the scattered light of two vills were just below them, and brighter night-fires flickered in the castle's enclosure, just beyond. She forced herself to remember that they too were hidden, lost in the dark black silhouette of the high fellside. Hati rubbed against her leg. That was all the reassurance she needed.

Hravn stopped, crouched, his raised hand signalling those behind him to keep low and close in. He pointed ahead, then gestured to his right. "That's the east-field track, the cross-tracks are probably a furlong down the hill." His low voice was just audible. "The church is two hundred paces beyond the track. We'll move singly: Edie, Ole, Orme. Ulf, bring up the rear. If you see anyone drop down and wait 'til it's clear. I'll see you in the church yard." A quick reassuring grin and he was gone, lost to the shadows and the rustle of the trees.

The track dropped into a shallow gill. Ealdgith moved lightly across the stepping stones then turned and paused, waiting for Ole to catch up. She was sure that he would appreciate her company. The night's raid was a big challenge for him after the day's trauma. Ole hesitated when he saw Ealdgith's still silhouette, worried that she had sensed a threat. She waved him forward, giving him a reassuring grip on the forearm when he joined her. "We'll go together, stay close, Hravn will be waiting."

On reaching the churchyard Hravn opened the gate in the high wall, slipped inside and decided quickly that a large shadowy yew tree by the side of the squat tower would provide cover and concealment. He crouched inside the gate and as each arrived he directed them to the yew. When Ulf arrived, he pulled him to the side. "Take your time, Ulf, we've a couple of hours yet. Find the house and the best route there and back, wait until business has stopped. Once it's quiet come back and lead us in." Ulf nodded, tapped Hravn on the shoulder and was gone. Hravn realised suddenly that Ulf needed no telling. The huscarl was a natural soldier and was enjoying himself.

Ulf paused outside the churchyard gate, then strode purposefully down the wynd to Hindrelag, confident that in his helmet and cloak he would be taken for a Norman soldier. He smiled to himself when a door opened, then closed quickly, as he approached. He had no problem finding Ora's house, it was the only building from which there was any noticeable noise. Ora was a tall, amply-built woman, hence her nickname of 'The Ox'. Ulf remembered her from before the harrying, running an alehouse with her husband. Her reputation for wantonness was well known. Ulf supposed that her husband was dead and that the alehouse had become a whorehouse, meeting the most basic of the garrison's needs.

The house was on the edge of the vill, just above the fishpond. Ulf stepped back quickly as the door opened, casting sudden light across the track. A man staggered out, laughing, then wound his way up the hill to Richemund as the door slammed shut behind him. The first of the drunks was leaving.

Ulf nipped into the ginnel at the side of the house. He could smell the cesspit behind a low wattle screen at the back of the house. There was no point in checking if the back entrance was open. The door hung, half-hinged, allowing light and sound to filter past. He could tell that Ora's clients were busy: a squeal, a slap, a sudden scream choked off, the repetitive squeaking of wood against wood. Ulf returned to the front and rested against a wall post in the ginnel opposite. He pulled the linen hood low over his forehead, wrapped his cloak tighter around his shoulders and took a birch twig from his pocket to chew. He might as well clean his teeth whilst he waited.

Whilst chewing, Ulf studied the house and tried to work out how many might be inside. He could hear two, maybe three, male voices, and several female. Once he thought he heard a child's sob, but he couldn't be sure. Time dragged and, as his thoughts turned to Cyneburg, the door opened again and two men stepped out, pausing to call back as if inviting someone to follow. They hesitated then seemed to decide that whoever was inside could stay. As they turned to stagger up the hill Ulf saw Ora glance after them then slam the door shut. A bolt rasped home.

Ulf glanced along the track, the vill was quiet. He crossed back to the ginnel by the cesspit. The back door was still open, but the light was just a glimmer. He heard snoring and two low female voices. It was time. He turned and made his way back to the churchyard.

164

Hravn nodded as Ulf told him that there were several women and possibly one drunk, snoring, man in the house. "Good. We'll go as planned. Take Orme and get in the back door, but no further. I will bang on the front and demand entry in Cumbric. If they think I'm from the guard they will open it. Look for the man and seize him. Orme, find Frida. I will deal with Ora, then Edie and Ole, talk to the women there. The hounds should be enough to stop any nonsense." The two men slipped away, keeping to the datker side of the narrow street. Hravn beckoned Ealdgith and others forward, then followed silently.

"Shut the Frigg up! You'll wake everyone." The forced low tones of the woman's curse amused Hravn. Ora must be a delight, but at least she was reacting to his banging on the door. As the bolt drew back he barged through shoulder first, slamming Ora back against the wall. She was tall and buxom. Hravn knew that she would have fought him if it wasn't for the tip of his short seax pressing into her throat, just breaking the skin. Her breasts heaved, pushing against Hravn, as she fought to recover her breath whilst her eyes flicked in panic between Hravn's cold black eyes and the wolfhound growling by her waist. "Quiet." Ora nodded and Hravn released the blade's pressure on her throat. Ora gasped as Ealdgith forced her way behind Hravn, followed by Ole and Hati.

"I have her. Frida's here." Orme called with relief from behind a partition.

"Hravn, here!" Ulf's low command was urgent.

Hravn glanced at Ole. "Hold Ora here, use your seax."

Ole nodded and stepped forward to replace Hravn. He stared Ora in the eye, whilst maintaining pressure on her throat with his seax. "You should know that Frida is my sister." His meaning was obvious. Ora twitched her eyes in acknowledgement, afraid to move her head.

Hravn pushed a partition aside. Ulf had a red-haired man pinned to a straw-stuffed mattress, his sword at the man's chest. Hravn gasped. This was his sisters' rapist. "Ulf, you know who this is?"

Ulf nodded. "He has to die, now."

Hravn stared at the man with loathing, struggling with his emotions. Revenge dictated that he had to die. They had to kill him, here in the house, but dispose of the body carefully, stage an accident. Murder would be investigated and retribution inevitable. But, what about Cori?

"Edie! Is Cori here?" Hravn shouted urgently, over his shoulder.

"No," she called back, "there's a young girl whose been badly used and is too shocked to talk, and four other women. I'm sorry." He turned back to the Norman, speaking in Cumbric.

"Do you understand me?" The man lay on his back, naked, shocked into sobriety. Ulf had pulled a coarse blanket off him. He shifted, propping himself up on his elbow until Ulf's sword point forced him back down. He nodded, his eyes fixed on Hravn. "Did you touch the girl you brought here today?" The man continued to stare. "Did you?" Hravn growled, bending down, into the man's face, as Ulf put pressure on his sword point.

"No. She was for tomorrow." He gave a thin smile. Hravn read contempt in his eyes.

"A year ago, you destroyed my father's manor, Raveneswet. Remember?" A shrug. "You had your men take six girls in a cart to the woods. All were raped, some were killed." A nod. "Three were my sisters." The man shivered. Hravn saw fear replace contempt as the man tried to pull backwards. "You brought the one that lived back here, didn't you?"

"Y...Yes." He was talking now. "She was too proud. The vicious bitch starved herself to death."

Hravn spat into his face. "She was my sister! You pimped her, didn't you? Ora works for you, doesn't she?" The contemptuous stare returned as Hravn's spittle rolled slowly down the scared face.

Ulf spoke calmly, without taking his eyes from the red-haired man. "Hravn. We need to act, now."

Hravn nodded. "We have to suffocate him, leaving no marks. When I move, hold his legs down."

Hravn's move was swift. Already stooped over the man, he snatched up the discarded blanket and, straddling his chest, rammed it into his mouth. Ulf sat on the thrashing feet, stilling the body and grabbed the naked testicles, squeezing hard. The man's wide-mouthed scream was choked by the coarse cloth thrust deep into his throat. Hravn lent with all his weight, gripping the jerking head, his eyes filled with loathing and hatred, determined to burn his need for revenge into the man's last living moments.

The violent jerking slowed to a twitching, then stopped. Ulf stood up, clasped Hravn's rigid shoulders and slowly raised him. "Come, it's over. We need to dress him in his clothes."

Hravn felt no emotion as he picked up discarded breeches and undershirt, and dressed the corpse slowly, finally wrapping the cloak with the boar's head crest around him.

Ulf turned, pulled the partition aside and pointed to Ora. "You! Bring a flask of ale." The woman, ashen-faced, hesitated, terrified. "You'll live, woman, but do as I say. Now, ale!" Ulf's low, commanding, growl prompted action. Ulf took the flask and slowly poured the still, brown, liquid down the man's throat. "He needs to reek of alcohol," he said as Hravn left to check on Ealdgith and the women.

Ealdgith stood up, taking Hravn's hands in hers. "You did what you had to, my love." She turned back towards a group of part-dressed women who, cowering on the floor, were watched by the hounds lying in front of them. "Frida is unharmed. Orme is with her by the door. She was tied to a post and forced to watch. I think they were conditioning her into submission."

Ealdgith crouched down and, taking a girl's hands in hers, raised her up; she was no more than twelve. "I don't know her name, she won't speak. Frida says that dead bastard used her tonight."

Hravn crouched down and the girl flinched as he gently held her trembling shoulders. "You're safe now. We will take you with us when we leave, very soon. Talk to Edie when you want to talk. We will take you home, if you want to go. Do you understand?" The girl nodded, terror turning to trust, as she looked into Hravn's eyes. "We will take you to a kind lady called Esma. She will look after you. Now, go and join Frida and Orme by the door."

Ealdgith turned back to Hravn. "I've spoken to the women. They won't leave. They know their families won't have them back, not now. They say his is the only life they have left to them."

Hravn shrugged. "I'm not surprised." He clicked his fingers at Ora. Ulf pushed her towards him. She stood in front of him, red-faced, but submissive. "Ora. Understand me. That bastard raped and murdered my sisters. One sister, Cori, was here and you let her die. I should kill you as I killed him. Instead, I will let you live, but you will run an alehouse, not a whorehouse. These women will work with you. If I hear that this remains a whorehouse I will burn it, with you in it. Is that clear?" Ora nodded. "That man," he pointed to the body, "left, by himself, drunk." He turned to the other women, "We were never here. This didn't happen. Is that understood?" All nodded.

"Edie, take the others and go straight back to the copse, wait 'til first light then go to the cave. Ulf and I need to clear up here, then we'll follow." He kissed her quickly and turned back to Ulf. Ealdgith moved towards the door and paused.

Ole was sitting with his back to the wall, the girl cuddled into him, his cloak around them both. He roused the girl and stood up, saying, "She's called Ada and she's from Aluretune. Her family are dead too." Ealdgith smiled at the girl. She had a pretty face, dark eyes and hair, with an air of innocence that belied the night's trauma. "Come, Ada, Ole will look after you. Stay close and follow me. Orme, bring up the rear." With that, they stepped into the night.

Hravn and Ulf dragged the body to the door. As Hravn went to open it Ulf stopped him and turned to Ora, grasping her under her chin, raising the bulky woman onto the tips of her toes. He held her neck against the wall. "I serve My Lady, as I served her father. You have betrayed her people." He paused, letting the meaning sink in. Ulf could tell from Ora's eyes that she understood. "If you fail in My Lord's bidding you know what will befall you." It was a statement, not a question. She nodded as he slowly released his grip.

Hravn bent down to the body and quickly searched the inner pockets of the cloak. He pulled out a weighty coin-sack and tipped all but the last few coins on the floor. "Take these Ora and turn your life around." He stuffed the sack back into the pocket, "I don't want it look as if he's been robbed. Now, Ora, open the door and check the street."

They lifted the corpse, draped an arm over each of their shoulders and walked down the track towards the fishpond. The door was bolted shut behind them. Ulf, who carryied the half empty flask of ale in his spare hand, said, "Take him to the top of the bank, it's steep there, we'll slide him straight in." The body was heavy and they were panting by the time they reached the top. Hravn glanced up to the stake-wall at the top of the bluff. The glow from the guard's fire silhouetted the outline of the edge. He sensed eyes staring down at them. Ulf glanced across at him, "Don't worry, those flames will destroy their night sight, they'll see nothing down here and, with this wind, hear even less." Ulf dropped his shoulder. Air groaned from the corpse's mouth as it fell to the ground. They rolled it onto its back and, seizing the feet, pushed it firmly down the grassy slope. A splash told them that the head, at least, was under water. Ulf dropped the flask at the top of the bank.

"A suitable marker for such a worthless sod." Hravn quipped, turning away after a last look at the part-submerged body of the man who had destroyed half his family.

"A waste of good ale, more like", scoffed Ulf.

*****

They slept long into the day and the sun was almost at its zenith when Ealdgith woke. She glanced around the cave and realised that, with Frida's arrival, their sleeping arrangements would need to change. The girl's arms were wrapped around Orme as he snored. Ealdgith knew that they would not be parted. Frida woke as Ealdgith blew on the ashes in the hearth. "Relax Frida, I'll warm some pottage for us all."

Frida smiled, shaking her head, "No. I'll do that. You are all the family I have now. It is I who should look after you...and thank you, Lady Edie." Ealdgith smiled and left Frida to it. She sensed it might be quite some time before Frida lost her instinctive formality.

Ealdgith wiped the last of the potage from her bowl with a lump of stale bread. "Hravn, I need to take Ada to see Bron. I think she will need an infusion of wild carrot or rue and I want to get it right. Do you want to come with us?"

Hravn looked up, puzzled at first as to why Ada needed to see Bron, then nodded, understanding the need for emergency contraception. "Of course, I'll stop off at my fader's on the way, then catch you up. He needs to know that we are back. We'll take Ada to Esma tomorrow."

Ole looked up and glanced at Ada, who was listening to the conversation, wide-eyed. "I'll come too, if I may, Edie?"

Ada shared Ole's pony, seated in front of him as they rode bare-back. She listened as he told her what Hravn and Ealdgith did, who Ealdgith really was and why it would be best for Ada to stay with Esma. He wanted her to stay, of course, but it wouldn't be safe and he would come and see her often. Hravn and Ealdgith looked at one another, smiled and rode ahead, feeling ever more like parents and very much older than they were.

Chapter 13

White blossom was bursting forth on hawthorns near the lower field outside Hyrst and hoverflies hung in the still, late spring, air. Ealdgith had spoken to Frida about contraception and needed to replenish her stock of herbs. She was sitting with her ealdmoder, under the narrow, thatched, porch, when an elderly man on a pony galloped into the vill. "Alfhildr? Where can I find Alfhildr?" He called, spotting the two women.

Ealdgith called back. "I know you. You're Ealhstan's uncle, aren't you?" Her heart jumped, "Is it Cyneburg?"

The man replied, "Yes, Lady. The birthing is upon her. Elfreda sent for Alfhildr."

Bron stood up. "Come, I'll take you to her,"

Ealdgith walked across to the old man, "Return and take Alfhildr with you. Tell Cyneburg that I will come too, with Ulf."

Ealdgith stuffed the herbs into her bag, kissed her ealdmoder gently, mounted her pony and galloped down the track after Hati, leaving a small trail of dust. At the ford she tethered her pony and then cursed the fellside as she clambered up through the trees to the cave. Hravn was away with The Bear, but Ulf was there, with Orme and Frida. Ole had found another excuse to visit Ada.

"Ulf!" She called as she neared the top of the slope. "It's Cyneburg. She is in labour. Elfreda has called for

Alfhildr." She paused, panting, as Ulf ran to her. "Come, get your horse. My pony is by the ford. I'll ride her."

Ulf held up his hand and gestured for her to slow down. "I need my helmet, I'll fetch yours too Edie. Remember the last trip? We'll follow the high ground above Marige this time."

Ealdgith's fell pony, bred for life on the harsh upland moors, coped surefootedly with the ground, whilst Ulf's horse moved cautiously across the tussocky grass. It was poor ground for horses and, consequently, a better route to avoid a hunting party.

Ealdgith glanced up at Ulf. He rode stern-faced, almost in a trance. "What's up, Ulf? Where's your normal good humour?" She teased.

"Sorry Edie. The truth be known, I fear what's ahead. I'll happily fight a man, but child birth! It's so brutal!"

Ealdgith laughed instinctively. "Oh Ulf. It's so natural." She paused, remembering Gunnar's heartbroken confession when they stayed at Morlund. His wife, Aelfgifu, had died in childbirth. "But I know what you mean. It's only my second experience and, if I'm honest, I'm a little nervous as well. But it is the most natural thing in the world, otherwise we wouldn't be here, would we. I spent a day with Alfhildr, she knows just what she is doing. Anyway, you won't be allowed in the room. You've got the easy bit."

Ulf chuckled. "I know Edie, I know. But it's the not-knowing that is hard to cope with."

When they arrived at Grinton, Elfreda ushered Ealdgith into the house. "I've partitioned a space at the back. Alfhildr is here and has placed charms about her. I have undone all the knots in the house and untied her hair. There is nothing to block the birth process." Ealdgith sensed that panic seized Elfreda. "That's good. Now, I have silver keys for Cyneburg to hold. We'll go to her, shall we."

Ulf found his way barred by Ealhstan. Cyneburg's father scowled at him. "You can sit on yon bank, if you want." He nodded towards the fellside above the house. "There's nowt you can do in there." Ulf knew that he was unwelcome. He stared back at Ealhstan. The man spoke at last. "I remember well what you said when you were last here. I've made my decision. If it is a boy, it will live. A girl is nowt but a waste. She'll be exposed and Cyneburg will just have to get over it."

Ulf continued to stare at Ealhstan. "We'll see," was all that he said as he moved to sit on the bank, staring at the door.

Her day with Alfhildr, attending a woman in Hyrst, had fascinated Ealdgith. As a thegn's daughter she had no reason to be involved in births within the manor and she had been a child when her twin sisters were born. Alfhildr was a bundle of energy. Tall, lythe and unmarried she controlled the birthing room with an efficiency and empathy that astounded Ealdgith. When Ealdgith had asked her about the charms and prayers that she used she had smiled secretively, saying, "people worry about what they can't control and look for reassurance in things they can. The women hereabouts believe in anything that might help, the charms to Freyja and the old gods, and prayers to Our Lady and Saint Dorothy. I leave them to their prayers and worry about what really matters: keeping the mother calm, her breathing controlled, cleanliness, boiled water, and feverfew and fennel to ease pain and cramp, flax oil for cleansing – those are my secrets, mind you safeguard them."

As Ealdgith stepped behind the crude partition of animal skins hanging from a rafter she was struck by the transformation. The floor had been swept and strewn with a deep layer of green bracken, she knew from Alfhildr's teaching that this kept evil spirits away whilst ensuring that the floor was clean and fresh. Tallow lights burned around the small area within which Alfhildr had to work. The green ferns clashed with Cyneburg's pale naked body. She looked almost animal-like, kneeling on all fours, groaning softly to herself as Alfhildr knelt in front of her, staring into her eyes, willing her to breath slowly and deeply. Alfhildr glanced up, "Good, Edie, Cyneburg is very close now. Can you take over here? Elfreda, do you have water ready? Take my little seax – hold the blade above a flame, the blade must be pure when I cut the cord. Thank you." Ealdgith knelt down, taking Cyneburg's hands in hers as Alfhildr eased her down onto her elbows. She smiled into her eyes but Cyneburg hardly saw her, her mind was far away, locked in upon herself.

The scream that Cyneburg uttered as she pushed her child into the world was so loud that Ulf was halfway across the farm yard before he could control himself. He stood at the door, waiting, listening. He heard muttered words, then a short, sharp argument. Was that Edie's voice? Moments later there was a smack and a cry, a baby's cry.

Ulf stepped through the doorway, he could hear more clearly now. "Moder! No! No!" Cyneburg's cry, which ended in a sob, was enough to draw him into the room, but not behind the partition.

He heard Elfreda say, "I must. You know your fader's decision. A boy we would keep, but a girl, well, we can't afford to feed an unproductive mouth. She must be exposed on the fell." He sensed that Alfhildr said nothing. Her job was done and she had no right to interfere. Elfreda anticipated Ealdgith's protest. "Say nothing, My Lady. You cannot keep a child, so have no right to demand that we do."

"No! But I can." Ulf stepped forward into the birthing room. Cyneburg gasped, embarrassed by her nakedness, relieved to see Ulf. The three women, Ealdgith included, turned to protest against his presence. He held his arm out to prevent Elfreda carrying the baby from the room. "Lady Ealdgith may not be able to care for a child, but I will care for Cyneburg and she will care for her daughter." He paused, looking directly at Cyneburg as she sat on the bed of ferns, marvelling inwardly at her beauty, seeing past her bedraggled hair, sweaty flesh and haggard face. "If that is what you want, Cyneburg? To be my wife?" She nodded, slowly, as tears trickled down her cheeks.

Elfreda gasped and stamped her foot. "No! She is needed here. Anyway, a child can't live in a cave."

Ulf wasn't fazed by her temper, and spoke calmly, quietly, but with considerable authority. "I will take her to the community in Wasfelte. I am sure The Bear will take her in. Cyneburg will be my wife and live there whilst I serve Lady Ealdgith and Hravn. I will not be gainsaid." Silence hung in the room. Ulf's offer was not only unexpected, it was unheard of; to take for your own, the child of a woman raped by your enemy. Ealdgith broke the silence. "Thank you, Ulf. You are truly remarkable. I know Hravn and The Bear will agree. You will not be gainsaid."

Ulf took the baby from Elfreda and knelt down by Cyneburg. "Here, hold your daughter. In a few days, when you are ready, I will return." As he placed the baby's head by her naked breast she stared up. "No, Ulf, we will leave today, once Alfhildr and Edie are finished with me." Her hand touched his. "Thank you."

Ulf sat on the bank whilst Cyneburg was cleaned and dressed. Hati lay by him, dozing, one eye half open watching for his mistress. Since Elfreda had stormed out of the house, he had seen no sign of her or her husband. He still couldn't quite believe what he had done. He was not an impulsive man, but Cyneburg held a sort of spell over him. It didn't worry him that her child wasn't his. A daughter was a daughter, and would always be loved. He relaxed and waited. It was a second chance for him, and he knew he would make it work.

Whilst they prepared Cyneburg to travel, Ealdgith bade Alfhildr return to Hyrst and ask Bron if she would take Cyneburg in for a few days. She knew her ealdmoder would care for her, and that the older lady's attention and wisdom would help ease her into motherhood and separation from her parents. Not that Ealdgith thought Cyneburg would miss her parents. She had not detected any fondness during her visits.

Ulf jumped up when Ealdgith held the door open for Cyneburg. He had the horse and pony ready for them. Cyneburg walked slowly, rather stiffly, carrying her baby in a woollen shawl. As Ulf bent to help her onto Ealdgith's pony she shook her head, "No, Ulf. That would be too much for me just now. I'll walk."

Ulf smiled. "No, Edie can ride the pony, carry your baby and lead the horse. I'll tie its reins to her saddle. Here, Edie, take the baby once you've mounted." He passed the baby to Ealdgith, then turned and swept Cyneburg up in his arms. "I'll carry you and, when I tire, we'll rest a while."

There was no sign of Cyneburg's parents as they left the farm and walked over the bridge. Cyneburg laid her head upon Ulf's shoulder and cried tears of relief and joy.

*****

Hravn's jaw dropped, mouth open, and stared at Ulf when Ulf told that he'd taken Cyneburg to be his wife. The big huscarl feared suddenly that Hravn was going to object, when he found himself embraced and punched in the chest. "Ulf, you old dog. That's most honourable. Well done! Speak to The Bear tomorrow and tell him you have my blessing."

"There's no need," Orme interrupted, "he's heading this way, with Edric – look!"

"That's odd, I've not long left him. He's not rushing though, that's for sure." Hravn was surprised to see his father trotting steadily down the track on his pony. "We'll go down and see them. You can give them your good news too, Ulf." They met at the ford.

"I thought it best to carry on our earlier conversation now that Edric is back." The Bear slipped off his pony and sat on a low boulder whilst the others gathered around. "You were right about the upper dale, Hravn. Edric found Rie to be partly occupied and half-torched. They certainly suffered last year. Hale though, has yet to see a Norman and the people were most welcoming, as they were in Fytun."

"That's good. It gives you an option." Hravn welcomed the news.

"Yes, Edric and I have decided. We will call a meeting of the settlements tomorrow. I will propose that we move there after haerfest, before the weather changes, and take all our winter grain with us."

"Do you suppose everyone will go, Fader? Some of those with Leofric may want to return to Marige or Mersche."

The Bear nodded, "I agree, that will be their decision. They may go sooner. If they do that might leave you more exposed here, though you could call on them there for supplies, rather than in Helwith. At least the other settlements will be further away from where the Normans may hunt."

"Fader, we will soon do as the Earl bids and raid further south. That will leave you as the only man here who is skilled with the sword. Edric has shown interest, and one or two others too, Aelf's sons as well. Edie and I are leaving the day after tomorrow to see the lie of the land and find those places best suited for an ambush. We'll be gone a week or more and I'd like Ulf to train Edric and the others. Are you happy for that?"

The Bear hesitated. "Not happy, but accepting. Edric has already asked me and I have heard of others. Your success has inspired them, and I know the Earl wants you to expand your cell. The more the young men join you, the harder it will be for those who are left, and so perhaps it is best we move to other vills up the dale. Yes, have Ulf gather them to him and train them."

"Thank you, Fader. I will not call on them until needed. You will have them to work for you and protect the settlements until then. When we return we should have more horses and weapons. There's still room for weapons and armour in the cave, but we can't take any more horses. Will you be able to build a new enclosure at Wasfelte? Mayhap you could use them for ploughing too?" The Bear nodded, accepting that his son was beginning to take charge. Hravn continued, "And now, Ulf has some news for you too and a favour to ask."

Chapter 14

"That's the perfect spot. The curved bend in the valley is just the place for an ambush." Hravn stood with Ealdgith and Ulf on a low hill overlooking a shallow, but steep-sided, valley that channelled the Massan to Ripum track through a dense strip of wild woodland that had never been cleared for farming. "The wood is just over a couple of furlongs long, I walked it, but the middle bit can't be seen from outside. If we control the entry points, and ambush in the middle, we could strike, clear the track and be away back up here in moments. The land behind us is in dead ground from anyone on the track. We'd have two furlongs in the open, after that it's just woodland again."

Ulf patted Hravn on his back. "I like it. Sweet and simple. We'll strip the bodies in this wood. Bury them in the ground beneath brush wood, bring the ponies forward from where we've tethered them within the wood line behind us, them take all the arms and mail away with us."

"We thought you'd like it, Ulf. There are a couple of other sites to show you too, though this is my favourite." Ealdgith grinned at Ulf. She had thrived on the freedom of the last two weeks. Living rough with Hravn and the hounds, hunting hare and deer, then lying with him under the stars at night. It had rekindled the excitement and challenges of their time a year ago, raiding for the Pendragons. But it was the new-found freedom to lie together that they had enjoyed most.

Ealdgith added, "Groups of men-at-arms ride the route three or four time a day. Usually three or four at a time, never more, and always a couple of hours apart. We think that if we can cover all our tracks, and make sure the bodies aren't found, then we could attack several times on stretches of this track, until they respond with larger groups."

Ulf nodded, "I can see why you've chosen to keep to the west of the Jor. We have the woodland behind us. If we were the other side we could be caught between the Jor and the Swale, and if we were east of the Swale we would be in open farmland on the plain."

Hravn glanced at the sun. "We'd best show you the other sites and then be getting back, Frida will be fretting."

Ulf laughed heartily and Ealdgith giggled, "I don't think so. She and Orme will be so tied up with each other that I doubt they know what day it is. Ole might be fretting though."

Ole wasn't fretting. He was sitting on watch, at the edge of the little camp in the woodland that he and Orme had constructed that morning, after their overnight ride. He ran to them. "Come on, Hravn, let me show you. See? We cut larch poles elsewhere in the wood, so there is no sign of cut wood."

Hravn was pleased. "A-frames with a ridge pole and overlapping waterproof cloaks to make a cover. Well done Ole, they're just what we need."

Ole beamed. "We made three, one for you and Edie, one for Orme and my sister and another for Ulf and me."

Ulf laughed, cuffing Ole playfully on the ear. "Mmm...I wonder who decided that? You'll have my snoring and grunting to cope with."

Ole skipped out of Ulf's reach. "I've a big prod-stick to sort that out!"

Frida looked up from the hearth and the pot she tended. "Well done Frida, I'm glad you're using old wood, we can't afford to make too much smoke." Hravn was very conscious of their security.

Ulf had other thoughts. "That smells good lass, I don't know how we lived before you came to us." She smiled, he yelped and turned around. "Edie! What the..."

"I'll kick your other ankle too, Ulf. What's wrong with my cooking?" Ealdgith poked a tongue at him.

Frida's smile widened and her face shone, she was content in the love and friendship around her.

Walking a short distance away from the camp, Hravn turned to see how well camouflaged it was. He caught sight of Orme returning with a large armful of newly cut branches. "It looks good Orme. Those mottled-green cloaks really blend in. Once you've broken up the outline of their edges with those branches it will never be seen."

Frida banged the side of the pot with a ladle to signal that the meal was ready. Whilst they ate Hravn told them his plan for the next day. "Get to sleep after this, I want us up for first light and away just after. Now, we'll need to take turns at standing watch."

*****

184

Hravn heard the clear sound of a curlew calling and nodded to Ulf. The curlew called four times. Ealdgith and Orme were posted as lookouts at either end of the wood. Ealdgith's call was the curlew, Orme's an owl. The number of calls signified the number of riders, whilst a fox bark was the alarm call.

Ulf stood, hidden behind a broad oak, and took a firm grasp of the trip-rope that ran across the track, buried under loose earth and pebbles. He heard riders approaching at a brisk canter and watched Hravn, waiting for the nod that would initiate the ambush.

Hravn lay close to the track, the hounds, to his right, were crouched ready to attack. He tracked the last rider with the cross bow. The four men-at-arms were bunched together and closing quickly. Fifty paces...forty...thirty... When the lead horse was ten paces from the rope Hravn nodded briskly then squeezed the trigger. Ulf flung himself backwards and, in the same movement, wound the rope around the tree trunk. The rope leapt into the air, pulled taught at knee height, tripping the lead horse which fell forward trapping its rider. Hravn's crossbow bolt punched through the last rider's hauberk, ripping through the mail and into his stomach. His horse reared as he fell backwards to the ground.

Sköll and Hati pounced. Sköll pinned the second rider by the throat as he hit the ground, falling backwards off his rearing horse. The third rider's mount panicked, and kicked wildly at Hati as the hound chased its legs in a flailing circle. The rider fell and jerked as Hravn sent another crossbow bolt into his chest.

"Off boys, Off!" Hravn leapt forward and, seizing both hounds by the collar, pulled them to the side of the track. He could tell that the men-at-arms posed no further threat. Hwhistled sharply for Ealdgith and Orme to run in, then kicked the man that Sköll had guarded. He was dead, his neck broken in the fall.

In the meantime, Ulf had already slit the throats of those whom Hravn had shot and was busy cutting the bolts out of the bodies. A sobbing moan drew Hravn's attention. The man pinned under the horse writhed, his pelvis crushed by the weight of the horse. Orme reached him first. He stood, hesitating; he'd never killed a man before. He thought of the destruction of Hindrelag, Agnaar, Thor, the rapes of Cyneburg and Ada, the abduction of Frida. In one swift movement, he drew his sword and stabbed the man through the heart. His compassion was for the horse that lay still, panting, staring up at him. "Hravn. The horse has both front legs broken." Ulf ran over. "Get me a cross bow." He took one of the blooded bolts, loaded the crossbow and carefully shot through the horse's pleading brown eye. It died, instantly.

There was no need for an order from Hravn, each knew what had to be done. Orme herded the three horses together and tethered them a short way down the track. Ealdgith called the hounds and then started to strip the bodies of their mail hauberks, weapons, boots and any serviceable clothing. Hravn and Ulf struggled to roll the dead horse off the fourth body, then called to Orme to lead the calmest of the horses across. Ulf used the trip-rope to lash the dead horse's hind legs together and then used it to make a rough harness for the horse to pull the carcass into the trees. Ten paces were all they could achieve, but it was enough. Ulf piled foliage over it and hid the marks where it had been dragged. "It'll be found within the week, the smell will attract attention," he called across to Hravn who had just led the pack ponies from the top of the hill.

186

"I know. I hadn't wanted a horse to die, but I suppose it's inevitable. We'll raid for the next three days and then be gone. The green men of Ripum's woods will no doubt be blamed." Ulf grinned back.

Having secured the Normans' arms and equipment on the pack ponies they hoisted the bodies onto the three horses. Once they were ready to move Hravn and Ulf walked slowly down the track, checking meticulously that they had removed all trace of the ambush. Blood was their biggest problem and they took time to scrape up stained earth and throw it well away before scattering fresh earth in its place. As Ealdgith and Orme led the animals up into the trees they followed behind, straitening crushed foliage and generally concealing their escape.

"That went better than I expected." Hravn was making a mental list of their hoard. "Four more crossbows and at least eighty bolts, plus swords and mail. We'll be able to equip Edric and the lads when we get back."

Ulf paused, thinking, and turned to Hravn. "I think we could use those crossbows tomorrow, instead of the rope. If we pre-load them we would have six bolts between the two of us. There'd be less risk to the horses that way."

"Agreed. Did you see the soldiers' markings? They were the same as those we ambushed with the hay waggon. All of them are Count Alan's men."

*****

The next two ambushes went just as well. The first was a merchant with a string of six pack ponies and two armed escorts. Hravn and Ulf shot the three bodies from their saddles with ease, the last hitting the earth only a couple of heart beats after the first. "Edie! Look at this!" Hravn called Ealdgith over as he opened the first of the ponies' panniers. "Silks, dresses and clothes for Count Alan's court. Someone will be mightily upset."

"There's more. Look!" Ealdgith exclaimed, as she opened the merchant's saddle bags. "Gold and silver coin, jewels too. No wonder he had an escort."

Ulf walked across, having quickly searched the merchant's body. "You may want these, Hravn, I've relieved him of his rings too," he said, passing him a parchment scroll and tossing a couple of heavy leather pouches in his hand.

Hravn handed the scroll to Ealdgith. She unrolled it and screwed her eyes up as she tried to read the heavy black script. "I can't understand it," she said at last. "I think it must be Latin."

Hravn laughed. "Then I know a man who can. We must find Father Oda. A man of the church and our Lord's agent; he will surely read Latin." He gestured for Orme to join them. "We've done well. There is enough here to pay our way for years to come, and to help The Bear. Let's get them buried well away from the track. A merchant with riches like these will be missed and searched for."

The second ambush was more challenging. They had pulled a recently fallen tree partway across the track to channel and slow any riders. Four had come at a gallop, their mixed forms of dress showing them to be the mercenaries that Hravn had anticipated confronting at some point, and they didn't behave as expected.

As the lead horseman slowed to avoid the tree the second urged his horse forward to jump over it. Hravn's bolt took the leader, but Ulf had to flick his point of aim quickly onto the third. Both men fell. The fourth wheeled his mount quickly and then spurred forward in a leap. Hravn just had time to raise his second crossbow and loose the bolt, catching the man in the midriff in mid jump. As his horse lent forward to land, the body tumbled in a summersault from the saddle. The surviving rider initially turned to gallop back to help his dying colleagues, then turned again to flee. Hravn sent the hounds after him whilst Ulf took aim with his second crossbow. The horse shied from the hounds and reared. The rider stood erect in the saddle as Ulf's bolt smashed into the small of his back.

Hravn smiled to himself as he added two more cross bows, two lances, a mace and four swords to his mental inventory. "Ulf, do you know how to use a mace? I think Edric has the build and strength to fight with one, what do you think?"

Ulf shook his head dismissively. "I think he'd do better with a crossbow, we all will. You and I could face a trained man-at-arms, but the others never will, not yet awhile anyway. It's much better to fight as we are now."

The fourth ambush was to be their last before they returned to the cave, via Jordale, and over the pass across the high moor to Grinton. Hravn had decided to return to the first day's ambush site. It was the one that provided the best concealment. In a re-run of the first day, Ealdgith signalled the arrival of four horsemen. Hravn and Ulf were lining their crossbow sights onto the first two riders when a fox barked urgently; its shrill harsh call resounding through the trees. A sudden chill ran down Hravn's neck and back. He lowered his cross bow and glanced at Ulf; he'd done the same. Both men flattened themselves to the ground and peered forward from under the cover of their green hoods. Hravn talked to the hounds, urgently, "Down! Down! Leave! Stay!"

The lead rider slowed, then stopped, looking around. Hravn held his breath. Had he seen something left over from their first ambush? Had the fox's call unsettled him? Four more horsemen galloped around the corner. The hesitant leader waved to them then spurred forward, resuming his gallop long the track. Hravn let out a long slow breath as the second group galloped by. "Thor's teeth, Ulf! I thought they'd suspected something." Ulf rolled onto his back, breathing deeply.

"Me too, but I think he just saw a good place for an ambush and wanted to keep in sight of his rear guard. Thank the gods for Edie's fox call."

Hravn nodded. "You know what this means?"

Ulf grinned at Hravn. "Aye, I do. The bastards are rattled and suspect ambushes. It's time we went home and left them to chase shadows."

The glare of the still-rising sun moved from behind the foliage above them. "Phew! It's hot!" Hravn swatted at a couple of flies that persisted in landing on his forehead. "Have you noticed that it hasn't rained for weeks?" He asked Ulf.

The huscarl nodded, "Aye, I reckon we could be in for a hot sumor. The ground's drying quickly too." Ulf gestured with his head to the dense wood to their left, where the heat of the sun had triggered a swarm of flies to rise in a sonorous buzz.

"That's nothing to do with the weather though, have you noticed the smell?" Hravn grimaced, wrinkling his nose. "The dead horse. I fear it will be noticed within the next few days, the smell will hang in the valley. You're right. It is time to leave."

Sumor

Chapter 15

"Come, meet the men." Ulf led Hravn across the meadow to meet the six men that Orme and he had trained a month earlier. Hravn stepped forward and shook hands with Edric, then Aelf's twin sons, Bada and Beowulf. Both were Orme's age and Hravn knew them from childhood. He gripped the first on his forearm. "It's good to see you again Bada...or is it Beowulf?" Hravn teased, it was a childhood joke. The stocky, blond, young men were identical, though a persistent tick in Bada's left eye always helped to tell them apart. The twins grinned. Beowulf spoke for them. "You too, Hravn, we wanted to join you in aefter-yule, but fader wasn't in favour. He's changed his tune now though."

Ulf continued on down the line. "I know these three rogues from Helwith. I thought I'd managed to escape them, but they seem to follow..."

"Yes, I know, like a bad smell." A swarthy, dark haired man interrupted and offered his hand to Hravn. "I'm Cola, named for my features, I guess."

Hravn laughed, then moved on to the next man, whom Ulf introduced as Dudda. Hravn gave him a welcoming smile, "And you must have been named despite your features." The tall, lithe man, was every bit the opposite of the tubby person that his name implied.

"I heard you speak last aefter-yule, Lord, but we weren't sure if you could live up to your promises. I was wrong, the grain and sheep you sent... well, a man who can deliver a promise is a man who I will follow."

Hravn looked sternly into his eyes. The two men were of a height, though Hravn was broader. "Some of my future promises may be less attractive...but I will deliver them. Welcome."

Ulf nodded, then passed on to the last in the line. The large huscarl towered over him. "Oz. He may be small, but he is the punchiest of the lot and sharp with it."

Hravn was impressed by the firm handshake and intensity with which the small man's deep brown eyes held his own. He had a long scar across his fair-skinned cheek. "Where were you from?"

"Mersche, Lord." Hravn nodded, picturing the deserted vill barely a league away and was impressed that the man would rather fight for him than return to it.

Hravn stepped back and turned to face the group. As he did so Orme and Ealdgith led a string of laden ponies towards them, followed by Ole and Frida.

"You now know me and you already know Ulf and Orme. Some of you do not know Edie." He turned to Ealdgith who removed her helmet, shaking her long fair hair free, looking every bit the Valkyrie with boots, breaches, padded leather jerkin and seax at her slender hips. Hravn sensed a frisson of uncertainty amongst those he had just met for the first time. "Lady Ealdgith is the daughter of our Lord Thor, who once held these lands. We lead together, her word is my word, and she will outfight anyone here, even Ulf."

Ulf broke any tension, laughing. "Aye Hravn, I still bear the bruises to prove it."

Ealdgith smiled thinly and scrutinised the new faces. She knew should would have to work hard to gain their trust, but was confident that she would. She had talked to Hravn about the implications of recruiting more to their cause and agreed that their relationship with the new men could not be as close as theirs with Ulf and Orme, both of whom had already been sworn to her father. If they were to lead effectively, they would need to maintain an emotional distance.

Hravn continued, and explained how they would work. Edric would be responsible for the new team whilst they served The Bear, but if they deployed outside the woodland, Ulf would be responsible for those from Helwith and Orme for Edric and the twins. "Now, let us issue you with your arms and mail. Our lord, the Earl Gospatrick, would call you his green men and has provided water proof cloaks and light cowls for us all, just like the ones Orme is posing in. There is a sword, helmet, and mail hauberk for each of you." He held one up, grinning. "The hauberks may need some repairs, we can tend to that. Let those holes be a reminder of the threats you will all face and the risks that we took to provide them for you."

Later, as they sat around the hearth outside the cave, roasting a roe deer that he and Ealdgith had caught the day before, Hravn took Edric and Ulf to one side. "Edric, I want you to look for another cave." Ulf nodded approvingly and picked his teeth with a birch twig. Hravn continued, "I want us to be one step ahead. If ever I sense that this cave is compromised, and many now know where it is, we may have to move very quickly."

*****

"What material is this? It is so fine and smooth."

"I don't know. See how the colours change in the light." Ealdgith and Frida were unpacking the merchant's paniers, having agreed with Hravn that they would decide what to do with the rolls of material, cotton, threads and needles that they had brought back from the raid.

"I might be good with a bow, but I am terrible with a needle. I could never apply myself, despite my moder's strictures," Ealdgith confessed, a little sheepishly.

Frida stared at her, briefly, in surprise. "Really? I love needlework. Moder taught me from an early age, I helped her make all our clothes." Frida picked up the silk again and held it to her cheek. "Now, this. I could make something with this."

Ealdgith smiled at her as a plan formed in her mind. "Why not? It would be foolish to waste your talent and...all this." She gestured to the bright colours that had tumbled from the paniers. "Why don't you choose all you want and make clothes for the three of you? I've a feeling Cyneburg might want a share and to prove to Ulf that she is a capable wife, why don't we talk to her?"

Frida's eyes gleamed with delight. "But what about you and Hravn? I could-"

Ealdgith interrupted her friend. "That's a lot to ask of you Frida. Thank you, but I might ask Bron. She could choose some for herself too. After that we should give some to Esma, now that she has Ada to clothe and feed, then Freya can share the rest with the women in her camp. Anyway, if I read my uncle's mind right, Wyrd will soon have Hravn and me knocking at Count Alan's door and we will both need more presentable clothes.

These could be just the answer. Making them would be too much to ask."

Frida looked stunned. "My Lady, surely not, you can't go..."

She faltered as Ealdgith pulled a wry smile and slowly nodded her head. "He's already asked us. Remember that old saying: 'Keep your friends close and your enemies closer still'? We need to find out what is in the Count's mind."

"Look Edie, here, with the needles." Frida shrieked with the delight of a young child. "These shears are beautiful, there are three, with handles of gold, silver and pearl. Oh! Where do I start?"

Ealdgith laughed, caught up with Frida's excitement. "Start with the green. After all, we are the green men and women of the woodland."

The next morning Hravn left early, with Orme, to ride to Esebi and make contact with Father Oda. He had chosen to take Orme to give him more experience and self-confidence. If Orme was to lead one of his two new teams he would need to be more assertive and able to think on his feet when alone and away from the woodland. Ealdgith took the opportunity to take the material to Bron and the women in the settlements. She knew that neither Ulf nor Ole would stay behind; the foursome chatted happily as they led the pack ponies down the track.

Bron had been as delighted as Ealdgith knew she would be; not only with the silks and linens, but also with the opportunity to meet Ole and Frida. Bron had taken Ealdgith's hands in hers when Ealdgith explained why she would like Bron to make a set of clothes for Hravn and her. The old lady had said: "Of course my dear, it will be a great risk that you will face, but if it is something you must do then it is for the good of us all." She had then turned to Frida and insisted that she join her in making all the clothes, adding that not only would she enjoy her company, but that it would be much easier to use the table under her porch than sit on the grass by a dark cave. Frida had been delighted and they could have stayed much longer, but only at the cost of shortening their other visits.

Ulf cantered ahead as they approached Wasfelte. Frida and Ealdgith exchanged knowing smiles as they watched the dust from his pony's hooves disappear into the distance. Ulf had last seen Cyneburg the day before their raid in the south, he longed to hold her close and to cuddle the baby girl to whom he felt increasingly bound. Cyneburg's last words still echoed in his head: "I'd like us to call her Adelind, as a sign of renewal, in hope that good times might return for us both."

The hut that Ulf had built for Cyneburg was in a little clearing to one side of the track, just before the larger cluster of huts that filled the clearing at Wasfelte. He had sensed that she had been happy to be a little separate from the crowded settlement. She had a desperate need for a little privacy after the trauma of her last year.

He paused, then stopped, as he heard singing. A soft melody, as gentle as the birdsong that floated around it, drifted through the trees. He stood spellbound, tears forming in the corners of his eyes. It was Cyneburg. He caught the soft sound of her words on the gentle breeze:

> *"He took her by her milk-white hand,*
> *And her by his grass-green sleeve;*

He mounted her high behind himself,
From her kinsmen he took his leave..."

He had never heard the song before; it sounded like
their song. Ulf dismounted and led his pony quietly to
where Cyneburg sat with her back to him, cradling her
daughter as she sang. She turned at the last moment.
He raised her up and kissed her fully, holding his new
family gently in his arms.

They sat as they waited for the others to join them. Ulf
cradled Adelind in the broad crook of his muscular arm
and gazed at Cyneburg as she continued to sing; until
Ole's noisy arrival shattered their peace. Cyneburg was
delighted to see Ealdgith, and delighted, too, to be
offered her choice of the array of silk, linen and wool.

Locherlega was their penultimate call. Ulf stayed with
Cyneburg whilst Ole galloped ahead. He was already
playing with Ada, teasing and chasing her, when Frida
and Ealdgith rode into the glade by the woodcutter's
hut. They slipped inside to surprise Esma and give her a
choice of fabric.

Esma shook her head as they sat outside the hut under
the shade of the turf-roofed porch. "Look at her. You'd
think narry a thing had happened to the wee lass. She
won't go near the men, not even Aelf, though she's
happy enough with me and the other women. I'm not
surprised though, her moder died when the next one
was born and her fader never took another wife. He
brought her up until he was slain."

Ealdgith looked up sharply, she hadn't heard the full
story of Ada's past. "What happened?"

"It was only days before you found her. He failed to pay
his rent. The red haired one that Hravn slew, had him

swing for it. The lass watched, then was taken. You know the rest."

The women watched Ada and Ole, the joy and innocence in their eyes belied the horrors both had seen. Esma sighed. "She won't talk of it though, nor of how she was...hurt. The only time she laughs like this is with young Ole."

*****

"What's up my dear? I can tell from the look of you that Esebi wasn't as expected." Hravn held out his hand to take Ealdgith's, as she walked back to the cave.

"The bastards never let up. We found Father Oda alright. You'd never suspect him of being the Earl's man, so pious, small, fussy, humble even."

"Yes, but he knows everyone's business." Orme chipped in. "People talk and he'll listen; and I'm sure they will listen to what he tells them."

"Did you talk about my uncle? Did he say much?" Ealdgith was impatient to find out what others knew.

Hravn gave a secretive smile. "Very little, and the least said the better. I think that shows that he can be trusted. My concern, and his, is the reeve for the manor. He's a rapacious bastard by all accounts. Takes more rent than his due, bullying and now...," he shook his head, "...intimidation and rape."

Ealdgith frowned and, as she glanced at Ulf, sensed that he had guessed what Hravn was going to say. "When last month's tax was due the miller wouldn't, I think probably couldn't, pay what was demanded. The reeve sent his men in to drag out the miller's wife." He stuttered, almost choking on his words. "They raped her, there, in the village. Two held the miller and the reeve took her first, his men then took their turn. Father Oda protested, but was thrown to the ground and trampled as they left on their way to Corburne."

Ulf slammed his fist backwards against the rock wall behind him. "You know what this means." It was a statement rather than a question.

Hravn answered, "Yes, we have to kill him before the people of Esebi do, because that will bring all hel down upon them, and others."

Ealdgith was all too aware of the implications. "We have to get to him, it has to look like an accident as it is right on our doorstep, which is not what my uncle wants. How?"

"Yes, Edie, I know! And the reeve is due again next week, the day after the Sabbath," Hravn said tersely as anger and frustration surfaced.

Orme surprised them. "Remember, Father Oda said that the reeve went to Corburne after Esebi." Hravn looked at him, quizzically. "To get to Corburne you cross the ford down-river from Esebi, and then follow a narrow track through the woods and up a very steep hillside. It's a single track with a long drop down through the trees to the river."

Orme left the thought hanging, until Ealdgith said, "And a good place for an ambush."

Hravn, nodded, and his mind whirred as he stared into the middle distance. He jumped up suddenly, grinned, and clasped Orme on the shoulder. "That's it, Orme. We'll go tomorrow at first light, have a look, choose the spot and start to plan. Just the four of us. Ole, I want you to stay with Frida. We'll take the long route, cross the river at Grinton, then keep well south of Richemund."

Ulf was enthusiastic. "Aye, we won't pass for Count Alan's men, but wearing mail, and helmed, we might pass for a band of mercenaries."

Ealdgith pulled a face. "Green men more like, and that's not something I want to put to the test."

The sun had clawed its way above the skyline of the moors over towards the sea as they rode fast, and hard, in a broad sweep over the high ground south of the Swale, taking care to stay out of sight of the high Richemund promontory. Hravn slowed the pace when the fields around Corburne came into sight. Ulf and Orme knew the land better and they led the way through the strips of woodland between the open fields. Orme eventually called a halt. "We can tether the horses here, then drop down through the trees to the track." Ulf eased his helmet off and wiped his brow, the heat under the steel was oppressive. Orme led them in single file down an increasingly steep slope. The waters of the Swale glistened below, in a silvery background to the dark green leaves. The cool of the dense woodland brought instant relief.

"I see what you mean Orme." Hravn was impressed. "Anyone riding up here will be forced to go slow and bend low over their mount to keep clear of the branches. They won't be keeping much of an eye on what's around them."

Ulf picked up Hravn's line of thought. "Aye, if man and horse went over the edge it would look like an accident."

"Or, just the man, the horse could have slipped and thrown him." Ealdgith was reluctant for unnecessary violence.

"Mmm...but how do we do that?" Hravn sucked his teeth in frustration.

Ealdgith was more positive. "Well, it depends how strong you feel...and how sturdy those boughs up there are." She pointed to the tall trunks that curved upwards and outwards, bending over the track. She grinned as three pairs of questioning eyes turned towards her.

"If we can drag the trunk of a dead tree onto the bank and suspend it from those boughs with a rope at either end, we could swing it across the track and knock everything in its way over the edge. We just need to get the ropes the right length and make sure that the boughs can take the weight."

Ulf chuckled. "Well done, Edie. That might just work. How's your climbing, Hravn?" Hravn laughed back. "Better than yours. We just need your brawn to heave on the ropes. What do you reckon Orme? We could climb those."

Whilst they would need to return with ropes to prepare the ambush site properly before the day itself, they gave themselves a head start: they found two logs that ponies could drag into place, cleared undergrowth to enable the logs to swing freely, and calculated distances and heights. As they finished, Hravn said, "I think we need to make sure the reeve and his men slow and bunch up at the point the logs will hit them. We'll dangle a fallen branch over the track so that the lead rider will need to slow and clear it."

Days later, the rising sun cast long shadows through the wood as they moved quietly into their final positions. Hravn's confirmatory orders were almost unnecessary. "Edie, cover the exit with a crossbow and have the hounds ready to chase anyone that tries to flee. Orme, you take the opposite end, in case they try to flee the way they came. Ulf and I will release the logs. Ulf, follow my lead." The logs were each held back by a short rope secured to a tree. The swift slash of a seax blade would be enough to sever the taught ropes and send the logs swinging across the track at chest height.

They lay in the woods and waited, smacking at mosquitoes that seemed to thrive in the unseasonal heat. "Wisst! Listen! There are horses crossing the river." Orme was nearest to the ford and gestured up the track to warn the others. He pulled his green cowl over his head and lay prone, tracking the riders with his crossbow as they came into sight through the trees.

Hravn waited for his moment, thankful that the reeve rode in the middle. The lead rider slowed and the reeve closed up on him. As he bent down to pull the low hanging branch out of the way, Hravn slashed through the retaining cord. The fifteen-foot log swung surprisingly quickly, caught the first and second riders and flung them over the edge. The horses reared, slipping and skittering on the loose earth, striving to keep their balance and stay on the narrow track. They succeeded and fled in a panicked gallop. The reeve hit the trunk of an oak and dropped twenty feet, straddling its roots. The lead rider missed all the trees, fell cleanly into the slow-moving water of the ale-brown Swale a hundred feet below, and sank out of sight, held down by the weight of his mail. Ulf's log slammed into the third rider, just clearing his horse's head. He, too, was thrown cleanly from his saddle, breaking his back with a chilling snap as he arched across a broad bough, before sliding down to snag on a craggy outcrop fifty feet below; his body was screened from sight, for the time being.

Hravn gave a low whistle, glancing across at Ulf who looked equally stunned at the speed and success of their attack. "Come! Quick! We need to get to the reeve, check he's dead and recover the taxes. The other two are certainly dead." Hravn called to Orme as he ran up the track. "Give Ulf a hand. Get the ropes down and clear all sign of the ambush. We need to push the logs over the edge too. Edie! Come with me."

They scrambled down the slope to the reeve. He was dead, his neck broken. Hravn unfastened a leather pouch from the man's waist belt and then felt inside his tunic for any more. There was a second one. "His own takings rather than Enisant's, I would guess," Ealdgith mused. Hravn emptied both pouches into his own and then returned them to the corpse. "Help me Edie. I want to tip him into the Swale." The body rolled, leaving a trail of snagged clothing, then sank into the dark water with a splash.

Hravn directed them to walk over the ambush site to remove all trace of their presence before shooing the Normans' horses away up the track. "The horses will probably return to Richemund in a day or two, but it might be a while before the bodies are found. Even then there is nothing to suggest a murder, only an unexplained accident." He was grimly satisfied.

As they scrambled back up the slope to their own horses Orme said, "We can follow the wood line around to the ford, if you like, and keep well clear of the track." Hravn nodded, "Orme, Ulf, can you stay on the hill above Esebi, when we get there, and keep watch. Edie and I will return the taxes to the priest, but I don't want to draw unwarranted attention."

The vill of Esebi was built on a tier of platforms cut into a broad semi-circle, above the flood plain, in the northern bank of the Swale. The small church of Saint Agatha's was to one side, set back from the river. When they crossed the ford, Ulf and Orme made their way through the trees to the top of the hill above the vill. Hravn and Ealdgith rode quietly into the vill and tethered their horses at the back of the low stone church. Ealdgith paused, took Hravn's hand and led him to a tall stone cross in front of the church. It towered above them. "It's wonderful, Hravn, look at the carvings; for Christ and Our Lady on the front and the old gods on the back – the faiths of all our people joined as one just as they should be. I wonder how long the Normans will let it stand?"

They slipped quietly through a heavy oak door into the dark cool within, straining to see in the low light. "Welcome Hravn, and Lady Ealdgith too, I presume." A low voice, deeper than she expected, came from within the sanctuary. Hravn answered, "Father Oda, are you alone?" The small, dark-robed, man came forward, his hand outstretched in welcome.

The priest's face was a complex picture of surprise, concern and pleasure when Hravn explained quickly that they had come to return the taxes that the reeve had extorted from his flock only a few hours before. "Thank you. I will make sure that they are returned and that all will know not to talk of it. I will also let our lord, The Earl, know."

Hravn gave him a warning look. "The bodies will doubtless be found sooner or later. Two are in the river and may be swept some distance unless the weight of their mail pins them to the river bed, one is caught on a ledge. When Enisant's men come asking, I suggest you say the reeve never came. They may demand back payment, which will have to be paid, but I hope that they won't demand the extra cut that the reeve was taking."

As they turned to leave, the priest put a cautioning hand on Hravn's arm. "There's talk in the vills about green men. Nothing specific, but enough to cause me concern. I'm not aware that the Normans have heard, but they will. They reward informers and someone will speak."

"But why?" Hravn asked, aghast.

"Why? Surely out of desperation, or risk starvation." Ealdgith was in no doubt.

Father Oda glanced at her with sudden respect. "Yes, My Lady, some are desperate, hunger can be stronger than loyalty, others want to retain what little power they have left; there are few you can really trust."

Chapter 16

"It's the shortest night tonight, I think. I rather lose track of the days living in the woodland." Hravn glanced over towards Ealdgith, as he lay on the river bank chewing the end of a long grass.

Ealdgith smiled back. "I think you're right. It's strange to think that the days will start to shorten, winter seems to have just passed."

Hravn put the grass down. "It's not just recently passed, Edie, we've had no proper rain for weeks. Feel the earth, it's drier than the dust in the cave and some of the springs are beginning to dry up. I fear we will have a poor harvest, with all the stress that will bring; and the woodland, it's already like a tinder box. One stray spark and..." He left the words unsaid. They both knew the consequences.

Ealdgith continued lying back on the grass, absentmindedly watching buzzards soar high overhead as the sun's heat soaked into her. "Hravn?" Hravn sighed inwardly. He knew a question was coming.

"Do you realise that it is a year since we promised ourselves to each other?"

It wasn't a question he was expecting. He rolled over and caressed her hair. "Yes, Edie. We've come a long way since then."

Ealdgith sat up. "We have, and I think we should go further. I think we should be married, properly." She turned, looking into Hravn's eyes. "Will you? Will you marry me, make vows in front of a priest? We weren't ready when we were with Brother Patrick, but we are now, and we have Father Oda."

Hravn looked up into Ealdgith's serious eyes, loving the way the sun teased out golden specks in the green. "Of course, Edie, of course. But why now?"

Ealdgith shook her head slowly, feigning a look of surprise. "Need you ask? We are as united now as we ever can be. I take steps, but one day there may be a child. But there is more. We don't know what the future holds, what plots Wyrd will weave. We have nothing, but we have a lot too. We have our freedom, we have men that follow us and will fight for us. We are sworn to my uncle and he to us; that must lead to something. I want us to be seen as the couple that we are: in the eyes of God, by our people and by all that we may meet."

Hravn could now see the conviction and resolve in her eyes, the playful gold glints replaced by cool silver. He nodded, imperceptibly, thinking. "I agree Edie. You're right. You're always right!" He pulled her to him, embracing her body with his hands.

They rolled apart and lay back on the turf. Hravn was suddenly very serious. "There are other reasons too, Edie. The laws are changing. The Normans are taking away the rights of wives to own property, the rights of women to own or do anything without the say so of a man. We must marry in the way of our people, whilst we still can. Let us see Father Oda tomorrow."

They left Ulf to go and visit The Bear and the settlements, in order to find out how they were coping with the drought, and Orme and Frida to look after the camp. Hravn and Ealdgith rode to Esebi in the early morning light. It was a long ride, through the Norman controlled woods, past the half deserted vills of Waston, Ghellinges and Schirebi, before looping back to the hill above Esebi. The couple attracted few looks from the bent-backed men as they rode slowly past the vill's western field, down towards the church. Smoke rose from domestic fires in a couple of the cottages off to their left. Their attention was off to their right, as they rode they both stared at the stone tower of the castle of Richemund that grew ever taller on the Hindrelag bluff, barely a league up the valley.

The heavy oak door creaked on its hinges as Hravn pushed it open. Ealdgith bade the hounds lie and watch the horses, then slipped inside. Father Oda looked taken aback. "News?"

Hravn chuckled. "No Father, other than news of a wedding. We'd like you to marry us." They tried hard not to laugh at the expression on Father Oda's face.

"Yes, Father, seriously!" Ealdgith reassured the priest. "We swore ourselves to each other last year, before we fled Westmoringaland, but we have never had access to a priest until now. Can you, please?"

"But of course, My Lady." The priest recovered from his surprise, "I'd just assumed that you were already married. Our Lord, Earl Gospatrick, spoke as if you were."

Ealdgith smiled. "That is reassuring." She hesitated, "Father, may I ask how it is that you are now here. I do not recall that you served my father? This manor was his."

Oda took a deep breath and gave Ealdgith a quizzical, penetrating, look. "You may, and you are right. I did not serve your father, but I have long served the Earl, we hold certain beliefs in common. The Earl was caught out by the harrying. He'd anticipated reprisals, but nothing of this scale. As soon as he bought back his earldom he used his influence with an intermediary to place me in this vill, where I am close to Count Alan's Richemund. It might surprise you, but the Count has some sympathy for our people's plight. He is a Breton and is not as brutal as other Norman lords."

Hravn laughed sarcastically. "Huh! Maybe not, but those who serve him can be. I can vouch for that."

Father Oda nodded. "I don't disagree. There are those, be they Norman, Breton or, sadly, English, that crave power with a brutality that is chilling to behold. Others, though, are more realistic and understand how power and loyalty are really gained. The Count is one of those, as is his steward, Enisant. The harrying was planned; carefully. Many of the fertile manors weren't harried. Esebi is one, and it is Enisant's now. He holds it in demesne. The freemen are now bondsmen, and just scrape by; but they weren't slain and didn't starve, as many others did." Hravn and Ealdgith nodded, keeping their counsel, as Oda continued, "It's important, too, that the Earl understands how Count Alan plans to reshape society hereabouts; and what plans the King may hold for the North."

"He's building a military centre, that's a certainty." Hravn interrupted, "Richemund dominates the land for miles round, sitting like a spider in the centre of a web of wooden castles, like Middelham. He's pulled the young people out of the vills on the poorer land and forced them to work in the more fertile manors...he's certainly reshaping society."

Oda was quiet for a moment. "You're shrewd Hravn, and perceptive. That's exactly what he is doing…and if the Earl is ever to lead another uprising he must understand how to engineer it."

Ealdgith's interruption surprised both men. "I fear he can't. Not now. We can resist and take our revenge on those who are brutal, but I cannot see that our people can ever rebel again."

Oda gave her an appraising glance, "I fear that you are right, My Lady."

She placed her hand on Oda's arm. "Thank you, Father, I understand and we all agree, but I think we digress."

Ealdgith's forthrightness surprised Oda, she read it in his eyes. He wasn't deterred. "Tell me about yourselves, and how you survived the harrying and came to serve the Earl?"

Father Oda showed little emotion as they described their mid-winter flight over the frozen hills and into the foreboding woods of the Mallerstang Forest. He listened intently, bent forward, nodding and encouraging them to talk. Then he jerked upright, his eyes alight. "Oswin? Brother Oswin from my brotherhood at Ripum?" They were both equally as startled by Oda's reaction.

"Yes Father. Do you know of him?" Ealdgith asked, intrigued.

"Yes, I do. Thanks be to Our Lord. This explains much. Brother Oswin left the community there some years ago in a much-troubled state of mind. He returned late last year saying that two young people had helped him face his own demons and find peace living with his fellow man. He sort fulfilment, and now looks after the leper sanctuary, enjoying the company there, working with those in need without fear or concern for his own health and future. I can see that we owe you a great debt."

"No Father." Hravn spoke for them both. "The debt will always be ours. We would not be here now if it were not for Brother Oswin. Tell us, do you also know Brother Patrick at Morlund?"

Father Oda looked intently at them both. He nodded slowly. "Sometimes it is wisest not to talk about those others who do the Earl's bidding.

Hravn understood Oda's reticence. "Father, it was foolish of us to ask. You are right. Let us talk about our wedding instead. We would like it here, with just my fader and Ulf with us. It is better that it is done in secret, though please do accompany us back to the woodland to celebrate afterwards."

"And Father," Ealdgith added, "are you able to record our vows in writing? These are very uncertain times and I am sure that we may one day be asked for proof."

Father Oda nodded seriously. "You are right, My Lady, particularly in your situation. I will of course prepare a parchment. Though, Hravn, I will decline your offer of a celebration. I must remain here with my flock. There are risks that it is not wise to run and at this time they need me more than usual. The granaries are empty and cannot be refilled until haerfest. We have the hay now, but it will be another few weeks until the grain comes in."

Hravn nodded his understanding. "I know Father, we all feel it. I've known mould on rye send men into a frenzy and the other week The Bear said that some at

Grenefell had baked loaves, eking out the last of their grain with poppy and hemp seeds, and fell into a stupor." He didn't confess that, thanks to their theft of grain earlier in the year, most of The Bear's people were just able to survive until their own grain could be harvested.

Ealdgith turned to him as they left, "What of Father Eadnoth? Is he still at Hindrelag? It was a spur of the moment question and Ealdgith wasn't sure why she suddenly felt the urge to ask.

"He is still there, My Lady. He tends his flock as best he can." Oda paused, obviously weighing his words. "It is difficult for him. He is of necessity close to all that is happening there. The needs of his flock are not in accord with the demands of his new lords. He does what he can, but is no longer held in the regard that he once was." Ealdgith nodded her thanks and understanding.

*****

Very early the next morning four grey figures slipped into the little stone church in the half-light of early dawn. The service was short and, of necessity, simple. The couple, unable to exchange financial gifts or a dowry, made simple vows to each other. When Father Oda asked if they had tokens to exchange each was surprised and delighted. Ealdgith was close to tears when Ulf passed her a heavy gold ring to give to Hravn and The Bear passed Hravn a delicate silver ring that Bron had given him for her. The couple embraced each other and their witnesses. As they turned back towards Father Oda he too surprised them, and bent down, straining to lift a small cask from behind the alter. "Mead, for the brýdeala, courtesy of Lord Enisant, though he does not know it."

Hravn laughed, grasped Father Oda by both shoulders, and embraced him. "Thank you."

"Ha! Hravn, do you know what this means?" Ulf slapped Hravn on the back as they walked away from the church.

Hravn gave him a quizzical sideways glance. "That I must always do Edie's bidding?"

"No, well that too," he laughed. "I meant that you are now also heir to Thor's lands, My Lord. I hope Count Alan never gets to hear."

Chapter 17

Hravn stood at the edge of the trees in the narrow wood that ran along the top of the crags above the cave. As he looked across the tall grass of the deserted fields he reflected on the waste of a good crop of hay. It would make good winter fodder for their horses, but if they harvested it then it may draw attention to their presence. He turned his mind instead to how to defend the cliff top entrance to the cave's chimney.

"I have it, lads. Come this way." He called to Orme and Ole who were lounging against an oak, holding a shovel, mattock and a couple of wooden buckets. "This oak is far enough back from the cliff edge for any of us to get past without the risk of falling over. I'll let you chose exactly where you dig, Orme, but if we start at the oak then choose a line that stays ten to fifteen paces away from the entrance and ends up at the cliff edge on the other side of it."

Orme nodded. "I'll dig a long line of pits, staggering them so that if they miss one they'll step in another."

"Yes, about a foot deep and three feet square, with short stakes in the bottom." Ole joined in laughing, "So they'll either break an ankle or stab their foot, is that the idea?"

Hravn grinned, pleased that they understood just what he wanted. "Aye, man or horse, either will stumble and the noise will give us enough warning. Cover them with thin branches and leaves. Pile the soil between the pits and cover it with brushwood. If anyone does venture across here I want to channel them into the pits. We just need to make sure that we follow the safe route in and out."

"Leave us to it, Hravn, we'll get it done in a couple of days." Orme was pleased to have a break from scrubbing chain mail and oiling swords. "Oh, and good hunting. Make sure you and Edie bring us something good for Frida's pot."

Rather than clamber down the chimney Hravn took the long way around to their camp by the cave. As he walked along the cliff top he thought back to their discussion a couple of days ago. Ulf was becoming increasingly concerned about the risk of betrayal, and wanted them to move to the caves near Ellepigerthwaite that Edric had found. Hravn had almost accused him of wanting to be nearer to Cyneburg, but had bitten his tongue when Ealdgith had agreed with Ulf. She had taken Father Oda's warning to heart and, as she had explained to Hravn later, she worried that Ealhstan could betray them out of spite and take a reward as recompense for loosing Cyneburg to Ulf. The line of pits was Hravn's way of securing their agreement to remain in the cave.

Hravn froze; the chill of fear ran the length of his spine. The high pitched, moaning, howl of a wolf echoed across the valley. It had come from behind him. As he turned the howl came again. He was sure it came from the high ground beyond Dune, the sound intensifying as it echoed down through the valleys. He took Sköll's head in his hands and ruffled his neck to calm him as the wolfhound threw his head back and yowled in response. Hati joined in too, his called resounding from the base of the crags below. Hravn knew at once what was happening. With the depopulation of the upper dales the wolf population was no longer under control.

That, and the drought, were forcing wolves to move closer to the fertile grounds of the lower dales. It was another reason why the Normans might come hunting.

Hravn skirtined around the bottom of the crags and called to Ealdgith, "Come on Edie, let's go and check those snares. These woods may be devoid of deer, but we might still catch a couple of hares." He really hoped that the snares had worked, he could almost taste the soft meat in his mouth. They hadn't eaten properly for days.

*****

The two lads worked hard. By the middle of the next day they had finished a first line of pits and were now digging a second line to cover any gaps. Orme stripped off his tunic and sweated in the hot sun as he dug. Ole cut thin, foot-long stakes and hardened their points over a low fire by the entrance to the chimney. As he stood up from the fire a distant flash of scarlet caught his eye. He paused, then froze.

"Orme! Riders. In the field, a furlong away. Get down." It was too late. Orme's naked torso, the sound of digging and the thin wisps of smoke from Ole's fire were enough to attract attention.

The five riders spurred their horses into a gallop, their heads bent low as they ducked under the branches of the outer line of trees. "Ole! The chimney! Get down the chimney. Warn Hravn." Orme yelled as he grabbed his sword and ran after Ole. As Ole slithered down the chimney Orme paused at the top and turned to face his pursuers.

It was a hunting party, not soldiers. The lead rider, bare-headed and scarlet-cloaked, was barely twenty

217

paces away. Orme could see that he was about to slow his horse and jump off, sword in hand, to confront him. The other men had dismounted and were running forward, swords drawn. He guessed that it was a knight with his squires. He hesitated. He should flee after Ole but, if the pits worked, what then?

The decision was made for him as the knight's mount stumbled into a pit. Orme heard the crack of breaking bone before the pain-stricken scream of the horse rent the air. The scarlet-cloaked knight pitched forward and screamed in unison with his horse, until his head crashed into the trunk of an oak with a neck-breaking thud.

Orme had no time to recover from the shock. It was a case of fight, not flight. A surge of adrenalin cleared his mind and stilled his nerves as he stepped forward to stand his ground on the inner edge of the line of pits.

Frida was inside the cave about to relight the fire in the hearth. The sudden noise of Ole's uncontrolled, slithering, descent panicked her. She screamed. Hravn and Ulf were in the cave entrance, talking. As they turned and ran in Ole collapsed into the hearth at the bottom of the chimney in a cloud of ash; Thor's skulls bounced after him. Hravn was about to laugh, until he saw the boy's stricken face. "Normans, at the top. Orme's still there," Ole panted, winded and choking on the cloud of ash.

Neither of the men paused as they scrambled past Ole and hauled themselves up the chimney. Frida pulled Ole to her and staggered with him to the cave entrance.

The four men ran at Orme. Although they had seen their lord thrown they hadn't realised that his horse had stumbled into a pit. Two came straight towards Orme as two others swept around to the sides intending to surround him. Orme focused on the two in front of him as he shifted so that he was directly behind a pit. Stripped to the waist and without a helmet he felt horribly naked, vulnerable to any touch of a sword. His only solace was that the pits were his shield, and surprise his greatest ally.

Orme stared into the eyes of the leader of the two men running at him. It was with surprise and relief that he realised the man was a youth, younger than him and clad only in a thin cotton tunic. H was no better protected and probably not as strong. The person behind was similar; Orme's confidence surged. He held the youth's gaze, deliberately distracting his attention from the ground in front of him. Orme stepped back as his attacker stepped on the pit, collapsing forward, screaming as his feet, and then his hands, were pierced by the wooden stakes. He knelt, screaming, pinned to the ground. The second youth stumbled as he tried to stop and avoid his friend. He pitched forward, arms outstretched, eyes wide with fear as he stared at the tip of the sword pointed at him. Orme lunged and rammed his sword into the exposed chest, feeling bone shatter, surprised at the ease with which it tore through heart and lungs. The young squire fell, almost ripping the sword from Orme's grasp as his body slid down the bloody blade.

As Orme tugged his blade free, blood spurted from severed arteries and drenched him in a scarlet spray. Cursing, he wiped the sticky liquid off his hands onto the back of his breaches in an attempt to prevent it spoiling his grip on his sword. He sensed movement to his right. The third squire, noticeably taller than the first two, was picking his way carefully between the pits. Orme spun around, his sword in the guard position, and saw that the fourth was doing the same. He backed towards the top of the chimney, this was a fight he couldn't win.

Hravn's breathless shout stopped him. "Orme! I'm behind you. Take the one on the left." Without looking behind, Orme sprang forward and swept his sword in a low arc aiming for the fourth squire's legs as he picked his way between the stakes. The youth parried and jumped, two footed, onto the edge of the pit. Orme used his momentum, and with his sword held shield-like across his body pushed forward, chest to chest. He saw fear in the squire's eyes and smelt it on his body. As the youth strained forward Orme jerked his head down in a vicious nod that shattered the squire's nose, forcing him backwards into the pit. Orme stepped back and, as a stake skewered the squire's heel, Orme's sword slashed across his stomach, disembowelling him. Bile rose in Orme's throat as the bloody mess collapsed in front of him in a twitching, stinking, screaming heap.

"Well done Orme, you're truly blooded now." Ulf's gruff compliment rallied Orme, though the pun was lost on him. He turned and saw that Hravn had taken the surrender of the last squire whilst Ulf had mercifully beheaded the youth pinned in the pit.

Hravn's prisoner stood shaking, looking at the three men and bodies of his lord and comrades. He was as tall as Hravn and possibly the same age. Their sumor afternoon's hunt, and sudden chance of some sport with a couple of peasants, had degenerated into a bloody nightmare. "S...silvatici?" He stuttered.

Hravn nodded then spoke in Cumbric. "Your life is forfeit. You cannot see us and then live to talk of it. You must surely know that?" The young man stared, then nodded. Hravn continued, calmly, his one-time reluctance to take life had gone. "Answer me truthfully and I will give you a quick death. If not..." He let the meaning sink in. The squire nodded again.

"Is the dead man your lord?" "Y..yes." The reply was hoarse, spoken dry-throated.

"Who is he and who does he serve?"

"Gwilherm du Guesclin. He serves my Lord Enisant."

"Thank you, and is he related to Enisant or Count Alan?"

"No, Lord." The squire was talking more freely, surprised but respectful that Hravn knew the names of his own masters.

"Who knew that you were hunting here today?"

"No-one, Lord, none that I know of. My Lord Gwilherm simply followed the woodland tracks and open lands. We sort deer but, found none and, having heard wolves yesterday, thought that we should hunt further west than we have before."

"I see, and what do you know of the silvatici? Did you expect to find any?"

The squire looked at Ulf and Orme. "No Lord. I know that they are in the woods above Ripum and some say they are in the hills south of the Jor, but I did not know that you were so close. I am surprised."

Ulf had slowly made his way around behind the squire. He watched Hravn's eyes. As Hravn flicked his eyes away from the young man's face Ulf stabbed a short thin blade into the side of the youth's neck, below his ear. Ulf held the body as it briefly twitched and then let it fall slowly to the ground. "Thank you, Ulf. Another of your rare skills. He spoke honestly and deserved a painless death."

"Hravn!" "Orme!" They turned. Ealdgith was running along the edge of the cliff top, followed closely by Frida and Ole. The hounds were well ahead.

"Stop! Stay! I'll come to you." Hravn was worried that one of them might run into a pit. He ran to the oak by the cliff edge, called the hounds to him, then shouted back to Ulf, "Ulf, kill the horse. We'll take the other four down to the enclosure."

As Ealdgith ran to him he grasped her in a close embrace before pointing out quickly the camouflaged stake pits. Ole ran up smiling, his face still caked in sweat, soot and ash. Hravn ruffled his head. "Well done Ole. Thank Thor you spotted them."

Hravn turned back to Ealdgith. "Don't say anything Edie. This has decided it. We're moving to Ellepigerthwaite, now. Come on, we need to dispose of the bodies."

As they walked across to Ulf, Hravn started to think through what they needed to do, but was distracted by Frida's scream when she saw Orme. Orme turned and grinned, the white of his face a hideous contrast to his blood-soaked chest. He laughed, still high on adrenalin, "Tis but a flesh wound Frida, come, give me a hug."

As Frida stepped back, ashen faced, Ealdgith pulled her close, "Just be pleased he's safe. It's bravado speaking. He'll feel the reaction soon enough."

"Orme, go and wash in the beck, you smell like the shambles already." Ulf saw Frida's distress and gripped the situation. "Don't tarry," Hravn called after him, "I have another task for you."

"Edie," Hravn took charge with a sense of urgency. "Ride to The Bear, tell him what's happened and get Edric and the others here as quick as you can. We need their help to move."

"Ulf, you were right about moving to Ellepigerthwaite, I should have heeded you. Strip the bodies with Frida and Ole, then push them into the chimney. I'm going to pile brushwood underneath and then we'll burn them to destroy any evidence of the fight. I'll bring ponies and a rope back. We can hang the horse from a tree, drain the blood and butcher it, at least the meat won't go to waste. Once we've finished up here we'll start clearing the cave and loading the ponies."

Hravn drove them hard, wanting to be clear of the cave as soon as he could, fearful that the smoke from the funeral pyre would attract attention. He was right to worry. As soon as he set light to the brushwood the draft from the cave entrance sucked air up the chimney as the dry timber caught alight. Flames roared up the rocky cleft consuming everything in their path with a stomach-turning sizzle. Ulf lent over the top of the crag and bellowed down to Hravn. "Get water, now! We need to dampen the turf at the top if we are to prevent a fire spreading." He turned to join Frida and Ole, stamping on the sparks belching out of the cleft.

Orme ran back up the slope, returning from the beck to the site of the fight. He'd scrubbed the blood from his arms and torso, cleaned his breeches as best he could and pulled on his tunic. He couldn't see the others and coughed as he choked in the thick, cloying, sweet but repugnant, smoke billowing from the chimney. He staggered backwards. "Orme, over here." He turned, blinking, and saw Hravn and Ulf some distance away, starting to strip meat from the carcass of the horse that swung, suspended, from the bough of a tall oak.

He ran across. "At least this smoke keeps the flies at bay," he joked. Frida stood up from the joint of horse meat that she was wrapping in its hide and flung herself into his arms.

Hravn laughed. "Enough, Frida. Orme, I cut this from the dead knight's cloak." He handed Orme a ragged piece of scarlet material with a yellow axe embroidered in the corner. "It must be his personal sign. I want you to take a pony and hang it from a tree by the Richemund-Ghellinges track. Make it look as if it snagged when he rode by, and make it visible. I want it to look as if his party were well away from here. His lord can ponder what befell them, but I don't want them looking this way...take care, others may be hunting."

Orme had barely left, with his horse at the gallop, taking the narrow forest ways that led around the top of Clapyat Gill, across the Richemund-Daltun track and eastward towards Ghellinges, when Ealdgith returned leading Edric and their band of new recruits. Hravn saw the group as they crossed the ford and ran down to meet them. Ealdgith led the way in a loop up to the top of the bank, below the crags, and along to the enclosure.

Hravn waved at the riders and gestrured for them to dismount and join him. They did so, grimacing at the smell of the smoke drifting from the cave's entrance. Perched on a ledge on the crags he summarised the situation and what was needed. "We're done here. The cave served us well, but we were surprised by a hunting party."

He grinned in acknowledgement of their expressions of admiration and awe when he described how Orme had held his ground and dealt with the attack. "We now need to get clear of here, quickly. I doubt we'll see others today, but there will doubtless be a search party in a day or two. We need to be gone, with no traces left. Whilst Ulf butchers the horse, Edric, load all the weapons, mail and stores onto the ponies and get them to the caves at Ellepigerthwaite. I haven't seen the caves yet, but I know the ones you mean. Edie, go with Edric and choose separate caves to live in and to use as a store. Edric, I've a mind that you and the others should move there too, so decide with Edie which cave you will use."

Hravn caught Ealdgith's look of surprise. "I know, we should have talked about this. I'll clear it with The Bear first, but if we must plan on facing more threats I want us grouped together so that we have the power to react if needed." Ealdgith nodded whilst Hravn continued, "I'll finish here, with Ulf and Frida. We'll wait for Orme, then I'll join you after I've spoken to fader."

The sun was dipping towards the hill tops across the valley, casting long grey shadows through the trees, by the time Orme galloped down the track. Frida's gasp of relief was shared by them all; it had been a long wait. In the meantime, they had wrapped large joints of horse meat with hide and ferns, thrown the bones and gore into the fire within the chimney, then choked the chimney as best they could with boulders. Frida and Ore had repaired the covers over the pits and scattered earth on the blood-stained ground whilst Hravn and Ulf had screened the cave entrance and pulled down the stakes that fenced the enclosure. Hravn knew that a searching eye would find signs of their presence, but he was sure that a casual glance would pass them by.

"Don't dismount, Orme. We're leaving." Hravn shouted as Orme rode towards them, panting as much as his pony. "Did all go well?"

Orme nodded, catching his breath. "Aye, the cloth will be found. The woods there are all being cleared. Working parties with oxen are hauling trunks back towards Richemund. I left it tagged to a hawthorn just on yon side of the track, a few furlongs from where they are felling. It'll be seen soon enough."

Hravn passed him a water sack. Orme gulped thirstily and nodded in acknowledgement as Ulf leant over and patted him appreciatively on the back.

Later, in the afterglow of sunset, Hravn picked his way carefully along the track from Wasfelte and across the ford over the beck that tumbled down the steep valley linking Locherlaga, at its head, to Ellepigerthwate and Helwith, before running into the Mersche Beck a league beyond Helwith. Their new home would be a lot more central but, as The Bear had pointed out, it tied them very closely to his people and they could no longer enjoy the independence that they once had. Hravn had agreed, and stressed that it would not be long until the second haerfest was over and The Bear moved his people to the safety of the upper dale at the vills of Hale and Fytun, and that thereafter both their sanctuaries would be a lot more secure. He dismounted and led his pony along the edge of the beck through dense thickets of mountain oak and rowan that crowded the valley bottom. They would need a better route in than this, he thought, as he cursed their luck and pondered about the myriad tasks ahead.

Sköll glanced up the slope and gave a low gruff bark. It was answered at once. Hravn heard low voices, on higher ground to his right. "Hravn, up here." Ealdgith's voice carried down to him on the still air. "The crags are still in the woods, but it is easier higher up. I'll come down for you." She picked her way deftly through the trees, embraced him, then took his hand to lead him back up the hill. "There's no chimney this time so we've made a hearth outside. I've spoken with Ulf and Edric, and in the morning, they'll have the lads build a long wattle roof and screen across the front of the caves. Orme will start on another stake-enclosure for all the horses and ponies where there's flatter ground further up the valley.

Hravn stopped, turned to Ealdgith and, pulling her to him, tilted his head to hers for a kiss. "Thank you, Edie. It's been a very long day and, as you say, we've lost nothing and we can start again, but I should have listened to you and Ulf."

Chapter 18

Edric felt a sharp sting on the side of his neck. He slapped hard, and cursed as he flicked away the sticky remains of a horse fly. He knew that his neck would swell and irritate him; it always did when bitten. The hot humid weather didn't help. For two days now the air had hung heavily, with a sultry yellow haze turning increasingly blue-grey over the western fells. He prayed for rain, they all did, but as yet it hadn't come.

"That's good work, Edric." He turned. He hadn't heard Hravn's approach behind him. Edric glanced down at the long lattice of woven branches that hugged the crags and covered the entrances to the four caves below. He nodded, pleased. It had taken his team longer than he had expected, but it was worth it. The lattice roof, supported on stout poles and covered with bracken and transplanted ivy, blended well with the trees and hid the encampment from view from both sides of the valley. Hravn's praise reassured him, just as the young man's calm leadership and sound planning inspired him. Edric had always valued his independence but, in Hravn, he had found someone he would happily follow and serve. "Thank you, Lord." Sweat stung his eyes and he wiped his brow with the back of his hand. "Hel's teeth! I wish it would rain."

Hravn laughed. "It will, soon enough. Look yonder." He pointed to the black spine of moors that rose between the Swale and the Jor, and merged into the oppressive sky above. Thin streaks of lightening played along the far horizon. "Lightning, but no thunder. We'll have a storm here within the hour. Let's get below."

The storm arrived with an explosive crash. Frida jumped and turned, wide-eyed, to Orme. Sköll and Hati whined and slunk into the cave. The lattice roof became suddenly alive, bouncing and thrashing as hailstones smashed onto it. Most bounced off, but some, larger egg-sized lumps, sliced their way through to shatter on the rocky floor below. Hravn raised his eyes and shook his head. "We wanted rain, but not this. Edie, Orme, we must get to the horses, they'll be terrified. Grab your helmets to protect your heads."

As he made for the door, Ulf burst in, his large hands covering his head. "That'll teach me to ride without my helm! Hravn, wait! I have a message from the Earl. Edie, My Lady, you'll need to read it."

Hravn nodded to Orme. "You go, take Edric and Ole. You can calm the horses better than anyone." He led Ulf and Ealdgith into the cave.

Ulf recovered his breath, then spoke. "I was with Cyneburg and The Bear when a messenger came from Oda. He'd sent someone from Esebi."

Ealdgith shook her head and interrupted. "Someone else who now knows where Wasfelte is."

Ulf nodded. "I know, Edie, but we must assume that he can be trusted. Anyway, he gave me this, saying that Father Oda said it is from his Lord." Ulf passed her a thick leather pouch. Ealdgith untied the draw-strings, to find a velum scroll that was tied and sealed, and a small, soft, leather pouch. She opened this with care and took out two gold rings that were identical except for their size. She glanced at the others. "My uncle's crest. See, that is his mark." She held the larger ring up for Hravn to take. "One for each of us, I think? Let's see what he has written."

Ealdgith walked to the cave entrance to get better light. The hail had abated to be replaced by heavy rain. Water dripped from the woven roof. Rather than read aloud she read the letter slowly, understanding it before explaining it to Hravn and Ulf. Ealdgith looked up and took a deep breath. With a meaningful glance at Hravn, she said, "He says that he has to know what is happening south of the Tees. Not just in the Count's lands, but further south in Snotingeham-scir if possible. He also wants to know if there is news of what the King has in mind for the North. He needs you, us, to make use of the letter of introduction he gave us and for you to work for the Count as a translator. He says that this is now more important than acts of resistance. The rings are for us, to show that we hold his trust and speak for him."

Hravn pulled a wry face and breathed deeply. "I rather thought that might be what he wanted." He paused, "So be it, if you're in agreement, Edie?"

Ealdgith nodded. "I am. I think it would work in our favour too. If you can gain the trust of those around the Count you might hear if there are any threats to the people here. I know The Bear will move his people, but that isn't for a couple of months. What do you think, Ulf?"

The huscarl smiled at Ealdgith. "I think you must do as the Earl asks, My lady." His formality surprised her. He continued, "You are right, it would help to know if the Count has anything in store for the lands around here. It might also be better if we halted our acts of resistance whilst we live so close to The Bear's people. I know it worries him. Intelligence is what the Earl needs now.

230

Only you and Hravn can get it for him. Once he knows what is being planned I am sure that he will want us to continue resisting. By then The Bear's people will be safely up the dale and we can think about a winter visit to your uncle's granaries. I can continue to train Edric and the lads, we can help with the haerfest here, and build up a reserve to see us through into next year."

"I agree, Ulf." Hravn was more confident. "Edie and I will find accommodation in Richemund. We'll take Ole with us. He can be our link back to you and he can accompany Edie during the day whilst I am with the Count. We must prepare a story that explains where we have come from." He grinned cheekily at Ealdgith, "You know that this means you're going to..."

"...have to wear dresses," said Ealdgith, resigned. She hesitated, thinking aloud, "I'm not sure if we should take just Ole. The Earl refers to you as Hravn of Ravenstandale, and we both wear his rings. That marks us out of people of standing and we should each have a servant if we are to play the role that he has in mind for us. I think Orme and Frida must come, as our servants; Ole too, as the errand boy."

Ulf chuckled, then spoke seriously. "You're right, Edie, but not just about the role play. You are our Lady, and Orme is sworn to you. Frida is too, though you have never asked her. They should both go with you, they would be hurt if they did not." Ealdgith smiled softly in reply. Try as she might, she still found it difficult to accept how others saw her.

The rain persisted for two days. The sultry atmosphere cleared and the temperature dropped whilst water cascaded from the leaden sky, sluiced down the rocks and rapidly filled the myriad becks with surging brown water. Summer dust turned to mud, but at least the caves stayed dry. Hravn groaned, "We're going nowhere in this, the best we can do is try and keep the horses under the cover of the trees."

Ulf nodded, echoing Hravn's despondency whilst he chewed a birch twig. "It's the haerfest that worries me. We've little enough as it is without the crops being flattened."

Ulf's worries were well-founded, but the damage was not as serious as he feared. The rain passed as quickly as it came. On the third day, they awoke to a clear sky, bright sun and the heady perfume of wet earth and drying foliage. Hravn stood in the doorway to the sheltered entrance and stretched. "Ulf, take the lads and see what you can do to help The Bear salvage the crops. Edie and Frida can prepare the clothes we'll need. Orme and I will go and find somewhere suitable for the Earl's man to live." He turned and caught Ealdgith's surprised look. "It's best Edie. We've a role to play and we need act it out. This is the tale I think we should tell, what do you say?" She raised an eyebrow and listened.

Hravn paused before starting. "You might be recognised and will need to explain why you haven't been around since the harrying. Let's say that your moder sent you away with the Earl's retinue after the Yule-tide feast, days before the harrying. She felt you were too boyish and needed schooling in the ways of a lady."

Ealdgith giggled, "I think I still do."

Hravn chuckled, "I'd say you were schooled as a Valkyrie instead."

"Anyway," he continued, "we'll say that we met at Bebbanburge. My fader had sent me to serve the Earl. He holds lands from the Earl in the head of the vale of

232

Eden. When your fader was slain, the Earl assumed guardianship and he agreed that we should marry. I took you back to Ravenstandale and we lived there for a year before The Earl summoned me to work for the Count. You know the lands of the Eden and can talk of them if asked."

"What about Orme and Frida?" said Ealdgith.

"They should just be themselves. Orme is Angle, Frida and Ole are Norse. They could be from the mixed communities of Cumbraland and Westmoringaland. Let's say that Frida and Ole's family serve Gunnar and that Orme is from Ravenstandale; his family serving my fader. We can tell them what little they need to know, but I doubt many will speak to them. They will be our servants after all."

Ealdgith laughed, jumped up and gave Hravn a kiss. "I like it. It's so simple and close to the truth." They turned.

Orme was lounging against the cave wall, grinning cheekily and clapping. "That sounds like a plan to me, Hravn. Even I can remember it. Though maybe you should teach me a few Cumbric curses to liven up my conversation."

Hravn laughed. "Come on then Orme, let's get the horses. Bring a pony with saddle bags too. We could all do with some brighter coloured cloaks, and you and I need new britches if we are to present ourselves to the Count. I'm aspiring to be a young Cumbric noble, I'll have you know."

"Not so fast, my Cumbric lord." Ealdgith pulled Hravn around to face her and tugged his straggly beard. "If you are play the part you need to look the part, and you

233

have the look of the wild man of the woods. You too Orme," she added, as Orme sidled out of the cave. "Frida, can you find those shears? We've beards to trim and hair to comb and plait."

Later, properly groomed, Hravn hoped, to the height of Cumbric fashion, they followed the track to Mersche, their horses' hooves splashing in puddles that were drying already in the sun. Steam rose from the wet ground and Hravn pondered that, although the rain might encourage growth, the woodland was still at great risk of fire. He slowed as they approached Richemund to allow Orme to catch up. "We'll start at the tailor's, next to the cobbler's. I'm sure the prospect of selling some of his finest cloaks will encourage him to recommend somewhere that will put us up."

The population of Hindrelag was growing quickly as the need for craftsmen sucked people in from the English south and Brittany. Hravn was surprised at the amount of ready-made clothing that was piled on tables and he seized the opportunity to properly dress the women of his expanded family. He even bought breeches and a cloak for little Ada, and enjoyed the irony of spending the dead merchant's coins to buy Norman clothes.

Hravn's confidence wasn't misplaced. As Orme packed neatly rolled scarlet and blue cloaks and breeches into the saddlebags, Hravn chatted freely to the tailor, cursed their luck with the weather during their crossing from Cumbraland, and was given a referral to a newly built inn and stables behind the main street. It was an impressive building, the size of a large hall and smelled strongly of fresh cut timber and newly lime-washed wattle and daub. Orme stood outside, holding the horses, with Sköll at heel, whilst Hravn pushed open the stout oak door.

The entrance opened onto a large central hearth where, despite the heat outside, a log fire was tended by three women who appeared to be preparing food. Smoke rose slowly to billow under the rafters and escape through two wide skylights. As expected, the hearth was surrounded by trestle tables and benches. It was the space beyond the central area that surprised Hravn and reminded him of a large stable. The walls were partitioned by high wicker screens into large stalls, each of which was closed at the front by a heavy fabric curtain. He wondered how many slept within each space.

Hravn assumed that the women were local and asked in English who was in charge. As he spoke a short, overweight, man called from the far end of the hall; his broken English inferring that he was probably Breton. "What do you want? We don't take English here, only those who serve the Count may take a room."

Hravn held up his hand in a gesture of appeasement and answered in Cumbric that he hoped the Breton would understand. "Not so fast, my friend. I am Cumbric, not English, and am here to serve my lord, the Count." The man raised an eyebrow and wiped his hands on his apron, "Indeed, at least your Breton is better than my English. We'll talk; come."

First impressions are often right. Hravn surmised that the inn-keeper was an opportunist and a bully, and adopted an arrogance that he sensed Normans would respect. "I am Hravn of Ravenstandale, a Cumbric lord in the service of Earl Gospatrick, and here at the request of Count Alan to serve him too. My family and staff need rooms, stabling too, and I understand that those who serve the Count are well served here."

The inn-keeper flinched, then held out his hand. "Welcome, Lord Hravn. Cumbric? I never knew that we spoke a common tongue."

Hravn gave a thin smile. "Neither did I. It's strange where fate leads us all." He took a small leather purse from his cloak pocket, squeezing it to make the coins clink. "I need beds for my wife, Lady Ealdgith, as well as her maid, my man servant and our groom." The inn-keeper watched the movement of the coins in Hravn's hand. "I'll pay for a month in advance. Perhaps room for four in a quiet corner? The boy can sleep in the stable." Hravn read hesitation in the man's face. "Mayhap you need to see authority from the Count?" He said, as he reached for the Earl's letter.

The inn-keeper's greed won. "No, I'll take your coins. There are two small rooms here, in the corner by the door." The inn-keeper held his hand out and Hravn tipped coins into the sweaty palm, and said, "I'll be back on the morrow."

*****

"No! No hounds in here! They can live in the stables." The inn-keeper rushed across the hall, waving his arms, as Hravn and Ealdgith walked in followed by Sköll and Hati.

Hravn paused, assuming the same imperious manner of the previous day. "Try and keep them out if you like...you must be a braver man than most, though. They'll sleep with us and, be assured, they won't foul the floor." With that, he turned and, with a slight flourish, introduced Ealdgith. "My wife, The Lady Ealdgith, niece to Earl Gospatrick." Ealdgith smiled, resplendent and more than a little self-conscious in the

236

green and yellow silk dress that Bron and Frida had made for her.

Orme suppressed a chuckle then, playing his part with aplomb, said deferentially. "We will prepare your room My Lord, whilst you attend upon the Count." Hravn left without a glance at the flustered, red-faced, inn-keeper.

Hravn and Ealdgith had discussed how to make their appearance at Count Alan's hall and agreed that, despite the difficulties that riding in a long dress posed for Ealdgith, to arrive on horseback would enhance their presence. Hravn helped Ealdgith adjust her skirts, and hide her legs with her cloak, before riding around to the gated entrance in the stake-wall. He paused, took a deep breath to calm his nerves and got his first real look at the castle and hall beyond. Ealdgith called the hounds to heel as Hravn walked his horse slowly up to two men-at-arms who controlled the gate, where he pulled the Earl's letter of introduction from inside his cloak. "I'm Lord Hravn of Ravenstandale. I serve Earl Gospatrick and am here to speak to the Count. These are my orders. You will see the Earl's seal and this is his ring that I wear." Hravn flashed his ring in the soldier's face.

The soldier stood back and scrutinsed Hravn before he glanced at Ealdgith. "The woman?"

Hravn raised an eyebrow. "The woman, as you so disrespectfully address her, is The Lady Ealdgith. My wife and niece to my lord, The Earl." He hoped his tone was sufficiently arrogant to persuade the soldier that he was no different to the many Norman knights that must be the bane of his life. "Where may I find the Count?"

The soldier stepped back in deference. "The hall, in the inner bailey." He nodded to a large wooden building at the opposite side of the enclosure to the part-built castle. Stabling is in the block beyond. Speak to the guard on the gate. There will be a man there to take your mounts and another to show you to the hall. Do not stray, My Lord, and keep those hounds close. The English tread with care inside these walls." Hravn nodded and spurred his horse forward. The undertone of threat was clear.

Ealdgith rode alongside Hravn as they moved deeper within the fortifications, where they halted, awed by the bustle of activity around them. The high promontory overlooking the Swale, that had once been Ealdgith's home, had become a budding fortress, a hive of industry and home to hundreds of men-at-arms, staff and masons. The broad area was bound by a stake-wall that enclosed a score of shingle or thatch-roofed wooden buildings to house artisan tradesmen, a bakery, washhouse and many more. Smoke and smells abounded, and men and a few women thronged with a sense of purpose and urgency, as if casual relaxation or conversation would be punished.

A stone building, larger than any hall they had seen, rose above the edge of the headland, and the foundations of other buildings were being laid next to it. Of Ealdgith's manor, there was no sign. Any grass had long since been worn away. The surface was dry earth or packed stones, that would turn to a sea of mud in the winter. In the middle of the enclosure endless teams of men carried stone blocks from a line of carts, and placed them at the base of a wooden scaffold that clung to the stone walls. Teams of masons were shaping the blocks, whilst carpenters split and formed lengths of new cut oak trunks that ox-teams dragged to a central pile.

Hravn glanced at Ealdgith. She was slowly shaking her head, her mouth clenched tight to choke a sob, as tears dampened her cheeks. "Come, Edie, don't dwell on what has been done. We have to keep calm and focus on what we have to do."

She nodded and forced a smile. "Help me to dismount. We'll lead the horses to the inner bailey. Keep the hounds on very short leashes."

Count Alan's hall was an imposing two-story wooden building with a steeply pitched shingle roof. Although two sets of doors opened into the ground floor, their guide led them up a flight of removable external stairs suspended below an entrance into the first floor. Hravn realised that the hall was a castle in its own right. A military force capable of building a defence such as this could never be beaten.

As they stepped over the threshold, past a stout oak door at the top of the steps, Ealdgith was struck by the all-pervading smell of cut timber that competed with the rank odour of close human habitation. It caught in her throat and was very different to the clean air of their woodland home. They were ushered into a small room off a corridor at the top of the steps. "Hravn of Ravenstandale, a Cumbric lord to see the Constable."

Ealdgith was conscious that their guide did not mention her name to the man-at-arms who guarded the entrance. In Norman eyes her status counted for little. Hravn sensed her discomfort, gripped her hand and forced a smile, and avoided looking at the soldier who stared at them from the doorway. "Stay strong, Valkyrie. Show them an English lady isn't daunted."

"Lord Enisant Musard de Plevan will see you now." The Constable's full title and the heavy Breton accent caught

Hravn unawares, it was a moment before he realised he was being summoned. They followed, the hounds held close, into a largish room towards the end of the corridor. Two mail clad men-at-arms guarded the entrance. Hravn was surprised by the spartan nature of the room, with plain timber walls. On one wall, there hung a red kite-shaped shield, a white diagonal flash its only marking. Daylight and warm air came through an open shutter, to highlight the face of a tall powerfully built man in his mid-twenties. His fashionable Norman haircut, the back of his skull shaven down to his neck, gave him a severe, almost demonic look. Ealdgith felt a shiver as his intense brown eyes glanced briefly at her. She held his look and refused to look down. His attention switched to Hravn.

Hravn seized the initiative and spoke first with an outward assuredness that belied how he felt. "My lord, Enisant." He paused. "My lord, the Earl Gospatrick, offers you and the Count my services as a translator. I am Cumbric and though I speak English, I am not English. As you hear, I speak a tongue that has much in common with Breton. This is my authority." He passed the parchment scroll to Enisant, assuming correctly that he could read Latin, and continued speaking whilst the Breton read. "Lady Ealdgith is my wife and the Earl's niece. We have travelled from Cumbraland and have rooms in the new vill. As I say, we are here to serve."

"Yes, yes." Enisant passed the scroll back peremptorily. "The Count has been expecting you, though we knew not when." He looked at Hravn with clinical scrutiny. "It is well that you have accommodation for there is none in the hall. You may eat here, as may you Lady Ealdgith, should you desire. You will work for the reeve, that is where we have the greatest need to communicate. We may also need you to be present when the Count talks to his English nobles, as a few still hold land from him." He glanced at Ealdgith. "Lady, there is nothing that the Count will need from you. You are of course welcome to join the other ladies here, few that they are, or mayhap you will concentrate on your husband's needs." Ignoring any reply that Ealdgith may have given, he turned back to Hravn. "Thank you, Lord Hravn. Report here tomorrow morning when the church bell sounds for Terce."

Hravn squeezed Ealdgith's hand as they walked back to the stables. "I'll be damned before I go back into that castle," she said through clenched teeth, "it reeks of their arrogance." He nodded grimly in reply. "I know, but I will. They have placed me just where the Earl wants."

Chapter 19

The main meal of the day was about to be served when Hravn and Ealdgith returned to the inn. They squeezed into the space that Orme had reserved on the long trestle table upon which all meals were served. The food was wholesome and more plentiful than they had seen in months. "Hey! You're the stable lad here not the lord, don't draw attention," Frida placed a restraining hand on Ole's arm as he reached for a third small loaf. They could tell from the conversation that most at the table were Breton or Norman, though a florid-faced merchant at the far end of the table spoke with a heavy accent that they took for that of Mercian London.

Hravn leant forward and talked quietly, summarising their encounter with Enisant. Ealdgith frowned when his name was mentioned, then surprised Hravn with the clarity with which she had thought through what they should do. "That arrogant Frenchman can go hang for all I care. Frida, you and I will do something to help our people instead. On the morrow, we will go to the church of Our Lady, seek out the priest, and offer to help those who need healing." Hravn started to speak but thought better; Ealdgith's look was not that of one to be gainsaid. "Hravn, you should take Orme with you tomorrow. As a lord, you should be accompanied by your man and whilst you may find it difficult to break free of the reeve, I am sure Orme will be able to talk more freely when you visit the vills and collect taxes."

Hravn's mood lightened. "You're right Edie, on both accounts. Don't look so puzzled Ole, you can go with Edie or, once you've cared for the horses, get to know

Hindrelag, chat to the local lads and get a feel for what people really think. There may be those to whom Edie and I need to talk."

The church bell rang for Terce as Hravn swung down from his horse and handed Orme the reins. "Once more into the wolves' lair," he teased, and forced Orme to smile, easing his tension. "Wait here, I'll be back with, or without, the reeve." Hravn trotted up the steps, with more confidence that he felt, and kept Sköll close to heel. He assumed that the man standing with his back to him, talking to a man-at-arms, was the reeve. The blue linen tunic, edged with gold embroidery, was a sufficient clue as to his status. The man turned at the sound of Hravn's footfall. His pleasant, friendly, smile, hedged by a neatly trimmed beard, immediately stilled Hravn's nerves. "Hravn, at a guess? And quite a hound too." Hravn was surprised that the man didn't appeared to be fazed by Sköll.

"Yes, his name's Sköll. I'm Hravn." He held out his hand, "And that is my man, Orme, with the horses."

"Good, good," said the reeve as he nodded his approval. Hravn could tell that the man was well into his thirties. His dark brown hair covered his ears and reached the nape of his neck and, in places, was becoming thin and grey. Hravn couldn't help but notice the contrast to Enisant. He shook Hravn's hand with a firm grip and said, "Riocus, I'm the reeve. With your man and your hound, I don't think we need my men to escort us. Come, we'll collect my horse from the stables. I'll explain how I work whilst we ride."

"We'll call at Schirebi and Elreton first, then return by Esebi. They are some of our more productive manors." Riocus bade Orme a brief good-day in halting English then, gesturing to Hravn to ride next to him, tweaked his reins and rode off towards the outer bailey gate. The reeve seemed more interested in Hravn's Cumbric background than in explaining his job. "I know others speak a similar tongue to mine, but did not know that they lived so far north. My uncle was a merchant and a seaman. He traded with Curnow and the lands of the Cymru, and said that the people there spoke with a common tongue."

Hravn felt immediately at ease with Riocus, and laughed. "It's strange. The English call the Cymru 'Wealas', which means foreigner, yet it would appear that the English are now foreigners in their country." Hravn spoke with an assurance and friendliness he didn't feel, finding it hard to speak as a Cumbric, and not as an Englishman.

Riocus warmed to his theme. "The old tales of my people intrigue me. Some are written down, but most have been passed from father to son. It is said that we Bretons once fled from the Saxons when they took the lands in the south of this island of Britain. It is where the name for my people comes from. It was a time of much fighting and honour, with a great Breton king called Arthur. Have you heard the stories?"

Hravn shook his head, intrigued. "No, not of Arthur, but my father's mother says that Cumbraland was once a kingdom called Rheged with a king called Urien, then the Bernicians came from Northumberland, followed by the Norse. The three peoples now share a common land, and look to the Scots' King.

Riocus laughed and slapped his thigh. "Ha! I see we have a lot in common, Hravn. Both our peoples have suffered at the hands of the English and then the Norse. He reined to a halt and turned to Hravn, suddenly serious. Orme stopped behind them, bemused. "The

Normans are like your Norse, maybe worse. They are the same pirates that came and stole lands and gold. We Bretons might fight alongside them, but many of us do not trust them. It's best you understand that. When they came, they took Frankish lands, took the daughters of the powerful for their wives, and set themselves up above the Franks. We cannot afford to have them as our enemy so we live alongside them. When Duke Willian took the English crown, it was a chance for many of us to make a better life, but I am not a Norman – remember that!" He spat.

Riocus smiled at Hravn's look of discomfort. "Do not be surprised. I serve the Count and his family, as my family has always done. He is the greatest soldier I know and a strong leader. When his cousin, the Duke, bade him join him in his quest for the English crown my destiny was sealed."

Hravn nodded and frowned, trying to understand. He said, "As you know, I am not from here, but the Earl, whom I serve, held many lands which were ravaged by the Count and are now forfeit. Is that the mark of a great leader?"

Riocus's eyes narrowed as he studied Hravn's face. "I will show you. You will see how the Count manages his lands. The people hereabouts are worked hard, but do not starve. You need to understand that they brought this upon themselves when they rebelled against their king. The Count was firm, but shrewd and fair. He made an example of some, but has kept English lords in charge of many of his manors and makes sure that sufficient food is produced to sustain the manors and his men-at-arms. Other Norman lords were brutal in their bloodlust. Their arrogant disregard for the future has meant that there are lands adjoining those of the Count that cannot sustain life and will be desolate for years to come. That's the difference between Norman and Breton."

Hravn nodded, stern-faced, thinking. He understood the complexity of the politics and wanted to avoid further discussion for fear that it would compromise him. "Come, lead on," he said at last, "it seems that I have a lot to learn."

The efficiency with which the reeve conducted his business surprised Hravn. His English, although faltering, was enough to get by in a brief conversation, and brief conversations were all that were needed. There was no attempt to get to know the people, nor to understand their needs, but simply to collect taxes. Hravn wondered if he was really needed. Though it was obvious that the reeve wouldn't be able to discuss a disputed matter, he rather doubted that the cowed villagers would speak against him.

Upon leaving Elreton, Riocus caught Hravn by surprise. "Make sure you only ever take that which is due. I had an under-reeve, Iusti was his name, I know he was taking double and keeping gold for himself. He disappeared before I could question him."

"Disappeared?" Hravn asked with a questioning innocence.

"Yes, only a few weeks back, along with his men, and no sign of them or their horses. I had my men search, but nothing."

"But why?" Hravn persisted. "Perhaps he took the proceeds and fled?"

Riocus laughed. "Possibly. If he knew I was to speak to him he may have feared the Count's wrath..."

"...or could the people of risen against him?" Hravn interrupted.

Riocus shook his head. "Do you really think so? You saw them just now, there is no spark in them. English! As you say, foreigners in their own land now."

As they rode on in silence Hravn felt a surge of relief.

*****

"Follow me, the Count will want to meet you, Orme too." Riocus's friendly aside, as they passed their horses into the care of a couple of stable-lads, caught Hravn unawares. He hadn't anticipated an informal summons, but he seized the opportunity to gain further access to his enemy's sanctum.

The Count sat on a low dais at one end of the great hall that was next to the room in which Hravn had met Enisant. The contrast could not have been greater. Embroidered tapestries, with scenes of hunting and, Hravn surmised, the Count in battle, hung from the walls. The Count's high-backed wooden chair had an almost throne-like appearance. This image was contradicted by the broad table in front of the Count, covered with an unscrolled map and several other documents. Enisant sat next to the Count and both looked up as the man-at-arms at the door announced the reeve's presence.

"Ah, Riocus. This must be Hravn of Ravenstandale, the Earl's man." He rose, stepped down from the dais and held out his hand in greeting. "Welcome." Hravn stepped forward, surprised and rather unsettled, by the informality. Orme took the leash from Hravn and stood back, holding Sköll close. The Count was tall, robust and, Hravn supposed, in his early thirties. With combed red hair, down to the base of his ears, and a thick well-trimmed beard, it was obvious where the sobriquet 'Rufus' came from. The Count's intense pale blue eyes held Hravn. They were the iron fist within the velvet glove of the informal welcome.

"Tell me of yourself, and what news of my friend Gospatrick? Is he much troubled by the Scots' King?"

Hravn fought a moment's panic as he strove to collect his thoughts and keep his reply as close to the truth as he could. The Count's scrutiny warned him that there was deliberate purpose behind the innocent question; he already knew the answer he sort. "The Earl is well, My Lord, I saw him only a few months back, when he came from Bebbanburge to Carleol." Although Hravn had never been to the principle Cumbric town, he was sure that the Count hadn't either. "The Scots are, as far as I know, quiet at the moment. They harried Cumbric lands along the Tyne a year ago, when the Earl was engaged elsewhere, but nothing since. My family's lands are well away from that border though, in the south of the vale of the Eden, towards Lauenesdale, alongside those now claimed by your king."

"And what of that border? It lies due west of my lands here, does it not? Is it peaceful?" Hravn was sure that the Count would know the state of the border, particularly in the Norman lands of Lauenesdale. He decided to tell a half-truth about his time with the Pendragons.

"Indeed, it does my lord. I would be wrong to say that it was peaceful. We have long had trouble with reavers, silvatici I think you call them, living in the remoter valleys and raiding into Norman and Cumbric lands, but it has been quieter there this past year since we slew one of their leaders."

The Counts eyebrow twitched, "Ah! Silvatici. Yes, a curse upon them. From what you say, they are an enduring problem. I had thought that they were perhaps one of our own more recent making - if you understand my point?"

Hravn smiled thinly and shook his head in reassurance. "No, my lord, they are more a legacy of the strife between English and Norse, with people taken from vills and sold to the Dyflin slavers." He felt surer of himself and couldn't resist a dig at the Norman occupation. "Though, I expect that those newly disposed hereabouts may want to exact a revenge."

The ice-blue eyes flicked again to Hravn's and chilled his new-found confidence. Had he said too much? "And there you have it, Hravn, my point precisely. I was just saying to Lord Enisant, the silvatici are the consequence of my over-zealous Norman brothers' actions. We must temper how we deal with the people on my lands."

The blue eyes warmed as quickly as they had frozen. The Count placed an arm around Hravn's shoulders and said, "Come, share a cup of wine with me and tell me more about the history of your people. I would know more about how they relate to mine. Have your man join us. Riocus, you too. I know this topic is a favourite of yours."

*****

Ealdgith heard the bells ring for Terce, and waited to allow time for the priest to attend to his duties, then walked with Frida down the dusty part-cobbled track from Richemund to Hindrelag. Both women wore silk

249

dresses and felt distinctly out of place as they passed rag-clad women who carried firewood. As they walked Ealdgith tested Frida with questions about Morlund and life on Gunnar's manor. They couldn't risk betraying themselves with ill-considered answers to probing questions.

The church door hung open. Ealdgith felt suddenly at home as she stepped into the small wooden hall with its low shingle roof and squat wooden tower. Two brass bells were suspended from a scaffold that protruded the top of the tower wall.

"Father, are you within?" Ealdgith called, not wishing to disturb the calm sanctuary of the church. If Father Ealdnoth was still the priest, she would have to great him warmly and explain her presence. Whilst she had fond childhood memories of the family priest, she rather hoped that he had moved on. It would make lying so much easier.

"Yes, here, by the alter. Wait, I will come to you." An elderly, stooped, man, bald with thin grey patches of hair clinging to the side of his head, walked stiffly towards them in the dim light. Ealdgith saw partial recognition and confusion in his eyes. She took a breath and spoke first.

"Father Ealdnoth. I had thought never to see you again. Your church, at least, has not changed whilst I have been away. How are you?" The old man wobbled slightly, seeking the support of a roof-post to hold onto. Ealdgith turned to Frida, "Quick, a chair." She stepped forward and held the priest by the arm to reassure him as Frida placed a chair and then returned with two more.

"Yes, Father, it is me, and this is Frida."

The old priest stared at her. "But you are dead. Surely? Did you not perish, with your family, on that fateful day?"

Ealdgith held his hands to reassure him. "No, I am here. Alive and not a wraith. By good fortune my mother had sent me to live with my uncle, the Earl, and to serve his wife as a maid. Do you recall that he was here for the Yuletide feast?"

The old man nodded, slowly.

"I was to learn more womanly ways. I escaped my family's fate, for that I am grateful. When the Earl heard of their death he became my guardian. I met a Cumbric lord and he agreed that we should marry. My husband is here now to serve the Count as a translator. He speaks Cumbric, English and Norse. I did not know it, but Cumbric has much in common with Breton and the Earl thought it might help our people if they could make themselves understood by their Breton overlords – though of course he didn't suggest it in quite those words when he spoke to the Count."

Father Ealdnoth smiled at last. "Much has happened, My Lady, as you must know. I serve my people, as you would expect, but I must also serve the Count and his Constable. It is a delicate path but I would rather work with them. If I fail I am sure that a Norman priest will replace me. That, I cannot permit. Our people have travails enough."

Ealdgith was reassured by what she heard and glad of the opening. "Father, maybe I can help. Whilst I have been away I have learned many of the healing skills. Some, I know, the Church does not favour, but healing is a way in which I can help. Perhaps I can assist you and administer to our people from the church." She hesitated, not wanting to give false hope to the priest. "Whilst I can, that is, for I cannot say how long my husband will serve the Count until he is called back by the Earl."

The old priest continued to hold Ealdgith's hands and regarded her with an intensity that surprised her. He spoke at last, "Thank you, My Lady. Yes, that would help. There are those who would benefit from your attention. I will have them come to the church." He hesitated. "I do not think it wise for you to venture far by yourself, even with that hound. There are too many men-at-arms and mercenaries about these days. They would not care about your status." Ealdgith glanced at Frida. It was a salutary reminder.

"Shall we return on the morrow, Father, and perhaps serve daily from Terce to Sext?

*****

Hravn read the excitement and enthusiasm in Ealdgith's face when he returned to their room in the inn. He held his finger to his lips and whispered, "Let's go for a walk down to the river. We can't talk here, there are too many ears and not enough walls."

Haerfest and Winter

Chapter 20

Days passed, and became weeks. Hravn and Orme rode with Riocus on most days to visit the many manors across the Count's vast estates. They even stayed overnight in cramped accommodation in the rebuilt castle at Euruic when taking tax from the Count's manors at Cliftune and Fuleford. It was a testing and intimidating experience for them both. Although they couldn't converse, Hravn knew that the Normans considered his Cumbric blood to be of no account. It was so different to his respectful, almost friendly, relationship with the open-hearted Breton.

Ealdgith and Frida throve on this opportunity to help the sick. Though few recognised Ealdgith, word soon got out as to who she was. Frida's natural practicality helped too. The respect, and gratitude, of those who had lost so much and now barely survived on a minimal diet almost brought her to tears. As she worked closely with Father Ealdnoth, she found that she was becoming as much a counsellor as a healer. Soon, she began to challenge Hravn to raise the matter of unpaid labour that their people were forced to provide for their lord.

When Hravn spoke about this with Riocus, it was with a great deal more tact than Ealdgith had shown. The blunt logic of Riocus's reply was hard to argue with. The northern English had rebelled against their king and they would never be allowed the opportunity of doing so again. This, the Normans would ensure. They needed enough food to sustain the garrisons that now held the land. The people would produce that food and enough extra to keep themselves alive. If there were too many people then some would have to starve, or move elsewhere. But, as Riocus kept emphasising to Hravn, Count Alan was not brutal. He knew the value of labour and he foresaw the day when he would demand military service from the people on his land. He would not, therefore, grind them down in the manner of his Norman colleagues, nor would he be overly generous. This new system had no need of free-men. They needed villeins; men who were bound to their lord. Each allocated a small holding of land to farm for his own needs and who gave a set number of days' labour free at their lord's demand. It worked, which was all that mattered. All Hravn could do was shrug and say that thank God that he had land in Cumbraland, where he could live in harmony with his people. If only this were true, he had thought to himself.

*****

"It's Hlafmaesse Day tomorrow, Hravn," Ealdgith told him with a smile as soon as she returned from helping at the church. "Father Ealdnoth's doing what little he can to give loaves to the needy, which means just about everyone in Hindrelag." Ealdgith referred to the traditional loaf mass with which they celebrated the end of the hungry period that preceded the grain harvest. "It'll be a poor do, though, with so little to spare."

Orme caught Hravn's eye from where he sat on the other side of the trestle table, and raised a questioning eyebrow. Hravn sat back, pursed his lips and narrowed his eyes in thought. Suddenly, his face brightened and he drew Ealdgith to him. "Now, there's a coincidence, Orme? We just happen to know where there is grain to be had."

254

Orme chuckled. "Do you mean the grain that was taken as tax just yesterday and passed to the garrison baker?"

"The very same." Hravn smiled at Ealdgith as she sat on his lap, and asked, "How many loaves do you think Father Ealdnoth might want?"

"More than just the five barley loaves Our Lord had to feed the five thousand," she quipped, before adding, "but...yes, I can see what you are thinking. It will cost us."

"Come on Orme." Hravn squeezed Ealdgith and stood up quickly, "Let us see that fat baker and place an order. We'll just say that they are needed for the church. The Count can hardly complain that I'm giving his grain back to his people if I am paying for it, can he now?"

Early the next morning Hravn and Orme, accompanied by Ole, led their two pack ponies to the bakery in the outer bailey and stuffed several score warm loves into the saddle panniers. The baker, ruddy-faced from too much good living, was a Saxon whom Orme had found out had served the Normans since a little after the death of the old king. He stood, smirking, avariciously tossing Hravn's silver coins in his hand. "I shan't ask what you want with so many loaves, my Lord, but your business is welcome anytime."

Ealdgith and Frida were already in the church helping Father Ealdnoth prepare. The elderly priest turned towards the door as the smell of freshly baked bread preceded Hravn's entry. Tumbling an armful of loaves onto a table he said, "Ask not Father, but the Count has had more than his fair share of our people's grain. At least now you can lead them in celebrating Hlafmaesse Day.

Hravn's early morning good humour didn't last much beyond mid-day. They took the track towards Ghellinges then on, northward across the old Roman road, to the vills bordering the Tees. As they passed through woodland devastated by recent logging, Hravn was all too aware that this area, at least, would not sustain hunting for a long time to come. He turned to Riocus, his casual question laden with meaning. "With all this felling, I can't see that there can be much wildlife in the woods hereabouts. Where do the lords hunt? Surely they must ride with hounds or a hawk?"

Riocus laughed. "Of course, they do; just try keeping a Norman lord away from the hunt. The Count would have a rebellion on his hands, and we've all had enough of those. This was hunted out 'ere the end of Lencten, but there is virgin woodland on the hills to the west. Some have already started to hunt it, though I hear that the Count intends to make it his own and take control of it."

Hravn glanced away and strove to keep his emotions under control. He took a deep breath and turned back to Riocus. "His own? Surely all the land is under the Count's control anyway?"

Riocus slowed to a halt and turned to Hravn. "I'll explain. The Count holds the land for the King, and then other Lords hold the land for the Count. However, he doesn't control who lives on the land, in particular the woodlands; and now we have the silvatici. It was Enisant's idea, but favoured by the Count." Hravn nodded, dreading what he was to hear. "The King has issued a new decree, called the Forest Laws, that will ensure that the Count can control the silvatici and please his lords."

Hravn looked briefly at Orme, by whom he was being watched closely, but he didn't understand the exchange in Breton and Cumbric.

"Forest?" Hravn asked. "Is that not just woodland?" Riocus shook his head. "No, and that's the brilliant simplicity of the Forest Laws. Forest is anywhere that the King deems to be a hunting area, be it woodland, scrub, moorland or even farmland. It all comes under the control of the King and, through him, the Count."

The implications of what Riocus said sank in. Hravn felt suddenly sick, but he strove to sound dispassionate and supportive. "Ah! So, if the Count has full control of the land he can control who lives there, and his lords can hunt it at their pleasure...and, if I understand you correctly, any silvatici living in the woods could be hunted too."

"Hah! You're shrewd, Hravn, and quick; exactly right". Riocus laughed, his eyes alight with excitement. "But there's more. The law now states that trees cannot be cut down for burning and that people in the forests cannot own dogs or bows and arrows. The punishment for hunting deer, all of which will now belong to the King, is blinding. Anyone living there without permission will be outside the law, and can be killed."

Hravn gave a low whistle, "That's harsh! But I see how it will stop the silvatici and any who support them. So, where will the Count's new forest be?"

Riocus shrugged and waved his arm to indicate the woods to their left. "Here, almost. It'll be all the woodland and upland, west of the track through Ghellinges."

"But surely there must be some who live there?" Hravn's voice showed genuine concern.

Riocus pulled a face. "I dare say there are, but as I have said before, the Count wants his people to work on productive manors downriver from Richemund. If anyone is living in the forest they can move...or be declared outlaws. The choice is theirs, but I know what I would do."

"When will this happen?" Hravn spoke too quickly.

Riocus did not, however, notice Hravn's haste to know more, and continued, "Soon, but not for a few weeks at least. The Count has been called to a meeting in Euruic with Odo, the King's half-brother. He is ruling whilst the King is in Normandy. The Count's told Enisant to wait until his return. Why? Are you keen to join the hunt?"

Hravn shook his head dismissively. "No, just interested. How will the forest be managed?"

Riocus tweaked his reins to make his horse walk on. "Come, we have work to do. But to answer you, there is a vill called Langethwait. It's in the dale beyond the woods, but within the area to be declared forest. The people there will be told to manage the forest. They pay little enough tax as it is. With a bit more work they should be able to pay more back to the Count, and be thankful for it."

Hravn rode on, his mind in turmoil. All their plans, all they had achieved, all would be destroyed. Thank goodness that The Bear was planning to move his people. They could no longer wait until the end of haerfest, that was a luxury. They must move now, and he must get word to The Bear. He had a sudden, panicked, thought: did Enisant know about the settlements?

"You said that it would control the silvatici. Do you think that there are any in the woods?"

Riocus paused before replying. "Maybe. The Count thought not, they all seem to be to the south, in the hills beyond Ripum, that's where all our trouble has come from. But someone from one of the vills that was harried last year came to see me yesterday. He wanted payment for information. He says that there are people in the woods and that some are armed. I said I'd give him a reward if what he claims is true.

"It could be so; one of our knights disappeared with his squires whilst out hunting a while ago. I've long wondered if the silvatici were to blame. I've told Enisant and we'll wait until the Count is back and decide how we will follow it through." He paused again, to think. "I've probably said more than I should, but the Count may well want you to help with any interrogations. If there are silvatici, he will want them alive, for a while anyway."

"Yes, my pleasure." Hravn lied, with as much as conviction as he could.

It was well into the afternoon before Hravn and Orme returned to the inn. Hravn had told Orme a little about his conversation with Riocus after they left him at the outer bailey, and he left Orme to hold the horses as he went in to find the others. "Ole, grab the horses from the stable please, I want us all to ride down to the waterfalls for a chat." Ealdgith gave Hravn a questioning look. She could tell that he was far from happy.

They tethered their horses to a tree and, at Hravn's request, sat the on rocks by the waterfalls below the high bluff. "Our worst nightmares are coming true," he said, and related what he knew about the Forest Laws and an informant.

Ealdgith was quick to judge. "It'll be Eahlstan, I'm sure, though we could never prove it. Ulf has never trusted him."

"Be that as it may, Edie," Hravn dismissed her accusation, "It hardly matters now. What this means, is that The Bear has two weeks, three at best, to get clear of the settlements and move all his people up the dale. Ulf and Edric will have to move all our equipment too. We have to remain here, for a while at least, as we can't leave the Count just yet. When we do go, it will have to be a clean break, because our departure will raise immediate suspicions about the role of the Earl. Orme, if you and Frida leave before Edie and me it will simply raise questions that I won't be able to answer. You'll both have to stay, and I have to wait until the Count returns from his meeting with Odo. If there is anything I can pass onto the Earl I must find out before we leave. Now, this is what I want you all to do." He looked at them individually, holding their gaze briefly, to impose his will.

"Edie and Frida. Take Ole, tomorrow, and go to Ulf; then take Ulf to The Bear. I want Ulf to understand my plan before he talks to my fader. Pack all our spare clothes and take them with you. We have to be ready to leave the inn at no notice, so we need a minimum with us, and what we do keep with us we will pack ready. You will have to stop working with Father Ealdnoth within the week. When we flee, it might be a case of Orme and me coming to the inn, collecting the three of you, saddling the horses and going. I need to know where to find you. I know it will be boring, but I can't see how else we can do it." He paused. "Stay overnight with Ulf if you need to. There's a lot to do and a fair distance to ride, too."

"Ole, keep the horses and ponies prepared, fed and watered, at all times. Scrounge spare grain and pack it in the panniers. Our animals are going to be worked hard and will need whatever food we can give them."

"Orme, stay with me at all times. As soon as I judge it's time to go I might find an excuse to release you so that you can get back to the girls. I might have to follow on once I escape Riocus."

"Now, Edie, tell Ulf that he has to persuade my fader that any haerfest that hasn't been gathered will have to be forfeit. All his people have to be clear of the woods before the Count enforces the Forest Laws. Riocus trusts me. He has even suggested that I help them interrogate any silvatici that they capture. I should be able to find out when and how the Count proposes to clear the forest. That will be the trigger for our departure. The Bear has to understand that he has to be clear of the woods by then. Tell him that I suggest that he moves the outlying settlements first, particularly the women and children, the men should stay to do the heavy lifting. Ulf and Edric can shuttle back and forth to Hale and Fytun, and get the spare weapons and suits of mail there. None of us can stay in the woodland now."

Hravn paused to take breath. "It's really that simple." He shrugged and held his hands palm up, "Any questions."

They shook their heads, speechless, glum.

*****

Two days later Ealdgith and Frida returned to the inn. Hravn was waiting for them, having persuaded Riocus that he needed time to himself to speak to a couple of the Richemund merchants. Ealdgith sank wearily onto the hard mattress and wiped her brow. "Phew, it's hot!"

Hravn glanced warily at the entrance to their stall. Frida hovered in the doorway, "It's alright, there's no one about. I'll keep watch whilst Edie fills you in."

"The Bear understands. He's not happy at losing the last of the haerfest, though most is in already. He rightly fears for their ability to survive the winter but, as he said, it's better to face the possibility of death in a few months than the certainty of death in a few weeks. Ulf is making a plan with Edric. He will keep a sword, crossbow and mail for everyone at the cave and move all else. He knows where our gold and jewels are and will keep them safe. Oh, by the way, Cyneburg and Adelind are living with him at the cave now, too."

Hravn gave Ealdgith a tired smile. "I'm glad. I thought she might. You've done well Edie, I thought my fader might be difficult."

Ealdgith cleared her throat. "He was, and still is, a bit. He insists on giving each of his settlements the choice of fleeing up the dale, moving to one of the wasted vills such as Grinton, or submitting to bondage in Richemund. I told him how hard it is for the people here, but he said that it is a choice that they must make, he can't do it for them. I fear that it will slow down the move."

"Hel's teeth!" Hravn struck the palm of his hand with his fist. "Fader's sense of fair play will be the death of him yet. If people leave the settlements and come to

Hindrelag now, Enisant will know that there are people in the woods and he may act before the Count returns."

"Where's Orme, by the way?" Ealdgith asked, suddenly.

"Oh, he's over in the outer bailey, picking up the gossip from the tradesmen and keeping an eye on the castle."

"Er! No, he's not!" Ealdgith laughed as Orme burst through the inn door.

"Hravn, the Count's back. He rode in apace, with his retinue following behind. Should we -"

 "- go and see what we can pick up?" Hravn interrupted and started to stand, until Ealdgith gently pushed him back onto his seat.

"No, wait, both of you. Wait until he calls for you, if he needs you, that is. Otherwise all you'll do is raise suspicion. Enisant is no fool. I'm sure he has his doubts anyway."

Hravn relaxed. "You're right Edie. Orme, we'll take our time, wander back over, and then see if Riocus wants us. We'll soon get a feel for anything that might be happening."

Ealdgith had been right to advise caution. Riocus was in a meeting with the Count's counsel. Something was very obviously up, judging by the coming and going of messengers, but the routine of the Count's hall wasn't upset. They waited, wondering. Eventually Hravn kicked the ground in frustration and turned to Orme, "We can't waste the day fretting. Come on, let's get the girls and go for a ride."

They didn't see Riocus until the next day's normal Terce-time meeting. Instead of riding off on their routine rounds Riocus gave Hravn something of a conspiratorial look and said, "Let's take a stroll over to look at the work on the castle, it's going to be one of the strongest I've yet seen. In stone, on a high rock above a river, it's just like some the Duke has had built back in Normandy."

Hravn glanced at Orme, and followed. Riocus was as open as ever. Hravn could only suppose that it was because he enjoyed the thought that their two peoples might once have been one, and that he felt he could trust Hravn as a kinsman.

"You probably saw all the rushing around yesterday. I'm going to be tied up for the next couple of days, so your time is your own. The Count's summoning all his lords, the English ones too, but he won't need you for the meeting." Riocus paused, and Hravn rather sensed that the reeve was telling him something in confidence.

Riocus continued. "He said that Bishop Oda was as bullish as ever. Apparently, he is busy hammering a rebellion in the Nordfolc fens. By all accounts it's the last in the country and the King is now going to start looking further afield. He said William is planning to return from Normandy in the New Year and then campaign against the Scots. The Count is to tell all his lords to prepare to provision an army. He doesn't want them to provide men, the Army will come with the King, but he does want them to ensure the safety and sustenance of the Army. The people will be worked hard and we are going to be busy taking payment in kind, stocking the Count's granaries and holding livestock. The Count is also going to move against the silvatici and ensure that all the open areas are clear. The Forest Laws will certainly help."

The Breton grinned at Hravn. "Keep all this to yourself, for now, but you are certainly going to be needed. I expect there will be some objections to overcome when we take more payments from the vills, and the Count will certainly need you if we do have silvatici to interrogate. Enisant will make sure that they speak, we'll need you to understand what they say."

Hravn fought to control a surge of anger, striving to keep calm and supportive of the reeve. "Of course, I'm not squeamish when it comes to torture, but what of my lord, the Earl? How is he to be involved?" Riocus shook his head. "He is not, as yet anyway. That is why the Count has not asked for your services to explain this to his English lords, and why I am telling you in confidence," Riocus hesitated, "Odo does not share the Count's faith in Gospatrick. He says that he is too close to the Scots and cannot be trusted. The King will not risk relying on him for support."

Hravn nodded. "I can see why, though surely the North's rebellion is behind us now that the Earl has sworn fealty to the King."

Riocus shrugged, "That's as may be. I'm only telling you because I am going to have to involve you, so its best you understand, then we can continue to work together."

He turned, clasped Hravn on the shoulder and headed back towards the hall. "Come. We'll meet again in three days. By then the lords will have been told and I will have a plan as to how we will raise the extra taxes."

*****

"Oh God!" Ealdgith exclaimed, when Hravn explained what Riocus had told him. "We can't stay now...and I fear that my uncle will be at risk too. Don't you see? It's obvious that the King doesn't trust him and, if he wins against the Scots, just as he beat the English, what need will he have of the Earl to hold his northern border?"

Hravn nodded, glumly. "I know Edie, I know. If the Scots succumb to the Normans, there will be no northern border."

Orme was equally grim-faced. "Edie's right. We can't survive here once the Count starts to clear all the woodlands."

"I agree, it's almost time. We'll use the next couple of days to speak to Father Oda. He needs to get a message to the Earl. I'm going to see my fader too, and urge him to move now, regardless. Edie, we'll quietly warn Father Ealdnoth, he should tell the people to start to hoard what they can. Orme, we'll keep to our meeting with Riocus, discover the outcome of the Count's meeting with his lords, and then we should cut and run."

They nodded agreement.

Chapter 21

Hravn and Ealdgith made the most of their three-day break. They had gone immediately to see Father Oda, who had assured them that the Earl would be informed within a week. The priest had looked sad when Hravn explained that they would be forced to flee the woodlands because of the Forest Laws and imminent campaign against the silvatici. "Tell the Earl to expect us in Bebbanburge before the year is out", Hravn had said as they left, adding "and get the people to start hoarding and hiding food".

The Bear had understood the urgency for action, saying that he would have the answer from the settlements by the end of the day, but that he was assured some had already started to leave. They had even managed to catch up with Ulf, just as he was leaving to lead the first of many pack-horse trains up the dale. Hravn had been thankful for the opportunity to get back to Wasfelte. He knew that he had neglected his moder for many months and he was grateful they were able to spend some time talking about how she would adapt to the change, and that she was taking Bron with them.

As a result of his frenetic three days, Hravn felt a little more optimistic that he would be able to stay one step ahead of the Count when he next went to meet Riocus. The reeve was late and Hravn was standing at the top of the steps into the hall, joking with the master-at-arms, when a young Breton household knight he had seen several times before, left Enisant's room, beaming. The Breton nodded curtly at Hravn, and interrupted their joke. "Send for my squire and have him warn off a dozen men-at-arms immediately, they'll need mounts too."

The master at arms forgot Hravn, and faced the knight. "Certainly, my Lord de Camois, but why the urgency?"

De Camois laughed. "We've got them, at last, those pig-shit 'men of the woods'. Enisant said two peasants came to the master mason yesterday, looking for work. They'd lived in the woods for a year or more as part of a much larger group that is now moving on. They're gathering at a place called Wasfelte. Enisant wants them rounding up and bringing in. I'm to take the peasants as guides, and to identify the ring leaders. We'll have them yet." He left, bounding down the stairs two at a time.

Hravn gasped and muttered, "Tell the reeve I'll be back later," but the master-at-arms was already heading down the corridor, calling for his runner. Hravn turned, leapt down the steps and called Orme, "It's too late! Some bastards have sold out to Enisant. He's sending a mounted party to Wasfelte now, to round everyone up and take the leaders." Orme gaped, lost for words, his face pallid as Hravn told him what to do. "Keep watching, follow when they ride out and see which track they take, then come back to the inn. I'm going there now. We'll be ready when you return." He clasped Orme's wrist. "Now, go!"

Leaping onto his horse, Hravn galloped out of the gate and back to the inn, his mind in turmoil. Ole was in the stables. "Ole, we go now! Ready the horses and get the saddle bags on the ponies." He ran inside, ignoring the inn keeper and pushed open the screen to their room. "Edie, Frida. Change into your riding clothes. We're leaving. There's to be a raid on Wasfelte." As Ealdgith ripped off her dress Hravn anticipated Frida's question.

268

"Orme will be here once he's confirmed which route is being taken." He hefted a saddle bag onto his shoulder and strode out to the stable.

Orme returned moments later. "They've taken the Mersche track."

"Hel curse them! We'll have to go by Hulders-wold. We'll never be able to warn fader now."

They left within minutes. The inn keeper watched, perplexed, doubts forming.

Hravn led, at a gallop. He knew they would attract attention, but wasn't worried. He had no intention of returning to Richemund. The others followed, barely keeping pace, even the hounds lagged. The speed of their flight demanded his attention and helped Hravn focus his mind. He slowed, then stopped, as the track past the gallows-field steepened. Ealdgith caught up with him at last.

"We need a plan before we rush headlong and compound this disaster."

"I know, Edie, I know. We just had to get away from Richemund. I couldn't risk Enisant or Riocus seeing me, or finding us. If they know about Wasfelte, what else have they been told?"

Ealdgith nodded. Orme watched; he had his own thoughts but wouldn't interrupt.

Hravn took a deep breath to calm himself. "We have to accept that De Camois will get to Wasfelte before us and that we will have no control over what happens there. I assume The Bear will be there, probably with more of our people than normal. I fear for them whatever happens. If Ulf and Edric are there, then there will doubtless be bloodshed and possibly little we can do. If Ulf and the others are at the cave then we might be able to take De Camois and his men by surprise, but if Ulf is up the dale we will still be too weak to achieve anything." Even as he spoke, Hravn was still thinking about what to do. He looked at Frida and gave her a confident smile.

"Frida, would you and Ole be happy to follow behind and lead the pack ponies from here to the cave? Ole, you know the track, don't you? She nodded, hesitantly. Ole grinned.

"The three of us will ride ahead. If there are problems we will come back for you. You will be safe. We may be gone when you get to the cave, so wait. Don't go to Wasfelte by yourselves. Ole, your job is to look after your sister, understood."

Turning to Orme and Ealdgith, he said, "I want us to get to the cave as quickly as we can. What we do next depends on where Ulf is. Agreed?" They nodded, there was nothing more to say. Hravn spurred his horse, "Let's go."

Hravn's eyes barely registered the track as he tore through the woodland. It was as if Sköll and Hati knew instinctively where they were headed, and they led, the horses following. Ealdgith stayed close to Hravn, Orme was some way behind. When they crossed the Mersche beck at Hulders-wold, and caught glimpses of Orme's tree-cut track markers, they knew that they were almost there. Skirting Ellepigerthwaite, they slowed as they dropped down onto the steep uneven ground leading to the cave.

Hravn held up his arm to call a halt. He was cautious, hearing shouting from the direction of the enclosure, but unable to see through the trees. He was soon reassured. It was Ulf, calling the horses.

"Edie, go with Orme and get yourselves armed. Orme you'll need everything, mail, sword, crossbow, spear, shield. I'll get Ulf."

Ulf turned when he heard Hravn's urgent call and started to run up the hillside to meet him. He interrupted Hravn's shouted warning that Normans were attacking Wasfelte. "I know. Oz was there. He had the sense to get away and warn us. The lads are getting armed and I'm getting the horses."

Hravn grinned as relief swept through him. "Thank Thor you're here, Ulf. I feared you'd be up the dale or worse, embroiled at Wasfelte. Let's get to the cave; we've got to plan this carefully then act quickly. However bad it is down there, maybe we can now do something to recover the situation; otherwise we've lost everything." He embraced the big huscarl, relieved to have him back by his side.

"Oz! Here lad! Come and tell Hravn what you saw." Ulf, shouted towards the group by the cave. The small, wiry man came running. Hravn noticed how exertion made the red scar stand proud against the pale skin of his left cheek; it made a chilling image. Although Oz was several years older, he was nervous of Hravn and held the younger man's status and achievements in awe. He cleared his throat nervously.

Hravn calmed him with a smile and friendly tap on the shoulder. "Come, tell me whilst we walk back to the cave. I need Edie and Orme to be in the picture too."

Oz glanced up at the sun to get a feel for the time of day. "I was riding down to Wasfelte an hour or so ago when I saw a dozen or more mounted men-at-arms in the woods, just in from the clearing. I dismounted and crept closer. They split into two groups, half dismounted and crawled to the edge of the wood, the others rode around to the main trackway in from Hyrst. Then they galloped into the clearing, spreading out and herding the people into the middle. Some panicked and ran, trying to get across the clearing to the stream. It was then that those in the edge of the woods stepped out and shot them down with crossbows. I think three fell."

Oz paused, then looked directly at Hravn. "Lord, they have two of our own with them. I recognise them from Helwith. One of them pointed out your fader and, as they made to seize him, Bada, the smith, stood in front of him holding a stave. He was gutted on the spot."

"My fader?" Hravn asked, trying to conceal the hesitation and worry in his voice.

"They bound him, Lord. Then pulled him into the centre of the clearing. I left then, to come and get Ulf."

"So," Hravn summarised, "there are a dozen of them, and when you left half were mounted and the others had left their horses tethered in the wood. Is that correct?"

"No, Lord. As I left they were dismounting. Some were binding people's hands behind them, others were clearing out the shelters."

"What about weapons?" "Just swords, Lord, and some with crossbows. All wore mail though."

Hravn turned to Ulf. "Whilst I'm getting dressed to fight, can you finish sorting out the men. They'll need horses, swords and crossbows, mail and helms too. Once you're ready I'll brief you all." He ran to the cave, undressing as he went. Ealdgith caught his eye. She was almost ready, with her long hair braided and held under her leather helmet. She wore a long seax on one hip and her short razor-edged seax at her belt. "Valkyrie or wildcat?" he teased. "Take your bow and three quivers of arrows, you'll need them for what I have in mind." Ealdgith smiled back, once she was committed to action the pre-fight nerves and initial nausea gave way to a cold focus.

Hravn's mind was in a whirl as he dressed automatically. In his mind's eye, he could see an aerial view of the clearing, the tracks in and out, the lie of the woodland and the stream and hillside that skirted the southern side.

"We're ready, My Lord." Ulf called into the cave. He addressed Hravn formally, to reassure the men outside.

Hravn stepped out, wearing his mail shirt, hauberk and helmet, with Nadr on his left hip and a long seax on his right. He grinned enthusiastically at the grim nervous faces looking enquiringly at him. "Gather close, whilst I tell you what we are to do."

"We're taking on trained men-at-arms, so be under no illusion just how difficult it will be. But, we have two great strengths: surprise and shock. The bastards have no idea that we are here, armed and trained. If we move quickly and keep the initiative we will keep them on the back foot and force mistakes. If we can kill or wound half of them at the outset we will have them two to one and, with that advantage, the day will be ours.

"My plan is based on what Oz saw, and the very good description of events that he has given me." He nodded his thanks, knowing that public praise would inspire the others. "We are going to move quickly, and we are going to move now. Quite how we engage them will depend upon the situation when we get there. I want us in two groups, so that we can play to our different strengths. Ulf, you, Orme and Edie are with me...and the hounds of course. Some of you have yet to see Sköll and Hati go for a man, but believe me, they are worth ten men each. Edric, you will lead the second group."

Hravn paused, to check their faces for understanding.

"My party will stay mounted. We have all trained in fighting on horseback. If, as Oz saw, they are still dismounted, we will ride them down at spearpoint and then engage with the sword whilst still mounted. Edie, once we've ridden through them stay mounted and use your bow to shower them with arrows. Aim for any flesh you see. I doubt you'll kill any who are wearing mail, but you will distract and disable. Avoid going one to one. Keep the hounds close and use them as you see fit.

"Edric, I want to avoid any of you getting involved sword to sword. Your strength is the cross bow. Follow our charge and dismount. You will be able to reload more quickly on foot. You must identify targets for each of your men, then all of you, aim your shots and kill.

"Once we have the odds in our favour I will then direct what we do next. Now, any questions?"

There was only one. "Prisoners?" asked Ulf.

Hravn pulled a face. "None. We can't risk any escaping either. That goes for the two who betrayed us as well."

He looked at Ealdgith, "Edie, if anyone runs, have the hounds take them down."

Ealdgith caught sight of Cyneburg, watching, grim faced, from the edge of the cave-shelter as she suckled Adelind. She waved to her. "Cyneburg, thank God you're here. Don't worry, Frida and Ole will be here soon with our ponies. Keep them here, with you. We will be back, I promise."

Hravn led the ten-strong band of warriors cautiously through the trees then, on gaining the track, at a gallop down the narrow valley and past Helwith towards Wasfelte. He slowed as they approached the final corner in the track, two furlongs before it opened into the Wasfelte clearing. They heard shouting and occasional screams. Hravn held his hand up to halt hem.

"Hold here, Ulf. Edie, we'll take a look." They jumped down and ran along the side of the track whilst Ulf took hold of their reins. As they neared the clearing they edged into the woods and, bending low, used the shelter of the broader trees to get close to the wood line. Hravn froze and choked a sudden cry. Ealdgith followed the line of his pointed finger. "Edie, The Bear!"

The Norman men-at-arms stood in a loose circle around three score villagers who sat in the middle of the clearing. On the near side of the circle two men held a third by the arms, forcing him into a kneeling position, whilst a Norman beat him slowly but purposefully with a length of knotted rope. They couldn't see his face, but by the size of the man and colour of his hair Hravn knew that it was his father. Hravn assumed that the two informers were the ones holding his father. Three other men lay on the ground, face down, alongside; beaten or waiting to be beaten. De Camois sat on horseback, to one side, watching. De Camois pointed to a woman at the edge of the circle and shouted an order to one of the men-at-arms who promptly dragged her forward. "Moder, no!" Hravn choked a scream. "They're torturing them, to find out about us!"

Ealdgith took charge. "Come. We attack now. Set Ulf against De Camois, take the hounds and free your parents. Orme and I'll hit those on the left of the circle."

They ran back, remounted and Hravn gave quick orders, restating Ealdgith's plan. He then led at a gallop, the hounds running in front and the others following close behind, their horse's hooves churning the dust on the narrow track. Heat, exertion, stress, the tight constraint of his helmet; all conspired against Hravn. He struggled to focus his mind as blood pounded in his temples.

De Camois came into sight. He saw the knight turn at the sound of galloping horses and raise his hand in greeting, doubtless mistaking them for reinforcements. Entering the clearing Hravn eased pace slightly to allow Ulf to move to his right and Orme and Ealdgith to spread out on his left. As De Camois' face came more into focus he saw the smile of greeting change suddenly to one of shock, then anger. He saw, rather than heard, the Norman's shouted command to his men.

Those at the far side of the clearing started to surge forward, pushing their way through the crowd, struggling in the crush of bound, seated bodies. He saw, too, the soldier beating his father drop the rope, draw his sword and raise it above is head. It swung down in an arc and severed The Bear's head in one swift blow. Hravn's wordless scream caught in the rush of air past his head. He grasped his spear tighter under his right arm and focused the tip on his father's killer. The soldier turned to face him, the blade of his blooded sword pointed directly at him.

Sköll and Hati saw the men holding The Bear, they saw the Norman slay him. Experience had taught them the danger of attacking men protected by chain mail; they chose their targets instinctively.

De Camois struggled to rein his horse around to face the attack whilst he tried desperately to pull his kite-shield onto his left arm, in order to protect his body from the imminent spear thrust. Ulf grinned.

Orme and Ealdgith chose the soldiers standing to the left of The Bear's headless body. The men turned to face them. Ealdgith forced herself to keep calm, her mind's eye recalling her practice charge against Ulf. Orme was surprised at how confident he felt; he had killed a Norman before and he would do it again.

The clash of arms swept the first line of Normans away. It was swift, brutal and effective. The hounds struck just ahead of Hravn, taking each of the renegade Saxons by their throats in two swift leaps that threw the bodies towards the crowd. The mass of people recoiled backwards, scrabbling to escape the horses and flailing hooves hurtling towards them, further blocking the way of the soldiers pushing through.

Hravn swerved to the left, clear of the slashing sword blade, and thrust his spear point at the murderer's throat. As it ripped through protective leather and exited from the back of the neck, he continued to turn his horse, drawing his sword as he searched for his next target. He couldn't risk going to his mother's aid or attend to his father's body, not yet.

Ulf continued to grin. He knew that the knight was his. At the last minute, De Camois stopped fumbling with his shield and flung himself down onto his horse's neck, in a desperate bid to avoid the lunging spear point. Ulf simply adjusted his point of aim to take the knight at the base of his neck. As the metal tip tore into lungs and heart the impact pushed the dying knight off the side of his horse. Ulf turned his horse tightly and swung behind the Norman's panicked mount, narrowly missing the packed bodies in front of him.

Ealdgith's heart leapt as she saw the soldier to her front swing his sword in a swift figure of eight pattern. How could she penetrate that arc of flashing steel, and survive? Changing the grasp on her spear from under-arm to over-hand, she raised her arm to give her more reach and, as she urged her horse in a sudden swerve to the left, she threw the spear directly above the flailing sword tip. Ealdgith doubted that the spear thrust would prove fatal. She was right.

Orme, meantime, hurtled his horse directly at his target, twitching his mount's course slightly to the left at the last moment, to ram his spear directly into the man's chest. Orme felt his arm lurch backward as the spear snagged on mail and leather and he let go at the last minute. He swung sharply, in time to to see the soldier on his back, legs kicking, clutching lamely at the shaft that had torn into his lungs and shattered his ribs. Then he saw Ealdgith.

Ealdgith's swerve to the left had slowed her momentum and taken her towards the edge of the clearing. She was struggling to control the winded horse, unsling the bow from her back and fit an arrow to the string. She hadn't noticed the wounded Norman, his right bicep slashed badly, running at her, sword in his left hand. She looked up and shouted, almost screamed, "Sköll, Hati. To me! To me!"

Orme pulled his horse's head around towards the soldier and urging it forward at speed into the man's back. As the soldier crumpled forward Orme swung his sword down, half severing the man's head. He flashed a grin at Ealdgith, turned and galloped to join Hravn.

The hounds leapt through the dense pack of people, snarling, snapping, thrusting their way, desperate to reach their mistress, their jaws wet with the blood of the dead renegade Saxons. Ealdgith took a deep breath, then took stock of the scene in front, seeing Orme join Hravn and Ulf as they circled four Normans standing back to back, parrying sword thrusts. Five more Normans were still struggling to make their way through the press of people. Edric and his four archers were just dismounting behind Hravn, running forward in a line to a position from they could shoot at the five Normans.

Ealdgith saw, rather than heard, Hravn's shouted commands. "Edric, No! Leave them. Take these down first. We'll pull back. Orme, Ulf! Disengage. Now!" Edric's men turned to their right, adjusted their aim and, as the three horsemen wheeled away they loosed a volley of crossbow bolts into the four Normans. From barely ten paces, they could hardly miss. The Normans froze momentarily as they realised their fate, then their bodies pitched backwards with the impact of the heavy steel-tipped bolts. As the crossbowmen bent forward to re-cock their weapons, Ulf dismounted briefly and made sure that the Normans were dead.

"Down! Lie down! Now!" Ealdgith screamed at the those in the crowd who were beginning to stand up. She saw what Hravn intended and worried that their own people would get caught by the next volley. The remaining five Normans realised too late. They turned to flee, back through the crowd. As three nearest the edge of the crowd broke clear and began to run, Ealdgith cantered her horse parallel to them and, guiding it with her knees, loosed arrow after arrow at them in an almost constant stream. Two fell, thrashing, their thighs pierced. The third ran on.

"Sköll, Hati, go!" Ealdgith's scream commanded the hounds, though they needed no bidding. The soldier managed another ten paces before he was pitched to the ground, the back of his neck half severed by powerful wolfhound jaws. "Off! Now! Guard!" The hounds stood over the twitching body, obeying their mistress's command, as she rode across to the two Normans. The men were trying to stand, hampered by the arrows embedded deep in their legs. Ealdgith ignored the pleading eyes and notched an arrow to her bow. "For The Bear," she said, as she shot the arrow directly into the face of the first man-at-arms. "For my people," she said softly, as she shot the second. She felt no guilt or compassion, only contempt and a dull sadness.

Ealdgith turned quickly, as the thrum and thwack of six more crossbow bolts resounded across the clearing. Two remaining soldiers twitched and fell into the crowd.

"On me!" Ealdgith called the hounds to heal as she cantered across to join Hravn. The fight over, he was already dismounting and bending down to gather his mother into his arms. Ulf tore a cloak off one of the dead Normans and placed it gently over The Bear's hacked body. Then, leaving Hravn and Ealdgith to comfort Freya, he called their men together to strip the Normans of their mail and weapons, to tend the wounded and collect the dead.

Chapter 22

Orme returned to the clearing with Frida, Cyneburg and Ole. As Ulf helped Cyneburg down from the saddle she surprised him, asking, "Ulf, can you show me the Normans' bodies, please." She smiled thinly at his frown. "Don't be surprised, you know the ghosts I have to lay to rest."

Ulf led her by the hand to where the Normans lay in a row, on their backs, whilst the men of the settlement dug a long burial pit. Cyneburg walked slowly along the line, then stopped and took a pace back, ashen faced. "Him...and him," she pointed. "They were two of the three." She spat at each of the bodies, then turned away, pallid but not tearful. "Ulf. Don't bury them, please. They aren't fit to be called men, let alone soldiers. You're a soldier, and honourable. They have no honour. Let the animals take them and spread their bones, it's all they deserve."

Ulf put his arm around Cyneburg as he walked her back to Frida. "I understand," was all that he needed to say. He watched Hravn as he stood up, leaving his mother and Ealdgith sitting by The Bear's hut, and walk to the centre of the clearing. At first, he thought Hravn was simply looking at the scene of their fight, then he realised that Hravn was staring into the middle distance, his eyes vacant, unseeing. He went to him, his friend and leader, and placed a hand on his shoulder.

"I'm deeply sorry about your fader. The Bear was the best of men and he died a hero's death, defending his people. He knew the risks and he shared them readily. Don't have any regrets."

Hravn nodded, understanding and accepting. "You're a good man too, Hravn."

"You know how to lead men. Believe me, they have more faith in you than they do in themselves. I would have bludgeoned my way through that situation just now. You didn't, you saw what we had to do and you inspired the men to do it."

Hravn turned, at last, to face Ulf. As he focussed on his huscarl he struggled to focus also on the present. "Thanks Ulf, you're right about The Bear, I suppose I always knew he'd die for his people." He paused, reflecting, "Sometimes I feel as if I too hold all our lives in my hands. Aye, that's why I do spend much of my time thinking about how to plan and fight, and how the lie of the land determines what to do. Today was all about surprise, shock, acting quicker than the enemy can react, then sequencing our action so that we always had the immediate advantage in numbers," He hesitated. "We were lucky, too, and I couldn't have done it without you, Ulf. You're the glue that binds the men together." He held out his hand in thanks and comradeship. "Come, gather the men. There is more that we have to do."

Cyneburg walked over and sat by Ealdgith and Freya. "Ealdgith, join Hravn, you're our leader too. You have to be there, with the men..." She hesitated, "And Hravn needs you. I'll stay with Freya."

Ealdgith perched with Hravn on The Bear's favourite tree stump, as their men drew close. "You did well today. We suffered a great loss." As he spoke, Hravn glanced towards The Bear's covered body. "But we had

282

a great victory too, and that is all due to you, each of you. I knew that we could beat them, and you justified my faith. I will be honest, I feared we would take casualties. The reason we didn't is your skill, your self-belief and, above all, your team work. Thank you." He smiled at each of them. "But," he lowered the tone of his voice, "we have a lot more to do. The Normans are determined to claim the woodland for themselves. They know we are here, and they will react once De Camois and his men don't return."

Hravn could tell from their expressions that some of the men had not anticipated a Norman response. He knew they still had more to learn. Ulf nodded in agreement as Hravn continued. "De Camois's orders were to round everyone up and to bring them into Richemund today. He disobeyed those orders when he tortured my fader here; Enisant wanted to control all interrogation from within the castle. When no one returns by nightfall Enisant will know that disaster has befallen them, he will know for certain that silvatici are in the woods, and he will react swiftly, with considerable force...that is certain."

Ealdgith looked up at Hravn and raised a questioning eyebrow. She didn't know what he had planned. He glanced down, and smiled. "Edie, what is the state of the woodland?"

She smiled, knowingly, guessing his intent, "Tinder dry. We could lose it all with a careless spark. The Count wouldn't like that."

Hravn laughed. "Yes, just so, Edie, just so."

He turned back to the men in front of him. "We will take the fight to the Normans, tonight. Surprise is our ally and the old gods fight for us. Logi will be on our side and ensure the Norns are with us. As Edie says, the woodland is a tinderbox and the wind is from the west. We will create a wall of fire to screen us from Richemund; one that the wind will sweep towards Richemund and threaten the very seat of their power. I don't care if half the woodland is lost if it buys us time to break clear, and get to Fytun and safety."

Hravn smiled at Orme's low whistle of surprise and waited a couple of moments, to let the implications of his plan sink in. "If I were Enisant, I would plan to attack us, here, at first light tomorrow, getting my men into position over night. It will be a clear and star-lit, and so this won't be difficult. We have to assume that he will do just that, and act now to stop him in his tracks."

Hravn looked to his left. "Edric."

"Yes, Lord." Edric tugged thoughtfully at his red-bush of a beard as he scurtinised Hravn with his grey eyes.

"Take your five and build me two fire-walls. Start where Clapyat Gill crosses the Mersche-Richemund track. Split into two teams. One team is to set a line of fires along the edge of the woodland from the gill to this side of Mersche, that should delay any attempt to take us from the southern flank. It's also the way De Camois came and should be your priority. The second team is to work up the gill, then cut across to Hulders-wald. The fires should spread quickly to the Richemund-Daltun track, and block any way in from the east and north. It will take Enisant, and the people of Richemeund and Hindrelag, days to get them under control."

The red beard twitched as Edric grinned. "Hah! Consider it done, Lord. We'll go now and be back by nightfall."

284

Hravn turned to his companions. "Ulf, Orme, gather the senior men from the settlements. They should all be here. Tell them to make sure that they move all their people and livestock here by tomorrow morning. I will speak to everyone then.

"Edie, let Cyneburg care for my moder. Take Frida and see what needs to be done for those who were hurt today. I can see that my fader wasn't the first they beat. I'm going to speak to moder about what she wants to do next, then I will see our ealdmoder and speak to the headman in Hyrst. He has to know what has happened, and what the Forest Laws will mean for his people." As she held her hand up to hold his, he drew her towards him. "Thank you, Valkyrie."

Ealdgith kept hold of Hravn's hand and led him towards where his mother sat. "I think we should speak to her together. She is still in shock. She has lost her husband and stands to lose us when we go to join the Earl." Hravn nodded, he feared it wasn't going to be easy to persuade his mother to take Bron and stay at Fytun.

Later, as he rode back from Hyrst, the setting sun cast long shadows in front of him and great palls of blue-black smoke rose across the eastern sky. The cloying smell of wood smoke was already heavy in the air. Hravn tried to order his thoughts. Freya had surprised him by saying that she would rather remain with the people she knew, and settle in Fytun, which was, she reminded him, a Norse vill. Bron had stoically accepted the news of her son's death and Hravn sensed that she had almost anticipated it, never really believing that the woodland settlements could survive for long. She had thanked him for the invitation to live with Freya, saying that she was sure that she could help the people of Fytun just as she had those of Hyrst. His worry now was what Ealdgith had said to him just before he had ridden off: "We must talk about Frida, there is something you should know."

"Hey! Leofric!" Hravn caught sight of the settlement headman as he was about to mount his pony. "A moment, please."

Leofric turned. "My Lord?" Hravn rode up and held out his hand in greeting. "Leofric, I won't keep you, though I have a favour to ask. The Bear is dead, and my duty to Earl Gospatrick means that I cannot stay with our people once they have moved. They will need someone strong to lead them, until such time at least as they are integrated with the people at Fytun and Hale." Leofric listened, sombre faced. "Could you be that man, Leofric? I have long thought you to be the strongest of my fader's leaders. Can you do this, for our people?"

Leofric paused, then relaxed. "Yes, My Lord, I can, but I cannot impose myself upon the people. Only you can do that. Most know, and respect, you."

Hravn grinned, considerably relieved. "Thank you, Leofric, I know you will serve them well. I will announce this when I speak to everyone in the morning. We will talk before then and plan how we will make the move, I have a few ideas."

Ealdgith waved as Hravn entered the clearing and walked to join him. "I've sent Ole to collect blankets and food from the cave. We will stay here tonight and doubtless Edric and the others will want feeding when they return." She placed her hand on Hravn's arm and turned him to one side. "Now, the matter of Frida. I think that she is with child."

Hravn's mouth dropped open, he was momentarily speechless. "What? Has she told you?"

Ealdgith smiled, "No, for I doubt that she knows herself, not for sure. But I can see the signs. I will talk to her, then she must talk to Orme."

Hravn was still thrown by the news. The thought of sharing childbirth and babies in their primitive conditions worried him. Cyneburg and Adelind were enough of a concern, though he would never complain to Ulf. "Edie, how will we cope?"

Ealdgith smiled at the sound of distress in his voice. "We will cope, never fear about that. Listen, when we leave here we are going to join my uncle. What better place to have a baby than at his hall? Getting there will not be easy, but Frida is fit and can ride. Just because she is with child, she is still capable and it will be several months yet before she struggles." She laughed. "Why do you think that there are so many children? We will help her, we all will. Though you will need to think carefully about the route we take."

Hravn nodded acceptance, then Ealdgith added. "There's one more thing to think about; Aelf told me he wants to come with us, and that means Esma and Ada too. Their sons are with us anyway and Aelf has always lived alone as a woodcutter. He isn't one for village life."

Hravn's reaction surprised Ealdgith. He paused and his mouth broadened in delight. "Really, Edie? That's good, it really is. I can see that when we leave here, we won't be just a war band, we'll be more like an extended family. Aelf's very practical and good at making bows. His sound head, and Esma's motherliness, will help keep the younger lads' feet on the ground and, oddly enough, Ada might keep Ole grounded too." He chuckled. "It's been a long, hard, bad day, Edie, but that really is good news." He gave her waist a tender squeeze, then said, "Right, that helps make my mind up. When we leave Fytun we will go by way of Kelda and then Kircabi Stephan, taking the old roads to Penrith and Carleol. It will be longer, maybe a hundred leagues and could take us a month, but it will be easier and we can pay to stay in inns in the towns." Ealdgith relaxed against him, as some of the stress of the last two months seeped out of her. They would be away from the Normans, at last, and they had a plan for the future.

"We can't relax just yet, Edie," said Hravn, jerking her attention back to the present. "We have my fader to bury."

She nodded and tears moistened her eyes. "I know, I wondered when, but didn't want to ask you just yet." He squeezed her hand. "Come, I asked Ulf and Orme to dig a grave and lay his body there. We will take moder. Will you stand with her whilst I say a few words and cover him?"

The little group walked quietly to the grave. Ulf had chosen the place well; under the shadow of a rowan tree, on softer ground near the beck, where the soil was deeper. Hravn gave a slight gasp when he saw his father's body. Ulf had taken great care to lay the big man on his back on a blanket, cleaned away the blood and reunited the severed head. The Bear's body had been covered with his best cloak, clasped about the throat with a brooch. Hravn was grateful that his father's eyes were closed. It was as if The Bear lay at rest.

Hravn held his mother's hand whilst Ealdgith held the other. He spoke quietly, for them all.

"The life and honour of the dead are carried in the memory of the living. Fader, you inspired us all. Our lives will honour you."

He stooped, lifted a handful of soil and threw it onto his father's body. His mother turned, as Hravn lifted a shovel, and Ealdgith led her by her hand. Ulf and Orme went to help Hravn as Cyneburg and Frida welcomed Freya back to the embrace of her people.

*****

Hravn stood on a cart that Ulf had arranged to be dragged into the centre of the clearing. As he cleared his throat, Ulf banged his spear-shaft against the cart and bellowed, "Listen in!" The crowd fell silent. Hravn was struck at how thin and ragged the people were. He knew then that they would never survive another winter in the forest, even if the Normans weren't hunting them down. He knew too, that the vills of Fytun and Hale would struggle to support them, but at least they would all be better off there. They would have to take with them everything that they had managed to harvest if they were to have that chance of survival.

"Many of you were here yesterday and know what happened. Those who weren't will now know of it. You must understand that our time in this woodland is finished. The Normans know that we are here, there were those amongst us who betrayed us, but that is not the reason why the Normans want us gone. The King has decreed that whole swathes of land, forests he calls them, are to be his for hunting – for the sport of his nobles. Any beast or man in these forests is now his, to be killed at his pleasure...and that means us...you."

Hravn gestured towards the freshly dug mass grave. "We fought a battle here yesterday and, yes, we won.

289

But we cannot do that again. We are too few, and yesterday we were lucky, the Norns were on our side." He pointed to the eastern skyline and the continuous line of smoke. "I have sacrificed half of the woodland, our woodland, to buy time, a few days at most, before the Normans beat the flames and come for us...for you. We must all be gone from here by then."

Many heads nodded assent, but Hravn could see others shake. Someone shouted, "Aye, you speak sense, but where? Into bondage? To the wasted vills from which we fled?"

"No." Hravn held the eyes of the crowd. "Not into bondage. I want you all to keep what freedoms you still have. Edric has been to the vills of Fytun and Hale. Those of you who were from this dale will know of them. They survived the harrying and the Normans have not ventured that far, not yet. The people there will welcome you. I say that you should join them."

A muttering of agreement, then another called. "Lord, you say 'you', not 'we'. What is it that you plan for yourself? Are you to desert us?"

Hravn knew that this question would come. "You are right. My fader led you, and he led you well, but I am not my fader. I serve the Earl, as does Lady Ealdgith, and we must return to him. We cannot beat the Normans here, but the fight continues and I will continue to fight them, as will those who have sworn themselves to me. But you are not warriors, you are farmers, tradesmen...faders and moders. The Bear is dead, but there is still one amongst you who will, and can, lead you and speak for you when you go to join the villagers of the upper dale. I have asked Leofric of Helwith. I have faith in him, so much so that my moder and ealdmoder will go with him too."

He paused, watching, judging the mood of the crowd, then clapped his hands to attract attention. "What say you then?" He opened his arms as if to draw the crowd towards him. "Will you embrace Leofric as your leader and follow him to Fytun and Hale?"

Hravn knew at once that the crowd were with him. With an ominous pall of smoke looming above them, through which the sun shone weakly, they had little option.

"Leofric, aye Leofric and Fytun. We will do as you bid Lord," their answers echoed across the clearing. He beckoned to Leofric to come forward and join him on the cart. Leofric smiled thinly, nodded his thanks to Hravn as he climbed up on to the cart, then began to speak. He had the loud, gruff, voice of one used to shouting at livestock.

"Thank you Lord Hravn, and thank you all. I will lead you to the best of my ability. I will be as fair as I am firm. We will start our journey today, now. Lord Hravn has already spoken to the headmen and they know what is to be done. We will take the route from here to Hyrst then down the scarp to Langethwait, up yon side of the dale and over the fell track to Hale, then Fytun. That will avoid Rie and any eyes there."

He paused for effect, to let the people get to know his voice. "We have this cart, and others that Lord Hravn has acquired these past months, as well as his horses and ponies. The carts should be right for the fell track and will carry all the grain and harvest that we have; smaller livestock too. I want all to be moved by dusk tomorrow, though Lord Hravn assures me that if anything of importance is left he will come back with his men and collect it."

Leofric paused again, to emphasise his next point. "Remember, once we have gone there is to be no coming back. I will not allow anyone here to be taken by the Normans for, if they do, they will doubtless force you to tell where we are."

He turned to Hravn. "Our Lord Hravn and Lady Ealdgith serve the Earl. They have risked much, and taken many Norman lives to help our cause these past months. Their lives would be forfeit, or worse, should they be taken. I will not risk that."

Chapter 23

"Take her, Edie." Hravn spoke very softly. Ealdgith stood five paces away, half hidden behind a high mossy boulder. Her shoulders tensed as she drew the bow string a little further back, then let her arrow fly. Hravn immediately stepped forward, drew, and released a second arrow. The red deer doe winced, staggered, bolted in a death run then collapsed several paces later; two arrows protruding from her heart. The rest of the herd fled through the fellside woods, the stags' rutting interrupted for the third morning running.

The couple turned towards each other, their faces alight with satisfaction. "More meat for the vill, I think we're earning our keep, don't you?" Hravn was ecstatic, "And that was a brilliant shot, Edie. I couldn't have taken her down from there."

He spun, poised to react to the sound of thrashing in the undergrowth below, then relaxed. "Come on Ole, bring the ponies up here. No wonder the deer fled, with all that noise you're making." As he caught sight of the lad's worried face, he added, "Relax, I'm teasing, Edie's to blame for scaring them off. Here, give a hand to lift this carcass."

As they rode back down the narrow, wooded valley, Ealdgith called across to Hravn. "I think we need to move on now, don't you? There's a chill in the air at night and we can't delay if we are going to go over the tops to the vale of Eden."

"Aye, it must be almost Winterfylleth," he called back. They had spent more weeks than they intended settling their people into the vills of Fytun and Hale, helping fell trees to build new houses, and hunting to provide extra food so that the newcomers wouldn't resent the burden they imposed. They had spent time with Freya too. The men of their new extended family, Aelf in particular, strove to build a small cottage for Freya and Bron, with enough room and light for Bron to continue to practice as a healing woman. The people of Fytun were already beating a path to her door and Hravn was content that his mother and grandmother were as well settled as he could hope. He knew that when they rode on, he would probably never see them again. "You're right, Edie. It is time. We'll talk to everyone tonight, and leave the morning after tomorrow."

Hravn became lost in his own thoughts as they trotted along. He realised how stressed he had become whilst working with Riocus; their recent break had done him good, Edie too. Wyrd had continued to look favourably upon them. A storm had hammered the north three days after they fled. It had made a miserable start to their stay in Fytun, but the two-day deluge had not only doused the forest fires, it had also washed away any trace of where they had fled. He had returned to the forest with Ulf a couple of weeks later. Sticking to the high ground between Hyrst and Langethwait they had seen large groups of men-at-arms in both vills. "Bastards!'" Ulf had spat. "They're one step further up the dale."

"'Aye," Hravn had acknowledged, adding "but they have no idea where we went. The most obvious route would be north to Stanmoir and over to Westmoringaland, just as I told the head men of both vills, knowing that they would need to ingratiate themselves with their new masters."

"You cunning young fox!" Ulf had laughed, and clapped him on the shoulder. With that they had turned their backs on the charred, blackened landscape.

As they drew near to Fytun, Hravn rode closer to Ealdgith. "Edie, take Orme with you tomorrow and go to see Frode and Edda at Kelda, and tell them that we will arrive the day after. It would be wrong to surprise them. Not a word to Edric and the others though, I want to test them on the journey up the dale. Take half of this deer with you. It will help Edda feed us all. They were all impoverished enough when we last stayed there."

She grinned, welcoming the chance to spend a little time with her friend from a year ago, then she paused, and said: "By the way, Bron and I spent time with Frida. She will be fine to ride. We think she will have an Ēostre baby." Hravn nodded, smiling; he'd seen the joy in Frida's eyes and the pride in Orme's face. New life heralded new beginnings.

Hravn concluded that evening's discussion about his future plans with a reminder that they were still a warrior band and that although they would be away from the Normans they would be travelling through Westmoringaland and Cumbraland. The Earl had told him that the wilder, eastern, parts of Cumbraland were lawless. They would need to take care.

He caught Edric's eye. "Your band of budding young warriors needs a wee bit more training, don't you think?" He looked at Oz and the others. "You've been idle too long lads, when we go we'll move as a war-band should. Aelf, I want you to be responsible for the safety of all the women, save for Edie of course. Edie, Ulf, Orme and I will lead. Ole, you will ride with us and act as my messenger. Aelf, your group will follow, a half furlong behind. Edric, you will bring up the rear a further half furlong behind Aelf, and take charge of all the pack ponies. I want you to rotate two of your group as scouts, changing them daily. They will ride ahead, using the higher ground to check the route. Ulf will brief them as to their duties each morning, before we ride out. If we do have a problem the four of us will be the first to react whilst Edric's group closes in on Aelf and protects the women and ponies with their crossbows. Oh, and Aelf, see Ulf and get some mail and a helm that fit, and a green cloak. How are you with a crossbow, by the way?"

Aelf chuckled, his leathery face creased with laughter. "I'm a woodsman, as you well know. A bow that I can't fathom, I've yet to see."

*****

The first day's journey was short, a mere half dozen leagues, but Hravn made the most of the opportunity to make sure they all understood the order of march. Ulf worked the two scouts hard, using Ole to relay fresh orders to them. As they wound their way slowly westward, keeping to the north side of the river, the dale narrowed, the way ahead repeatedly hidden by steep bluffs. They skirted the little Norse vills of Gunnar's Saetr and Meuhaker, preferring to keep their own council as to who they were and where they were going.

Just past Meuhaker, Cola galloped back to them, his horse's hooves skidding slightly as he reined to a halt by Hravn. "Lord, the valley splits ahead and there are two rivers. One comes from the north, the other from the west, as we are headed now. I cannot say which is the one to follow."

Hravn gave a wry smile, and Cola guessed that he knew the route already. "Kelda is on the Swale. Rejoin Dudda, one of you go north, the other west, then regroup and decide which of the two rivers is the Swale. Do it within the hour."

Cola touched the side of his head in a gesture of respect and understanding, then wheeled his horse and galloped back to Dudda. He was enjoying scouting; it was challenging, yet reassuring, that Hravn always seemed to be at least one step ahead of them. Hravn turned to Ole. "Tell Aelf and Edric we'll take a break for an hour. Have Edric form up with Aelf, and to post two men on watch." Ole, gave a wide grin and saluted as he had seen Cola do. Ulf sat back in his saddle, chuckling to himself as he beamed at Hravn.

Cola chose his route wisely and in well under the hour he was back, Dudda following, to brief Hravn that the northerly river was indeed the Swale. They should cross a little further up, where there was a ford. After that the river ran through a gorge and they would be best following the high ground over the shoulder of the hill in front. Kelda lay just beyond. He went happily to join Edric for a quick meal, smiling inwardly at Hravn's words of praise.

As they rounded the shoulder of the hill, they looked down upon the vill of Kelda, a familiar and welcoming cluster of low, inter-linked longhouses. A small group stood in the central clearing, where smoke rose from a cooking fire. Ealdgith laughed, "Odda said that she would have venison stewing when we arrived."

"I can almost smell it from here" Ulf smacked his lips and quickened his pace.

The small settlement, which hung on the edge of survival in the remotest of dales, made the party very welcome. Frode clasped Hravn as if welcoming his brother. "My Lord, it is good to see you again. When you left us last year, I thought your plans for resistance were doomed, though I dare not say it. Now, you have a war band and family of followers, with more weapons than I've seen in my lifetime. Edie told us yesterday of what befell you. It is an honour indeed for us to host you."

Hravn stepped back, grinning. "Thank you, Frode. We are privileged indeed to have such friends. We will only stay the one night, though. I want us to get to the vale of Eden, and then to Carleol. Mayhap we'll rest there a few days before heading to Bebbanburge." He laughed, continuing, "Some war band though, we have one lady with child and another expecting one. I'm still training most of my men..." he paused, summoning Ulf over to them, "...if you want to meet a real warrior, then meet Ulf."

Odda had organised the younger women of the vill. Hravn smiled to himself as he watched them serve bowls of venison stew, and was sure they had needed little bidding to cook for his men. He glanced across to where Ealdgith was deep in conversation with Odda, just as she had been a year ago, and marvelled at how two women from such different backgrounds could be such close and immediate friends. He was pleased that Odda drew the other women of his extended family into the conversation, they were bonding well.

"Aelf!" He called to the woodcutter, who was looking rather lost within the company. Come and meet Alfr, he and I have spent many an hour talking about lead mining." Leaving the two together he re-joined Ulf and Frode, "So, which route over to the vale of Eden do you recommend, Frode? I really don't want to tramp across that God forsaken peat moor again."

Frode laughed. "You'd be headed in the wrong direction, if you did. Just follow the river up, go left at the first fork, then right at the second. The ponies will be fine, and those big beasts," he said, eyeing the horses, "will be alright if you take it slowly. There's a pass that takes you down to Nateby and Kircabi Stephan. You'll do it in a day."

Frode's advice was sound. They rode early the next morning, settling easily into their line of march, with the twins scouting ahead. As they followed the second branch of the river up the now very narrow dale, a wall of mist blew across the fell tops in front, dropping in feathery shrouds over their route. Hravn sensed unease and called a halt, signalling for everyone to close in on him. "I doubt if many of you have been on the high tops in the mist before. Fear not, we're crossing into my family's lands and, like a good Herdwick, I'm hefted to the fells. Stay close and, if the mist drops further, keep those in front and behind in sight. Call out if you lose touch. I'll lead for now, the scouts can rejoin Edric." He led off, guiding his horse carefully as he slowly followed the feint track across the grassy, boulder strewn, fell-side. The others followed, shiny droplets forming on their clothes.

The mist cleared as they crossed the pass. A low westerly sun broke through the clouds, casting the high Cumbric fells into dark shadow in the distance, whilst the back-lit, low round hills of Eden beckoned from the broad valley below. Hravn knew that they had time in hand. As they stopped to marvel at the low rolling hills, bounded by fells on all sides, Hravn looked across to

Ealdgith. Tears trickled down her cheeks and he reached out to touch her arm. "Edie, what is it?"

She smiled, sheepishly, and rubbed her cheeks with the back of hand. "Remember, when we rode away from Morlund last year, how I said that I was leaving a place that felt like home? Now, I feel as if I am home again. I know we can't stay, but it is so beautiful, peaceful...I'm being daft. Come, we'll ride ahead and find rooms and stabling for the night."

Hravn, squeezed her arm. "I know, Edie. I thought that maybe you were thinking of the Pendragons and the way they terrorised the valley to our left. I hope that is all behind us now. But, yes, you're right. It will be easier for the two of us to persuade an innkeeper, than for him to be surprised by a dozen mail-clad horsemen on his doorstep. I'll tell Ulf."

Ealdgith was right. The innkeeper was surprised enough to see a man and a woman, both armed, let alone a band of warriors. He was pleased, though, to take Hravn's gold, and even happier when Hravn said that he wanted three men to sleep in the stables. He didn't want to be held responsible for any prying eyes and hands overnight. The sleeping arrangements were rudimentary and Ealdgith decided in the end that all the women should share one room, leaving the men in the other two.

Cyneburg and Frida had both found the long day's riding difficult, especially Cyneburg, who was struggling to produce enough milk for Adelind. Ealdgith arranged for a small bowl of whey to be brought for her and she watched while Esma helped Cyneburg start to wean her daughter. She made sure that Cyneburg drank as much milk as she could, convinced that it would help in the production of her own. Later, she spoke to Hravn and told him that they must plan to stay in an inn every night. They couldn't risk Adelind failing to thrive after all that Cyneburg had endured. He agreed, adding, "Edie, make sure Ulf understands. I rather think Cyneburg will want to keep this from him. He needs to know, and he will understand, there is no shame in it."

Ealdgith smiled, stretched up and kissed Hravn, "You're better men than many, Hravn, you and Ulf."

Their night in Kircabi Stephan set the scene for many nights to come. As they rode north through Aplebi, they joined the old, stone-flagged, pot-holed, Roman road that ran arrow-straight through Penrith to Carleol. Hravn judged their time in the saddle and covered about ten leagues a day and, to ease the strain on both women, stopped at inns or sought sanctuary in small farmsteads along their route. Their ride to Carleol was one of peace and tranquillity, very unlike Carleol itself.

They paused on the low ridge overlooking the ancient city. Only Ulf, Orme and Hravn had ever seen such a sight, on their infrequent trips to Euruic. The others, even Ealdgith, were awed. Smoke from domestic fires hung over the city of tight-packed thatched roofs huddled either side of the wide boat-filled river flowing slowly towards the estuary on the horizon. Beyond the roof tops a red stone wall, and the stumps of collapsed buildings, showed the outline of the old Roman fort and town. A fetid smell drifted towards them.

Hravn called the older men to him. "We'll ride in as one close body. When we find shelter, Edric, keep the lads away from the ale and other temptations and Aelf, keep Ada close. There will no doubt be slavers all too willing to take young girls for sale in Dyflin. I know the trade has been stamped upon, but it still persists."

Ealdgith understood Hravn's concern. They too, had been threatened with sale into slavery only a year before; though she doubted Ada would stray. She had noticed how inseparable Cyneburg and Ada had become, and thought that they had probably talked, shared the horrors of their experiences, and that this had forged a close bond between them. More often than not Ada now rode with Adelind bound to her, to give Cyneburg a rest; whilst the young woman looked upon her as a younger sister.

Hravn found shelter in an old inn that occupied part of a stone building in the old town. The rooms were rudimentary and damp in places, but it provided the space they needed. He and Ealdgith managed to take a small room for themselves, to obtain a little privacy that they had long lacked, and longed for. As they lay, relaxing in each other's arms on the straw-filled mattress, Ealdgith said, "We should stay for a few days and rest. The journey from here on will be harder, and we need to eat well when we have the chance."

"Aye, we've still fifty leagues to go, and we need to buy provisions. I want to have clothes and boots made for those who are still in rags, Aelf and Esma especially." He hesitated, then added, "Edie, you should know we have used up more of our coin than I had expected, all the silver has gone, though there is still gold and the merchant's jewels. We may be more dependent upon your uncle's generosity than we thought, when we reach him."

Ealdgith laughed, "You should have no fear on that account, he's been generous to us so far." She changed the tack of their conversation. "It's paying for a household that costs so much. Have you noticed how everyone has settled into a role? We've become more than just a large family, it's like the old days, back at the manor at Hindrelag."

Hravn took time to answer. "You're right. I hadn't planned it, not consciously, but yes, I see it: Ulf and Orme are huscarls, Aelf my armourer and quartermaster, Edric our Constable with his men-at-arms, Frida your maid, and Ada cares for Cyneburg. Even Esma is now more like the housekeeper." He pulled Ealdgith to him. "And you're my lady, as well as my Valkyrie."

She giggled. "I wonder what Oswin would say? He never did like you calling me 'Valkyrie'." Hravn's kisses stilled further conversation.

Whilst in Carleol Hravn sought directions to Bebbanburge and was told simply to follow the Stanegate until someway past the watershed it was crossed by another stone road leading north. Otherwise, their time there was uneventful, as was their onward journey, until they came to the wall beyond Twisla.

Chapter 24

"Hravn! Stop. See there. Cola and Dudda are coming back. Something's up." Ealdgith's eyes had again beaten them all. Hravn held up his hand to halt the column, and waited, hemmed in by scrubby woodland. The scouts galloped along the stone road, uphill, and halted beside Hravn, almost as breathless as their mounts.

"Lord," Cola spoke for them both. "There's a stone-built town and fort ahead. The stone road runs right through them. I've never seen the like before, mayhap it's from the days of the old people. But there are men there, mounted. Ten, I think, blocking the way into the fort. There's no way around; they are expecting us, I am sure." Hravn nodded, thinking, whilst Ulf edged closer.

"Are they armed?"

"Aye, Lord. Spears and swords, from what we could see, but no mail or bows."

"Do you think it's an ambush? Did they see you?"

Cola answered the second question first. "No, Lord. We tethered our horses and went on foot. The old town lies this side of the fort. It has high stone walls, with a wide arched entrance. From what we could tell, there's a cross track, a little further on, in the middle of the fort, old buildings line the roadway in. There are three men facing our way, on the stone road, just beyond the arch, three more on the junction and two each on the other two tracks, we could see their heads over the top of the collapsed walls. It seemed that they expect us and could send the men at the back by the flank, once we stop."

Ulf interrupted. "Are you sure they are just ten?"

"Aye, we made our way on foot through the houses, there is no one else there, though I can't say what lies beyond."

Hravn gave a grim smile, "Thanks Cola, you too Dudda. You've done well, very well. Stay with us now." He took a deep breath, momentarily lost in thought. "Ulf, Edie, I think Cola's right. It is an ambush. The Earl spoke of lawlessness in the wild lands between the kingdoms, that's pretty much where we are now."

Ealdgith agreed, "We've two options, as I see it. Take a long detour and risk attack elsewhere, or face them down. By the look of it we can't just ride around the fort, the trees are too dense and grow right up to the walls. If Cola's right, we have the edge in numbers."

Ulf scratched his whiskers with the back of his thumb nail, thinking. "Edie's right. We should face them down. You've taught me the benefits of surprise and taking the initiative. They think they will surprise us, whereas it is we who can now surprise them."

Hravn smiled as his plan clarified. "Well said, Ulf. We'll ride towards them, slowly, casually. When we see them, we'll stop short and entice them forward. Cola and Dudda can make their way through the houses and cover our immediate flanks. When I judge it time they can take out two of that vanguard of three with an arrow apiece. The hounds can take others, if needs be. That will reduce the odds to two to one. He waved Ole forward. "Tell Edric to close in on Aelf and give the ponies to Cynburg and Frida to lead. Edric is to flank the women, with crossbows at the ready.

"Cola, Dudda, you've heard the plan. Cola, take the right flank; Dudda, the left. I want to entice that first three-some forward, when we close with them, get in position to shoot at the man nearest you. My signal will be when I look directly at you and nod. Understood?"

They moved off, walking their horses.

The old town enveloped them, as they became hemmed in by collapsed houses overgrown by scrub. It felt to Ealdgith as if the spirits of the old people watched, waiting. The fort-wall loomed in front of them, a gateless archway framed the entrance. Hravn could see three horsemen under the span of the arch. Fifty paces beyond that three more horsemen stood astride the Stanegate. He halted thirty paces from the gate. Aelf and Edric stopped further back, fearful of being outflanked and penned inside the old town. A temporary stand-off ensued.

"Come forward and talk, you cannot expect us to ride into that fort without assurance of safe passage." Hravn shouted in Cumbric. When there was no response he repeated his request in English. Eventually, the three men rode forward. Hravn noticed that the group on the cross-tracks followed, at a distance, and that others moved to replace them. He hoped that he had drawn the opposition into the open.

As the men rode closer Hravn could see that they were ragged, unkempt and gaunt. The leader held a drawn sword, the blade shiny and well honed. "Outlaws," Ealdgith whispered.

"Aye, but well-schooled, they look after their weapons. Take care," Ulf muttered.

The three stopped again, ten paces off. Their leader spoke. "This fort is under my control," he waved his hands at the walls behind him, "as is this beautiful town that you choose to visit...if you want to follow the road then you perforce must enter." His fake smile chilled Ealdgith, and annoyed Hravn, "But, those who visit must pay for their passage, the larger the party the bigger the fee." He took an exaggerated look at the string of horses behind Hravn. "Quite a household you have there...quite some fee." The menace in the voice was obvious.

Hravn mimicked the fake smile. "I think not. Do you know to whom you speak? Are these lands not those of My Lord, the Earl Gospatrick?"

The reply surprised Hravn. "Hah! It matters not. I don't answer to the Earl, or any man; and I care not to whom I speak. I care only for the coin you must pay, though you may care about the blood that you will shed, or the honour those pretty ladies will lose." The sudden lewd smile was far from fake.

Ealdgith interrupted the flow, "Take care, you will die ere any lady is touched. On that, you have a lady's word."

Ulf couldn't help but smile, "And on that you can rely, so take heed. I suggest you let us past; now!" He said, with no smile at all.

Hravn held up his hand, as if to placate everyone. "Come let us meet and talk." He urged his horse a couple of paces forward. The man copied, almost instinctively.

Ealdgith guessed what he was doing and called the hounds to heel. As the man edged forward the two men behind him followed, they were now in front of Cola and Dudda. Ealdgith watched as they moved slowly into position, crossbows aimed at the two escorts. When he was within five paces of the man, Hravn nodded, twice. Two crossbow bolts slashed into the escorts with such short-range force that the bodies were flung out of the saddles. Ulf and Orme took Hravn's nods as their own cue to ride forward, drawing their swords and closing behind the, now solitary, man.

Hravn gave a very genuine smile. "I suggest you dismount, now, and lead us all through the town. Tell your men to stay where they are until we allow you to return." The tap of Ulf's sword on his shoulder ensured no hesitation.

The man walk with them for a good half league beyond the fort's southern gate, before Hravn called a halt. "You can return. I want you to remember our names, and that we all serve Earl Gospatrick, across all his lands and beyond. I am Hravn of Ravenstandale."

"Lady Ealdgith," added, Ealdgith.

"Not forgetting Ulf, you little skita," said Ulf, prodding him with his sword point. Sköll snapped at the man's hand as he walked past, drawing blood.

"Oh, and Sköll and Hati, too," Ealdgith added, scornfully.

*****

They rode on, and used the many half-collapsed forts along the old wall as shelter from squalls of rain

308

blowing in from the west. Having discussed their options as they rode, they agreed that the benefit of a night in an inn was worth the risk of staying on the northern edge of Norman lands. By sundown they had crossed south over the River Tyne and reached Corbricg and the welcome sight of a rundown inn, where they spent a night, before heading north on the stoney road known as Deer Street. Onward, by way of Routhebiria and Alnewich, and towards the coast just south of Bebbanburge.

Blót-month, the time of sacrifice, was already upon them and most of the shrivelled, brown, leaves had been whipped from the trees by seasonal winds. The temperature had dropped, too, and their oiled-wool cloaks came into their own, keeping the biting wind and driven rain at bay. Just east of Alnewich, Dudda, who was probably the most Christian of them all, rode frantically back from the summit of a ridge, where he was scouting ahead of the group.

"Lord! Lord!" He called frantically, his horse rearing up as he reined it brutally to a halt, alongside Hravn. He crossed himself urgently, before speaking. "Lord. We are at the end of the world. The land stops beyond yon ridge, and there is nothing but a grey void. What has happened? What..." Dudda hesitated, perplexed at the reaction on the faces surrounding him. Orme looked confused, but the others were grinning and laughing.

Hravn held out his hand in reassurance. "You have nothing to fear, Dudda. You bring good news, indeed."

Ealdgith looked at the pain and confusion in the young man's face and, feeling suddenly guilty, said, "Dudda, that is the sea. I too, took fright when I first saw it, but fear not. Hravn tells me that our forefathers came from a land far to the other side of it. It is not, as you must fear, the end of the world, it is just the edge of our country, and it is good news, for it shows that we are close to my uncle's hall."

Hravn sent Ole back to Aelf and summoned everyone to close in. "The sea lies beyond, and the Earl's hall cannot be much further," he said. "Most of you will never have seen the sea. Do not be afraid of it, it is beautiful in its own way, but take care and respect it. Do not drink from it for I hear it is not like spring water; that it is very salty and liable to send men mad if you do, but you can touch it and bathe in it. Come, we will ride to see it before we go to the Earl. Please, as we ride, keep to the formation that we have used so long. We are safe here, but I know for sure that the Earl will be watching us, and I know Lady Edie will join me in wanting to make sure that he has the best first impression of us all."

Hravn led the way down, through open woodland and past a few herdsmen minding pigs as they snuffled through fallen leaves. As they met sandy soil they dismounted and led their horses across a low dune and onto a wide beach that hugged the coast as far as they could see. The sea, flat and grey, reflected the heavy grey clouds above, and broke in a series of low gentle waves only fifty paces away. Ealdgith grimaced at the sharp smell of salt and seaweed that hung in the hair. The others closed in behind them. Ole leapt from his horse and ran to Ada, holding his arms up to her. "Come, come," he beseeched her, "let's go to the sea."

Ada had Adelind strapped to her and looked pleadingly at Cyneburg, who nodded, smiling. Ole helped Ada down and took her hand as she ran, heavy footed, first in dry sand and then more tentatively across pungent seaweed, and bleached driftwood and dead crabs strewn along the tideline. Her free arm supported Adelind as she stopped just short of the water and bent to touch it cautiously, before putting her finger tips to her lips. Ole hesitated, then ran forward, following a retreating wave. Turning to gesture to Ada, he yelled in annoyance as the next wave broke over his legs, sending him running back, red-faced, embarrassed by the ripple of laughter. All their concern about the sea had gone.

"Well done, Ole! You'll learn. Now, let's go to meet our Lord."

As they remounted, Frida spoke for them all, remarking, "How our lives have changed."

"Aye lass." Esma smiled as she looked beyond Frida to a high rocky bluff. "And they are about to change again, look yonder." Esma gestured towards a collection of large halls surround by a high stake-wall that covered the top of the Bebbanburge outcrop. The fort dominated the flat coastland and their thoughts.

Once clear of the sand dunes, Ulf geed everyone back into formation. Hravn grinned as he looked back at his very orderly, purposeful, war-band. He hoped that the Earl would be equally impressed.

Ealdgith's expression, as they rode up the metalled track leading to the first gate in an outer stake-wall, was a mixture of joy and awe. "To think, it's taken nearly two years for us to reach here, since we fled in that awful winter. Just look at it. Even Richemund isn't as grand."

"Aye, Edie," Hravn agreed, "and this isn't quite the arrival we first planned. I hope your uncle accepts that we have a household with us too."

As they halted a trap in the stout, iron shod, door slid open. Hravn spoke. "Lady Ealdgith and Hravn of

Ravenstandale. We have business with My Lady's uncle, Earl Gospatrick."

"Welcome, My Lord. You are expected." The high double doors swung backwards to reveal a corridor leading to the crag-top stake-wall and a further door within a tower; the door opened as they approached and continued through.

"Uncle!" Ealdgith shouted with joy, flinging herself down from her horse and running to the Earl where he stood in the centre of a wide cobbled courtyard in front of a high wood-tiled hall.

"Welcome to your new home, Edie," he said, sweeping her up into a close embrace. Hravn dismounted slowly and walked to the Earl, and bowed slightly as he held out his hand. Earl Gospatrick laughed, "Not so formal Hravn, welcome." He stepped forward to embrace Hravn. "Now, come, my men will take care of your people and show them to the quarters I have prepared. We will gather in the main hall shortly, but first we must talk." He placed a hand on each of their shoulders and steered them up the steps into the hall. Sköll and Hati followed.

Ulf watched, shrugged at Orme, then grinned as he dismounted. "Come on, lad, I think we've work to do."

Gospatrick led them to his private chamber, and handed Ealdgith a glass of mead and Hravn a tankard of ale, before settling them in chairs by a table with an oil lamp. Ealdgith relaxed as she read pleasure and pride in his eyes. Hravn was still cautious, unsure how the Earl would respond to news that his standing with Count Alan had been compromised.

The Earl saw Hravn's reservation. He spoke to reassure. "Well done, both of you. You are a credit to yourselves, and to me. Oda got your message through to me, and then sent a further one. I have heard about the clearance of the settlements and the burning of the woods. Tell me the detail later, but to get your people safely away and then report here with a very credible war-band is a great achievement by any measure. My men have monitored your progress these past few days, and have been most impressed. That tells me two things, Hravn: you're a leader and a soldier."

Hravn smiled, relieved. "Thank you, My Lord." Ealdgith beamed.

"Now, tell me briefly what you understand to be the King's plans and the Count's intent?"

Hravn glanced at Ealdgith, then took a breath. "I understand, Lord, that the King considers that you are too close to the Scots' King. He sees the Scots as a threat and that the North will not be secure until they submit to him. Only he can achieve that, and he will come north once he has dealt with rebellion in the east. This will probably be in early sumor. The Count is to support the campaign logistically, rather than with men. I'm sure the King wants to ensure that the North does not have the chance to rise again, and he therefore won't take men away from the Count. The Forest Laws will also help achieve this, by denying the people the right to live in the woodlands, and by treating all who live in wasteland as outlaws and cut off from any contact with the people. That has destroyed any scope for resistance in Ghellinges-scir, and elsewhere to the south. There may be scope to raid into Norman lands south of the Tyne, from a sanctuary in your lands to the north, but this would draw attention to you." Gospatrick nodded, listening, his chin resting on pointed finger tips.

Hravn looked the Earl in the eye, "I am sorry that our flight showed me to be your man, and compromised you in the eyes of the Earl."

"Hah! Worry not." Gospatrick laughed, "He's always had his doubts about me. You took a great risk, both of you, by infiltrating his household. Your warning about the King's plans is worth a lot more to me than problems caused by confirming the Count's suspicions. I fear my time here may be limited, but we will talk of that another day."

Gospatrick stood and placed his tankard on the table. "Come, I have made my guest hall ready for you and your household. Consider it yours. First, though, follow me. Your people should be in the great hall by now. I would talk to them all."

Both gasped as they followed Gospatrick. The great hall was larger than any they had seen before and it glowed in the light of dozens of oil lamps that highlighted rich colours in the tapestry covered walls. Fresh rushes lay on the floor, scenting the air, and fires blazed in two hearths. The warmth hit them like a hot wall, after so long living outside.

Gospatrick guided them to a low dais alongside the central wall, and then turned to face the throng gathered in front of him. They saw at once that their own people were in the front, surrounded by the Earl's wider household. The Earl lent forward, holding out his hand to a tall lady in a blue silk gown. The gold braid around her waist echoed the lustre of her golden hair, her face the colour and texture of ivory. "My wife, Lady Aethelreda."

Ealdgith felt immediately out of place in her breaches, mudded boots, well-worn leather jerkin and mottled green cloak, her faced tanned by a life outdoors and her braided hair bleached by the long hot summer sun. Hravn, too, felt suddenly scruffy and mis-placed. His hair was long and unkempt, and several days' black stubble covered his chin. Although his mail shone bright, having been well scrubbed by Ole the day before, it still bore the holes and abrasions it had suffered in their fight at Wasfelte.

"Ealdgith, Hravn, you are always welcome." Aethelreda smiled sweetly and spoke with a hard Saxon-Wessex accent. Ealdgith could feel the eyes of the women in the Earl's household looking askance, whilst some of the men stared scornfully at her warrior-like appearance.

Gospatrick noticed the looks and, with a few words, turned frowns of judgement to smiles of respect. "Gentlemen, ladies, let us welcome my kinswoman, Ealdgith, her husband, Hravn, and their household. They will be living with us for many months to come. Edie is my cousin, though since the slaying of her family in the harrying, I, we," he glanced at Aethelreda, "look upon her as our daughter. Over the last two years Lady Ealdgith and Hravn have done me great service. They have killed several of those who were reaving on my Westmoringaland border, they have led a successful resistance across Ghellinges-scir whilst bettering the lives of many of their people and, just recently, they infiltrated the household of my rival, Count Alan, and secured information that is of significant importance for our own future security. Hravn calls Lady Ealdgith 'his Valkyrie', and with good reason. She has killed more men in her own defence than have many men in this room. I would wager that she could, singlehanded, better any man here..." He grinned at the disbelieving faces, "...not that, that, is to happen. They are part of my household and you will serve them as you serve me. Now, there is a small ceremony in which we shall all share."

The Earl turned to Hravn. "Hravn, please kneel." Hravn felt his pulse quicken, he had no inclination as to why he was commanded to kneel. As he knelt, the Earl turned to the table behind him and lifted the sword that lay there. Then facing Hravn, he gently touched Hravn's right shoulder with the tip. "Hravn, do you swear fealty to me?"

Hravn gulped as he realised what was happening, then, taking a deep breath, spoke clearly. "I promise on my faith that I will in the future be faithful to you, My Lord, never cause you harm and will observe my homage to you completely against all persons in good faith and without deceit."

The Earl lifted the sword. "Arise, Sir Hravn."

As Hravn stood, Ealdgith went to embrace him, tears of surprise and joy streaking her cheeks. Gospatrick raised his hand. "Edie, wait, there is more." He turned to them both.

"Sir Hravn, Lady Ealdgith, there is work that I would have you do. Before Yule-tide you are to represent me to the Scots' King and report the matters that we have just now discussed. Edie, you may be pleased to meet his Queen, she too is your kinswoman. Thereafter, I want you to sow unrest south of the Tyne. Earl Waltheof is too close to Bishop Walcher for our good, and needs to be distracted. That done, please clear any outlaws from my lands along the wall, I know you've made a start already. When all is done, you will return to the land of your forebears, Hravn, and hold my southern Westmoringaland border for me."

Hravn and Ealdgith exchanged glances as their hopes suddenly surged.

The Earl continued. "Hravn, I am granting you the lands from my southern border on the headwaters of the Lauen and the southern watershed of the Eden, north to Ravenstandale and Crosebi Raveneswart. Edie, I will grant you, in your own right, the lands of Hep and Ulueswater, The western watershed of the Eden, north to the northern watershed of the Eamont. Together, you will hold the border of the upper vale from west of the Eden at Kircabi Stephan, embracing the lands of your good friend Gunnar of Morlund, to those Cumbric passes west of Penrith. I want you to remove any vestiges of the Pendragons and ensure that the border routes to the south and west are under your direct control. I do not want the Normans to have any excuse for coming further north. It is something that I know you will enjoy," he said with a glint in his eye. He paused, then added, "I hear that there are reserves of lead, and mayhap silver, to be found there. Though some of the lands are poor, I am sure that you will generate wealth to sustain the household that you will need."

Hravn struggled to keep calm, the sudden honour, responsibility, the value of the gift, and the faith that Earl Gospatick so obviously had in them both, was overwhelming. "My Lord, how can we thank you?"

Gospatrick stilled him. "It will be a challenge, to be sure. Therefore, I am appointing a troop from my household to join yours. Employ them as you desire, from now until such time as you have secured my Westmoringaland and Cumbric borders; they should return thereafter. In the meantime, your costs are my costs. Your household is most welcome. Please, clothe and feed them at my expense." He held out his hand to Hravn, before firmly embracing Ealdgith.

The Earl clapped his hands. "Now! There is a feast for you to prepare for."

Hravn stepped down from the dais, leading Ealdgith by the hand. As he released her he clasped Ulf and Orme on their shoulders. "Ulf, Orme. Edie and I want you to do us the great honour of becoming our huscarls."

As he did so, Frida touched Ealdgith's arm. "My Lady, I have laid out your dress for the feast. Shall we go and get you ready?"

Ealdgith grinned and poked the tip of her tongue cheekily at her friend and self-appointed maid. "Thank you Frida. Yes, let's. I fear that I may be seeing far too many dresses for some time to come."

~~~~~

Hravn and Ealdgith will return in 'Retribution' – a tale of the year 1072.

Glossary

Aefter Yule. After Yule. January; the month after the Yuletide festival that became Christmas.

Aere Yule. Before Yule. December.

Atheling. Old English. A royal prince eligible to be king.

Blót-month. November.

Breeks. Breeches. From Old English, brec. Northern dialect.

Brýdeala. Bride-ale or marriage-feast.

Burh. A Saxon fortified settlement. Typically a timber-faced bank and ditch with a palisade on top, enclosing a manor house and settlement.

Castle. A European innovation, castles originated in the 9th and 10th centuries. Many castles were originally built from earth and timber, but had their defences replaced later by stone. The motte and bailey castle was introduced to England by the Normans. It consisted of a circular moat surrounding an earth mound (Motte) upon which a wooden keep (Tower) was built. The Baily was a wooden palisade inside the moat encompassing the motte and flat land upon which the castle's domestic buildings were built.

Cell. (1). A cell is a small room used by a hermit, monk, anchorite or nun to live, and as a devotional space. (2). A small group forming a nucleus of political activity, typically a secret, subversive one such as a terrorist cell.

Churl. The lowest rank of English freemen.

Dale. Old English and Norse for a valley.

Ealdmoder. Grandmother.

Earl. An Earl is a member of the nobility. The title is Anglo-Saxon, akin to the Scandinavian form: Jarl.

Ēostre. Easter

Fader. Father.

Fell. Norse for a high hill, mountain or high moorland.

Fettling. Northern English. Various meanings, including: to sort out, fix or repair.

Freyja. Norse. Goddess of love, fertility, and battle.

Furlong. Old English. An eighth of a mile or 200 metres.

Fyrd. The local militia of an Anglo-Saxon shire, in which all freemen had to serve.

Haerfest. Harvest.

Hall. Old English: Heall, a large house.

Hefted. The instinctive ablity of some breeds of sheep, including Cumbrian herdwicks, to know intimately the land they live on.

Hel. Queen of Helheim, the Norse underworld.

Hide. An area of land capable of supporting an extended family of up to 50 people.

Hlafmaesse Day. Lammas Day, or loaf-mass day. Traditionally the first of August, when the first grain from the harvest would be used to bake bread.

Holmganga. Norse: "going to an island", a special place for a duel governed by rules of combat.

Hundred. Most of the English shires were divided into 'Hundreds;' groups of 100 'Hides'.

League. A league is a classical unit of length. The word originally meant the distance a person could walk in an hour. Its distance has been defined variously as between one and a half and three miles. I have used the Roman league which is 7,500 feet or one and half miles.

Lencten. Spring.

Logi. Norse god of fire.

Longhouse. A Viking equivalent of the English manor house, typically 5 to 7 metres wide and anywhere from 15 to 75 metres long, depending on the wealth and social position of the owner.

Manor. An estate of land. The manor is often described as the basic feudal unit of tenure. A manor was akin to the modern firm or business. It was a productive unit, which required physical capital, in the form of land, buildings, equipment and draught animals such as ploughing oxen and labour in the form of direction, day-to-day management and a workforce. Its ownership could be transferred, by the overlord, In many cases this was ultimately the King.

Moder. Mother.

Nadr. Norse. Viper or adder.

Norns. Norse. The Norns were female beings who ruled upon the destiny of gods and men. They roughly correspond to other controllers of humans' destiny, the Fates, elsewhere in European mythology. (See Wyrd.)

Ratch. Yorkshire slang. To rummage.

Reave. To plunder or rob. Reaver: a raider. From Old English: reafian.

Reeve. An administrative officer who generally ranked lower than the ealdorman or earl. Different types of reeves were attested, including high-reeve, town-reeve, port-reeve, shire-reeve (predecessor to the sheriff), reeve of the hundred, and the reeve of a manor.

Seax. The seax is a type of sword or dagger typical of the Germanic peoples of the Early Middle Ages, especially the Saxons. The smallest were knives, the longest would have a blade over 50 cm long.

Shire. Groups of hundreds were combined to form shires, with each shire under the control of an earl.

Silvatici. Norman term for the 'men of the woods' or the green men.

Skíta. Old Norse: shit.

Staddle Stone. Supporting bases for granaries, hayricks, game larders, etc. The staddle stones lifted the granaries above the ground thereby protecting the stored grain from vermin and water seepage.

Sumor. Summer.

Thegn. A member of several Norse and Saxon aristocratic classes of men, ranking between earls and ordinary freemen, and granted lands by the king, or by lords, for military service. The minimum qualifying holding of land was five Hides.

Vill. Medieval English term to describe a land unit which might otherwise be described as a parish, manor or tithing.

Wapentake. An administrative area. The Dane-law equivalent of an Anglo-Saxon Hundred.

Warg. In Norse mythology, a warg is a wolf and in particular refers to the wolf Fenrir and his sons Sköll and Hati.

Winterfylleth. October. It marked and celebrated the beginning of winter.

Wyrd. Norse and Anglo-Saxon. Fate or personal destiny. Wyrd was one of the three most important Norns. The Norns were female and ruled upon the destiny of man.

Yule. The two months of the bleak midwinter. Aere Yule ('Ere Yule or Before Yule) is our December and Aefter Yule (After Yule) is our January.

Historical Note

Rebellion in the North.

In the darkest months of the winter of 1069/70 William the Conqueror led an intense campaign to destroy once and for all the independent nature of the people of Northern England, and in particular those living in Yorkshire and Durham, east of the Pennines.

The North had never been subject to the same degree of royal control that the rest of England had. For the past two hundred years, the region's history was one of competition between Danish rule from York and Anglo-Saxon rule by the old kingdom of Northumbria.

1066 changed all that. The failed Danish invasion that culminated in the battles of Fulford and Stamford Bridge, near York, and then the Battle of Hastings shattered England's Anglo-Danish ruling class. Norman rule had arrived.

King William initially appointed an Englishman, called Copsig, to rule the North from York. Copsig was not northern, his imposition of high taxes to pay for Norman mercenaries was resented by the people and he was killed when he tried to expand his rule into Northumbria. Gospatrick of Northumbria then bought the earldom of the North from King William. He refused to impose high taxes and when, in 1068, earls Edwin and Morcar of Mercia rebelled against Norman rule, he supported them. They were joined by the young Atheling (Prince) Edgar, the last Saxon with a true claim to the English throne.

It was a revolt against Norman tyranny, but was seen by the Normans as a challenge for the crown.

The uprising failed, Norman castles were built at Warwick and Nottingham, earls Morcar and Edwin submitted to the King, and Gospatrick fled to Scotland. The men of York also submitted. The Normans built York castle and imposed heavy taxes. Northern assets were seized, but Northern power was not destroyed.

In early 1069 the new Norman earl, Robert de Comines, plundered northwards to Durham. He was ambushed and killed in Durham, triggering a second rebellion led by Edgar the Atheling and earls Gospatrick and Maerleswein.

The rebels laid siege to York castle but King William reacted quickly, marched north, broke the siege, plundered York and built a second castle. The rebels hid in the Dales waiting for the King's departure; which was just before Easter. Norman control was consolidated but was bedevilled by constant hit and run raids.

The Northern nobility continued to rebel and encouraged King Swein of Denmark to take the crown, with Northern financial backing. In September 1069 King Swein sent a fleet of 240 ships, raided in North Lincolnshire then took York, supported by a Northern English army. The Normans were ambushed by the rebels at York; the city was largely burnt and the garrison was killed outside the castle. Norman power north of the Humber had been destroyed.

The rebels planned to hold York over the winter, expecting a Norman attack in the spring. The Danes couldn't support themselves in the destroyed remains of York and moved to North Lincolnshire for the winter.

Norman reaction was swift and unexpected. The King marched north, forcing the Danes back across the Humber. The rebels quickly re-grouped and for three weeks held the crossings through the marshland that dominated the area between the rivers Aire and Don.

The Normans outflanked the rebels, captured York and bought off the Danes, who departed raiding the Northumbrian coast as they went. The rebels fled back into the hills and valleys, expecting the Normans to stay in York over the winter.

King William held his Christmas court in York then planned to ensure that the North could never again sustain a Danish force or a rebel claim against his authority and crown.

The Harrying

Harrying is the persistent destruction of an enemy's land and people. It is a long-established form of warfare and was constantly used by the Normans, in Normandy and England, to control rebellious areas and to ensure that regions could not provide support for an enemy.

Orderic Vitalis, an Anglo-Norman monk, writing 50 years after the harrying wrote: *"The King stopped at nothing to hunt his enemies. He cut down many people and destroyed homes and land. Nowhere else had he shown such cruelty. This made a real change. To his shame, William made no effort to control his fury, punishing the innocent with the guilty. He ordered that crops and herds, tools and food be burned to ashes. More than 100,000 people perished of starvation. I have often praised William but I can say nothing good about this brutal slaughter. God will punish him."*

John of Worcester, a contemporary monk, said that from the Humber to the Tees, William's men burnt whole villages and slaughtered the inhabitants. Food stores and livestock were destroyed so that anyone surviving the initial massacre would succumb to starvation over the winter. Some survivors were reduced to cannibalism. Refugees from the harrying are mentioned as far away as Worcestershire in the Evesham Abbey chronicle.

These are just two of the many emotive accounts about the harrying, many claiming outright genocide and the creation of a wasteland that lasted for decades.

But what really happened?

The Normans didn't have the manpower to destroy the entire population of Yorkshire whilst retaining control across the rest of England, preventing other rebellions and maintaining castle garrisons. They also had to ensure that the North could continue to sustain the new castles and garrisons that they would have to establish in order to secure the region and prevent Danish or Scottish invasion.

Total destruction wasn't necessary. All the Normans had to do was to dislocate and impoverish Northern society. They did this comprehensively in a pre-planned and coordinated manner that has parallels in the subjugation of France after 1940.

Between early January and March 1070, they carried out multi-pronged advances through the vales of York and Pickering, into Holderness and West Yorkshire, swept through the Aire marshes and north across the Tees as far as Jarrow and the Tyne valley.

The Norman army would have lived off the land as it went, taking food, slaughtering livestock, burning granaries and homesteads, killing and raping at will. Their commanders must also have been mindful as to where they intended to build future castles and which communication routes they intended to control.

Small groups of men, moving through a strange land and lacking the means to communicate, would have cut paths of destruction that left some communities unscathed and devastated others.

Many northerners would have starved, dying of cold and hunger in the bitter winter. The old, the infirm and the very young must have perished. Others, particularly in the outlying regions, would have fled as refugees to Cumberland, Northumberland and Mercia.

Most survivors would have entered the service of the new Norman land holders, working as bondsmen providing free labour.

Where the will to resist was not broken gangs of outlaws and bandits formed in what became known as the 'free zone' in the upland valleys and woods where they were outside direct Norman control. The Normans called those who lived here 'silvatici', or 'the men of the woods'. Perhaps this is where the legends of the 'green man' and Robin Hood come from?

The strategic importance of the area around what is now Richmond must have been identified very early on, possibly before the harrying. Construction of one of the earliest stone castles in the country was started in 1070/71. Richmond, or Richemund, means strong hill. It was here that Count Alan the Red of Brittany controlled the lands given him by his relative, King William. Richmond castle dominates the fertile lands of the lower Swale and Ure valleys and controls the old Roman roads north and west along what are now the A1 and A66, as well as routes into what was then Scottish

Cumberland and Westmorland, along the valleys of Swaledale and Wensleydale.

King William had achieved his aim. The North could never again threaten his control of England.

The Legacy of the Harrying

The best account of the impact of the Harrying of the North is the Doomsday Book. This was a nationwide audit ordered by King William in 1086 in order that he could regain control of the national finances and ensure that he knew what taxes each of his barons should pay him.

Sixteen years after the harrying many settlements are described as 'waste'. This has often been taken to mean that they were uninhabited wasteland. But, is that realistic? These villages are recorded by name. If they had been destroyed and uninhabited for a generation they would surely have been forgotten and not recorded.

It is more likely that the Doomsday Book commissioners failed to visit villages due to their inaccessibility, or that the villages were simply not productive and could not generate any tax for the Crown, hence their description as 'waste'.

What is known is that by 1086 the population density of most of Yorkshire was half that of Nottinghamshire and North Lincolnshire, and that the number of plough teams, which indicate the productivity of the land, were two to three times greater in Nottinghamshire.

Populations became concentrated where the Normans had a strategic interest: on roads, where they had built castles, the entry routes into the North and on the more productive lowland areas.

In 'The Norman Conquest of the North' Willian E Kapelle comments that it is perhaps significant that the Normans were very conscious of their social status and refused to eat bread made from anything other than wheat flower. Medieval wheat would only grow in warmer, drier, regions and land over 400' high was unsuitable. This could be one reason why the land of many upland villages was taken out of production and declared waste.

There was considerable social dislocation and upheaval. Estates were moved en-masse to a Norman overlord and the middle ranking nobility largely disappeared. Prior to the invasion much land was owned by freemen. This changed and by 1086 there were three times as many freemen in Nottinghamshire than in Yorkshire. In 1066, there were more freemen in Northallerton and Scarborough than there were in the North and East Ridings in 1086, by which time 80% of the Yorkshire population were villeins, who provided the maximum amount of free labour to their over-lord. There was also a significant increase in desmesne land, with up to three quarters of an estate reserved for the manorial lord's personal use.

Although overall productivity was significantly lower by 1086, estates in the key areas were more productive, reflecting how the Normans directed the people's work to their will.

This was certainly the case around Richmond. In 1086, the villages upriver from Richmond and Leyburn were waste, whereas many of those down-river were more productive. It is also of note that several English lords survived, retaining their estates on behalf of Count

Alan. Lord Gospatrick, a relative of Earl Gospatrick, was one.

Richmond itself isn't mentioned in the Doomsday Book, but two manors are. One is called Hindrelag. This is possibly the original English settlement, which may have been located in the vicinity of St Mary's Church. The other was 'Neutone'. This was possibly a new settlement built outside the bailey wall of the new castle of Richemund, possibly where Newbiggin now is.

The harrying was the end of the Northern rebellions but it was not the end of major raids into the North. Scots raided across Stainmore in 1070, the Northumbrians raided into Durham and Yorkshire in 1074, Scots harried Northumberland in 1079, and in 1080 the King's half-brother, Bishop Odo, raided Northumberland.

The North was finally secured after 1080 by the castles of Pontefract, Richmond and Newcastle.

Earl Gospatrick.

Gospatrick (meaning: servant of Saint Patrick) is something of an enigma. Gospatrick (or Cospatrick) was a popular name within the House of Bamburgh, with a Gospatrick of that generation in each of the three family lines descending from Earl Uhtred the Bold. One Gospatrick was assassinated by Tostig in the mid 1060s, one was a major landholder across Yorkshire who managed to retain his lands after the harrying, the third was the grandson of Uhtred and Aelgifu and, through his father, the Cumbrian prince Maldred, a great Grandson of Malcolm 2nd of Scotland.

Medieval Childbirth.

The little that we know about early medieval childbirth suggests that delivery techniques were universal and changed little over time. Only women were present. The normal birth position was for the woman to kneel on the floor, with helpers ready at her knees or supporting her arms. As the birth progressed, she would shift to a knee-elbow position, and the child would be received from behind. Runes and songs were offered as age-old remedies for difficult births, probably performed by a helping woman trained through experience and apprenticeship. This practice continued into the Christian era, with prayers replacing Germanic charms and songs. Even today, folk traditions persist that all doors should be unlocked, as a locked door could block the birth process. The mother might also choose to wear keys, perhaps as jewelry, during labor and should also be sure to untie and unknot everything that she can in her room as knots are also thought to delay or complicate the birth.

Medieval Contraception.

Queen Anne's Lace is also known as wild carrot, and its seeds have long been used as a contraceptive. The seeds block progesterone synthesis, disrupting implantation and are most effective as emergency contraception within eight hours of exposure to sperm, a sort of "morning after" form of birth control. Taking Queen Anne's Lace led to no, or mild, side effects (like a bit of constipation), and women who stopped taking it could conceive and rear a healthy child. The only danger, it seemed, was confusing the plant with the similar-looking but potentially deadly poisons hemlock and water hemlock. Rue is a hardy, evergreen, somewhat shrubby plant. In England, Rue is one of our oldest garden plants, cultivated for its use medicinally, having, together with other herbs, been introduced by the Romans, but it is not found in a wild state except rarely on the hills of Lancashire and Yorkshire. Rue leaves can be eaten as a contraceptive or drunk within an infusion as emergency contraception or to induce abortion. Ingested regularly, rue decreases blood flow to the endometrium, essentially making the lining of the uterus non-nutritive to a fertilized egg.

The Silvatici and the Murdrum Laws.

In the years following the Conquest, as the French expropriation of English lands intensified, large numbers of English thegns fled overseas, many eventually finding their way to the Byzantine empire where they were soon to become the main element in the Varangian Guard. Other thegns plus the vast majority of common English people did not have this option, they had to stay in England. Some took to the woods. The Anglo-Norman monk Orderic Vitalis tells us that the Normans called these 'resistance fighters' silvatici – the men of the woods. The English, it is said, called them the same thing in their own language: green men. A tradition of resistance and rebellion against unwanted masters that lies at the heart of the later Robin Hood ('Robin du Bois') legend.

To help protect the conquerors, Frenchmen as they called themselves, from being murdered by the English, King William introduced a new law known as the 'murdrum' or, more probably, reintroduced an earlier law imposed by King Cnut for the muder of Danes.

Marc Morris writes in 'The Norman Conquest': By this law if a Norman was found murdered, the onus was placed on the lord of the murderer to produce him within five days or face a ruinous fine. If the culprit remained at large despite his lord's financial ruin, the penalty was simply transferred to the local community as a whole, and levied until such time as the murderer was produced... The murdrum fine conjures the vivid picture of Englishmen up and down the country, continuing to vent their anger against their Norman occupiers by picking them off individually whenever the opportunity presented itself.

Forest Laws

Laws were one of the hallmarks of the feudal system that King William imposed on England after 1066. In the case of forest laws, Norman law superseded the earlier Anglo-Saxon laws in which rights to the forest (not necessarily just woods, but also heath, moorland, and wetlands) were not exclusive to the king or nobles, but were shared among the people. Feudal forest laws, in contrast, were harsh, forbidding not only the hunting of game in the forest, but even the cutting of wood or the collection of fallen timber, berries, or anything growing within the forest.

The English forest laws were designed to protect the beasts of the chase (i.e. deer and wild boar.) and their habitats. They precluded poaching and taking wood from the forest. The punishments for breaking these laws were severe and ranged from fines to, in the most severe cases, death.

Because of these forest laws the local peasants who lived on the land faced severe restrictions on their lifestyles. They were banned from enclosing their land by fencing or other means as this restricted the hunt. The forest laws were therefore extremely unpopular with the local population, who were unable to continue in their way of life that had existed up until the Norman rule. They were not allowed to protect their crops by fencing, they could not use the timber from the woodland for building houses and they were not allowed to hunt game to provide food for their families. As the 'underwood' was also protected they also faced a severe restriction on their ability to gather wood for fuel.

27210452R00204

Printed in Great Britain
by Amazon